"**W** is for wonderful,
worthy and world-class.

"*W is for Wasted…*
is all those things and more.

"*W is for Wasted*
in all the word's iterations, as it
turns out, is further proof of the amount
of care Grafton continues to invest in this
stellar series. Lesser authors churn books
out; Grafton continues to knock them
out of the park."
—*The Courier-Journal*

IS FOR
WASTED

SUE GRAFTON

BERKLEY BOOKS, NEW YORK

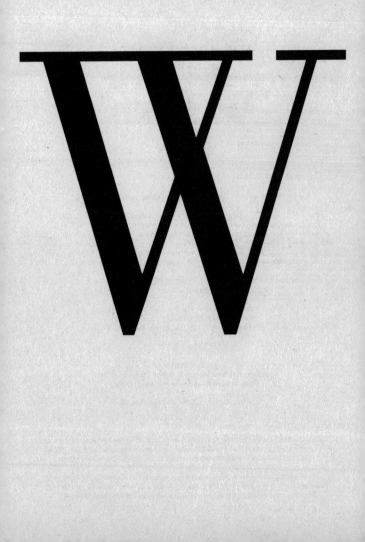

THE BERKLEY PUBLISHING GROUP
Published by the Penguin Group
Penguin Group (USA) LLC
375 Hudson Street, New York, New York 10014

USA • Canada • UK • Ireland • Australia • New Zealand • India • South Africa • China

penguin.com

A Penguin Random House Company

W IS FOR WASTED

A Berkley Book / published by arrangement with the author

For information, address: The Berkley Publishing Group,
a division of Penguin Group (USA) LLC,
375 Hudson Street, New York, New York 10014.

ISBN: 978-0-425-27157-5

PUBLISHING HISTORY
G. P. Putnam's Sons hardcover edition / September 2013
Berkley mass-market edition / August 2014

PRINTED IN THE UNITED STATES OF AMERICA

10   9   8   7   6   5   4   3   2   1

For Margo and Jeff Barbakow

and

Terri and Steve Bass.

Friends forever . . . and that's what it's all about.

ACKNOWLEDGMENTS

The author wishes to acknowledge the invaluable assistance of the following people: Steven Humphrey; Judge Brian Hill, Santa Barbara Superior Court; John Mackall, Attorney at Law, Seed Mackall LLP; Ted Steinbock, M.D.; Chief of Police Cam Sanchez, Senior Forensic Technician Michael Uullemeyer, Administrative Specialist Thalia Chaltas, Sergeant Dave Henderson, and Detective Gregory Hons of the Santa Barbara Police Department; Robert Failing, M.D.; Larry Gillespie; Florence Michel; Ken Ralph and Mike Foley, Casa Esperanza Homeless Center; Renee Burdick, American Express Travel; Brian Robertson and Heather Schuyler, Robertson International Travel; David Dyne, M.D.; Dana Hanson, funeral director, the Neptune Society; Director Donald Miller, M.D.; Associate Professor of Medicine Brian Clem and Research Technologist II Miriam Reynolds, James Graham Brown Cancer Center, Louisville, Kentucky; Supervisor Christine Estrada, Lead Clerk Dolores Buendia and Judicial Assistants Kimberlee Taylor and Victoria Stuber, Santa Barbara Superior Court Records; Denyse Avila, Superior Court Clerk's Office; Employee Benefits Manager Melissa Jammer and Customer Service Manager Barbara Allcock, Anderson Financial Services; Wayne Palmer; Terri Lang; Jeanie Purcell Hill; and Dale Charpentier.

And a special thank-you to Alice Hildreth Fix for the use of her name.

PROLOGUE

Two dead men changed the course of my life that fall. One of them I knew and the other I'd never laid eyes on until I saw him in the morgue. The first was Pete Wolinsky, an unscrupulous private detective I'd met years before through Byrd-Shine Investigations, where I'd served my apprenticeship. I worked for Ben Byrd and Morley Shine for three years, amassing the six thousand hours I needed for my license. The two were old-school private eyes, hardworking, tireless, and inventive. While Ben and Morley did business with Pete on occasion, they didn't think much of him. He was morally shabby, disorganized, and irresponsible with money. In addition, he was constantly pestering them for work, since his marketing skills were minimal and his reputation too dubious to recommend him without an outside push. Byrd-Shine might subcontract the odd stretch of surveillance to him or assign him a routine records search, but his name never appeared on a client report. This didn't prevent him from stopping by the office without invitation or dropping their names in casual conversations with attorneys, implying a close professional relationship. Pete was a man who cut corners and he assumed his colleagues did likewise. More problematic was the fact that he'd rationalized his bad behavior for so long it had become standard operating procedure.

Pete Wolinsky was gunned down the night of August 25 on a dark stretch of pavement just off the parking lot at the Santa Teresa Bird Refuge. The site was right across the street from the Caliente Café, a popular hangout for off-duty cops. It might seem odd that no one in the bar was aware that shots were fired, but the volume on the jukebox exceeds 117 dB, roughly the equivalent of a gas-powered chainsaw at a distance of three feet. The rare moments of quiet are masked by the high-pitched rattle of ice cubes in dueling blenders where margaritas are whipped up at a rate of one every four and a half minutes.

Pete's body might not have been discovered until daylight if it hadn't been for an inebriated bar patron who stepped into the shadows to take a leak. I heard about Pete's death on the morning news while I was eating my Cheerios. The TV set was on in the living room behind me, more for the company than the content. I caught his name and turned to catch a night shot of the crime scene blocked off by yellow tape. By the time the news crew had arrived, his body had been loaded into the ambulance in preparation for transport to the coroner's office, so there was really nothing to see. In the harsh glare of artificial light, a somber female reporter recited the bare facts. Pete's immediate family must have been notified by then or she wouldn't have mentioned him by name. Pete's death was a surprise, but I can't say it was a shock. He'd often complained of sleeping poorly and had taken to wandering the streets at all hours. According to the reporter, his wallet had been stolen along with his watch, a knock-off Rolex with a faux-platinum band. I guess robbers these days can't distinguish the genuine article from the fake, which meant that Pete's death wound up being more about impulse or cheap thrills than profit. He was a man with a propensity for risk, and it was only a matter of time before Lady Luck caught up with him and pushed him off the cliff.

The story about the second dead man is more complex and takes longer to articulate, especially since the facts emerged slowly over a matter of weeks. The coroner's office called me on a Friday afternoon, asking if I could ID a John Doe who had my name and phone number on a slip of paper in his pocket. How could I resist? Every good mystery takes place on three planes—what *really* happened; what *appears* to have happened; and how the sleuth, amateur or professional (yours truly in this case) figures out which is which. I suppose I could put everything in perspective if I explained how it all turned out and then doubled back to that phone call, but it's better if you experience it just as I did, one strange step at a time.

This was October 7, 1988, and it looked like things were as bad as they were going to get. On the national front, congressional spending was a whopping $1,064.14 billion and the federal debt was topping out at $2,601.3 billion. Unemployment hovered at 5.5 percent and the price of a first-class postage stamp had jumped from twenty-two cents to twenty-five. I tend to disregard issues over which I have no control. Like it or not, the politicians don't consult me about economic policies, budget cuts, or the gross national product, whatever *that* is. I might voice an opinion (if I had one), but as nearly as I can tell, nobody pays the slightest attention, so what's the point? My only hope is to be the master of my own small universe, which is centered in a Southern California town ninety-six miles north of Los Angeles.

My name is Kinsey Millhone. I'm a private investigator, female, age thirty-eight. I rent office space in a two-room bungalow with a kitchenette and a bathroom on a narrow side street in the heart of Santa Teresa, population 85,810, minus the two dead guys. Since I'm the sole proprietor and lone employee, I operate on a modest scale, supporting myself by doing missing-persons searches, background checks, witness location, and the occasional service of process. From time to time I'm hired to establish paper trails in legal, financial, or property disputes. On a more personal note, let me say that I believe in law and order, loyalty, and patriotism—old-fashioned values that might seem woefully out of date. I also believe in earning an honest living so I can pay my taxes, cover my monthly bills, and tuck any surplus into my retirement account.

When I reached the coroner's office, I was ushered into a bay with the curtain discreetly pulled around the ceiling track. Though curious, I wasn't apprehensive. I'd done a quick survey and could account for the people I knew and loved. There were those who orbited my world in a wider gyre, but I couldn't think of one whose death would have had a significant impact.

The dead man was stretched out on a gurney with a sheet pulled up to his chin, so there was nothing of an intimate nature in evidence. He was not someone I recognized. His skin tones were gray, underlined with a pale gold that suggested liver issues of a profound and possibly fatal nature. His features had been softened and flattened in death, angles worn as smooth as stone over which water has poured for thousands of years. The human spirit does more than animate the face; it lends character and definition. Here, there was none.

The decedent (to use the official term) appeared to be in his early seventies, white, and overweight in the manner of those who forgo their nine servings of fresh fruits and vegetables per day. Judging by the bulbous nose and broken veins across his weather-darkened face, he'd enjoyed alcohol in sufficient quantities to pickle the average adult. Sometimes the dead seem to sleep. This man did not. I studied him at length, and there was not even the faintest suggestion that he was breathing. Whatever spell had been cast over him, the effects were permanent.

His body had been discovered that morning in a sleeping bag on the beach where he'd hollowed out a place for himself in the sand. His campsite was just below a bank of ice plant that flourished between the bike path and the beach itself, a spot not immediately visible to passersby. During the day, the area is popular with the homeless. At night, the fortunate among them secure bed space at one of the local shelters. The unlucky ones are left to flop where they can.

The beachside park closes thirty minutes after sunset and doesn't open again until 6:00 A.M. According to Municipal Code 15.16.085, it's unlawful to sleep in any public park, public street, public parking lot, or public beach, which doesn't leave much in the way of open-air habitats available free of charge. The ordinance is designed to discourage transients from sacking out on the doorsteps of area businesses, thus forcing them to set up makeshift quarters under bridges, freeway overpasses, bushes, and other places of concealment. Sometimes the police roust them out and sometimes they look the other way. Much of this depends on whether the local citizens are feeling righteous about the poor or indifferent, as is usually the case.

Preliminary examination suggested the man had been dead for close to eighteen hours by the time the coroner's investigator got in touch with me. Aaron Blumberg had been hired by the Santa Teresa County Coroner's Office in the mid-'70s, just about the time I left the Santa Teresa Police Department and went to work for Ben Byrd and Morley Shine. The year I opened my office, Aaron was recruited by the Kern County Sheriff's Department, from which he'd recently retired. Like many law-enforcement junkies, he was ill suited for a life of leisure, and he'd returned to the local coroner's office some six months before.

He was a man in his sixties with a softly receding hairline. The top of his head was covered with gray fluff, like the first feathering out of a baby bird. His ears were prominent, his cheekbones pronounced, and his smile created long creases that bracketed his mouth like a marionette's. We stood in silence for a moment and then he checked my reaction. "You know him?"

"I don't. I take it he was homeless."

Aaron shrugged. "That's my guess. A group of them have been congregating in that grassy patch across the street from the Santa Teresa Inn. Before that, they camped in the park adjacent to the municipal swimming pool."

"Who called it in?"

He took off his glasses and polished one lens with the end of his tie. "Fellow named Cross. Seven o'clock this morning, he was out on the beach with a metal detector sweeping for coins. He had his eye on the sleeping bag, thinking it had been dumped. Something about it bothered him, so he went out to the street and flagged down the first black-and-white that came by."

"Was anyone else around?"

"The usual posse of bums, but by the time the paramedics arrived, they'd all drifted away." He checked his lenses for smears and then resettled the glasses on his nose, tucking a wire stem carefully behind each ear.

"Any signs of foul play?"

"Nothing obvious. Dr. Palchek's on her way out. She has two autopsies on the books, which puts this guy at the end of the line, pending her assessment. Since Medicare went into effect, she doesn't do a post on every body brought in."

"What do you think he died of? He looks jaundiced."

"Not to be flip about it, but what do any of these guys die of? It's a hard life. We have one just like this every couple of months. Guy goes to sleep and he never wakes up. Could be hepatitis C, anemia, heart attack, alcohol poisoning. If we can ID the guy, I'll canvas the local clinics in hopes he's seen a doc sometime in the last twenty days."

"No ID at all?"

Aaron shook his head. "Note with your name and phone number and that was it. I inked his fingers and faxed the ten-print card to the DOJ in Sacramento. Weekend's coming up and those requests are going to sit there until somebody gets around to 'em. Might be the middle of next week."

"Meanwhile, what?"

"I'll check his description against missing-persons reports and see if there's a match. With the homeless, their families sometimes don't care enough to fill out the paperwork. Of course, it works the other way as well. Street people don't always want to be located by their so-called loved ones."

"Anything else? Moles, tattoos?"

He lifted the sheet to expose the man's left leg, which was shorter than his right. The knee cap was misshapen, raised in a thick knot like a burl. The flesh along the fibula was laced with red ropes of scar tissue. At some point in the past, he'd suffered a devastating injury.

"What happens if you never find out who he is?"

"We'll hold him for a time and then we'll bury him."

"What about his effects?"

"Clothes on his back, sleeping bag, and that's it. If he had anything else, it's gone now."

"Ripped off?"

"That's possible. In my experience, the beach bums are protective of one another, which is not to say they might not confiscate the stuff he had no further use for."

"What about the note he carried? Can I see it?"

He reached for the clipboard at the bottom of the gurney and freed the clear plastic evidence bag in which the slip had been placed. There was a picket fence of torn paper along the top, the leaf apparently ripped from a spiral-bound pad. The note was written in ballpoint pen, the letters uniform and clean: MILLHONE INVESTIGATIONS with the address and phone. It was the sort of printing I'd emulated in the fourth grade, inspired by a teacher who used a mechanical pencil and the same neat hand.

"That's my office," I remarked. "He must have looked me up in the yellow pages. My home number's unlisted. Wonder what a homeless guy wanted with a PI?"

"I guess they've got problems just like everyone else."

"Maybe he thought I'd come cheap since I'm a girl."

"How would he know that? Millhone Investigations is gender neutral."

"Good point," I said.

"At any rate, I'm sorry for the wasted trip, but I thought it was worth a shot."

"Absolutely," I said. "Do you mind if I ask around? Somebody must know who he was. If the guy needed help, he might have confided in his cronies."

"Do anything you want as long as you keep us in the loop. Maybe you'll find out who he is before we do."

"Wouldn't that be nice?"

I sat for a moment in the parking lot, jotting notes on a succession of index cards that I keep in my bag. There was a time when I trusted more to memory. I was raised by a maiden aunt who believed in rote learning: multiplication tables, state capitals, the kings and queens of England and their reigns, religions of the world, and the periodic table of elements, which she taught me by the judicious arrangement of cookies decorated with blue, pink, yellow, and green frosting, numbers piped onto each in a contrasting color. Oddly enough, I'd forgotten that particular exercise in child abuse until the previous April, when I walked into a bakery and saw a display of Easter cookies. In a flash, like a series of photographs, I saw hydrogen, atomic number 1; helium, atomic number 2; lithium, atomic number 3, working my way as far as neon, atomic number 10, before my mind went blank. I am still able to recite long portions of Alfred Noyes's "The Highwayman" at the slightest provocation. In my experience, this is not a useful skill.

When I was young, such pointless mental gymnastics were the perfect training for a game played at various birthday parties I attended. We were briefly shown a tray of objects, and a prize was given to the little girl who remembered the most. I was a whiz at this. In fourth grade, I won a pocket comb, a

ChapStick, a small bag of marbles, a box of crayons, a nicely wrapped bar of motel soap, and a pair of plastic barrettes . . . really not worth the effort in my opinion. Eventually, mothers became annoyed and hinted broadly that I should share the bounty or cede the floor. Having a keen sense of justice even at that age, I refused, which pared down the number of invitations to zero. I've learned in the years since that the simple expedient of written notes relieves the beleaguered child in me from burdening my brain. I'm still resistant to sharing bounty I've acquired by fair means.

Pulling out of the parking lot, I thought about the oddities of life, that something as insignificant as a slip of paper could have a ripple effect. For reasons unknown, the dead man had made a note of my name and phone number, and because of that, my path had touched his. While it was too late for conversation, I wasn't quite prepared to shrug and move on. Maybe he'd meant to make the call the day he died and his mortality caught up with him before he could act. Maybe he'd thought about calling and changed his mind. I wasn't looking for answers, but it couldn't hurt to inquire. I didn't anticipate long-term consequences. I pictured myself asking a few questions, making little or no progress, and then letting the matter drop. Sometimes the import of a minor moment makes all the difference.

1

On my way back into town, I stopped at the car wash. For years I owned VW Bugs, which were cheap to run and possessed a certain quirky charm. A full tank of gas would get you almost anywhere in the state, and if you suffered a fender bender, you could replace a bumper for pennies on the dollar. This more than made up for the minimal horsepower and the smirks from other drivers. I'm a jeans-and-boots kind of gal myself, so the lack of glamour suited me just fine.

My first VW, a beige 1968 sedan, ended up in a ditch after a fellow in a truck ran me off the road. This was out by the Salton Sea, where I was conducting a missing-persons search. The guy was intent on killing me but managed to inflict only modest damage to my person while the car was a total loss. My second VW sedan was a 1974, pale blue, with only one minor ding in the left rear fender. That car went to an early grave, shoved into a big hole after a slow-speed chase on an isolated stretch of road up in San Luis Obispo County. I've heard that most traffic fatalities occur within a two-mile radius of home, but my experience would suggest otherwise. I don't mean to imply that the life of a private eye is all that dangerous. The big threat is my being bored half to death doing title searches at the county courthouse.

My current vehicle is a 1970 Ford Mustang, a two-door

coupe with manual transmission, a front spoiler, and wide track tires. This car had served me well, but the color was an eye-popping Grabber Blue, much too conspicuous for someone in my line of work. Occasionally I'm hired to run surveillance on an unsuspecting spouse, and the persistent sight of a Boss 429 in close range will blow a tail every time. I'd owned the Mustang for a year, and while I was no longer smitten with it, I was reconciled to Mustang ownership until the next kick-ass miscreant had a go at me. I figured I was just about due.

In the meantime, I tried to be conscientious about maintenance, with frequent servicing at the local repair shop and a weekly hosing down. At the car wash for $9.99, the "deluxe package" includes a thorough interior vacuuming, a foam wash, a rinse, a hot wax, and a blow dry with 60-horsepower fans. Ticket in hand, I watched the attendant ease the Mustang into a line of cars awaiting the conveyor track, which would ferry it from view. I went inside the station and paid the cashier, declining the offer of a vanilla-scented doohickey to hang on my rearview mirror. I moved over to the waiting area's long spectator window and peered to my right, watching as the attendant steered the Mustang forward until it was caught on the flat mechanical tramway. A white hatchback of unknown manufacture followed right behind.

Four panels of trailing cloth bands wagged soap and water back and forth across the top surfaces of the car while whirling cloth skirts pirouetted along the sides. A separate cylinder of soft brushes caught the front grille, merrily scrubbing and polishing. There was something hypnotic about the methodical lather and rinse processes that enveloped the Mustang in a blanket of sudsy water, soap, and wax. That I considered the process enthralling is a fair gauge of how easily entertained I was at the time.

I was so engrossed that I scarcely noticed the guy standing at the window next to me until he spoke.

"That your Mustang?"

"Yep," I said and looked over at him. I placed him in his early forties, dark hair, good jawline, slender frame. Not so good-looking as to annoy or intimidate. He wore boots, faded jeans, and a blue denim shirt with the sleeves rolled up. His smile revealed a row of white teeth with one crooked bicuspid.

"Are you a fan?" I asked.

"Oh, god yes. My older brother had a 429 when he was in high school. Man, you floored that thing and it tore the black-top off the road. Is that a 1969?"

"Close, a 1970. The intake ports are the size of sewer pipes."

"They'd have to be. What's the airflow rate?"

"Eight," I said, like I knew what I was talking about. I walked the length of the station's window, keeping pace with my car as it inched down the line. "Is that your hatchback?"

"I'm afraid so," he said. "I liked the car when I bought it, but it's one thing after another. I've taken it back to the dealer three times and they claim there's nothing they can do."

Both cars disappeared from view, and as we moved toward the exit, he stepped ahead of me and pushed open the glass door, holding it for me as I passed in front of him. One car jockey slid into the front seat of the Mustang while another took the wheel of his car, which I could see now was a Nissan. Both cars were driven out onto the tarmac, where two sets of workers swarmed forward with terry-cloth towels, wiping away stray traces of water and squirting shiner on the sides of the tires. A minute later, one of the workers raised a towel, looking over at us.

As I headed for my car, the Nissan owner said, "You ever decide to sell, post a notice on the board in there."

I turned and walked backward for a few steps. "I've actually been thinking about dumping it."

He laughed, glancing over as a second worker nodded to indicate that his car was ready.

I said, "I'm serious. It's the wrong car for me."

"How so?"

"I bought it on a whim and I've regretted it ever since. I have all the service records and the tires are brand new. And no, it's not stolen. I own it outright."

"How much?"

"I paid five grand and I'd be willing to let it go for that."

By then he'd caught up with me and we'd stopped to finish the conversation. "You mean it?"

"Let's just say I'm open to the idea." I reached into one of the outer flaps of my shoulder bag and took out a business card. I scribbled my home phone number on the back and offered it to him.

He glanced at the information. "Well, okay. This is good. I don't have the money now, but I might one day soon."

"I'd have to line up a replacement. I need wheels or I'm out of business."

"Why don't you think about it and I will, too. A friend of mine owes me money and he swears he'll pay."

"You have a name?"

"Drew Unser. Actually, it's Andrew, but Drew's easier."

"I'm Kinsey."

"I know." He held the card up. "It says so right here."

"Have a good one," I said. I continued to my car and then waved as I got in. The last I saw of him, he was heading left out of the lot while I took a right.

I returned to the office and spent a satisfying half hour at my Smith-Corona typing a report. The job I'd just wrapped up was a work-related disability claim through California Fidelity Insurance, where I'd been accorded office space for many years. Since CFI and I had parted on bad terms, I appreciated the opportunity to ingratiate myself, a reversal made possible because the executive who fired me had himself been fired. This was a gloat-worthy turn of events and the news had lifted my spirits for days. The recent job had been gratifying for more reasons than the hefty paycheck. The responsibility of an employer for the health and safety of employees is governed by state law, and the follow-up to a workplace accident usually falls to the insurance company. Not all private insurance companies write worker-comp policies, which requires a property and casualty license. In this case, the injured man was married to a CFI executive, which was why I was brought in. Being skeptical by nature, I suspected the fellow was malingering, coached by a spouse well acquainted with the means and methods for milking the situation. As it turned out, I was able to document the man's incapacitation, and his employer made sure he was afforded the benefits he was entitled to. Cynicism aside, it makes me happy when two parties, whose relationship could turn adversarial, resolve their differences to the satisfaction of both.

When I finished typing the report, I made two copies on my newly acquired secondhand copy machine, kept one for my files, and put the original and one copy in an envelope that I addressed to CFI, which I dropped into the nearest mailbox as I headed for home. I was caught up on work, and for the moment I had no new clients clamoring for my services, so I'd awarded myself some time off. I wasn't thinking in terms of a bona fide vacation. I'm too tight with a buck to spend money on a trip and there wasn't any place else I longed to be in any event. As a rule, if I don't work, I don't eat, but my checking account was full, I had three months' worth of expenses covered, and I was looking forward to a stretch of time in which to do as I pleased.

Once I'd reached Cabana, I followed the wide boulevard that ran parallel to the Pacific Ocean. We'd had fog and drizzle the day before and the skies were sufficiently overcast to generate a fine mist. As it happened, rainfall total for the month would later register a touch over 0.00 inches, but for all I knew, the sprinkle heralded an epic tropical storm that would soak us properly. The lingering damp suggested a change of seasons, Santa Teresa's version of summer giving way to fall.

A mile farther on, at the intersection of Milagro and Cabana, I turned into one of the public lots and nosed into a parking spot that faced the Santa Teresa Inn. I figured as long as I was out and about, I'd try to make contact with those who might be acquainted with the man in the morgue. This was a neighborhood I knew well, the halfway point in my usual three-mile morning jog. It was now late afternoon and the beach path was populated by a cross-flow of walkers and cyclists, tourists peddling foot-powered surreys, and kids maneuvering their skateboards as though surfing the pipeline.

The homeless I saw in the early morning hours were often still huddled under a deadweight of blankets, sheltered by shopping carts piled high with their belongings. Even for nomads, the urge toward ownership is apparently irresistible. Regardless of social status, we derive comfort from our *stuff*; the familiar warp and weft of our lives. My pillow, my blanket, my small plot of earth. It's not that the homeless are any less invested in their possessions. The dimensions of what they own are simply more compact and more easily carted from place to place.

The sun was making its slow descent and the air was getting chillier by the minute. I set my sights on a trio lounging on sleeping bags under a cluster of palms. As I watched, they passed a cigarette from hand to hand and took turns sipping from a soda can that had probably been emptied and refilled with a high-test substitute. In addition to the censure against snoozing in public, consumption of alcohol is also prohibited by municipal code. Clearly, the homeless can't do much of anything without risking arrest.

It didn't take much sleuthing to locate the spot where the John Doe had been found. Just beyond a shelf of ice plant, someone had constructed a tower of carefully balanced rocks, six by my count, each stone settled on the one below it in an artful arrangement that appeared both stable and precarious. I knew the sculpture hadn't been there the day before because I'd have spotted it. At the base, a motley collection of glass jars had been placed, each containing a bouquet of wildflowers or blooms confiscated from the yards of home owners in the area. While jogging, the only way I have to keep my mind occupied is by a free-form internal commentary about external events.

I focused on the three transients, two of whom were regarding me without expression. They didn't seem overtly threatening, but I'm an undersize female—five foot six, one hundred eighteen pounds—and while capable of defending myself, I'd been taught to keep my distance from any assemblage of idlers. There's something edgy and unpredictable about those who loiter with no clear purpose, especially when alcohol is folded into the mix. I'm a person of order and regulation, discipline and routine. That's what makes me feel safe. The anarchy of the disenfranchised is worrisome. In this case, my wariness was superseded by my quest for information.

I approached the threesome, taking a mental photograph of each in turn. A white kid somewhere in his twenties sat with his back against a palm. He sported dreadlocks. The sparse shadow of facial hair suggested he'd shaved maybe once in the past two weeks. I could see a sharp angle of bare chest visible in the V of his short-sleeve shirt. The sight of his bare arms made me cross my own for warmth. His shorts seemed light for the season. The only items of substance he wore were heavy-duty wool socks and a pair of hiking boots. His legs were cute, but that was about it.

The second fellow was African American, with a full head of springy gray hair, frosted with white. His beard and mustache were carefully trimmed, and he wore glasses with metal rims. He was probably in his seventies, decked out in a pale blue dress shirt under a herringbone sport coat with frayed cuffs. The third fellow sat cross-legged in the grass with his back to me, as round-shouldered and squat as a statue of Buddha. He wore an imitation leather jacket with a rip under one arm and a black knit watch cap pulled down to his brows.

I said, "Hi, guys. I don't mean to intrude, but did any of you know the dead man who was found out there this morning in his sleeping bag?"

As I gestured toward the beach, it occurred to me that the detail about the sleeping bag was superfluous. How many dead men in any guise had been discovered at the beach in the past twenty-four hours?

The fellow with his back to me rotated to get a good look at me and I realized my mistake. It was a woman, who said, "What business is it of yours?"

"Sorry. I should have introduced myself. Kinsey Millhone. What's your name?"

She turned away, murmuring a four-letter word, which was audible, owing to my keen appreciation of bad language. I'm occasionally rebuked for my salty tongue, but who gives a shit?

The white kid spoke up in an effort to present a friendlier point of view. Without quite meeting my gaze, he said, "That's Pearl. This here's Dandy and I'm Felix."

"Nice meeting you," I said.

In a gesture that I hoped would convey both goodwill and trust, I held out my hand. There was an awkward moment and then Felix got the message. He shook hands with me, smiling sheepishly, his gaze fixed on the grass. I could see grungy metal braces on his teeth. Was the welfare system in the business of correcting malocclusions these days? That was hard to believe. Maybe he'd been fitted as a teen and had run away from home before his dentist finished his work. His teeth did look straight, but I questioned the wisdom of sporting orthodontia for life.

Dandy, the older gentleman, spoke up, his tone mild. "Don't mind Pearl. It's almost supper time and she's hypoglycemic. Brings out a side of her we'd just as soon not see. What's your interest in our friend?"

"He had my name and phone number in his pocket. The coroner's office asked me to ID the guy, but I'd never seen him before. Were you aware that he'd passed away?"

Pearl snorted. "We look like fools? Of course he's *dead*. Why else would the coroner send a van? He was laying out there still as stone an hour and a half after sunup. Down here, come daybreak, you better be on the move or the cops will bust you for loitering." Her lower teeth were dark and widely spaced as though every other one had been yanked out.

"Can you tell me his name?"

She measured me, sizing up my capacity to pay. "How much is it worth to you?"

Dandy said, "Come on now, Pearl. Why don't you answer the lady? She asked all polite and look how you're doing her."

"Would you butt out? I can handle this myself if it's all the same to you."

"Fellow passed on. She wants to know who he is. No reason to be rude."

"I asked why it's any of her concern? She ain't answer me, so why should I answer her?"

I said, "There's nothing complicated going on. The coroner's office wants to contact his next of kin so his family can decide what to do with his remains. I'd hate to see him buried in a pauper's grave."

"What difference does it make as long as it don't cost us anything?"

Her hostility was getting on my nerves, but I didn't think this was the time to introduce the notion of sensitivity training when she was already "sharing" her feelings. She went on. "What's it to you? You a social worker? Is that it? You work for St. Terry's or that clinic at the university?"

I was doing an admirable job of keeping my temper in check. Nothing sets me off quicker than belligerence, warranted or otherwise. "I'm a private investigator. Your friend must have found my name in the yellow pages. I wondered if he'd had a problem he needed help with."

"We all need help," Pearl said. She held out a hand to Dandy. "Gimme up."

He stood and pulled her to her feet. I watched while she dusted imaginary blades of grass from the back of her pants.

"Nice making your acquaintance," Dandy said.

The white kid took his cue from his companions and stubbed out the last half inch of the cigarette. He stood and took one last sip from the soda can before he crushed it underfoot. He might have left it in the grass, but since I was standing right there watching him, he tucked it into his backpack like a good Boy Scout. He gathered his sleeping bag, bundled it carelessly, and secured it to his backpack with a length of rope.

Clearly, our chummy conversation was coming to an end. I said, "Anybody know where he was from?"

No response.

"Can't you even give me a hint?"

The white kid said, "Terrence."

Pearl hissed, trying to shut him up.

Meanwhile, I was drawing a blank. "Which is where?"

Felix was staring off to one side. "You ast his first name."

"Got it. Terrence. I appreciate the information. What about his last name?"

"Hey! Enough. We don't have to tell you nothing," Pearl said.

I was about to choke the woman to death with my bare hands when Dandy spoke up.

"You have a business card? I'm not saying we'll get back to you, but just in case."

"Of course."

I reached into my shoulder bag and took one out, which I handed to him. "I jog most weekday mornings, so you can always look for me on the bike path. I'm usually here by six fifteen."

He examined the card. "What kind of name's Kinsey?"

"My mother's maiden name."

He looked up. "You happen to have any spare smokes on you?"

"I don't," I said, patting my jacket as though to verify the fact. I was about to add that I didn't have any spare change either, but it seemed insulting as he hadn't inquired about my financial state. Pearl had lost interest. She grabbed her shopping cart and began hauling it toward the bike path, wheels digging into the soft grass.

When it was clear the three were moving on, I said, "I appreciate your help. If you think of anything useful, you can let me know."

Dandy paused. "You know that minimart a block down?"

"Sure."

"You pick up a couple packs of cigarettes and it might put Miss Pearly White in a mood to chat."

"She can bite my big fat ass," Pearl said.

"Thanks a bunch. Really fun," I sang as they ambled away.

2

I retraced my route, this time hanging a right onto Bay and then a left onto Albanil. I found a parking place two doors down from my studio and let myself in through the squeaking gate. I continued around to the backyard and skirted the flagstone patio. I unlocked my door and tossed my shoulder bag on a kitchen stool.

My studio was created when my eighty-eight-year-old landlord, Henry Pitts, built a spacious new two-car garage and converted his former one-car garage into a rental unit. At the time I was looking for a place near the beach. I'd been scouting the area on foot in hopes of spotting a For Rent sign when I came across the notice he'd posted in the neighborhood laundromat. We met, chatted briefly, and agreed to a three-month trial period during which we could decide if the arrangement suited us.

From the first, I thought he was adorable—tall and lean, with bright blue eyes, a healthy head of white hair, and a wicked smile. As it turned out, Henry and I were perfect for each other, not in any romantic sense, but as good friends living close to each other. Not infrequently I'm on the road for work purposes, and during the periods when I'm home I tend to keep to myself. Henry is similarly self-sufficient and as committed to independence as I am. I'm tidy and quiet. He's tidy and gregarious, with a strong sense of decorum, which means he minds his own business unless I'm in need of a dressing-down, as is sometimes the case. He's a retired commercial baker and he was happy to have someone on whom to lavish his freshly made cinnamon rolls and chocolate-chunk brownies. Soon we were making the trek to the neighborhood tavern for dinner a couple of nights a week. He would also issue an impromptu dinner invitation when he'd made a beef stew or a big pot of vegetable soup.

When I first moved in, I was thirty-two years old and he was eighty-two, an age gap I considered negligible. What's fifty years' difference between friends? I've been his tenant now for going on seven years and can't imagine living anywhere else. The only blip on the radar screen was an unfortunate incident when a bomb exploded and blew the roof off my place. Henry assumed the role of general contractor during the reconstruction, redesigning and furnishing the whole of it as though he'd been doing it all his life. He fashioned the remodel after a ship's interior, complete with a porthole in the front door.

Given the plunging late-afternoon temperatures, I was happy to be back in my cozy little place. The space is compact. Numerous built-in cabinets and cubbyholes provide more storage space than you'd think possible. Though a mere fifteen feet on a side, the downstairs comprises a living room, a makeshift corner office, a full bath, and a five-foot bump-out to accommodate a galley-style kitchen. A small spiral staircase leads up to a sleeping loft with a Plexiglas skylight above the bed and a bathroom with a window at tub level that looks out into the trees.

By way of modern conveniences, I have a stacking washer and dryer, a microwave oven, and a lightweight vacuum cleaner for my few square yards of cotton shag wall-to-wall carpet. I don't often cook, unless you want to count heating a can of tomato soup as a culinary accomplishment. Those of us who don't cook seldom have to worry about a sink full of dirty dishes, so a dishwasher would have been beside the point. After breakfast, I wash my cereal bowl and spoon, juice glass, and coffee mug, and leave them in the dish rack to air-dry until I need them again. Lunches I eat out, except for days when I take a sandwich, an apple, and cookies to munch while I'm sitting at my desk. On the rare nights when I have dinner at home, I put together one of my favorite sandwiches and serve it on a folded paper towel that I can then toss in the trash. This, by the way, is yet another argument for being single. Whatever I choose to do, there's no one to complain.

Henry was tied up that night, catering a small dinner party for Moza Lowenstein down the street. Rosie's Tavern was closed for the week because Rosie and William had flown to Flint, Michigan, the day before to help care for Henry and William's sister, Nell, who had undergone a second surgery on the hip she'd broken in the spring. She was just getting out of rehab, and Rosie and William had agreed to be on hand until the following Friday, offering assistance when she was discharged. William is Henry's brother, older by one year. Their sister, Nell, at ninety-nine, is the oldest of the five Pitts "kids," with Charlie and Lewis, ages ninety-one and ninety-six respectively, filling in the gap.

An addendum to the plan was that Rosie was having her building fumigated while they were out of town. In anticipation of the process, the restaurant kitchen and storage areas had been emptied, and Henry's second and third bedrooms were now jammed with all manner of foodstuffs. I didn't inquire too closely what had motivated the purge. Rosie's devil-may-care Hungarian dishes often feature animal organs, finely minced and sauced with a slurry of alarming black specks and chewy bits. I didn't want to think about mice, weevils, and cigarette beetles.

I knew Henry would report on the family drama at the first opportunity, which I anticipated in the next few days. In the meantime, I was on my own, a happy circumstance for someone of my sometimes prickly disposition. I changed into my sweats and put together a deluxe hot hard-boiled-egg sandwich and poured myself a glass of Chardonnay. After supper, I curled up on the sofa with a mystery novel until I put myself to bed.

The next day, Saturday, I cruised the beach area hoping to see my homeless pals. I didn't intend to make this my life's work. I thought the coroner's office had a better chance than I did of picking up a proper ID on Terrence Last-Name-Unknown.

However, since I'd scored the dead man's first name the day before, my modest success was now spurring me on. Pearl's antagonism was a motivating factor as well. If she'd known me better—or at all—she'd have realized that her surliness was more of a challenge than an insult.

I was still debating the purchase of the cigarettes Dandy had implied might open the floodgates where Terrence was concerned. I questioned the ethics of supplying the trio with tobacco products as a means to an end. Given current scientific research, I think it's fair to point out that smoking's not a healthy practice, and I was reluctant to foster the habit among those who could ill afford it. On the other hand, as Pearl had so tartly observed in our first conversation, what business was it of mine?

Having sacrificed my principles, I was left with the burning question (as it were) of which brand to buy. I had no way to evaluate the virtues of filtered cigarettes versus nonfiltered, or mentholated versus nonmentholated, so I was forced to throw myself on the mercy of the minimart clerk, who appeared to be fourteen years old—too young to *buy* cigarettes let alone sell them to me.

I said, "I could use some help here. What's the cheapest brand of cigarettes you have?"

He turned and picked up a pack of Carlton's, which he placed in front of me.

"Is this what the homeless smoke?"

Without a change of expression he reached under the counter and pulled out a generic brand I'd never heard of.

"I need two more." I'd already decided I'd better provide a pack for each so no feelings would be hurt.

He put two additional packs on top of the first.

"How much?"

"A buck nine."

"That's not bad," I said. I don't smoke myself, so I didn't know what to expect.

"Each."

"*Each?* Are you kidding me?"

He was not. I paid for the three packs and tossed them into my shoulder bag. Three dollars plus change seemed like a lot to pay, but maybe I could claim the deduction on my Schedule A when tax season rolled around.

There was no sign of the threesome as I drove along Cabana Boulevard on my way home.

Sunday, I made another trip to the beach, my Grabber Blue Mustang attracting the usual curious stares. If my homeless friends wanted to duck me, it wouldn't be hard to do. I drove at a speed so slow it made other drivers honk. I passed the recreation center and followed the wide curve that skirted the lagoon that served as a bird refuge. I knew Pete Wolinsky had been shot to death somewhere along here, but it seemed ghoulish to park and search out the spot.

I rolled through the small parking lot along the water's edge and drove back the way I'd come, scanning both sides of the road. This was clearly unproductive, so I shifted to Plan B. At Milagro, I turned right and drove to the homeless shelter. Harbor House was situated in the middle of the block. The lot is narrow, the building itself set back from the street. There were eight parking spaces in front, all of them in use. I parked on the street. A metal accordion gate had been pulled across the front door and secured with a padlock. A hand-lettered sign pasted on a side window said NA SUPPORT GROUP MEETS MONDAY AT 2:00.

While Narcotics Anonymous might not meet on weekends, surely the shelter itself was open. I backed up six steps and peered in both directions. To the right of the building, a heavy-duty fence prevented passage. To the left, a double-wide drive ran between Harbor House and the service station next door. I followed the asphalt path. Tucked between the building and the drive, a stucco arch opened onto a courtyard where a small group of men and women had gathered to smoke. Landscaping was an afterthought: two palms, a few shrubs, and random patches of grass. Sand-filled coffee cans did double duty as receptacles for cigarette butts and freshly hawked-up goobers. Though I felt out of place, what worked to my advantage was that in turtleneck, jeans, and scuffed boots I looked like everyone else.

A metal folding chair was planted in the archway, but no one manned the entrance and no one took notice as I crossed the patio to a door that stood open to the air. I went in, wondering if I'd be asked about my reasons for being on the premises.

Being rule governed, I operate in a world filled with imaginary restraints. I'm happiest when signs are posted—NO SPITTING, NO PUBLIC URINATION, NO WALKING ON THE GRASS. I might not obey but at least I knew where I stood.

For the record, I should say this: I don't romanticize the plight of the homeless or project sentiment where none is required. My take on the indigent is that some are there because of temporary setbacks, some by default, and some for lack of an alternative. Some are needy, some are off their meds, some have opted out, some have been ousted from facilities where they might be better served. Many are there for life and not always by personal choice. Alcoholic, addicted, aimless, illiterate, unmotivated, unskilled, or otherwise unable to prosper, they sink to the bottom, and if they're down for any length of time, they lose the capacity to climb back out of the hole into which they've fallen. If there's a remedy, I don't know what it is. From what I've seen of the problem, most solutions perpetuate the status quo.

The room I entered was large, furnished with an assortment of couches and chairs, many occupied. The foot traffic in and out was constant. A handsome gentleman in his midsixties was perched on a rolling chair behind the counter to my right. There was a woman ahead of me in this two-person line and I waited my turn. She removed a laminated card from her jeans pocket. By shifting slightly, I saw that it bore her name, an ID number, and a photo likeness.

She pushed the card across the counter. "Hi, Ken. Could you check to see if I have mail?"

She leaned on the counter and peered over the edge. On the desktop below there was a ceramic mug full of toothbrushes, still sealed in cellophane packaging. "Can I have one of those?"

By way of reply, he held up the mug and watched as she selected a red toothbrush and put it in her fanny pack. He said, "I heard you were sick. Feeling better?"

She made a face. "I was in the hospital two days. I passed a kidney stone—little bitty thing about the size of a grain of sand—and I'm puking my guts out and shrieking like a banshee. The ER doc thinks I'm faking to score a few Vicodin and that pissed me off. I raised a stink until the other doc signed an order to have me admitted. I finally got a shot of Demerol, no thanks to the asshole who turned me down."

"But you're okay now?"

"I'd feel better if my check came in. I got two bucks left to my name."

He took her ID card and turned away, using his feet to scoot himself from the counter to a metal file cabinet behind him. He put the ID on top and began a finger stroll through the files. After a moment he said, "Nope. Not today."

"Can you go through the bin? Might be a big manila envelope with some other paperwork. They said it went out Tuesday, so it should be here."

He leaned down to a large white plastic United States Postal Service bin, where oversize and bulky packages were lined up. He took his time, looking at the name on each piece.

"Sorry." He rolled himself back to the counter and returned her ID. "Did you talk to Lucy? She was looking for you."

"I saw her Thursday, but not since. What'd she want?"

"No idea. You might take a look at the board and see if she left you a note."

She stepped away from the counter and disappeared around the corner at the far end where the bulletin board was apparently mounted on the wall.

Ken turned his attention to me. "What can I do for you?"

I toyed with the notion of a ruse, but I couldn't see the point. "I'm looking for information about a fellow named Terrence. I don't have his last name, but I'm hoping you'll know who I mean. He died a couple of days ago."

"We can't give out information about our clients. The social worker might help, but she's not here today."

"What about Dandy or Pearl?"

His expression remained neutral, as though even acknowledging the existence of a client would violate protocol. "Can't help. You're welcome to come in and take a look."

Surprised, I said, "Really? You don't mind if I walk around?"

"This isn't a private club. Anyone can join," he said.

"Thanks."

I circled the common room, which was spacious enough to accommodate the twenty-five people present without any suggestion of crowding. There was a big television set in one corner, but the screen was dark. There was a lone bookcase in evidence, the shelves lined side to side with an ancient-looking set of encyclopedias. One fellow had commandeered a couch for napping purposes, and he was curled up with a jacket over him. There were a few ongoing conversations, but in the main people weren't doing much. An exception was the two women who sat at either end of a Naugahyde couch with knitting projects. One unraveled row after row of a pink sweater, which shrank in her hands, reduced to a lap full of kinked yarn. The other woman struggled with size-19 needles and a ball of thick green wool. The article she was knitting was impossible to identify, something with bumps and irregular edges and holes where stitches had gotten away from her. I don't knit often these days, but I'm acquainted with the perils. The same aunt who browbeat me into memorizing the rivers of the world by length (the Nile, the Amazon, the Yangtze, the Mississippi-Missouri, the Yenisey, the Yellow, on and on) also taught me to knit and crochet—not for the pleasure of it, but with the intent to promote patience. This for me at age six when no child is content to sit for more than a minute at a time.

More to the point here: no Pearl, no Dandy, no Felix, and I'd gone as far as I could go. The dead man was dead. If he'd needed my help, it was already too late to be of service. First thing in the morning I'd call Aaron Blumberg and pass along what I'd learned. Armed with a first name and a description of the deceased, he might track down a doctor who could fill in the blanks. "A bum named Terrence with a bad limp" was hardly definitive, but it was a step in the right direction. Meanwhile, my participation was at an end.

3

Monday, I tried three times with no luck to reach Aaron Blumberg at the coroner's office. I left messages, asking him to call me when he had a minute. I could have taken the opportunity to detail the scanty facts I'd picked up, but I was hoping for a pat on the head for my resourcefulness. I spent most of the day puttering around the office, feeling distracted and oddly out of sorts. I left early, arriving home at 4:15 instead of the usual 5:00 P.M. I passed Rosie's twice in my search for a parking place and noted the building was now draped in enormous rectangular tarpaulins that were clipped together along the edges. The red, white, and turquoise stripes gave the place the look of a circus big top. I parked the car around the corner on Bay in the only semilegal spot I could find.

When I reached the backyard, Henry was hard at work in shorts, a T-shirt, and bare feet, his flip-flops tossed aside on the flagstone walk. His face was smudged with dirt, his white hair dampened by sweat, and his shins flecked with mud. His nose and cheeks were rosy from the autumn sunshine. He'd apparently spent the past couple of hours aerating the lawn in preparation for overseeding the grass. Some sections he'd attacked with a rototiller, then leveled the ground with a weighted roller he'd rented for the occasion. A scoop of fine lawn mulch had been piled to one side with a shovel resting against the wall.

He'd recently acquired a cypress potting bench that was now attached to the garage. The unit boasted a zinc top and two drawers where he kept his gardening gloves and the smaller of his gardening tools. On the shelf below he'd placed his galvanized watering cans and a big bag of sphagnum moss. The adjacent wall was designated for the larger tools—his wood-handled garden forks, trowels, cultivators, and graduating sizes of pruning shears. Painted outlines assured that each piece would be returned to its proper place.

Along with his other fall projects, he was transplanting three dozen marigolds from the original plastic commercial nursery containers to terra-cotta pots. He'd already lined my modest porchlet with half a dozen of these rust-and-gold arrangements, which I thought quite festive.

"You've been busy," I remarked.

"Getting the jump on winter. Another couple of weeks we'll lose daylight saving time and it'll be close to dark by this hour. How about you? What are you up to?"

"Nothing much. I was asked to ID a guy at the morgue, but I'd never seen him before."

"Why you?"

"He had my name and number on a slip of paper in his pocket. Blumberg, the coroner's investigator, assumed we were acquainted."

"What was that about?"

"Who knows? He was a homeless fellow, found dead in his sleeping bag on the beach. This was Friday morning. I've been trying to get a line on him but haven't picked up much. Business is down so at least it gives me something to do. You need help?"

"I'm just about done with this phase, but I'd love the company. I haven't seen you since, what, Thursday?"

"Yep. After Rosie and William left," I said. I set my shoulder bag on the porch and I settled on the step where he'd laid his three-ring binder for ready reference. While Henry returned two pieces of lawn equipment to the garage, I spread the binder open on my lap and studied the list of items he'd checked off. He'd emptied, scoured, and refilled the bird feeders; harvested the last of the summer herbs for drying; pulled faded annuals from flower beds; and transplanted his perennials. He'd also scrubbed and hosed off the outdoor furniture, which was currently air-drying before he stacked it in the storage shed until spring.

When he reappeared, he detached a sprinkler head from the hose and began to round up the length of it in a neat coil.

"What's next?" he asked.

I put a tick mark by the job he'd just completed. "Once you finish the lawn, all you have left is to air the wool blankets and comforters before you remake the beds. How's Nell?"

"She's doing well, but William's turned into a royal pain in the butt, and I mean literally. She'd been home from rehab less than an hour before he started complaining his sciatica was acting up."

"He has a problem with sciatica? Since when?"

Henry waved off the idea. "You know him—highly suggestible and just a tiny bit competitive. I talked to him Friday and heard the whole tale, symptom by symptom. He said it was fortunate he'd taken his cane along though it was barely adequate given the extent of his disability. He's had to borrow Nell's walker so he can hobble from place to place. He thought Rosie should rush him to the nearest emergency room, but she was busy fixing dinner, so she made Charlie take him instead. The good news—or the bad, depending on your point of view—is the doctor suggested an MRI and William's decided to have it done here. He says he's in dire need of a nerve specialist and asked me to set up an appointment."

I said, "Wow. He's not due back until the end of the week. I'm surprised he'd put up with the delay."

"Well, here's how it went. I started calling around, assuming it would be weeks before a slot opened up, but Dr. Metzger had a cancellation for tomorrow morning at nine. William's booked the first flight home."

"What about Rosie?"

"She'll stay until the end of the week as planned. I'm sure she's happy to have him off her hands, and I gather the other sibs are equally relieved. They plan to teach Rosie to play bridge, which William never got the hang of anyway. He gets in at five, which means once I pick him up at the airport, I'll be at his beck and call. He claims he can barely bend over to tie his shoes."

"Five o'clock? Great. As in thirty minutes from now?"

He straightened up. "*What* time is it? It can't be that late."

"Four thirty-five by my watch."

Henry said a word that was so out of character, I had to laugh.

"I can pick him up," I said, getting to my feet. "It'll give you a chance to finish your chores and take a quick shower."

"I hate to ask you to do that in the thick of rush-hour traffic. I'll go as I am. I don't smell that bad." He gave his T-shirt a whiff and made a show of crossing his eyes while he held his nose.

"The airport's a twenty-minute drive. It's no big deal. You can pour me a glass of Chardonnay as soon as I get home."

"I'll do better than that. I'll buy you both supper at Emile's-at-the Beach, assuming William can sit that long."

"You got a deal."

Construction of the Santa Teresa Municipal Airport was begun in the early 1940s and the terminal opened for business with six gates that served two national airlines and three puddle jumpers. The pint-size structure was done in the usual Spanish style—a stucco exterior, a red tile roof, and a blaze of magenta bougainvillea artfully draped across the entranceway. Boarding and deplaning were accomplished on foot by way of a rolling set of stairs. Baggage claim was located outside the building in what looked like an extensive temporary carport.

I pulled into the parking lot at 4:59 P.M. just as a United flight was trundling along the runway toward Gate 4. It was a small commuter craft, one of the no-frills short hops where the best one could hope for in the way of food-and-beverage service is a box containing two small pieces of Chiclets chewing gum. The flight attendant would offer the gum in a wicker basket and you were welcome to help yourself as long as you took only one. I was in no particular rush, thinking William would be last off the plane, hampered by his painful, possibly life-threatening condition.

I passed through the ticketing area and out the French doors into the small grassy courtyard. I took my place near the chest-high stucco wall and watched through the length of window glass along the top as a uniformed gate agent pushed a wheelchair toward the prop jet. The engines shut down. Stairs were rolled into place. After a brief delay, the door was wrenched open, and William appeared, his cane hooked over his arm. The natural eddies of air along the runway ruffled his white hair and tugged at his suit coat. A stewardess followed in his wake, supporting him gently by the elbow as he came down the stairs. He didn't actually smack her hand, but he was visibly offended by the gesture, and he jerked his arm free. He was properly attired for travel in the same dark three-piece suit he wore for funerals and visitations. He took his time, descending the portable stairs like a toddler, first one foot down and joined by the other before he undertook the next. The remaining passengers crowded against the doorway, trying to determine what the traffic jam was about. William was not to be hurried. He was an elegant gentleman, with the same lean frame Henry had been graced with. When he reached the tarmac, he turned and waited at the foot of the stairs, leaning on his cane while the other passengers pushed past him, giving him cross looks.

The pilot appeared next, carrying a bulky red canvas duffel bag with a mesh panel on each end. Behind the pilot, the copilot, or possibly the flight engineer, stepped out of the plane toting William's black rolling suitcase. Somehow he'd not only claimed the right to deplane first, but he'd enlisted the assistance of the entire crew. They'd probably jumped at the chance to be shed of him. Whatever the motivation, William seemed to take the personal ministrations for granted.

As far as I could tell, he was fine—ambulatory at any rate. He had the pilot place the canvas duffel in the wheelchair, which he manned himself, pushing it toward the terminal. When he caught sight of me, he winced and placed a hand at the small of his back as though stricken with sharp pain. The copilot/flight engineer extended the handle on William's suitcase and tagged after him dutifully, pulling it along behind. As William and his merry band approached the terminal, I moved out to meet them and took over responsibility for the suitcase, murmuring my thanks to the crew.

William paused and leaned his weight on the handles of the wheelchair. "Let me catch my breath," he said. "It's been a rough trip. Three stops and just as many changes of aircraft."

I suspected he was hoping to generate a touch of sympathy, which I offered obligingly before he could up the ante. "You must be exhausted," I said.

"Not to worry. I just need a moment."

"Why don't you take advantage of the wheelchair and let me push you? It'll save you a few steps."

"No, no. I like to do for myself . . . while I'm able," he added. "You might bring the car around. I doubt I can make it as far as the parking lot. I'll rest on one of the benches out front."

"What about checked bags?"

"This is it."

I decided I might as well take the duffel as long as I was heading for the car. I could put it in the trunk and then swing around and pick him up. I grabbed the satchel by the handle and lifted it from the seat of the wheelchair. It was heavier than I'd anticipated and the contents shifted as though he'd packed a bowling ball without securing it properly. I said, "Whoa! What have you got in here?"

I set it down and leaned over so I could peer through the mesh. A hissing white cat, topped with patches of caramel and black, put its ears back and spat. I jerked away, my heart hammering. This cat was the equivalent of the one in horror movies, jumping out when you're expecting the guy with the bloody butcher knife. "Where did that come from?" I asked, patting my chest.

"I brought the cat," he said complacently. "I couldn't bear to leave it behind. Lewis was going to take it to the pound."

"I'm not surprised. Talk about a cranky beast."

"Not as cranky as it would have been if I hadn't prevailed. I wanted to have the cat with me in the cabin, but the ticket agent refused. I knew there'd be room under the seat in front of me, but she said it was the cargo hold or nothing. Her supervisor was just as argumentative until I mentioned my attorney."

"Why do you have a cat at all?"

"This is the stray Charlie took in months ago. Lewis has been opposed all along, which just goes to show what a heartless fellow he is."

I said, "Ah. This is the cat Nell toppled over when she broke her hip."

"Well, yes, but it wasn't the *cat's* fault. Even Nell admitted she should have watched where she was stepping."

William scratched affectionately on the top of the canvas

duffel, which caused the cat to rocket around the interior and then ricochet from end to end. "Very playful," he remarked.

The cat began to claw at the side of the carrier so vigorously, the zipper inched down a hair. I'd have tugged it back into place but I didn't dare put my hand anywhere near the carrier. I didn't think the cat could reach me with its claws, but I wasn't sure the cat knew that.

I returned the carrier to the wheelchair and pushed it as far as the entrance. In no way was I going to tote the cat through the parking lot to the car. I left William on a bench outside, the duffel at his feet, while I retrieved the Mustang, paid the parking fee, and brought it around to the front. William leaned over and said something to the cat, then jumped back as I had. He was apparently so caught up in the cat's playful antics that he'd forgotten about his infirmity. I put his rolling bag in the trunk and wedged the cat carrier into the space behind the driver's seat while William took his place in the front, wincing in pain.

"Are you all right?"

"I'm fine. Don't mind me."

I put the car in gear and eased away from the curb. I hadn't driven ten feet before the cat let out a long continuous howl, its tone moving up and down the scale as though yodeling. "Does it always do that?"

"Oh no. Just in the car on the way to the airport and all three flights. Airline passengers can be very unpleasant when things don't go their way. The woman in front of me had a horrid little girl who screamed and cried the whole time, but did anyone complain about that? No, sir."

"Is it male or female?"

"I'm not sure. I think you're supposed to peek at something underneath, but the cat doesn't care for the idea. Charlie would know. He took it to the vet."

"Does it have a name? Joe? Sally? That might be a clue."

"We referred to the cat as 'the cat.' I'm sure Nell or Charlie would have come up with a name, but Lewis kept threatening to toss it out and neither of them wanted to get attached. If you think about it, I saved its life, a selfless act on my part."

"Good for you," I said. "I must say I'm surprised Rosie agreed to go along with the plan. Where are you going to keep it?"

William and Rosie occupied a two-bedroom apartment above the tavern. I'd never actually seen the place, but Henry assures me the rooms are small and dark and crowded with oversize furniture.

William said, "Oh, it's not for me. I thought Henry would enjoy the companionship."

"Does Henry know about this?"

"Not yet."

"Oh, boy."

"You think that's a problem?"

"Far be it from me to say."

We drove for a while in silence except for the cat, which was now growling and making relentless work of canvas scratching in between thumps and flinging itself from side to side. I was trying to visualize Henry's reaction, which I knew would be genuine and heartfelt and probably high pitched. I've never lived with a cat myself, but I'd always assumed there was paraphernalia involved. I looked over at William, saying, "What about a litter box? Isn't that where cats do their business?"

He blinked. "That's not necessary, do you think? Nell let it out in the backyard."

"But we live on a busy street. The cat will get hit by a car. Henry's going to have enough adjustments to make without the cat doing caca on his couch."

"You may have a point. We better stop at the market. You can go in while I mind the cat."

I think it was occurring to William that his plan was ill advised because his back problem seemed to take a sudden turn for the worse. He emitted a short yelp and sucked air through his teeth.

"Are you sure you don't want me to drop you at the house and come back?" The minute I suggested it I knew William would be too smart to introduce the cat without someone else close at hand. Henry would tone down his response if I was present.

"The pain comes and goes. Sometimes it's no more than a mild tingling or dull ache. Sometimes a burning sensation. The urgent-care doctor said it could be due to a slipped disc or spinal stenosis. I'll have to have *tests*."

"You poor thing," I said. To William, a "test" was the prelude to a terminal diagnosis.

I left the 101 at Capillo and took surface streets in a zigzag detour to the nearest market. I left the howling cat in the car while William limped to and fro in the parking lot, flicking pitiful looks in my direction.

I went into the store and wandered up and down the aisle devoted to pets, throwing items in my cart. The litter box was an easy choice, but there were five or six kinds of litter, and I had no idea what cats preferred in the way of toilet soil. I finally picked the one with the four cute kittens on the package. I threw in a bag of dry food with only the briefest of debates about chicken versus tuna flavors. Then I bought ten small cans of wet food, choosing items I thought I'd like if I were in the cat's place, only not as hostile. I nearly stopped at the pay phone to call Henry, but he'd probably assume I was playing a practical joke.

Thus it was that I searched out a parking space for the second time that afternoon, this one three doors down from my studio. I put myself in charge of William's rolling bag and I even went so far as to remove the cat carrier from the backseat, lugging it in one hand as I maneuvered the rolling suitcase with the other. William held open the gate and then trailed along behind me most reluctantly, I thought. I carried the duffel as far as Henry's back door and set it down.

"You can do the honors," I said. When I looked back at William, he was bent double, staring at the walk as though searching for a lost dime.

"Back's out," he said.

Henry opened the kitchen door. "Good heavens," he said as he moved to William's side. Between us, we helped him up the few shallow steps and into the kitchen. Moaning, William sank into Henry's rocking chair. I went back for the suitcase and that's when I saw the cat's paw appear through a gap where it had worked the zipper down.

I've never been present in a delivery room in the tender moment when a child is born, but I picture it much like this. The slit was no more than an inch long when the cat began to push through the opening. After the first paw, its head emerged and shortly after that, one shoulder, followed by a second white paw with a very long front leg attached. Cats are amazingly agile, as was plain to see. I watched, hypnotized, as though witnessing a miracle. "Hey, William?" I said, but by then, the cat had wiggled free and streaked off toward the shrubs.

Henry snapped to attention. "What the hell was that?"

Weakly, William said, "Surprise!"

4

Tuesday morning I rolled out of bed at 6:00, brushed my teeth, and pulled on my sweats and running shoes. A baseball cap eliminated the need to deal with my hair, which was flat on one side and standing straight out on the other. When I left the house, the only hint that the cat was still in the vicinity was a pair of mouse feet and a long gray tail on my welcome mat. I tied my key into the laces of one shoe and set out at a slow clip, hoping to warm up before I began to jog in earnest.

Henry's dinner invitation from the night before had been superseded by our efforts to persuade the cat to come out of the bushes. Since William was incapacitated, it fell to Henry and me to crawl around on the newly aerated lawn, coaxing the cat with kitty treats and threats, all to no avail. Once it got dark, we'd been forced to abandon the attempt and hope that the cat would at least remain where it was until morning.

The day promised to be warm. In typical California fashion, the damp and chill of the week before had been replaced by temperatures slated to reach the low eighties. A lingering marine layer hovered like thick white batting, but that would burn off by midday. As though in proof of this, a column of bright yellow sunshine illuminated the ocean just offshore, looking as though a monster hole had been punched in the clouds.

I completed the three-mile loop and slowed to a walk. I hadn't seen my homeless pals and I wondered how many times the notion of their whereabouts would cross my mind. It was like having a tune lodged in my head, endless replays of a melody I couldn't seem to block. The week before I'd known nothing of the dead man and nothing of his friends. Now I was troubled by their absence. In deciding to dismiss the matter, I'd succeeded only in tempering its effect. Terrence still hovered on the periphery while I waited for someone to step forward with a few concrete facts. I suppose I'd assumed that once I knew what his story was, I could forget about him entirely and his cronies along with him.

Home again, I showered, dressed, ate my cereal, and read the paper. When I left the studio, there was still no sign of Henry, William, or the cat. Either Henry had lured it inside or it had remained stubbornly out of reach. I left the mouse parts where they were in case the cat was looking forward to a snack later in the day. I hadn't even known we had mice on the property and now the population was down by one.

Driving to the office, I spotted a pedestrian in a familiar herringbone sport coat poised to cross the street half a block ahead. He gave a quick look in each direction and then fixed his gaze on the sidewalk as he stepped up on the curb, heading in the same direction I was. I slowed and peered closely. Apparently, Fate wasn't done with me because sure enough, it was Dandy in baggy black trousers and a pair of bright white running shoes. I pulled over to the curb and rolled down the car window on the passenger side. "Dandy? It's Kinsey. You want a ride?"

He smiled when he caught sight of me. "That'd be nice. I was on my way to your office."

"Hop in and I'll deliver you to my door."

I flipped the locks. Dandy opened the car door and slid into the passenger seat, bringing with him the cloudy smell of old cigarettes, which seemed to cling to his clothes. His pale pink dress shirt was freshly ironed and had the stiffness and sheen of spray starch. I had to guess he'd spiffed himself up in anticipation of the visit. I could smell soap and shampoo and the saturated scent of alcohol wafting through his skin. It was an odd combination; his efforts at personal hygiene undercut by his habitual intake of whiskey and nicotine. I experienced a

piercing sense of protectiveness because he seemed so un-
aware of his effect.

He held up my business card. "I never met a private eye, so
I thought I better see for myself."

"The office isn't much, but you can be the judge. I take it
Pearl wasn't panting to see me again."

"She doesn't like to walk. Me, I hoof it all over town. I
apologize for her being rude the other day."

"Is she always that hostile?"

"I wouldn't fret if I were you. It's nothing personal. Terrence was a good friend and his death was a blow. She hasn't
been handling it well."

"Why take it out on me? I didn't even know the man."

"She's disputatious, though she's not as tough as she'd have
us believe. She may give you a hard time, but she's a pussycat
at heart."

"Yeah, sure."

I took a right turn off Santa Teresa Street onto Caballero
Lane, which was one block long. My office was the center one
in a line of three small stucco cottages. In addition to the
cheap rent, the location was close to the heart of downtown, in
walking distance of the public library, the courthouse, and the
police station. I pulled up in front. There were ample parking spots available because the bungalows on either side of me
were empty and had been since I moved in. Dandy got out and
waited while I locked the car and joined him on the walk. He
had a courtly air about him. Maybe it was the dress shirt or the
hint of humor in his eyes. I thought he seemed surprisingly
intelligent, and then I had to stop and correct myself. Being
homeless and being smart aren't mutually exclusive states.
There might be any number of reasons he was on the street.

I led the way up the front steps. I unlocked the door and
opened it for him. "I'm putting on a pot of coffee if you're
interested."

"I'd like that," he said as he followed me in.

"Make yourself at home. I'll be right back."

"Thank you."

I rinsed out the coffeepot and slotted it onto the machine,
putting a fresh filter in the holder, which I popped into place.
Over my shoulder, I could see Dandy in the outer office, where
he browsed the various law books and texts in my collection,

everything from *California Criminal Law* to a 1980 edition of *Shooter's Bible*. There were also the technical tomes about burglary and theft, *Scott's Fingerprint Mechanics*, arson investigation, the criminal mind-set, and Adelson's *Pathology of Homicide*.

When he drifted into the inner office, I left the coffee brewing in the kitchenette and joined him. It crossed my mind, just briefly, that he might try pilfering an item, but then I remembered I didn't have anything of value. No cash, no dope, no prescription medication, and no bottle of booze in my bottom drawer. If he wanted a ballpoint pen, I'd be happy to gift him with one.

He'd taken a seat in one of the two guest chairs, clearly curious about my domain. I took my place on the other side of the desk and tried seeing the place through his eyes. As it happens, my office is devoid of personal touches. I have an artificial ficus tree that I think lends the room a hint of class, but the fake plant is about it. There are no family photographs, no travel posters, no bric-a-brac, and no paperweight advertising "Bail Bonds, Quick Response." For the most part, my desktop was clear, all of the paperwork consigned to folders tucked away in the file cabinets lining one wall.

He smiled. "Cozy."

"That's one word for it," I said. "Can I ask a personal question?"

"As long as I'm not under oath."

"I was wondering what brought you to Santa Teresa."

"This is my hometown. I grew up three blocks from here. My father taught math at Santa Teresa High back in the forties and fifties."

I made a face. "Math's not my strong suit."

"Nor mine," he replied. His smile activated dimples I hadn't noticed before. His teeth were charmingly buckled and flashed white against the dark of his complexion.

"Did you go to Santa Teresa High by any chance?" I asked.

"Yes, ma'am. I graduated class of nineteen and thirty-three, long before you were born. I attended City College for two years, but I couldn't see the point."

"Really? Same here. I went two semesters and then quit. Now I wish I'd stuck it out, but I sure don't want to go back."

"Better to get an education while you're young. My age, it's too late."

"Hey, mine, too. Did you like school? I hated it. High school, at any rate. I was a low-waller, smokin' dope half the time." Low-wallers were the kids who loitered before and after classes on a low wall that ran along the backside of the school grounds.

"I was straight A's. Then life came along and I guess while you went up in the world, I went down."

"I wouldn't call this up."

"Up from where I stand."

I didn't know if he viewed himself as a victim or a realist. I could hear the coffee machine gurgle to a halt and I got to my feet. "What do you take in your coffee?"

"Milk and two sugars, please."

"Sugar for sure. Milk could be a problem. Let me see what I can do."

I left the office and went down the hall to the kitchenette, where I opened my pint-size refrigerator and gave the milk carton a sniff. Slightly off, I thought, but I've heard that sometimes the residue of milk on the pour spout sours before the rest. I filled two mugs with coffee and added milk to mine, checking for the telltale curdling that suggests beaucoup bacteria at work. No evidence of spoilage, so I added a big dollop to his coffee and returned the carton to the fridge.

I handed him his mug and two paper packets of sugar and resettled myself in my swivel chair. I held up a finger. "Before I forget . . ." I leaned down and extracted the three packs of cigarettes from the shoulder bag at my feet and pushed them across the desk. "Consider this a bribe."

"Much appreciated. I'll pass along a pack each to Felix and Pearl."

"Pearl, in particular. I was hoping to elevate myself in her opinion."

There was a dip in the conversation. My usual practice is to let the silence lengthen until the other fellow gets squirmy enough to speak his mind. This time, I took the lead. "I'm assuming you didn't walk all this way to pay a social call."

"Not entirely. Don't take this wrong, but your asking about Terrence really set Pearl off."

"As I'm keenly aware. What's the big deal?"

"She says you smell like a cop."

"That's because I *was* a cop, once upon a time. I was with the STPD two years and then I got out. I like playing by the rules when it suits, but I don't like answering to anyone."

"Understandable," he said. "Then again, Terrence hadn't been dead a full day when you came sniffing around. Her words, not mine."

"'Sniffing' seems an odd choice. I told you I was hoping to locate his family, which is not a federal offense. Right now, he's a John Doe. His name might be Terrence, but that's the extent of what we have. The coroner's office is swamped this week, so I said I'd see what I could find out. What's she think I'm up to?"

"She's suspicious by nature while I'm the opposite. I believe most folks are honest until proven otherwise."

"My policy as well," I said. "What else is bugging her? We might as well put all our cards on the table as long as you're here."

"She thinks you're not being honest about who you're working for."

"What, like I'm an undercover agent? I'm self-employed. None of my work has anything to do with Terrence, dead or alive. You don't believe me, you can search my files."

"You don't work for St. Terry's?"

"Nope."

"You're not associated with the hospital or the university in any capacity at all?"

"No way. I'm freelance. I'll swear to it," I said. "I don't have clients in the medical profession or any related field. And that includes dentists and podiatrists. I don't know how else to assure you of my sincerity."

"I'll pass that on to her."

"Are we square?"

"As far as I'm concerned."

"Good. Then it's my turn. Why did Terrence need the services of a PI? I asked before and I didn't get an answer."

"He didn't spell out the particulars, but I know what was on his mind. He believed he had kin in the area. Growing up, he had an uncle he very much admired. The two were close when he was a kid, but he hadn't seen the man for years. Said he came to visit his uncle here shortly after the man moved to Santa Teresa. Later he heard the fellow died. He hoped to connect with family members, assuming there were any left."

"He never mentioned his uncle's name?"

"No. I happened to overhear him talking about it to someone else."

"Why pick me when there are half a dozen private eyes in town?"

"You know a fellow named Pinky Ford?"

"Of course. How do you know him?"

"He's a man about town, in some sense of the word. I haven't seen him in weeks, but he lives in a big yellow Cadillac he parks here and there. Terrence was asking around and Pinky told him you were a decent sort."

"I'd like to think so."

Dandy cocked his head. "How do you know Pinky? He doesn't seem like your type."

"Long story I'll save for another time."

"I may take you up on it," he said. "Meantime, what else can I tell you about Terrence?"

"Do you know where he was from?"

"Bakersfield. I don't know if he was born there, but the way he told it, that's where he lived most of his life."

"You met him at Harbor House?"

"That's right. He arrived here in January on a Greyhound bus. He'd been in prison up at Soledad. He said it was a life sentence, but that's all I know. He didn't like to talk about it. He slept a couple of nights under a freeway overpass and figured out it was a bad idea. The panhandlers with cardboard signs aren't as nice as the rest of us. You stand by the road begging, that's a different work ethic. Terrence tried the Rescue Mission, but they wouldn't take him unless he swore off alcohol, which he wasn't about to do. He heard about the shelter and when he showed up, the first person he met was Pearl. She introduced him to Felix and me. Harbor House, you don't have to be sober, but you'd better not be obstreperous. Make trouble and you're out."

"It seems like a cool place," I said. "I stopped by the day before yesterday looking for you."

"Sunday, we throw darts. Sports bar down the block has a weekly tournament."

"Are you any good?"

"Depends on what day it is and how much I've had to drink."

"I noticed the woman in line ahead of me had a shelter ID card. At least I think that's what it was. I wondered if Terrence had one. I ask because he didn't have any identification on him when the coroner brought him in."

"Oh, he had a card. I'm sure of it. Harbor House issued one so he could take his meals with us. Someone walked off with all his stuff, so maybe it was in his cart."

"He wasn't a Harbor House resident?"

"Not him. He didn't want a bed. Nights, he didn't like to be around other folks. He spent most of his time drunk and he hung out with another fellow in the same sorry shape. Now and then he tried cleaning up his act without much success."

"So he was in Santa Teresa, what, eight or nine months?"

"Sounds about right. He loved it here. He said he was never going anyplace else. March, the other fellow died and Terrence went on a bender that landed him in jail. After that he sobered up for a couple weeks. Then he started in again and one day collapsed in the street. He was lucky he didn't die that round. Pain meds and alcohol are a bad mix."

"No fooling. Pain pills? What was that about?"

"Up at Soledad, some fellows went after him with lead pipes. Busted up his leg bad, leaving him with a limp and a load of agony. He didn't sleep well because of it. He had to get up now and then and walk around so it wouldn't seize up. That was another reason he preferred to be outdoors, so he wouldn't bother any of the rest of us."

"I saw the damage to his leg when I was at the morgue. What triggered the attack?"

"He wouldn't say. Some things you'd ask and all he'd do is shake his head. When he spiraled down the second time, he ended up in St. Terry's. They put him through detox and then into rehab. Next thing I heard, he was on the street again. I didn't think he'd last a week. I figured it was just a matter of time before his demons got ahold of him and took him down."

"Is that what happened?"

"Naw. He got into a program that put him back on his feet."

"Apparently not for good."

Dandy smiled. "There's no such thing as 'for good' when

you're one of us. It's 'for good' until the first drink or you're back to chipping heroin. Meth, if you're really on a downward slide. Terrence went back to his old ways and that was the end of him. Pearl didn't want to believe he'd started drinking again. Broke her heart, if you want to know the truth. He finally got clean and then he couldn't maintain. Might sound odd coming from me. Nobody knows better than another drunk how hard it is to quit. Pearl believed he'd cleaned up his act. He gave her his word and she took it seriously."

"Do you know when he was last seen by a doctor? It would help if the coroner's office found a physician who'd sign off on the death certificate."

"There was a doctor headed up the program. He's the one terminated Terrence for disobeying the rules. I know he wasn't feeling well the last couple of weeks. Much as he drank, it wasn't any big surprise. He was a wreck of a human being and then he died and that's the end of it."

"What about his family? Any kids?"

"He burned that bridge a year ago. He was on the outs with his ex-wife and estranged from his kids. I don't know the whole of it, but I gather his kids as good as slammed the door in his face. He claimed he did everything in his power to make things right, but they weren't buying it."

"What was the issue?"

Dandy's smile was benign. "Being drunk's the issue. What else you got? He gave up on his kids because they gave up on him. That's the kind of pain for which there's no relief."

"It must have been hard on him."

"He learned his lesson that round. He wanted to be clean and sober before he contacted his kinfolk, which is why he carried your name in his pocket for months. He needed a go-between, someone to smooth the way for him. After what happened with his kids, he was through with surprises, I can tell you that."

"Meaning what?"

"The way he told it, his kids had no clue he'd come knocking at the door. He'd called and told 'em he wanted to make amends, but I guess they never thought they'd actually see him again and good riddance from their perspective. I believe he'd had a fair amount to drink by the time he got there. I fussed at him good when he told me how he'd gone about it. Said, bro, it's not cool. It's not cool at all. When there's bad blood, you don't do that—show up drunk and think your kids are going to welcome you with open arms. Doesn't work that way."

"Family's tough. It's like walking through a minefield, hoping you won't get blown to bits," I said. "I wonder what he was in prison for."

"He never said. Something bad must have gone down."

"I'm sorry he didn't call me."

"He might have been too sick. With him back on the booze, he was probably ashamed of himself. He disappeared for a month last summer and then he came back."

"Disappeared to where?"

"Los Angeles, but I don't know what he did there. Give a fellow his space is my attitude."

I tilted back in my swivel chair and propped my foot on the edge of the desk. "Depressing, isn't it?"

"Not every life turns out."

"Which I should know by now," I said. "The coroner's investigator says all Terrence had on him were the clothes on his back and the sleeping bag he died in. Didn't he own anything else?"

"'Course he did. Had a shopping cart where he kept his cookstove, his books, and a custom-made tent. All gone by the time we got to the beach on the morning he died. He also had a fancy backpack with an aluminum frame. Somebody walked off with everything."

"That's too bad. What kind of books?"

"These were textbooks mostly. He loved anything to do with plants. Trees, shrubs, container gardening, propagation. He knew everything there was to know about California oaks. Drop of a hat, he'd talk your ear off. It was hard to shut him up once he got started."

"Was he a teacher?"

"No, but he sure knew a lot. He said before he went to prison, he'd been working on a landscaping degree. He was a tree trimmer by trade, which was how he supported his family, but he wanted to be a landscape architect. Nights and weekends, he took classes."

"Must have been a bright guy."

"Very. He was a sweet man, too." Dandy shifted in his

chair. "Something else. Pearl didn't want me to tell you this, but I don't see why not. She thinks he had money. Lots of it."

"Really. Do you agree?"

"Yes, ma'am. I'm not sure where it came from, but he didn't live check-to-check like the rest of us. He kept a roll of bills in his pocket this big around." He made a sizable circle with his thumb and index finger.

"But that makes no sense. If he had money, why was he living on the streets? Why not rent a room?"

"He didn't care to spend his money that way. You might feel safe sleeping in your own bed, but to him, it was a night-mare. Furnished room was just like a cell to him. Too hot, too small, too noisy. Camping out feels like freedom. Even I know that and I never *been* in jail. Except a time or two . . ." he added, just to keep the record straight. "Point is, what he could afford wasn't relevant."

"So where do you think the money came from?"

"Beats me. He might have gone to prison for embezzle-ment. He might have robbed a bank. He didn't seem like the sort who'd do either one, but what do I know? Any rate, he knew what he wanted done with it when he passed."

"Such as what?"

"All I know is he went to that office-supply place up on State? He bought him a kit full of legal forms so he could draw up his last will and testament."

"That was enterprising."

"Yes, it was. He filled it out and had us sign as witnesses. Felix, Pearl, and me."

I could feel my head tilt, like a dog picking up a high-pitched whine inaudible to us humans. "How long ago was this?"

"July. I believe it was the eighth."

"So on the eighth of July, you witnessed his signature?"

"So did Felix and Pearl. We all did."

"Then you must know his full name."

Dandy's change of expression was nearly comical. I'd nailed him and he knew it. He'd been neatly sidestepping the matter of Terrence's identity, but he'd forgotten to censor the secondary references. Once I'd called him on it, he wasn't quick enough to fabricate a cover story. He looked at me as though I were blessed with psychic powers. "I'm right about that, aren't I?"

"I never lied. I wouldn't do that."

"But why didn't you speak up? We've been talking all around the subject and you knew his name the whole time."

"You didn't ask."

"I asked the first time we met. That was the whole point. I came down to the beach to find out who he was and I asked you straight out. The three of you were sitting right there."

"Pearl said not to tell."

"Are we still in grade school? Who made her the boss? I'm trying to do something nice for the man. Doesn't that mean anything to you? Whether he was on good terms with his kids or not, they have a right to know he's gone."

I noticed he'd stopped making eye contact and he was busy picking at a snag on the knee of his trousers.

I said, "So what was his name?"

I didn't think he'd answer. I watched him shift in his chair, wrestling with his conscience. On one hand, there was Pearl, the Holy Terror. If she found out he'd leaked the information, she'd break both of his clavicles, put him on the rack, and stretch him until she'd torn off his arms. On the other hand, there was me, all-around good person, generous with my coffee, and only occasionally guilty of sticking my nose into other people's business. "Dandy?"

"R. T. Dace. He went by his middle name, Terrence, but you never heard it from me."

I turned an imaginary key in my lips, locking them shut before I tossed away the key.

5

Fifteen minutes later, I dropped Dandy at the Harbor House. He hadn't asked for a ride. I'd offered . . . nay, I'd insisted. I wanted to get rid of him so I'd have a chance to think about what he'd said. Having chided him for withholding information, I'd been less than forthcoming myself.

I'd actually heard the name R. T. Dace before. Twice as a matter of fact. I couldn't remember the dates, but I knew of two distinct occasions in which people called to ask for him. What the heck was that about?

I left the shelter trying to recall the circumstances in which the phone calls had come in. It was distracting, trying to pin down the reference in a moving vehicle while hoping to obey traffic laws and avoid running over pedestrians. I turned into one of the public parking lots that looked out over the beach to the ocean beyond. I pulled into a slot and killed the engine. I laid my head back and closed my eyes, slowing my breath, working to silence the chatter in my head.

The inquiries had come months before, probably midsummer. I'd taken the first call at the office. I remembered that much. I tried to picture the cases I was working at the time, but my mental screen was blank. I set the point aside and focused on the fragment of conversation that had stuck in my mind. I was eating lunch at my desk when the phone rang. I put a quick hand against my mouth, chewing and swallowing in haste before I picked up. "Millhone Investigations."

"May I speak to Mr. Millhone?"

The caller was male, on the young side, and his voice, while deep, suggested an underlying anxiety. I was already thinking it was a sales call, some boiler-room trainee learning the ropes. I'd pushed the caution button in my head while I tried to guess the nature of the upcoming pitch. Telemarketers inevitably say "How are you today?" in a tone that's patently insincere, using the question as a means of engaging you in conversation. I said, "There isn't a Mr. Millhone."

The fellow cut in, but instead of the expected spiel, he said, "This is Dr. . . ."

I blanked on the name instantly because I had zeroed in on the voice, thinking it might be one I recognized. "What can I do for you?"

"I'm trying to reach Mr. Dace."

"Who?"

"Artie Dace. I understand he doesn't have a phone, but I hoped you'd put me in touch with him. Is he there by any chance?"

"You have the wrong number. There's no Mr. Dace here."

"Do you know how I can reach him? I tried the shelter, but they won't confirm the name."

"Same here. I never heard of him."

There was a brief silence. "Sorry," he said, and the line went dead.

I remembered dismissing the call the moment I hung up, though I half expected the phone to ring again. Wrong numbers seem to come in clusters, often because the calling party tries the same number a second time, thinking the error is connected to the dialing process. I stared at the handset and when the phone didn't ring, I shrugged and went about my business.

The second call came within a matter of days. I know this because the name Dace had been planted recently enough that I hadn't yet deleted it from memory. I'd closed the office early and I was having my calls forwarded. Henry and I were sitting in the backyard when the phone in my studio began to ring. I'd left my door open for just this reason, in case a client tried to reach me. When the phone rang a second time, I leaped to my feet and trotted into the apartment, where I caught the phone on the third ring. "Millhone Investigations."

"May I speak to Mr. Millhone?"

This time the caller was a woman and I could hear noise in the background that suggested a public setting. "This is Kinsey Millhone. What can I do for you?"

The woman said, "This is the Cardiac Care Unit at Santa Teresa Hospital. We've admitted Mr. Artie Dace and we're hoping you can give us information about what medications he's on. He's in and out of consciousness and unable to respond to questions."

I squinted at the handset. "*Who's* this?"

"My name is Eloise Cantrell. I'm the charge nurse in the CCU. The patient's name is Artie Dace."

This time, I'd picked up a pen and pulled over a scratch pad, making a note of the nurse's name. I added CCU. "I don't know anyone named Artie."

"The last name is Dace, initials R. T."

"I still can't help you."

"But you do know the gentleman. Is that correct?"

"No, and I don't understand why you're calling me. How did you get my name and number?"

"The patient was brought in through the emergency room and one of the nurse's aides recognized him from a prior hospitalization. Medical Records located his chart and the doctor asked me to get in touch."

"Look, I wish I could help, but I don't know anyone by that name. Honest."

There was a stretch of silence. "This isn't in regard to his hospital bill. He's covered by Medicaid," she said, as though that might soften my stance.

"Doesn't matter. I don't know anyone named Dace and I certainly don't know what medications he's on."

Her tone turned cool. "Well, I appreciate your time and I'm sorry to have troubled you."

"No problem."

And that was the extent of it.

I opened my eyes and looked out at the ocean. Maybe Dace *had* tried to reach me, but he'd been ill at the time. The doctor whose name I'd missed and the charge nurse, Eloise Cantrell, had probably discovered my name and number in his trouser pocket the same way the coroner's office had. His handwritten note had said Millhone Investigations along with my office number. Both callers had erroneously assumed that Millhone was a man. Dandy had just told me Dace carried the information with him for months, hoping to sober up before he asked for help.

Though there were still gaps in the story, I was feeling better about the string of events. There's something inherent in human nature that has us constructing narratives to explain a world that is otherwise chaotic and opaque. Life is little more than a series of overlapping stories about who we are, where we came from, and how we struggle to survive. What we call news isn't new at all: wars, murders, famines, plagues—death in all its forms. It's folly to assign meaning to every chance event, yet we do it all the time. In this case, it seemed curious that Pinky Ford, whose life had touched mine six months before, had made another appearance, this time connecting me to the man in the morgue. It did help me to understand how some of the lines connected. Dace's choosing me wasn't random. He was acting on the recommendation of a mutual acquaintance. The referral hadn't netted me a job, but there was always the chance that a casual mention would result in future employment. In the meantime, the two phone calls regarding him and my name and number on that paper in his pocket were no longer mysterious in the overall scheme of things. I paused to correct myself. There had actually been three calls, the last one being from the coroner's office.

Now that I thought about it, I'd had a number of hang-ups on my office answering machine. There must have been six in all, someone calling while I was out and electing not to leave a message. There was no reason to assume that the caller was the same in every instance and no reason to imagine it was R. T. Dace on the other end. But it was possible. Nothing to be done about it at this point, and I felt a momentary, formless regret.

As long as I was only three blocks from home, I decided to stop off and see what kind of luck Henry was having with the cat. I'd left that morning long before William's appointment with the neurologist, and I was interested in an update on his condition as well. I found a parking spot across the street from Rosie's place and noticed that the tenting was down. I could see a workman closing the downstairs windows, and I assumed that both the restaurant and the apartment upstairs had undergone a thorough airing out.

I locked my car, walked the half block, and made my way into the backyard. There was no sign of Henry, no sign of the cat, and no sign of William. Henry's kitchen door was open, and when I tapped on the frame, there was a lengthy delay and then William hobbled into view from the direction of the living room. He held the door for me and I stepped into the kitchen.

"Henry's not here, but he's due back momentarily. Have a seat and don't mind me if I stand. Hurts too much to get up and down. I'm better off on my feet."

"I see the termite tenting's down. Will you be staying here or going home?"

"I'll go home if I can manage it. I'm sure Henry will be glad to see the last of me."

"What about all the kitchen equipment and supplies? Won't they have to be moved back in?"

"I suppose that can wait until Rosie gets home."

"I'll be happy to help. If you'll direct our efforts, Henry and I can do the work."

I pulled out a kitchen chair and settled my shoulder bag on the floor nearby. William leaned against the counter with his cane to provide balance. I could see past him into the backyard, so I knew I'd spot Henry as soon as he appeared. "How'd your doctor's appointment go?" I asked.

"Dr. Metzger did a thorough examination and didn't seem to think an MRI would be necessary for now. He made a point of saying 'for now.' 'Always have ammunition in reserve' was the way he put it. He prescribed an anti-inflammatory, pain medication, and a muscle relaxant. I'm also to do physical therapy three times a week. I have a heating pad that I'm to use before therapy and an ice pack for after."

I sensed William's discomfiture that his medical prognosis had been downgraded from near death, past acute, down to the mundane level of pills, ice packs, and PT. Added to that shame was his miscalculation with regard to the cat. I said, "Well, thank heaven you came home when you did. If you'd stayed in Flint four more days, no telling how bad your sciatica would have been. At least you're under the care of a specialist."

"The doctor said so as well, that I'd done exactly what he would have done in my shoes."

"Absolutely. Good for you," I said. "When do your physical therapy sessions start?"

"Tomorrow afternoon. I believe the facility is not far from here. Of course, I don't want to be a burden, so I might take a cab. I hate to put Henry out."

"Where'd you sleep last night? I thought both his guest rooms were stacked with items from the restaurant."

"He offered me the couch, but I thought it best that I sleep on the floor. Once I managed to get down, which was no easy task, I kept my knees elevated so my back remained flat and properly supported. I slept as well as I could under the circumstances."

"What's the situation with the cat?"

"Henry caught the cat and he's taken it to a veterinarian who has an office not too far from here. He tried everything to persuade the cat to come out of the bushes, but I'm afraid he didn't have much success. He finally looked up the vet in the yellow pages. He was hoping she had a Havahart trap he could borrow, but hers was on loan to a group that rescues feral cats. She recommended a bit of cooked chicken and it worked like a charm. The cat even allowed itself to be tucked into the carrier for transport. I don't know if I mentioned it, but the poor cat has no tail. Just a stump covered with a tuft of hair. I have no idea what happened to him. Henry says the cat's pathetic— ugly, bad tempered, and uncooperative."

"Not too uncooperative or Henry couldn't have gotten him in the carrier."

"You're right. I hadn't thought of that," he said. "I don't mind Henry being mad at me, but I don't want him to take it out on the cat."

"Henry wouldn't do that, do you think?"

"He has no use for it and he made that plain, but I don't know what he meant. He's hardly speaking to me, so I didn't have a chance to press him on the point. He wants to be rid of the poor thing for sure."

"You don't think he'd have the cat put down, do you?"

"The mood he's in, he's capable of anything. He refuses to have it here. Especially after all the pain and suffering Nell's been through."

"Couldn't the vet find a home for it?"

"That remains to be seen. Henry has no patience. He called Lewis, and Lewis said the same thing he's been saying all along: take the cat to the pound and put an end to it. Henry says whatever happens, it's my fault for not asking in advance. He knew a fellow bitten by a stray who was stricken with cat scratch fever. His arm swelled up to three times its normal size. He was in the hospital for a week. Henry says why take the risk? Fleas and god knows what diseases. He says the cat's fate is on my head."

"Henry said that?"

"Words to that effect. I thought I was doing a good deed, but there's no predicting Henry. He can be hard-nosed."

I caught movement and looked up in time to see Henry's station wagon ease along the drive. He paused while the automatic door went up and then pulled into the garage. I heard the car door slam and he appeared a moment later, hauling the carrier, which was clearly lighter and most decidedly empty.

Stony-faced, he came into the kitchen and set the carrier to one side. "That takes care of that," he said, and then looked over at me, his tone shifting from cranky to something more pleasant. "You're home early."

I murmured a response, realizing that I was sorely disappointed with the man. He was in no way obliged to keep the cat simply because William had taken it upon himself to transport it across country. Henry had never expressed any interest in animals and I'd never known him to mention a pet. Still, I counted on him to do the right thing, even if he wanted to be a grouch about it.

He turned to William. "You owe me fifty dollars."

William wasn't going to argue. He was already chastened by Henry's anger and repentant at having caused such an uproar. He had to feel worse about the cat than I did. He took out his wallet and counted off the bills, which he handed to Henry. "May I ask what this is for?"

Henry said, "The vet has to put the cat to sleep and that's what it costs."

Both William and I said "Oh" in tones of regret and bewilderment.

"What's the matter with you?" he asked, looking from my face to William's.

I said, "If I'd known you were going to have it put down, I'd have taken it myself."

"What are you talking about? She's not *killing* the cat. She's cleaning his teeth and he has to be sedated. I'm to pick him up at five."

I said, "Really? Well, that's great!"

He seemed to be feeling self-conscious as he went on. "The vet says he's a Japanese bobtail, which is a rare breed. As a matter of fact, this is the first one she's seen in her entire career. Bobtails are active and very intelligent, easily trained to a leash. And talkative, she said, which I'd noticed myself. Two people in the waiting room spotted him and volunteered to take him off my hands that very minute, but I didn't like their looks. One had a yappy dog the cat took an instant dislike to, and the other was a young woman who looked irresponsible to me. She had pierced ears and peroxided hair that stood up in spikes all over her head. I told the vet I wouldn't dream of putting the cat in the care of someone like that."

"Well, that's wonderful," I said, patting myself on the chest with relief. "So he's a male?"

"He *was* male. Apparently, he was neutered some time ago. The vet says neutering tempers aggression and will keep him from spraying and getting into fights with other cats. She also pointed out he has what they call heterochromia, meaning his eyes are different colors. One is blue and the other is a golden green. Odd-eyed kittens are more expensive than the ordinary ones."

William stirred, wanting to ask a question without generating any more ire on Henry's part. "Have you thought about a name?"

"Of course. The cat's name is Ed."

William blinked and said, "Good choice."

I said, "Excellent."

6

PETE WOLINSKY

May 1988, Five Months Earlier

Pete ignored the phone when it rang, letting his answering machine pick up while he sorted through the mail that had piled up over the past week. Idly, he tuned in to his outgoing message, thinking as he always did that his recorded voice sounded manly, mature, and trustworthy.

"Able and Wolinsky. We're currently out of the office, but if you'll leave your name and number, we'll get back to you as soon as we return. We value your business and look forward to serving you with efficiency and discretion."

There was actually no Able. Pete had adopted a mythical partner so his agency name would appear first in the listings for private investigators.

The caller didn't need to identify himself since he rang up six to eight times a day. "Listen, you son of a bitch. I know you're there, so let's cut the bullshit and get straight to the point. If you don't pay what you owe, I'll come over there with a meat cleaver and chop off your shriveled dick . . ."

Pete listened with amusement. Synchronicity being what it was, it was Barnaby on the line again, calling on behalf of Ajax Financial Recovery Associates, whose officious written demands were spelled out in the letter he held in his hand while the goober from the self-same company spewed venom. In truth, the dunning notices were almost as bad as the daily calls and both were getting on his nerves—abusive tirades generated by clowns who weren't qualified for real jobs. What kind of fool spent his days in a cubicle badgering gainfully employed citizens about debts that might or might not be owed? Most debt collectors were rude, obnoxious, devious, and unprincipled. He filtered their calls, deleting a message the minute the caller announced his purpose. If he was careless and picked up the line, allowing one of his creditors to get through, he'd blast him with a handheld siren that would render a fellow deaf for the better part of an hour. He made an exception for Barnaby, whose threats were more vicious and imaginative than most. As soon as he'd recorded another week's worth of diatribes, he'd file a complaint with the FTC.

He tossed the Ajax letter into the trash along with the other overdue notices, a summons, two default judgments, and the threat of a lawsuit. The only envelope left contained a preapproved credit card offer, which made him laugh aloud. Those assholes never gave up. He adjusted his glasses, leaning close to the application as he took a few minutes to fill in the particulars. He used his own name with an X as his middle initial. The rest of the personal information—employment, bank accounts—he invented on the spot, wondering if the company would actually be foolish enough to issue him a card.

It didn't bother him so much that he was broke. It was the unpleasantness he objected to, having to suffer the screaming and insults, being interrogated about his intentions, which forced him to make up excuses or, worse yet, tell outright lies. He didn't enjoy the dishonesty, but what choice did he have? Business was slow and had been for the past year and a half. The rent on his small office was three months in arrears. He avoided the premises when possible because his landlady was likely to pop up without warning, angling for payment. She insisted on cash, refusing to accept Pete's checks after the third one was returned for insufficient funds.

He glanced at his watch, startled to see the time had gotten away from him. It was 9:43. He had an appointment at 10:00, a job prospect that had come as a happy surprise. Fellow named Willard Bryce—young man by the sound of him, clearly unaccustomed to requiring the services of a private eye. During their phone conversation, Pete had pressed, trying to get a line on the problem, but the fellow was reluctant to specify. Pete was imagining a matrimonial issue, always depressing to contemplate.

He removed his sport coat from the rack, hung his scarf around his neck, locked the office door behind him, and went out to the car, brooding about his lot in life. In his heyday, he'd hated having to stoop to domestic cases, which were emotional and messy and seldom netted much in the way of returns. Confirm a woman's intuition that her husband was cheating and suddenly she'd reverse herself, denying the truth even when the photographs were laid out in front of her. If Pete managed to convince her, she'd be too bitter or too upset to pay his fee. On the other hand, if he assured her of her hubby's innocence, the wife would claim he hadn't done his job. Why pay a PI who couldn't come up with the goods? Why was that worth thirty bucks an hour? she'd ask, peevishly.

Working the husband's side of the equation was no better. Pete would tease out the ex-wife's property holdings, providing proof she'd bought a condominium in Hawaii while at the same time claiming her meager spousal support was inadequate to her needs. By the time a court date was set to review the facts, the husband would have piled up legal expenses so steep that he wouldn't have the bucks to pay the PI who'd provided the ammunition.

He drove north on the 101, waving in response to the sour looks from passing drivers. His 1968 Ford Fairlane wouldn't exceed fifty-five miles an hour. The muffler was noisy and the once fire-engine red paint had faded to a harsh flamingo pink. It was a sweet drive for a twenty-year-old vehicle with 278,000 miles on the odometer. On cold mornings, it took a fair amount of coaxing before the engine turned over, sending up dark puffs, like smoke signals, visible in his rearview mirror. He'd bought the car at what he could see now was the height of his career. It ate up gasoline at a rate of fifteen miles to the gallon, but it was otherwise low maintenance.

He didn't want to dwell on the fact that the prospective client lived in Colgate, but it didn't bode well. Colgate was a lackluster sprawl of tract homes, built on land that had once supported citrus and avocado orchards. Colgate residents were workaday folk—plumbers and electricians, auto mechanics, store clerks, and trash collectors—not poor by any stretch, but getting by on wages that barely kept up with inflation. Actually, they all made more than he did, but that was neither here nor there.

He'd been a damn fine detective once upon a time and he was still good at what he did. If he cut corners on occasion, he figured it was strictly his business. He'd learned early on that in his line of work, it didn't pay to be too fastidious. As long as he delivered the goods, his clients looked the other way. Most made a point of not inquiring too closely about his methods. For years he'd sidestepped the Business and Professions Codes that governed the practices of private investigators. By his reckoning, he'd violated most of them anyway, so why get all prissy at this point? His clients didn't seem to care what he did as long as nothing blew back on them. So far he hadn't been *caught*, which was, after all, the point. As long as he wasn't apprehended in the course of an illegal act, he wasn't subject to censure. He was immune from threats of having his license yanked since he hadn't operated with a valid PI license for some years. Those who hired him understood that whatever their needs, fees would be paid in cash before he embarked on a job and little would be committed to paper. A contract was sealed by gentlemen's agreement, confirmed by a handshake, and accompanied by a nod and a wink.

Once in Colgate proper, he turned off the main street onto Cherry Lane, leaning forward to catch house numbers. The address he was searching for turned out to be a twelve-unit apartment complex, built during the fifties by the look of it, not shabby but with the glum air of postwar construction. He found a parking spot, locked the car, and walked back to the entrance. An iron gate opened into a spacious courtyard partly shaded by young trees. Now he pictured a schoolteacher or the general manager of a fast-food restaurant, though why either would be home at this hour was anybody's guess. Maybe the problem was a business dispute or a slip-and-fall claim, something involving an insurance company, which would allow him to pump up his bill into the four-figure range. Pad his hours, pad expenses, exaggerate the difficulty of the job, and then string it out.

Apartment 4 was on the ground floor near the rear of the building. He rang the bell and then turned to do a quick survey of the premises. No kids' toys in evidence and no swimming pool. In the central grassy area, a set of metal lawn chairs and a glider had been arranged in a conversational grouping that suggested an occasional gathering of the residents. These were probably the kind of folks who looked after one another. Always admirable, he thought. The shrubs needed pruning and the flower beds were riddled with weeds, but the basic landscaping design was good.

The door opened and when he turned to face his prospective client, he made quick work of covering his surprise. The fellow had had the crap knocked out of him at some point, though Pete guessed the injury wasn't recent. Willard Bryce had propped himself upright using a pair of lightweight aluminum forearm crutches with rubber handgrips and vinyl-coated contoured arm cuffs. His left leg was intact, but the right was half gone, his pant leg empty from the knee down. There was also something about his pelvic area that suggested irreparably crushed bones. There were no visible scars in evidence, so there was no way to guess what had happened to him.

His red hair was clipped close to his skull and his light blue eyes seemed faded under pale ginger brows. His eyelids had a pinkish cast as though itchy from an allergy. His upper lip and chin were shaded with a two-day growth of facial hair. He was thin. His dress shirt was open at the collar, exposing a bony, hairless chest. He'd rolled his sleeves up above his elbows, and his pale arms were hairless as well.

The young man held out his right hand, saying, "I'm Willard Bryce, Mr. Wolinsky. I appreciate your coming out."

"Happy to oblige," Pete said. He shook Bryce's hand, watching Bryce's reaction to his own appearance, which usually netted him second looks. Pete was very tall and stooped, with disproportionately long arms, legs, fingers, and feet. He suffered a curvature of the spine and his breastbone dipped inward. He was extremely nearsighted and his mouth was crowded with a mess of teeth.

"Come in," Willard Bryce said. He turned and crossed the living room on his crutches, moving with ease as he swung himself forward, leaving Pete to close the door behind him.

This was one of those apartments where the living room took a short left-hand turn into a dining L, which was separated from the open kitchen area by a pass-through. Two tall stools sat at the counter, providing an eating area. Living room furniture was the standard matching tweed sofa and armchair, plus a La-Z-Boy upholstered in dusty brown suede cloth. The seating was arranged around a coffee table with a television set on the opposite wall. The color scheme was beige on beige. The small dining table and four wooden chairs were relegated to the periphery to make room for a big drafting table, located by the window where the light was good. A corner desk held a computer with two floppy disk drives. The black-and-white monitor was turned on but presented no more than a blur from where he stood. Willard sank into the La-Z-Boy and placed his crutches to one side. On a table next to him, he had an oversize sketchbook and an assortment of drawing pencils.

Pete settled onto the couch. He unwound the scarf from his neck and held it loosely in his hands, leaning forward slightly with his elbows on his knees. Ruthie had knit him the scarf and he liked the feel because it reminded him of her. "Looks like you've suffered a world of hurt," he said. "Mind if I ask what happened?"

He wouldn't ordinarily have made mention of the young man's condition, but he didn't want to spend the entire meeting avoiding reference to something so obvious. Maybe this was a product-liability suit, in which case he could add an automatic five thousand dollars to his bill. He'd get paid whether the jury found for the plantiff or not. If the plantiff prevailed and was awarded punitive damages, it might net him a handsome bonus.

"Automobile accident when I was seventeen. Car went off the road and hit a tree. My best friend was driving and he died instantly." No mention of rain-slick roads or high speeds or alcohol.

"One of those unfortunate twists of fate," Pete suggested, hoping the comment didn't sound too trite.

Willard said, "I know this sounds odd, but if it hadn't been for the accident, I wouldn't have felt so compelled to succeed."

"Not odd at all. I noticed your drafting table. You're an architect?"

Willard shook his head. "Graphic design and illustration with a specialty in comic art."

Pete was at a loss. "You're talking comic books?"

"Basically, though it's a much broader field."

"You'll have to pardon my ignorance. I didn't realize a fellow could make a living off comic books. You have formal training for a job like that?"

"Of course. I got my degree from the California College of the Arts in Oakland. I work freelance—currently with a couple of guys I went to school with. My buddy Jocko does the writing. I'm what they call a penciler. There are two other fellows who do the inking and the coloring."

"I read a lot of comic books when I was a kid. Tales from the Crypt and the like."

Willard smiled. "I know that one well. The company was originally Educational Comics. William Gaines inherited the business from his dad. In 1947, he and an editor named Al Feldstein came up with the concept, which was a smash success and generated hundreds of imitators. Weird Chills, Weird Thrillers, Web of Mystery. I have hundreds of those old classics."

"Is that right? And now you're writing them yourself."

"As part of the team. I also do freelance editorial cartoons as well. I'm lucky circumstances allowed me to pursue my dream. My parents are still convinced I'll starve."

"Well, I admire your gumption. I'll have to take a look at your work sometime," he said, hoping the fellow wouldn't jump right up and fetch his portfolio.

"I think of this as my bread-and-butter money until I can launch the project closest to my heart."

"And what would that be?"

"A graphic novel. Are you familiar with the form?"

"I'm not, but I'd imagine it's much like it sounds. Comic book starring a superhero of some type?"

"The graphic novel's actually a separate genre. A version called manga's been popular in Japan for years and encompasses all kinds of stories. Action-adventure, horror, detective. I'm not saying mine's manga. That's strictly of Japanese origin."

"Is that right? And yours is about what, if you don't mind my asking?"

"I've created a character called Joe Jupiter, who's been crippled in an accident."

"Writing what you know, so to speak."

"Except I take the setup in a different direction. He enrolls in an experimental protocol and ends up acquiring supernatural abilities after being injected with a powerful new drug that's supposed to regenerate nerves and cells. Through some fluke— I'm still working on that aspect—instead of being cured, Jupiter develops unusual powers of telepathy and mind control."

"No telling what kind of adventures that might lead to," Pete remarked.

"My wife thinks it's too much like science fiction, which isn't my intent. Of course, there's an *element* of fantasy, but the premise is reality based."

"Not my area of expertise, but I can definitely see the possibilities. Is yours a lucrative trade?"

"If you hit it big, absolutely," Willard replied. The pink in his eyelids had intensified, like a curious form of blushing. Pete wondered which he was exaggerating—the earnings potential or his chances of making it.

Pete kept hoping he'd state his problem and get on with it. So far, he had no idea what the job was and no clue if the fellow had the money to pay. "You're a married man."

"I am."

"How many years is that now?"

"Four and a half. We moved here a year ago from Pittsburgh, which is where we met. My wife's an associate professor at UCST. She does pharmaceutical research, which is what triggered the Joe Jupiter idea."

"Promising field." Pete fixed his gaze expectantly on the young man.

Willard said, "Which actually brings me to the reason for my call."

Pete said nothing, worried that Willard would get off point and start talking about himself again.

"As it, uh, happens my wife applied for this position without realizing the man in charge of the project was someone she'd worked with before."

"When was this?"

"When she took this job or when she worked with him before?"

"You already said you moved here a year ago. I'm assuming that was for the job."

"Right. They were both undergraduates at Florida State.

This was several years back. I guess they were involved in a romantic relationship. Nothing serious from what she says. She was the one who broke it off."

"Because . . ."

"I'm not really sure."

"Passing fling perhaps?"

"Something like that."

"What's his position now?"

"Head of the research lab. There are guys above him, but essentially he runs the show."

"I'm surprised he wasn't part of the hiring process—the interview or some such."

Willard apparently hadn't thought of that, so Pete left the subject and moved on, saying, "Any rate, now they're thrown into regular contact, you're worried sparks might fly."

"I wouldn't say *worried*. I'm concerned. It's not that I don't trust her." The sentence came to an abrupt halt.

"However . . ."

"There's a professional conference in Reno during this upcoming Memorial Day weekend. I knew she was planning to attend. What I didn't realize until a couple of days ago was that he'd be there as well. He's presenting a paper."

"I don't believe you've mentioned your wife's name."

"Mary Lee."

"The two plan on traveling together?"

"Not as far as I know. She hasn't said anything to that effect."

"One way or the other, you'd appreciate assurance everything's on the up-and-up."

"Exactly."

"This fellow have a name?"

"Dr. Reed. Linton Reed."

"Bit of a wunderkind," Pete said.

"Pardon?"

"Fellow must be on a fast track, given they started out the same. Sounds like you're talking star power if he's already heading up a lab."

"I guess."

Pete took out a weather-beaten spiral-bound notebook and jotted down the name before he went on. "Are you talking medical doctor or a Ph.D.?"

"Both. He went through a program at Duke that combined the two. His Ph.D. is in biochemistry."

"Admirable. And he lives where?"

"Montebello. As I understand it, his wife comes from money. Quite a lot of money, as a matter of fact. Her family's well known in town—very prominent—so he definitely married up."

"You're telling me he'd risk all of that in order to pursue a relationship with your wife?"

"I really have no idea."

"Have you met him?"

"I have, yes."

"Good-looking fellow?"

"Women seem to think so. I'm not impressed."

Pete pinched his lower lip, then shook his head. "Might not be anything to it, but it always pays to be informed. Unfortunately, what you're talking here is an expensive proposition."

"Money's not the issue. I wasn't sure if this was the type of case you handled as a rule."

"You're asking about my personal qualifications? May I call you Willard?"

"Please do."

"Appreciate it, Willard. Point of fact, domestic happens to be a specialty of mine. My forte's exactly the sort of situation you describe. Not to toot my own horn, but you ask around and you'll find out I'm a man who not only gets results, but I'm known for my discretion. That's a rare combination. I'm not saying there aren't younger practitioners coming up behind, but there's no one as well trained. I'll admit I'm old-school, but you couldn't be in better hands."

"Good. I'm glad to hear it."

Pete waited.

Willard cleared his throat. "When you say 'expensive,' I'm not sure what kind of money you're talking about. I hope I'm not putting you on the spot."

"No need to apologize, but here's what you should be aware of. You're talking short notice here. This is the seventeenth, which means I have ten days to get my ducks in a row. I'm talking about equipment, airline tickets, a rental car once I'm on site. Once I find out where the conference is taking place,

I still need time to study the layout, establish personal contacts, determine who's staying where . . ."

"I can give you most of that."

"Good thing. Because I'm a man who likes to be prepared."

"You'll provide receipts?"

"No question. I'll submit an invoice same time I hand over my written report. Of course, I'll be needing an advance."

"You mean right now?"

"As good a time as any."

"What did you have in mind?"

"Twenty-five hundred should be sufficient."

"Oh. Well, fine. If you'll take a credit card, I can use my business account."

"Won't work. I'm not set up for it. I'll take a check, but let's be honest about this, I won't get in gear until it clears the bank."

The tips of Willard's ears turned a brighter shade of pink. "The problem is my wife pays the bills and reconciles the checking account. I don't want her asking who you are or what this is about."

"Cash, then."

"That's just it. I don't keep cash like that on hand. I have five hundred. The rest I can reimburse you. I swear I'm good for it."

"Mr. Bryce . . . Willard. Forgive my impertinence, but I run a business here. I don't mind a few out-of-pocket expenses, but we're talking round-trip airfare right off the bat. I may have to make two trips depending on what comes up. Hotel and meals. On top of that, I may have to grease a few palms, if you get what I mean. Trust me, you don't want me leaving a paper trail. Something comes to light and that sweet wife of yours will be all over you, thinking you have no confidence in her."

"I have money in a separate account. I could have it for you this afternoon, I suppose."

"Give me a call and I'll be happy to swing back by." Pete got up, thinking they were done.

Uncomfortably, Willard said, "Can I ask you something?"

"What's that?"

"You carry a gun?"

Pete blinked. "Do you have need of one?"

"No, no. Not at all. I'm working on three panels where a gangster pulls a gun on Joe Jupiter and I've never handled one. If I show a close-up, I want to get the details right."

"I couldn't agree more," Pete said. He removed the semi-automatic from his shoulder holster, released the magazine, and checked to make sure there wasn't a round in the chamber before he offered it to Willard butt first.

Willard took the gun and hefted it in his hand. "Wow. What is this?"

"Pocket pistol. Smith and Wesson Escort. I have a Glock 17 that I carry on occasion, but that little gun's my baby."

Pete spent a few minutes explaining the features while Willard checked it from all angles, turning it this way and that. He placed it on the arm of the chair and picked up his drawing pad. He folded the cover back and made a few quick pencil sketches, his eyes moving from the gun to the page and back. Pete was impressed with the rapidity with which he captured the weapon in a few simple strokes.

Willard set the sketch pad to one side. "You have a permit?"

Pete returned the gun to his shoulder holster. "I do. Issued in Tehama County, up north. Tehama you have densely wooded areas, lot of rainfall, and not many folks. Marijuana's the big cash crop. I had a side business scoping out these little farmlets buried in the woods. I'd find 'em, map out the coordinates, and pass the information along to law enforcement. Job didn't offer benefits, so I got my concealed-carry permit as part of my compensation."

"Is it legal here?"

"Permit's valid statewide. Both my guns are registered," he said.

"Well, that's good."

Pete shrugged, saying, "Anything else you need?"

Willard shook his head. "I'll call when I have the cash."

It wasn't until Pete was in his car again that he started to laugh, delighted with the way the meeting had gone. He turned the key in the ignition and pulled away from Willard's Cherry Lane address. He drove a block and took a right onto Colgate's main thoroughfare. He had his choice of two travel agencies and he selected the smaller one. There were oversize travel posters taped to the plate-glass window, their once vibrant hues faded to a palette of misty pinks and blues. The one that caught his eye depicted a cruise ship moving along a wide still body of water. He leaned closer. BOUTIQUE RIVER TOURS. ENCHANTING DANUBE was what it said in small print.

At the desk inside he picked up a glossy brochure from a display near the door and slid it into the inner pocket of his sport coat. Something about the scene made his heart swell with hope. There were two agents at work, both women, and he chose the older one, who invited him to have a seat. Her name tag indicated she was Sabrina. Pete introduced himself, and in a matter of minutes he made round-trip reservations to fly from Santa Teresa to Reno on Friday the twentieth, returning on Monday the twenty-third. Because of the short notice, the fare for United Airline tickets was a hefty thirteen hundred bucks. He put the charges on the only one of his credit cards with any margin to spare. Sabrina printed the tickets and handed them over, along with a copy of the itinerary and his receipt, all neatly tucked into a ticket envelope with the logo of the agency emblazoned on the front.

He walked half a block to a UPS outlet and used their Xerox machine to run off multiple copies of the travel documents, which he slid into a blank manila envelope. Later that day, having picked up his retainer from Willard, he drove into Colgate for the second time and parked across the street from the travel agency. He waited until he saw Sabrina emerge, ostensibly to run an errand. As soon as she was out of sight, he went in and conferred with the other travel agent, expressing embarrassment that his plans had changed. She wasn't the least bit curious. At his request, she rescheduled the flights for the Memorial Day weekend, departing on Thursday the twenty-sixth, returning late on Monday the thirtieth. She applied the money he'd paid for the first tickets to the second, and he applied the difference in fares to the credit card he'd used earlier. Expense was no issue. He wouldn't be paying the card off in any event. He voiced his appreciation, but her gaze had already moved to the customer coming in the door.

He returned to the office, waited for his copy machine to warm up, and photocopied the new itinerary and the second set of tickets, which he intended to cancel in a day or two. On the set he had, he changed the relevant dates, neatly typing the new number over the old, and photocopied the copies, satisfied that the result would pass superficial examination. Anyone with a knowledge of forgery techniques would spot the clumsy effort, but he was confident Willard had no such expertise.

He slid the file folder into the box he was packing. No point in leaving sensitive papers in view since his landlady used a master key to get in on occasion, to poke around. Soon Pete would be forced to run his business from his home. For now, he was pleased. He'd effectively run up close to three thousand dollars' worth of travel expenses without ever leaving the state. Truly, he was a man who loved his work.

7

At 4:50, Henry left the house, carrier in hand, to retrieve the cat from the veterinarian's office. I took the opportunity to retreat to my studio. Once inside, I set my shoulder bag on a kitchen stool and stood there, trying to decide what to do with myself. There was no point in going back to the office. It was technically closing time and I'd already goofed off most of the day. Since new clients were temporarily in short supply, I had no paper searches, no phone calls, and no reports to write. It was too early to worry about supper and much too early for a glass of wine. Rosie's was still closed, which meant that I'd be fending for myself in any event. I'd just about worked through my repertoire of sandwiches and I was down to my last can of soup.

More from boredom than dedication, I scoured the kitchen sink, put the few clean dishes away, and wiped down the counters. I found a cache of dust rags and made short work of all the surfaces in my living room—desk, end tables, windowsills, and shutters. I got down on my hands and knees and crawled along the baseboards, rag in hand, sweeping away dust and soot. On a prior occasion, this was how I'd discovered that my studio was bugged and from that point on, I'd added base-boards to my must-do list.

As was usually the case during one of my Cinderella moments, I wondered what other kick-ass private eyes were doing at this hour. Probably blasting paper targets at the shooting range or practicing their martial arts moves, busting bricks in half with their bare hands. I'm never going to be that tough. What I lack in brute force I make up for in persistence and sheer cunning. I'd been behaving myself of late, which wasn't really my style. Being a good girl has such a low adrenaline quotient I might as well take a nap.

I put away the cleaning rags, then hauled out the vacuum cleaner, plugged it in, and began the process of mowing my shag carpet. The vacuum was sounding shrill and there didn't seem to be any suction. Specks remained untouched and the shag itself showed none of those satisfactory tracks that speak of a job well done. I flipped off the power and turned the machine on its back to have a look. This was pointless, as I'm no more knowledgeable about the workings of a vacuum cleaner than I am about the internal combustion engine.

When I heard someone knocking at my door, I assumed it was Henry wanting to properly introduce the cat. I crossed to the front door and peered out the porthole. Felix was standing on my porch, looking off across the yard. He was wearing yet another short-sleeve shirt, this one polyester with a Polynesian motif—parrots, thatch-roofed huts, palm trees, hula girls, and surf in garish yellows and blues.

I opened the door. "What are you doing here?"

I knew I sounded accusatory, but I was dismayed by his showing up at my residence.

He didn't actually shuffle his feet, but he shifted his weight, looking down at my welcome mat, where I could still see the mouse parts the cat had left.

"I seen your car out front and thought you might be home." His shorts were the sort that basketball players wear, a flabby black material, extending well below his knees. The fabric was perforated with tiny holes that were probably meant for ventilation in the heat of hard play.

"How did you know where I lived?"

He glanced over his shoulder and then down again, anything to avoid making eye contact. It was the first time it occurred to me that Felix might be slow. It was also possible he was stoned or drunk. I made a mental note to find out the nature and extent of his substance abuse.

He lifted one shoulder. "Other day you said you jogged, so I waited until you went by this morning and followed you home."

"You saw me this morning? I didn't see any of you."

"I was down at that bathhouse when you run by. I left the shelter early because I was curious where you lived. Dandy and Pearl stayed in and had breakfast. They won't hardly miss a meal. Bacon, eggs, and biscuits the church ladies cook up. I watched you turn around and I fell in behind when you passed the second time."

"Why would you *do* that? This is my home. You want to talk to me, you don't show up here. You go to my office like everyone else."

"Something I thought you should know."

"I can hardly wait."

"Pearl knows who stole Terrence's backpack."

I stared at him briefly while I sorted through my responses. I was offended at the intrusion, but I wasn't sure he understood the concept of personal boundaries. At the same time, it wasn't my place to lecture him about social norms. More to the point: my curiosity took precedence. "You want to come in?"

"Naw. That's okay. I'm fine out here."

"Well, it's chilly and I don't want to stand around letting the heat out."

I stepped back and he inched his way into my living room. He exhibited no interest in the place. He scarcely lifted his gaze from the floor, so I took heart that he probably wasn't casing the joint. I closed the door behind him and gestured at one of my canvas director's chairs. Sitting was apparently outside his comfort zone.

Since he remained standing, I followed suit. "What's the story?"

"Pearl was at the liquor store and she saw one of them fellas that hang out at the off-ramps with cardboard signs. She saw this one guy toting Terrence's backpack plain as day. She recognized it from the frame and even the same color bungee cords. She knew where he was headed. Bums have this hobo camp up the hill from the bird refuge? She waited 'til he was out of sight and then followed him and hid in the bushes to have her a look—"

"Pearl hid in the bushes and no one spotted her?"

"I guess not. She said there was no sign of Terrence's cart, probably because they couldn't have drug it up the hill. But she saw his cookstove and waterproof bags where he kept his gear. Also, his camo box."

"'Camo' as in 'camouflage'?"

"Like different color spots painted on to look like leaves. She's wanting to get his stuff back, but there's too much to haul even if I help out."

I said, "Uhn-hun."

"She said she just wisht she knew someone with a car and right away I thought about you."

I said, "Ah."

"She was wondering what you'd think about lending her a hand."

"I'd think it was dumb. Pearl can't stand me so why would I help her?"

"She said please."

"She did not. I'd bet you a dollar she doesn't even know you're here."

"Naw, not really. Way I figure it, she couldn't ast no one at Harbor House and you're the only other person we know that has a vehicle."

"Well, I'm flattered you thought of me, but the idea is lame, not to mention dangerous. You can't raid a hobo camp and hope to get away with it."

"I told her the same thing, but she's made up her mind. She'll get caught if she tries doing it on her own."

"Oh, for heaven's sake," I said, crossly. "I'm not going to participate in her harebrained scheme."

"Whyn't you just talk to her?"

"I don't want to talk to her."

I could see his gaze track across the floor, a rough approximation of his tiny mind at work. Finally, he said, "If you want, I can fix that." He was pointing to the injured vacuum cleaner.

"What do you know about vacuum cleaners?"

"I can see where the belt's come off. Won't take a minute to fix, if you want me to. Only . . ."

"Only you want me to talk to Pearl in exchange."

"That'd be nice. Maybe you can argue her out of it."

"I'll get my jacket."

I crossed to the coat closet, watching him over my shoulder as he dropped to one knee. He had the belt back on in a jiffy, making me wonder if I'd sold out too cheap.

Thus it was that late afternoon on Tuesday, I found myself driving along Cabana Boulevard with a dreadlocked white boy in baggy shorts seated to my right. I was hungry and slightly cranky, which is the only way I can explain the lack of foresight. In my own mind, I wasn't committed to the idea of helping Pearl. I was giving the *appearance* of cooperation, reserving the right to back out if she gave me any guff.

I swung by Harbor House and sent Felix in to find Pearl. "And put some clothes on," I said as he closed the car door. He responded with a foolish grin and I watched until he disappeared from view. Even out at the street, I caught a whiff of their supper. Chili or lasagna or spaghetti and meatballs— *something* that smelled wonderful. Sitting down to a home-cooked meal three times a day must be like having a mother, someone who genuinely cared about seeing that your plate was cleaned and your tummy was full. The shelter provided the equivalent of a family home and an ever-shifting supply of siblings.

I wondered what it would take to feed 150 homeless people three meals a day. Dandy, Felix, and Pearl didn't seem to question the fact that bed and board were theirs for the asking. In exchange for what? While I was growing fond of the three, I saw them as perpetual adolescents who'd never leave home. I'd seen the residents performing various chores around the place, but what incentive did they have to go out on their own? Their basic needs were provided for as long as they behaved. To me, the bargain seemed off-kilter. I was taught the virtues of hard work, and the trio's complacency chafed at me. I could understand the needs of the infirm and the mentally ill. The able-bodied? Not so much. I'd heard the issue argued both for and against, but I'd never heard an equable solution.

It was still full-on daylight, but the air was taking on that odd cast that signals the gradual fading into twilight. The outside temperature was almost imperceptibly cooler. I turned on the heater and pressed my hands between my knees for warmth. I was hoping to see Dandy, thinking that if he'd gotten wind of the raid, he might be able to talk some sense into them.

Ten minutes passed and Felix emerged in black jeans and a black sweatshirt, as though prepared to knock an old lady on the head and snatch her pocketbook. He had a black rag tied around his dreads like a ninja or a sushi chef. Pearl followed in his wake, packed into blue jeans the size of those featured in the before photos in articles about weight loss of gargantuan proportions. She also wore jogging shoes, her black leather jacket, and her black knit watch cap.

She came around to the driver's side of my car, and I got out and stood there, not wanting her to have the advantage of towering over me. Felix had opened the passenger-side door and he was about to slide into the back when he realized Pearl and I were going to have a powwow. Not wanting to miss the fun, he scampered around the front of the car and took his place at her side. I thought at first this was to show unity, but when she took out a cigarette, I realized he was only interested in bumming a smoke. She held out the pack and he took one, then pulled a Zippo from his pocket and lit both cigarettes. The two inhaled with such satisfaction, you'd have thought they'd just made love.

"He tell you about the backpack?" she asked. She still sounded belligerent, but maybe that was her normal tone.

"The gist of it. Why don't you fill me in?"

"Man, I was PO'd. I go up to that minimart for a pack of smokes? There stands one of those Boggarts with Terrence's backpack."

"Boggarts?"

She fixed me with a look of disbelief. "Bad fairies. Like Knockers, only worse. My Scottish granny used to tell me stories about Boggarts when she tucked me in at night. This lot has taken over a camp in the woods where they live like hooligans. They'll steal anything that's not nailed down."

"How do you know the backpack was Terrence's?"

"Because he'd wrote his name on the front with a waterproof marker pen. I saw it with my own eyes less than two hours ago. I followed the guy and watched him hang it on a tree branch like the bears might be after it. I intend to go up there and get it back. So what do you say?"

"Why don't you just leave well enough alone?"

"Because it belongs to Terrence."

"But you can't just go in there and *take* it."

"Why not? If they stole it from Terrence, why can't I steal it back?"

"What if they catch you?"

"They won't. They're out panhandling at this hour. It's like regular shift work—five to seven except they don't punch a clock. Besides, there's only three of 'em."

"And three of us," Felix pointed out.

Pearl ignored his observation. "First, we check to make sure they're all at work. If Boggarts are busy, we go in, get the stuff, and take off. No big deal."

"If it's that easy, what do you need me for?"

"It's not just the backpack. It's his cookstove and all his books. Terrence loved his books. He kept them in this water-proof box so the weather wouldn't get to them. Plus, he's got two big bags packed with stuff. Me and Felix together can't carry that much."

I nodded toward the shelter. "Aren't you going to miss supper?"

"Well, yeah, but that's not the worst of it. We're not back by seven the place is locked up and we got no place to sleep unless we have a good excuse, which we do in this case. Otherwise, they put us at the back of the line and we have to start all over waiting for a bed. Might take months."

"What's your excuse?"

"I told Ken at the desk Felix and me were going to church."

"Really. You said that? And he believed you?"

"Naw, but he knew better than to call me a liar. I've punched the lights out of guys for less. Anyway, don't worry about it. Place closes, we'll go somewheres else."

"Pearl, be reasonable. You know what's going to happen. The minute one of those bums sees you with the backpack, they'll know you took it and they'll come after you. And then what?"

"'Then what,' who cares? They can't complain when they stole it off Terrence in the first place. Robbing a dead guy? How cold is that? They sure as hell won't be filing a police report. All I'm asking is you stand by with your car and help put the stuff in the trunk. Then we take off."

"Where is this place? Felix said it was over by the bird refuge."

"Up that nature trail. The path snakes back in there until it butts right up against the zoo. There's a service road runs along the hill at the property line. We go in that way, from the backside."

"How do you know this?"

"Everybody knows. Bums been camping there fifty years or more. Started as a hobo city during the Depression. Guys out of work hopped on trains and went clear across the country, riding the rails. They used to elect their own mayor and everything. Access road is their escape hatch, in case the cops bust in."

"How do you know there aren't twenty guys up there?"

"Because the Boggarts invaded the place and that's how it is now. Everybody else took off. Nobody wants to mess with them three. They're bad news," she said.

"What if they happen to be there?"

"They won't be. I just got done telling you. They're busy manning the ramps at this hour because people are coming home from work, happy to pass out dollar bills to bums claiming their car's broke down. Can't they figure it out? There isn't a *car*. Bums don't have cars."

"I love your confidence," I said.

"Fine. You don't believe me? We can check the off-ramps first to make sure all three Boggarts are accounted for. Camp's deserted, we go in and grab the stuff. Ten minutes max and we're outta there."

I could feel a roiling anxiety rise through my body like nausea. "This is a bad idea."

"You got a better one?"

When I didn't reply, she went on in a warning tone. "You don't help, we'll just turn around and find someone else. I want that backpack and I mean to have it."

"Come on, Pearl. Would you cut it out? This is ridiculous. If you're that desperate for a backpack, you can buy one at the nearest army-navy store."

"Not like this one."

"And why is that?"

She broke off eye contact. "You don't need to know."

"What, like there's a secret compartment where Terrence kept his Sky King decoder ring?"

"Go ahead and make fun. That backpack is valuable."

"I'm not moving an inch until you tell me why," I said.

Felix looked from me to Pearl and back. "Her lips is sealed," he said, "But mine ain't."

She squinted at him. "Would you shut your mouth? We're having a conversation here that's no concern of yours."

He leaned closer to me with a proud smile, like a little kid who swears up and down he can keep a secret when he can't.

Pearl banged him on the head, but it was too late.

"Backpack's where Terrence hid the key to his safe deposit box."

"A safe deposit box," I said, making a declarative sentence of it instead of a question.

"Like at a bank," he said, as opposed to those at the laundromat.

I closed my eyes and let my head sink in despair. If Terrence had a will . . . which Dandy claimed he did . . . he probably kept it in a safe deposit box. Which might also contain information about his ex-wife and kids and any final wishes he might have about disposition of his remains. This was exactly what I'd been looking for for the past four days. "I don't know how I get caught up in shit like this."

Pearl said, "Atta girl! Now you're talking."

8

I slid in behind the driver's seat. Felix squeezed into the back while Pearl crushed her cigarette underfoot and then settled into the front. I felt a flutter in my chest like I'd swallowed a hummingbird. I turned the key in the ignition, put the Mustang in gear, and pulled away from the curb. I took a right on Milagro and moved into the lane that ran parallel to the freeway, allowing southbound cars to merge with oncoming traffic. In the interest of being thorough, I took the first exit, which emptied just shy of the bird refuge. I'd never seen the bums work that area and I realized now it was because that particular ramp was too close to home. If a patrol car cruised by, there was no way to disappear without the risk of drawing attention to their camp.

When cross-traffic allowed, I got onto the southbound on-ramp, which was clear of panhandlers just as the other on-ramps turned out to be. I suppose the reasoning was that people getting *onto* the freeway had a fixed destination and were therefore focused on the drive and less inclined to interrupt the journey for donation purposes, whereas those getting *off* the freeway, their progress halted by traffic lights or stop signs, had more time to read the signs beseeching motorists for help and thus were more likely to haul out the old wallet or change purse.

I drove an elongated figure eight nearly a mile in length, cruising the ramps where the Boggarts typically stationed themselves. I noticed I'd freely adopted Pearl's term for the panhandlers, which seemed tidy and to the point. I didn't believe they were "bad fairies." I wasn't even sure that they were *bad*, but the word "Boggart" had a certain air to it that seemed to encompass the minigang of thugs. By trekking back and forth, we spotted two of the three bums. I came back around to the Cabana Boulevard off-ramp, slowing as I exited. At the bottom of the slope, sure enough, the third Boggart was standing on the berm, holding a battered cardboard sign. Crudely lettered in pencil, it read:

> Down on my luck and hungry
> Any small donation appreciated
> God Bless

Pearl said, "That's the one had the backpack."

I gave him points for correct spelling. With just an occasional glance to my left, I kept my gaze fixed on the car in front of me. I already knew the fellow by sight. He was tall, with the muscle mass of an athlete whose trophy days were done. I placed him at six feet with a build that had probably been pumped up by steroids once upon a time. His head was shaved and he wore a red baseball cap that he removed from time to time so he could smooth his bald pate before settling the cap back into place. He wore jeans and a red flannel shirt, the nap worn thin at the elbows but otherwise looking like a proper safeguard against the chill. His expression was blank, revealing no negative reaction to those who passed without making a contribution. Maybe next time around the stingy ones would feel guilty enough to hand over a dollar bill. Meanwhile, he was prepared to stand there without complaint until some righteous driver passed money to him through the window.

Both Pearl in the front seat and Felix in the back had turned their heads to the right as though studying the view from the passenger-side windows. Out of the corner of my eye I saw the Boggart's focus drift in our direction and fix on Pearl, conspicuous by reason of her size and the telltale black knit watch cap. He squinted at the sight of her. He had no reason in the world to think we were up to no good. Then again, like the paranoids in every walk of life, he had no reason to think we weren't. He tracked the rear of the Mustang as I turned right onto Cabana. It might have been my Grabber Blue 1970 Mustang he found so fascinating, but I doubted it.

I continued around the big bend in the road and took a right at the next light, turning onto the street that fronted the zoo, which was closed for the day, its entrance barred by a gate with a wooden arm. The parking lot was empty, and even at a distance I could see that the wrought iron gates were locked. The turnstiles behind them were in shadow.

Felix leaned forward, arms on the front seat, talking into my right ear. "Keep on this road around to Milagro."

I did as instructed, wondering if this was how a bank robber felt when he'd been assigned to drive the getaway car. There was a produce market on the corner a couple of blocks farther on. It was open for business seven days a week with an expansive parking lot on the far side. I'd passed the market any number of times. I'd even shopped there on occasion, impressed by the lavish displays of fresh fruits and vegetables. I caught the scent of celery as I drove by—I swear I can smell celery half a block away—and wished I were eating a bowl of homemade vegetable soup instead of being cooped up with a homeless pair who reeked of cigarettes. I turned right onto Milagro and then right again into the parking lot.

The Union Pacific rail lines run between the highway and the periphery of the lot, which was topped with a mix of gravel and asphalt. There were ten or twelve cars parked close to the market, but the remainder of the lot was empty. I drove to the far end, where I could see the pavement shrink to a narrow road that snaked upward and out of sight. I followed the road. The hill rose gradually with trees on either side forming a canopy overhead. The roadbed was not quite wide enough for two cars to pass, but I didn't picture much in the way of traffic.

I kept my speed to a minimum as I trundled along the lane. I was driving maybe two miles an hour, noting the backside of the zoo structures as they appeared to my right. It was odd to see the facility from this perspective. Where the public areas were defined by walkways that wound among the animal enclosures, the hinterland was all business: garages and storage sheds; lengths of fence that could be moved and bolted into place where needed; service trucks, fork lifts, and utility vehicles; artificial jungle plants and fake boulders that could be called into use to create the illusion of the wilds. As a child, I'd ridden on the narrow-gauge kiddie train that circled the property, so I'd seen glimpses of the same inner workings.

I let Pearl direct me to a spot along the fence she said was closest to the camp.

"You better turn the car around in case we have to get out in a hurry."

"What hurry? The guys are gone," I said.

"But supposing they come back is all I'm trying to say."

Oh great, I thought. I would have liked a place to pee, but it was too late for that and the urge was probably only a manifestation of a creeping attack of nerves. There was scant turning-around room available. I only succeeded by constantly backing up and inching forward, with Felix standing where I could see him in the rear- and side-view mirrors making hand gestures to signal left, right, and stop. Give the fellow an orange plastic baton and he could have offered the same guidance to an airline pilot arriving at the gate.

When I'd completed the 180-degree reorientation, I pulled on the emergency brake, killed the engine, and got out. The fence was a heavy-duty chain link with poles buried in concrete containers at ten-foot intervals. Someone had used cable cutters to open a seam that ran up along the side of one pole. The section of fencing was still bent upward where it had been pressed into use. Right away I thought about that high school geometry concept I never imagined would serve me in real life. The pole and the ground formed a right angle, with the hypotenuse measuring a lean thirty-six inches. Pearl was wider than a yardstick and I wasn't sure how she'd manage to condense her girth sufficiently to fit through the gap. However, this invasion was her big hot idea and I wasn't about to volunteer to take her place.

It looked like the emergency exit hadn't been used for some time. The weeds were thick and the ground underfoot was spongy, a natural mulch of decomposing leaves and bark. The smell suggested decay, not of flesh but of plant material. Felix and I pulled up the stiff triangle of fencing while Pearl got down on her hands and knees and then lowered herself on her stomach. Being prone didn't seem to make her smaller or more compact. Pearl's fake leather jacket added mass to her already bulky frame. The raw cut tines of chain link formed a crooked line. Some of the tines pointed down and some upward, like the traffic teeth at a parking lot exit, intended to discourage you from changing your mind and backing up.

Felix said, "Whyn't you take your jacket off?"

"Why don't you shut your trap and let me do this my way?"

Felix and I exchanged a look and he shrugged.

She managed to hunch her way through the opening at an agonizing pace, but Felix and I knew better than to offer further tips. On the other side of the fence, she struggled to her feet and brushed herself off, dislodging dirt and twigs. Felix left me to hold up the flap of fencing while he slipped through after her.

The two began descending the hill, half slipping along the softened ground. A few yards farther on they disappeared into the tangle of saplings, fallen trees, and weeds. For a moment I could follow the rustle and thump. Pearl huffed and grunted briefly, and from that point on, sound was muffled and uninformative. She'd told me Terrence's backpack was stashed in a tree and his book collection was stored in a waterproof box. How would she manage to carry both? The rest of his belongings were apparently stuffed in waterproof canvas bags, which I pictured her dragging up the hill. Surely, she and Felix would have to make more than one trip. Her claim that the job would take no more than ten minutes was patently absurd. Why is it that other people's plans so often seem ill thought out while our own make so much sense?

I checked my watch. Not even a minute had passed though it felt like ten. The on-ramp where we'd seen the nearest panhandler was between the lanes of north- and southbound traffic, a ten-minute walk if he decided to leave his post and return to the camp. From my vantage point, I could see intermittent stretches of Cabana and a section of the parking lot across from the Caliente Café. I watched a car pull in and park. A woman got out with a jogging stroller and strapped her baby in the seat. At that distance, she was scarcely half an inch tall, an elf in my eyes.

I stayed close to the fence, clinging like a prisoner hoping to be liberated. I peered into the growth of trees down the hill from me but saw nothing. Traffic sounds didn't penetrate the quiet. Above and behind me, the zoo property acted as a buffer, muting the low rumble of the Pacific Ocean on the far side of it. The slope in front of me dropped at an angle through the brush, extending maybe an eighth of a mile before it leveled out. The ground then rose up again to meet the railroad tracks, which were shielded from view by dense shrubs and a line of trees.

Without conscious intent, I tried to calculate the odds of the nearest bum returning prematurely. To me, the chances seemed iffy. I had to assume that on prior occasions, the Boggarts had seen Terrence with Dandy, Pearl, and Felix, sprawled on the grass, trading smokes or passing around a common jug of wine. The homeless seemed to be subdivided into smaller populations, not necessarily friendly toward one another, but not hostile either. Under ordinary circumstances, the Boggarts probably wouldn't have stolen another fellow's cart, but death had upset the balance in the social order and they'd used this to their advantage. Why, then, wouldn't it occur to them that Terrence's pals might try to recoup the loss?

As though in reply, I caught a punctuation mark of red in the parking lot below, a semicolon of cap and flannel shirt that appeared and disappeared so quickly that I blinked. Had I imagined it? I didn't think so. Tentatively, I called out, "Hey, Pearl?"

The vegetation was so dense that the word was rendered flat, pasted against the thicket like a printed flyer announcing my alarm. As nearly as I could tell, the sound didn't carry even one foot. I had no idea what the distance was between the point where I'd spotted the bum and the location of the camp, but what difference did it make? Felix and Pearl hadn't been gone long enough to accomplish their aims, which meant he'd be walking in on them before long.

How could I stand at the fence and do nothing? An ambush was imminent and Felix and Pearl probably hadn't had the good sense to designate one of them as a lookout. I would have preferred being more certain of what I'd seen. If I was wrong, I could help tote stuff up the hill. If I was right, at least they'd have *some* warning. I dropped to the ground and turned over on my back, holding up the treacherous flap of chain-link fence with one hand while I dug my heels into the dirt and used the leverage to hunch my way under.

Once on the other side, I scrambled to my feet and took off down the hill, the stern tug of gravity slowing my pace. The soil conditions created the sensation of running across a mattress, but I labored on, struggling for balance. I reached the thicket and raised my arms above my head. The undergrowth was dense and I thought I'd be wading into the brush for some distance. Ten steps more and I broke into the clearing, nearly falling over in my surprise. The first thing I spotted was an aluminum-framed backpack, propped against a tree with Terrence's name neatly lettered on the canvas. Beside it was what looked like a seaman's soft-sided duffel stuffed to the top.

The camp itself was a revelation. I took in the layout at a glance before I turned my attention to Felix and Pearl. The Boggarts had suspended tarps from clotheslines that neatly divided the space into "rooms," one of which was furnished with a plastic table and chairs confiscated from god knows where. Hammocks were strung between closely spaced trees, looking like traps for airborne creatures not yet in captivity. Tents had been erected as shelter from the elements. Plastic milk crates, arranged in various configurations, served as storage for their provisions. On a picnic table sat a big insulated cooler for foods that required refrigeration. Beach umbrellas protected some of their belongings, but many items had been left in the open air with no apparent harm.

The "mess" was in a tent of its own. Hijacked electric lines were connected by a series of bright orange extension cords that disappeared in the grass. A hose with a spray nozzle lay close at hand and provided running water as long as the zoo paid its bills. Big garbage cans with the lids secured in place were marked SANTA TERESA WASTE MANAGEMENT, which meant that by judicious placement among similar cans, the Boggarts could have their trash picked up on a regular basis, as did everyone else in town.

The only thing lacking was an indoor flush toilet. The smell in the air suggested weeds and bushes had been adapted to that use. I supposed being downwind of the zoo had its advantages.

There was scant time to marvel at the wholesale thievery because Pearl and Felix were busy trashing the place. It was a sorry impulse with gleeful undertones. Felix had overturned a large metal footlocker and the contents were now strewn across the ground. He bent and picked up an item that he secured behind his back in the waist of his jeans, moving so efficiently I didn't have a chance to see what it was. He shoved other items in a second canvas duffel, apparently intent on packing Terrence's belongings along with anything else of value, whether Terrence's or not. He was as methodical as a soldier stripping the enemy dead.

My attention snapped to Pearl, who had kicked over an oil drum that now lay on its side, heavily dented where she'd stomped it dead center. This was a makeshift incinerator emptied of half-burned logs. Firewood from a nearby stack had been supplemented with books, which must have made good tinder. The blackened spines of once whole texts had tumbled out of the drum like bones, doilies of charred paper spilling over the hard-packed dirt.

"What are you *doing*?" I asked in a hoarse whisper. I'd meant to warn them, but I was so taken aback, I couldn't gather my wits about me. The big guy was probably already making short work of the hill.

When there was no response, I hissed, the sound harsh and unexpected. Pearl scarcely seemed aware of me, but Felix lifted his head abruptly. As it turned out, even the hiss was pointless because the bum in the red flannel shirt chose that moment to stride into the camp. He knew instantly what was going on and his rage was a sound that started low in his throat as he crossed the littered ground. He grabbed Pearl's jacket and shoved her. Off balance, she fell backward with a thud. Any other woman would have had the air knocked out of her, but Pearl was made of sturdier stuff. She tried to sit upright so she could get to her feet, but the bum kicked her squarely in the side and then landed on her chest with both knees.

Felix bent and picked up a piece of firewood, which had been hewn from a young tree with a diameter about the size of a dinner plate. The log had been split into four sections, the raw wood visible in a wedge as sharp as a fixed-blade machete. He moved toward the bum with a measured pace, his face blank. Gone was any suggestion that he was mentally slow. I saw now that his thinking was straightforward. Subtlety wasn't high on his list and he lacked the facility for reflection. He was practical. He saw what needed to be done and he did it. In this case, the bum attacking Pearl needed to be hit with a hunk of wood, which Felix managed with dispatch. The bum toppled over in exactly the manner you'd expect for a man who'd just been hit with a hunk of wood.

I didn't wait to see what happened next. I made a quick run to the tree, where I snatched the backpack from its resting place. I was surprised to find it nearly weightless, offering little or no resistance. I'd imagined having to drag it along behind me, but while it was unwieldy, it was easy to carry. I grabbed the nearby canvas duffel and dragged it into the dense shrubs, pulling it in one hand while I held the backpack in front of me like a shield. Advancement was almost impossible. I plunged through the path of crushed and snapped undergrowth created by our approach. I broke out of the woods and began to struggle up the hill toward the fence. I was breathing hard and sweating, and my shoulders burned. I like to think I'm in good shape, but clearly that was not the case. Behind me, I hoped Felix and Pearl knew how to protect themselves. The last I'd seen of them, they were doing okay. Rescuing the backpack had been the goal, and if we failed at that, then the venture was all risk with no payoff. Once I'd tossed the backpack and the duffel in the trunk of my car, I'd go back and offer what I could in the way of help.

When I reached the fence, I dumped the duffel temporarily and shoved the backpack through the hole, irritated when the frame got caught in the chain link. I jerked to free it and shoved again, all the while talking to myself, murmuring, "Come on, come on." This time the canvas got snagged on a sharp hook of raw wire. I tried again, pushing the flap of fence with the pack itself until the gap was wide enough for the frame to pass through. I dragged the duffel bag to the hole, sat down, and kicked it through to the other side.

Behind me I heard a rustling on the hill, dead leaves and twigs responding in a series of pops and whispers. I'd hoped to slide through the fence myself so I could throw both items in the trunk, but there was no time for that. I turned as Pearl staggered into view, her face a livid pink with exertion. Behind her Felix charged out of the woods and loped up the hill. Neither had managed to snag the second duffel from the camp. Felix lost his footing every third or fourth step, which made progress agonizingly slow. Pearl seemed to run without forward motion. Felix was clearly moving faster, but the distance between them appeared the same because of the angle of my view.

Behind Pearl I saw the bum. Blood trickled down the side of his cheek, already darkened by a bruise. Felix flew at the fence like a chimp. His feet created toeholds, one above the other, as he propelled himself upward, climbing with surprising agility. He would have reached the top and tumbled down on the other side if Pearl hadn't cried out. Her exclamation was rendered in the ancient language of panic. Felix released his hold on the fence and dropped back to the ground.

The Boggart had gained on Pearl, and it was clear she couldn't move fast enough to outrun him. He was a good ten years younger and perhaps not physically fit, but in better shape than she was. In a canny way, she knew her weight was an advantage, the sheer mass of her being a force to contend with. Breathing hard, she turned to face the bum and planted her feet. As he reached for her, she pulled her fist back and punched him without ceremony. His head barely moved as he absorbed the blow. He shook himself like a wet dog while Pearl started up the hill again. The bum lunged forward and grabbed her by the foot. She kicked at him repeatedly, forcing him to release her. Before she could scramble out of his reach, he grabbed her again and pulled her feet out from under her. I saw her sprawl forward and then he was on her.

Felix moved toward the two. He was operating on autopilot, converting raw adrenaline to action. He approached with deliberation, his arm out straight, his hand extended in front of him. Pearl was still down. The burly man swung an arm up, a knife gripped in his fist. Pearl managed to turn to one side as the blade came down, slashing the tough faux leather sleeve of her jacket. Felix stretched forward and the bum recoiled, uttering a harsh cry. Belatedly, I realized Felix had hit him with a shot of pepper spray. The panhandler rolled away from Pearl, blinded and howling. Unfortunately, Pearl had inhaled the same irritant. Her cough was sudden and relentless, as debilitating as the spray that caught the bum in the face.

Pearl got herself up on all fours, coughing uncontrollably. Felix pulled her to her feet. Behind them, the bum bent helplessly from the waist. The pepper spray had created a fiery distraction, excruciating pain that might have stopped a lesser mortal but wouldn't delay him for long. Felix grabbed Pearl under one arm and the two of them lumbered toward the fence. I slid under the fence in one continuous motion, knowing I didn't dare pause for fear of getting myself snagged. I came up on the far side, rose to my feet, and hauled up the curl of fencing far enough to allow Pearl to hunch herself under. Her jacket caught in a stretch of raw tines that tore into the dense fabric like fishing hooks. Felix was, by then, on my side of the fence, having scaled it and rolled over the top before he thudded to the ground. Pearl's jacket was impaled and she was stuck halfway under the fence with little room to maneuver. She backed up abruptly, shed the jacket, and rolled over onto her back, this time head first. She dug her heels into the soft ground as I had, kicking her way through while Felix and I raised the raw chain link as far up as we could. We hauled her by the arms and pulled her to safety. She was breathing heavily and she moaned, more from fear, I suspect, than from pain. Her eyes were pink and swollen from the cloud of pepper spray, and her cough picked up again. Her nose ran as steadily as the trickle from a hose. We urged her toward the car, but she stopped where she was, hands on her knees. "I gotta get my jacket!"

"No, you don't!"

She ignored me, dropped to her hands and knees again to rescue the garment, which she managed with one quick jerk. Felix and I each grabbed one of Pearl's arms, supporting her on either side while she stumbled between us. Once we reached the car, we left her sitting sideways in the passenger seat with the door ajar. I opened the trunk. Felix snatched the backpack and the duffel and tossed them in. I banged the trunk shut.

Together we lifted Pearl's feet and swung them into the car, slamming the door on her side. Felix came around to the driver's side and squeezed into the back. I flung my shoulder bag in after him. I got behind the wheel, slammed the door shut, and released the emergency brake. I felt the car move slowly.

I started the engine as the Mustang picked up speed and we continued rolling down the hill, gathering momentum.

I directed my comment to Felix by way of the rearview mirror. "Cool move. I didn't know you carried pepper spray."

He flashed me a metallic smile. "I don't. I stole it from them."

9

At the bottom of the hill I gunned it through the parking lot and took a squealing turn onto Milagro, only belatedly checking to make sure there wasn't a cop car in range. I didn't for a moment imagine the Boggart was hot on our tail, but I was shot through with adrenaline and couldn't suppress the urge to flee. A block farther up on Milagro, I took my eyes off the road long enough to look at Pearl. "Why did you tear up the camp? What were you thinking?"

"They burned his books. They were using them as fuel—"

"So what? He's dead. The books don't mean anything to him. Who knows what they'll do to get even with you."

Pearl held up a hand. "Stop. I gotta get out."

"Are you going to be sick?"

"No, I'm not going to be *sick*, you dumb shit. I need a smoke."

Felix said, "Hey, me, too!"

"Oh, for heaven's sake," I snapped.

I searched for a stretch of curb that would allow me to ease out of the flow of traffic. In truth, I didn't trust myself to drive at that moment. I was wired and needed time to compose myself. Milagro was a busy thoroughfare, and I felt distracted and out of sorts. I activated my left turn signal and took the side street that bordered the McDonald's parking lot. The light had faded and the few trees on the grassy strip between the street and the sidewalk created a shadowy haven. I spotted a long gap between two parked vehicles and did a nifty job of parallel parking, which I notice is usually better done without too much thought.

I killed the engine and listened to the tick of hot metal while Pearl got out. Felix followed her out the passenger-side door. I emerged on my side and leaned against the door frame, legs extended behind me as though to loosen my hamstrings. I rested my cheek on my outstretched arms and waited for my heart to slow. Ten feet away, I could see Felix's hands shake. Beads of sweat appeared on Pearl's forehead in response to the unaccustomed physical exertion. Her eyes still watered from the capsicum and tears trickled down her cheeks. She sniffed and then leaned to one side and blew her nose through her fingers, which she wiped on her jeans. I don't know why I expected anything more from her.

A quick look at my watch told me it was 7:10—too late to take them back to the shelter, which by now would be locked for the night. In theory, they would have been safe at Harbor House, but I knew it was the first place the Boggarts would check if they decided to retaliate.

Felix fumbled a pack of cigarettes from his shirt pocket.

I said, "Why'd you bum a cigarette from her when you already had a pack?"

"She don't mind."

"The hell I don't."

Felix's pack of cigarettes was smashed and the first two cigarettes he pulled out were broken in half. He tossed the first away.

"Gimme that," Pearl said. She snatched the second cigarette, which was little more than a stub with strands of tobacco hanging out. He offered her a light and then extracted a third cigarette and lit it for himself. Almost simultaneously they inhaled, sucking smoke so far down into their lungs I thought they'd hyperventilate. I experienced a brief flash of what it felt like to light up in times of stress, but I don't think I actually whimpered aloud.

"You two are nuts," I said. "Cigarettes are expensive and they're bad for you."

Pearl scowled. "What's it to you? Clearly, you never smoked a day in your life."

"I did, *too*. I smoked for two years before I gave it up."

"Then you ought to be more compassionate."

"I'm not the warm fuzzy type. I thought that's why we got along so well."

She smiled, exposing her four bottom teeth with wide gaps between. "Lord help me. I think I'm getting attached to you."

"God forbid."

She took a final drag from her cigarette and crushed the butt underfoot. "Whoo! Better. Whyn't we take a look at what we got here?"

"By all means," I said.

I grabbed my shoulder bag from the backseat and dug through the contents for my penlight, which I flicked on. I closed the car door and walked around to the rear, where the three of us convened. I popped open the trunk and removed the backpack. I handed it off to her, then reached for the duffel and set it on the pavement between us.

Pearl flipped the backpack upside down. The frame was constructed of hollow lengths of aluminum tubing, each of the four ends capped with a rubber shoe. Pearl removed one and turned the frame right side up again. She gave it a couple of shakes and I heard the tinkle of metal on pavement. I shone the light down on the long flat key that had fallen out of the frame. She leaned over with effort and picked it up. I held out my hand and she placed it in my palm. I studied it in the beam of my penlight.

The key to Dace's safe deposit box had notches of varying depths along one side. I turned it over. No bank name, no address, and no box number. "This is blank."

Pearl said, "Of course it is. You find that, they don't want you to walk in and claim stuff that ain't yours."

I said, "You couldn't do that anyway. To get into a safe deposit box, they ask for your ID and your signature, which has to match the one they keep on file."

"No kidding?" Felix said. "Even if the box is yours for real and you got the key and everything? That don't seem right."

"I don't suppose either one of you knows where Terrence did his banking."

Pearl said, "Nope. Though you gotta figure it's somewhere in walking distance. That limp of his, he couldn't go far."

"Unless he took a cab," I said.

"Good point."

I offered her the key. "You might as well keep this. You worked hard enough for it."

"Hey, no. You hang on to it. Once you figure out where the box is, you can let us know. I'm curious why he'd keep his valuables in a bank when that's exactly where a bank robber's going to hit first."

She set the backpack aside and loosened the mouth of the canvas duffel. She peered in and then upended it, shaking out the contents. A wad of old clothes tumbled out, drab, worn, and smelling of mildew. I flashed a beam across the pile. The only exception to the whole raggedy-ass collection was a neatly folded cotton shirt with a button-down collar and long sleeves, the fabric a brightly colored green-and-yellow plaid. When she picked up the shirt, a pair of glasses and a photo ID fell out.

"That's Charles," she said. "Terrence's friend who died."

"What was Terrence doing with his stuff?"

"Keepsake. Terrence had a sentimental streak and that was really all the fella had."

The remaining items were a washed-out gray, cheap goods he probably plucked from a garbage can or a Salvation Army bin.

"What kind of world is it that when life ends all that's left looks like junk?" she asked. She picked up the plaid shirt and rolled it around the glasses and ID, which she shoved back into the duffel, followed by everything else. I was waiting for further comment, but she was staring off down the street. I didn't think we'd netted much for the risk we'd taken.

"That's everything?" I asked.

"Pretty much."

"So now what?"

She said, "You want, we can put our heads together while we have us a bite to eat. QP with Cheese would really hit the spot."

I stared at her with interest. "What a truly fine idea."

• • •

Pearl and Felix settled into a booth near a window looking out onto the side street where the Mustang was parked. I stood in line waiting my turn, then placed our order, paid the tab, and watched while our meal was assembled: three QPs with Cheese, two Big Macs, three large orders of fries, and three Cokes. The Big Macs were for them, though I'd have been willing to suck on the paper wrappers if they offered me the chance. I crossed to the table with the tray and distributed the food. I noticed Pearl kept the backpack beside her, the canvas duffel tucked between her feet.

We ate without saying much, each of us intent on the fragrant blend of meat and cheese, grilled to a fare-thee-well, tucked in a soft bun, and liberally doused with the ketchup we squeezed from little plastic envelopes. I'd picked up extra salt packets, and we spared ourselves nothing in the way of additives, preservatives, and sodium chloride.

I let Felix bus the table, after which we returned to the car and got in. "Where should I drop you?"

Pearl said, "Anywhere at the beach is fine. We'll figure it out from there."

I fired up the Mustang, cruised down one block and over one, eventually turning right onto Milagro. I headed for Cabana Boulevard. The combination of junk food and the sharp drop in my stress levels had left me logy and longing for sleep. In an attempt to make conversation, I said, "How'd you two end up on the street? That can't be much fun."

Felix leaned forward on the seat, inserting himself between the two of us like the family dog on an outing. "More fun than you'd think. I run off when I was fifteen and went to live with my dad."

Pearl smiled at him. "This guy's epileptic. Had a brain injury, didn't you?"

"Yep. My mom come after me with a ball-peen hammer. Soft-faced instead of hard, which she said was a lucky break for me. She give me such a whack she knocked me out cold. When I come to I was seeing stars and didn't have a clue where I was at. Didn't bleed much, but my head hurt bad. After that, I started having fits—ten to fifteen a day."

"She claimed he only did it to embarrass her," Pearl said.

"That's right. She didn't take me to the doctor for two

years. Said the fits was phoney-baloney I came up with just to bug the shit out of her. Couldn't prove it by me. I'd be fine and then I'd be down on the ground pissin' myself."

Pearl said, "By the time she took him for help, the seizures damaged his brain."

"She said I didn't have much brains to begin with, so no big loss," he said. "I'm fine as long as I take my pills."

"That's right. And don't you forget," she said, and pointed a finger at him.

He smiled, happily, grungy braces glinting on his teeth. "She's tough. Her and Dandy watch out for me."

"Better than your mom did, that's for sure."

I caught his eye in the rearview mirror. "Who paid for your braces?"

"My dad."

"What happened to him?"

"He got tired of me, I guess. One day he went off and didn't come back. After that, I was on my own."

"What about you, Pearl?"

"I was afraid you'd get around to asking. I'm chronically unemployed. Never had a job my whole life. None of my family did. I take that back. Once my daddy was hired on a construction crew for two weeks and two days. He said it was way more work than it paid. He maintained it was just one more way to take advantage of the poor. After that, the state took care of us," she said. "How about yourself? The business you're in, what do you do all day?"

"It varies. Process serving, paper searches at the courthouse. Background checks. Sometimes I sit surveillance. Once a case is wrapped up, I write reports and send out invoices so I can pay my bills."

"Now see, right there. That's dumb. I don't have bills. I don't owe anyone a dime, so in that respect, I'm better off than you."

I stared at her briefly, thinking she was pulling my leg.

"Up here is fine," she said, indicating the intersection where Cabana Boulevard met State Street.

I pulled over to the curb across the street from the public parking lot near the wharf. "You have a place to sleep?"

"As long as the cops don't hassle us," she said.

I was skeptical, though in truth the only alternative I could think of was an invitation to stay at my place, and how would that play out? The two of them on my sofa bed? Felix on the sofa and Pearl in bed with me? "I can give you a few bucks for a motel," I said.

"We don't take handouts. Boggarts do that," she said.

"Sorry. My mistake," I said.

Felix said, "That's all right. You didn't know. Thanks for dinner. It was a treat. I kept me a couple packets of ketchup in case I get hungry later."

The two of them got out, Pearl toting the backpack while Felix carried the duffel in his arms like a dog.

"Thanks for the help," she said, holding up the backpack.

"You two better keep an eye out," I said. "Those guys will be cruising to get even."

"Doesn't scare me," she said. "Bunch of bozos."

As I pulled away, I kept an eye on them in the side-view mirror. They waited patiently, clearly unwilling to move while I still had them in my sights. Wherever they intended to hole up for the night, they didn't want me to know. What a pair: Pearl, round as a beach ball, and Felix, with his gummed-up braces and his white-boy dreads. Why did the sight of them make me want to weep?

Wednesday morning, having worked my way through my usual routine, I went into the office, where I put on a pot of coffee and opened the mail from the day before. Despite the fact that business was nonexistent, I'm happier at my desk than just about anyplace else. I took out my index cards, intending to jot down a few notes, when the phone rang.

It was Aaron Blumberg returning my Monday-morning call with apologies for taking so long.

"Don't worry about it," I said. "I know you've been busy. I figured you'd get back to me when you had the chance. Have you heard from Sacramento?"

"Not a peep," he said. "What about you? Anything on your end?"

"Actually, I've picked up quite a bit," I said. I gave him a quick summary of the blanks I'd filled in, including the dead man's full name and the fact that he'd lived in Bakersfield for some years. I also told him about Dandy, Pearl, and Felix as my source for much of the information. "According to the scuttlebutt, Dace was sentenced to life in prison, but no one seems to know what he did or why he was released. I'd love to find out what that's about."

"Me and thee both. Give me the name again."

"Last name, Dace. First initial, R—but I don't know what it stands for. Richard, Robert. His beach buddies are convinced he had money because he went to the trouble to draw up his last will and testament with the three of them serving as witnesses. I didn't see the document among his effects, but you might try his sleeping bag in case he sewed it into the lining or something of the sort. I have what they claim is the key to his safe deposit box, so that's another possibility, and probably a better bet."

"I'll take a look at his sleeping bag," he said. "You know where he was incarcerated?"

"Soledad, though I take it that was a subject he didn't care to discuss."

"Nice. I'll pull up his criminal history on my computer. Date of birth?"

"Don't have that. You worked in Kern County not that long ago. Seems like Bakersfield PD or the sheriff's department could fill you in."

"I'll see what my buddies have to say. You know where he did his banking?" In the background, I could hear Aaron tapping out a note to himself on his computer.

"I don't, but I was just setting out on a scouting mission if that's okay with you. I know bankers can be tight-lipped, but I'm hoping someone will at least confirm a customer relationship. It'll help if I can drop your name into the conversation like I've been officially blessed."

"Do that. Once we know which bank we're dealing with, I'll see if we need a court order to get into the box. Did you find out what he was doing with your phone number?"

"He was hoping to contact family in the area and needed an intermediary. I was recommended by a pal of mine named Pinky Ford. You remember him from the warehouse shoot-out last May?"

"Oh, man, do I ever," he said. "You did good. R. Terrence Dace from Bakersfield. I'll get back to you as soon as I get a line on him."

Once in my car, I went back to the beach and began driving the surface streets, starting from the point where Terrence pitched his tent. I'd decided Pearl was right about his doing his banking business in walking distance. While he could have taken a cab, it was money he probably wouldn't have wanted to spend. A man who won't pay for shelter isn't likely to pay for taxi rides.

There were five banks in Montebello, another twelve in downtown Santa Teresa. Nine were scattered over a six-block strip of State Street and another three on Santa Teresa Street, which runs parallel to State. Once I plotted my course, I began with the closest financial institution and worked my way outward.

Doing a canvass of any kind can be tedious unless you're in the proper frame of mind. I took a Zen-like approach. This was the job I'd assigned myself. It wasn't about finding the right answer; it was about patience and diligence. I surrendered to the process, ascribing the same importance to this work as to anything else I did.

This is the gist of the conversation I initiated in every bank I entered. First, I'd ask the nearest teller if I could see the bank manager, who was usually visible at his desk in a modest glass cubicle or maybe seated at a nondescript desk on the floor. After I introduced myself to the manager or assistant manager, I'd show my current driver's license and a photostat of my investigator's license, and then hand over my business card. I'd mention R. Terrence Dace and ask if he'd been a customer. I'd explain that the key to a safe deposit box had been found among his effects. I'd toss Aaron Blumberg's name out at the first opportunity, indicating that the coroner's investigator would make arrangements to open the box in the presence of a bank officer once we knew where the deceased did his banking. Mention of the coroner's investigator worked like magic. Operating on my own, I doubted anyone would have given me the time of day.

I hit pay dirt in the tenth bank when the teller referred me to an assistant vice president named Ted Hill, who nodded at the mention of Dace's name.

"Mr. Dace was a valued customer. I'm sorry to hear he's passed on."

"I gather he was ill for some time," I said. "The coroner's office wondered if a court order would be required to get into the box."

"That's not necessary. We're happy to cooperate with the public administrator's office. Tell Mr. Blumberg we'll do anything we can to help. Have him call and we'll set up an appointment at his convenience."

And just like that, the lid to Pandora's box flew open. It would take me another day before I understood how many imps had been freed, but for the moment, I was inordinately pleased with myself.

10

I left the bank and drove home. I'd promised to help move supplies and equipment from Henry's guest rooms back into the storage areas off the kitchen at Rosie's Tavern, and I wanted to make good on the offer. I found a parking space and walked the short distance to the studio, noting that Henry's station wagon was already sitting in the drive, the back hatch open in preparation for loading. I rounded the corner just as Henry emerged from the house, toting a cardboard box laden with packaged goods. I half expected to see William in the backyard leaning on his cane, but he was nowhere in evidence.

"Where's William? I thought he'd be supervising."

"I dropped him off for his physical therapy appointment. I'll pick him up in an hour. In the meantime, I thought I might as well start loading up. Seems silly to drive half a block, but I refuse to haul it all by hand."

"I have a quick call to make and then I'll pitch in," I said. "Is there a scheme in the works or is it grab and go?"

"I've been picking up items in random order. When William gets back, we'll park him in Rosie's kitchen and he can tell us how he wants the shelves arranged."

"How's he doing?"

"Don't ask."

"What about the cat?"

"Ed's fine. He slept in my bed with his head on the pillow next to mine. And don't roll your eyes."

"I won't. I swear."

I rolled my eyes as soon as my back was turned, but I was smiling as I did so. I unlocked the studio and set my shoulder bag on the nearest stool. I put a call in to Aaron, who picked up on the second ring. I gave him Ted Hill's name and the name of the bank. "It doesn't sound like he's going to be a butt about getting into the box," I said.

"Do you want to be there?"

"Absolutely! I'd love it."

"Good. I'll talk to Hill and get back to you."

I left the studio door open in case Aaron called back while I was moving items. Henry was better at loading than I was, so I delivered boxes and left it up to him to determine how to stack and stow them in the back of the station wagon.

The cat supervised our efforts, climbing in and out of the car, walking across the seat back, and perching in the spot with the best view, usually right where Henry intended to put a box. The vet had told Henry the cat was less than two years old, and it was clear he'd retained many of his kittenish ways. I'm not going to report every cute thing the cat did, but I noticed both Henry and I had taken up baby talk in our inane, ongoing conversational exchange with him. Henry swore Ed understood English, though he didn't seem that interested in what we had to say. Whatever the cat's native tongue, his tone of voice couldn't be the same high-pitched, goofy one Henry and I had adopted in our comments to him. I always knew having a cat around would do this to me, which is why I've resisted. I'd thought Henry and I were of like minds, but clearly he'd lost his.

Aaron called at 6:00 that night. We'd completed the move. Henry and William were still over at Rosie's, reorganizing the goods and equipment. They'd insisted they didn't need my help, so I'd come home to shower. The phone rang as I was coming down the spiral stairs in a fresh pair of jeans and a sweatshirt.

"We're meeting Ted Hill at the bank at nine," Aaron said when I picked up the phone. "He's got a nine-thirty appointment at the Colgate branch, so he'll have one of the tellers oversee our efforts. Once he's sure the situation's under control, he'll leave us to our work. Why don't I meet you at that little coffee shop across the street and buy you breakfast before we go to the bank?"

"Great. To what do I owe the pleasure?"

"Department has a slush fund we use to pay the occasional confidential informant. I told the coroner you'd rustled up some good intel, saving me the work. I suggested you should be compensated for the time you put in."

"Well, on that basis, I'm happy to accept."

In the morning, I skipped my run. I could have made an earlier start or shortened the distance to carve out sufficient time, but I was in the mood to take a day off. I slept in until 7:15, scandalously late by my standards. To celebrate the change of pace, I put on a pair of pantyhose, my black flats, and my black all-purpose dress. This versatile and completely wrinkle-resistant garment is the only bona fide dress I own, good for cocktail parties, funerals, and semisolemn occasions in between. I flapped a ceremonial rag across the shoulders where a fine layer of dust had settled. After that, I figured I was good to go.

I found a space in the parking structure adjacent to the coffee shop. Aaron had been watching for me and he rose to his feet politely when he saw me come in the door. I joined him in a booth by the window, where we could watch foot traffic out on the street—clerks, judges, court reporters, lawyers and their clients heading for the courthouse. A black-and-white bus, designated as the Santa Teresa County Sheriff's Department transport, pulled up at the curb and a parade of orange-clad and shackled inmates emerged from the vehicle and shuffled into the building, accompanied by three uniformed corrections officers.

Aaron's hair was damp from his morning shower, comb tracks still evident as he handed me a menu and checked for the specials of the day. He wore a sport coat over a blue-and-white-checked shirt with a folded necktie visible in the pocket. He looked up as the waitress approached, coffeepot in hand. She filled our cups and delivered small pods of half-and-half from a pocket in her apron. We ordered, Aaron opting for bacon, scrambled eggs, and wheat toast, while I asked for the steel-cut oats, which came with small containers arranged on a separate tray: brown sugar, raisins, blueberries, butter, candied pecans, and a small pitcher of cream, for which I substituted milk. We chatted about inconsequential matters, and once the waitress delivered the food, took time out to eat.

Aaron ate faster than I did and when he finished the last bite of toast, he ran his napkin across his mouth and then tucked it under his plate. "I heard back from Sacramento late last night with a match on the prints, which confirm Dace's identity. I thought I'd fill you in on his criminal history before we go over to the bank."

"Ah. You must have talked to someone in Bakersfield."

"I pulled up his file and then put in a call to one of the sheriff's department homicide detectives."

"Am I going to like this?"

"You might. The story's actually more interesting than you'd think. Dace spent twelve years in prison on a felony murder conviction that was overturned a year ago."

"Who'd he kill?"

"I'll get to that. He'd had some earlier, minor skirmishes with the law. A couple of DUIs. A charge of drunk and disorderly that was later dismissed. Nothing of significance. For years, he ran his own tree-trimming company while he worked on a degree in landscape architecture . . . which he never got, by the way . . ."

"So I heard. Dandy tells me he was a bright guy, and very knowledgeable."

"Apparently so. He had a reputation for being a hands-on kind of boss. He could push a crew, but he was more than willing to get up there himself when it came to proper pruning. In 1968, he took a bad fall; broke his shoulder and his left hip, which put him out of commission for a while. During his recovery he got caught up in prescription drugs and heavy drinking, which he had a penchant for in any event. Some of this you may know."

"Not exactly, but close enough. I heard about the pain pills and alcohol," I said. "I can't imagine how you get from trimming trees to felony murder, but I'm all ears."

"Well, he started on a downward spiral. You know how it goes. Once word got out about his boozing, his clients started dropping him, which meant his business went into the toilet. His wife threatened to kick him out, saying she didn't want the kids exposed to his bad behavior. He managed to hold his marriage together, but things weren't good by a long shot and the only work he could get was day labor. Bunch of them would stand out on a corner, like hookers, while prospective employers cruised by in their half-ton trucks, looking them over and quizzing them about their skills. He and another fellow named Herman Cates picked up a couple days' work trimming trees . . ."

While I listened, I worked on my oatmeal. I pushed the raisins to the bottom of the bowl so the heat would plump them. Then I folded in the milk and sugar. My Aunt Gin favored a couple of pats of butter, but that's too decadent for my taste.

Aaron was saying, "What Dace doesn't know is this guy Cates is a registered sex offender and he has his eye on the teenaged girl in a bikini, sunning herself in the yard next door. She's abducted that night, and two days later they find her body stuffed in a sewer pipe half a mile away. She's been raped and strangled with the cord from the rope-and-pulley system on the very pruning saw Dace was using that day."

I lowered my spoon. "Are you sure about this? I never even met the man, but I find that hard to believe."

"Sheriff's department didn't have a problem with it. Cates was identified from a palm print left at the scene and he's the one who implicated Dace. Eventually, Cates ended up on death row in San Quentin, but Dace insisted all along that he was innocent. His wife got on the stand and testified he was home the night the girl was kidnapped. Jury figured she was lying through her teeth. Vote on the guilty verdict was unanimous and the judge sentenced him to life in prison. He spent the next twelve years writing letters to anyone and everyone."

"I've had letters from inmates and they always sound like crackpots. Long, garbled tales about political conspiracies and corruption in the legal system."

Aaron leaned forward. "Here's the kicker. Two years ago, Cates finds out he's terminal. He's diagnosed with stage four lung cancer, three months to live at the outside, and he decides he doesn't want to die with a bad conscience. He finally tells the authorities Dace wasn't the guy, that it was someone else."

"Amazing."

"That's what *I* said. You'd think Cates's recanting would be sufficient, but no deal. Prosecutor thinks it's bullshit. Dace's original defense attorney is retired and suffering early stage dementia so he's no help. The judge doesn't want to hear about it and there's no one willing to go to bat for him. Twenty-five letters later an attorney finally agreed to look into Dace's claims. He went back and reviewed all the old police files and the evidence in storage, including a bloody shirt Dace had always sworn wasn't his. The attorney got a judge to sign an order submitting the semen sample and the bloody shirt for DNA testing that wasn't available back then. Sure enough, results ruled him out."

"What about the real guy?"

"He'd been killed in a prison riot two months before. Dace was freed but his life was in pieces, as you might imagine."

"Humpty Dumpty."

"That's about it. This was a major embarrassment for the department. Let's not even talk about the DA's office. No one believed Dace was innocent. Some still won't accept the fact because who wants to take responsibility when you're that far off? Dace's attorney uncovered a host of other issues. Crucial reports were 'lost.' Exculpatory evidence was swept under the rug."

Aaron glanced at his watch and signaled the waitress for the check. "There's more, but it can wait."

We finished the last of our coffee and Aaron paid the bill. We went out into the morning sun and crossed the street to the bank without saying a word. Dace's story made chitchat seem inappropriate.

Ted Hill had been watching for us and he held the door open as we approached. Aaron introduced himself and the two men shook hands. Both of us provided photo identification. Aaron had brought a letter from the coroner, identifying the John Doe as R. T. Dace, verifying the date and cause of death, and asking the bank's cooperation in the matter of the safe deposit box. Hill barely paid attention. Once he'd made up his mind to help, the official folderol didn't seem to matter to him. Hill introduced us to a teller named Joyce Mount, who would accompany us into the vault. Ted Hill excused himself and suggested Aaron call him later in the day.

Aaron and I went into the vault with Ms. Mount. Aaron used the key we'd found in Dace's backpack and the teller used the master. In fewer than ten seconds, the safe deposit box was on the table in front of us. Aaron and I pulled up chairs side by side. The teller remained on hand as the bank's representative, probably as curious as we were about what we'd find.

Aaron removed the contents of the box and fanned out the papers on the table. He had a notebook and he kept a written inventory, cataloging each item as he examined it and passed it on to me. The first was a savings account passbook. He flipped through, looking at a number of entries, and then checked the final balance. He blinked, made a note, and handed it to me.

The account had been opened nine months before on January 8, 1988, which must have been shortly after Dace arrived in town. The initial deposit was $597,500. The last transaction, a withdrawal of $200, was date-stamped October 1, 1988, leaving a balance of $595,350.

I said, "Whoa. I heard he had money, but I had no idea the total was anywhere close to this. I figured a couple of hundred bucks. Where'd it come from?"

"That's what I didn't have a chance to tell you. He went after the state and sued 'em for twelve million dollars—a million for every year he was incarcerated. After weeks of haggling, he agreed to a settlement. At six hundred thousand dollars, the state got off cheap. He probably could've held out for more, but he wanted his life back. He had his freedom. His reputation was clean again and he was eager to see his kids."

At least I understood now why the bank valued Dace as a customer. Maybe they pegged him as eccentric; all that money and he was still living like a tramp.

The next item was a plain white number-ten envelope that contained school pictures of three kids—a boy and two girls—who I assumed were his. The first name, the name of the school, and the year, 1973, were noted on the back of each photo. A boy, Ethan, appeared to be in his midteens at the time the picture was taken. The middle child, a girl named Ellen, was probably fourteen, and the youngest, Anna, might have been eleven or twelve. By now, the girls would be in their late twenties, the boy in his early thirties. Aaron and I both studied the faces before returning the photos to the envelope.

The next document was a divorce decree in which Evelyn Chastain Dace was named as the plantiff and R. Terrence Dace, the defendant. Dissolution of marriage had been granted in August 1974. This document was followed by a quitclaim deed signed by R. Terrence Dace as grantor, in which he had conveyed the described house and lot to Evelyn Chastain Dace, including all oil, gas, and minerals on and under the property owned by the two of them as joint tenants.

The manila envelope that surfaced next was packed with a number of newspaper clippings from the *Bakersfield Californian* and the *Kern County News*, covering the period between February 28, 1972, and November 15, 1973, detailing the murder of a teenage girl who'd first been reported missing the morning of February 26, 1972. The black-and-white newspaper photo of the victim was enough to break your heart. She was a beautiful young woman with long, dark hair and a bright smile.

I skimmed, picking up a paragraph here and there. It helped that Aaron had given me the broad strokes. Knowing how the story turned out put the bits and pieces into context. Herman Cates and R. Terrence Dace were tried separately, court dates and appearances stretching over a protracted period while both defendants were assigned court-appointed attorneys, who probably requested time to prepare.

Herman Cates and a second suspect, R. Terrence Dace, were accused of the abduction and murder of fifteen-year-old Karen Coffey, a freshman at Bakersfield High School. Dace denied any involvement and the state's case rested, in large part, on the eyewitness testimony of a neighbor who claimed that she saw Dace on the property the day of the abduction . . .

Dace's defense attorney presented an alibi defense, that he was home with his wife the night of the murder and therefore didn't have an opportunity to commit the crime. Mrs. Dace's testimony was supported by a next-door neighbor, Lorelei Brandle, who was at the house during the time in question. The defense also challenged Cates's credibility in tying Dace to the crime. The jury was unimpressed, and after deliberating for four hours, convicted Dace of felony murder. Dace was sentenced to life in prison without the possibility of parole and began serving his time in January 1974.

It wasn't difficult to imagine the sequence of events. After Dace's conviction and sentencing, his wife filed for divorce, insisting that he quitclaim the house to her. Or maybe he'd voluntarily relinquished claim in light of his disgrace. Once he was freed from prison, sued the state, and collected his settlement, the money must have looked like a way to make amends. I could imagine him arriving in Bakersfield, eager to contact his children so he could tell them his name had been cleared. Big mistake. According to Dandy, the reunion was a disaster. In the end, they'd severed their relationship and he'd traveled to Santa Teresa in hopes of reconnecting with whatever remaining family he could find.

Occasionally, the teller would lean forward and look at an item herself, but for the most part she seemed content to observe without comment.

Aaron came to Dace's social security card and a California driver's license that had expired in May of 1976. He made a note of the social security number, Dace's full name, and his address at the time the license was issued. "The initial 'R' stands for Randall," he remarked.

"Good to know."

He passed both documents to me after he added the information to his inventory.

I checked the date of birth on his driver's license. "Catch this. He was born in 1935, which means he's fifty-three years old. He looked more like seventy when I saw him."

"Nobody ever said drink, drugs, and cigarettes were the fountain of youth."

"I guess not."

Aaron read and passed along paperwork related to the settlement, showing Dace's receipt of the money, his signature attesting to the fact that this was settlement in full, that he held the state harmless, and so forth. I added that document to the mounting pile of those we'd reviewed.

The next items Aaron passed me were three sixteen-page folios Dace had put together for his children. I recognized his characteristic printing style. The three booklets were handwritten and hand-bound. The first covered edible California plants; the second, medicinal herbs; and the third was devoted to California wildflowers. Included with the text were delicate drawings, some done in pen and ink and some in colored pencil. There was a note attached to each, indicating which child was meant as the recipient. There was no way to know whether he'd put the folios together while he was still in prison or after his release, but I was struck by the care he'd taken. He couldn't have executed the intricate illustrations if he was drunk. These were like poems made visible, precise and lovingly rendered. For the first time, I realized Terrence Dace was a talented man, with an innate intelligence and sensitivity few people in his life had reason to appreciate. How many hours had he spent on the project, and how much affection had he lavished on the drawings and the text? I hoped someone would track down his kids and deliver these in his behalf. It might make a dent in whatever ill will they bore him. The guy deserved better.

The next envelope Aaron picked up was five inches by eight and closed with a metal clasp. Aaron opened it and removed four black-and-white photographs. They were the old-fashioned Kodak prints edged in white. Aaron noted the topmost photo and studied it briefly before he picked up the next. I did the same thing as he passed each one along. Even the teller leaned forward to have a look. In the first, a towheaded boy of six was perched on the shoulders of a rangy, good-looking man who was grasping the child's feet to anchor him in place. The background showed glimpses of flat, empty land. I could see a crumpled fence and two young trees. I pictured farmland and open countryside. On the back of the photograph, in pen, the note said ME AND UNCLE R, SEPTEMBER 1941. The boy had to be Terrence Dace. I'd seen him only once, in death, and while it was a stretch to trace the similarities between the child and the wreck of a man he'd become, the faint link was there.

The second photo showed the same towheaded boy, progressed to age ten. This time he and his Uncle R sat on the front stairs of a white frame house, Uncle R on the top step with Terrence seated between his uncle's knees one step down. The affection between the two was unmistakable. Behind them, I could see a portion of a screen door. Off the bottom step there was a boot scraper shaped like a dachshund, and on the right, partially obscured, was a cast concrete planter filled with marigolds in desperate need of watering. Now I picked up the family resemblance; the same flop of straight hair, the same tilt to the eyes. This one was also marked ME AND UNCLE R. The date was June 4, 1945.

The third and fourth photos were indoor shots, one with a Christmas tree showing in the background. Uncle R wasn't visible; in fact, I was guessing he was the photographer. Young

Terrence, now perhaps twelve, was the proud possessor of a .22 rifle, the box and wrapping paper still in evidence at his feet. No date on the back. The fourth photo was taken in the kitchen, the same house and the same holiday, judging by Dace's shirt, which appeared in both. Terrence and his Uncle R toasted the season with clear-glass punch cups held aloft. The drink might have been eggnog, something creamy-looking. The curve of whiskey bottle to the right suggested that Uncle R had greatly improved his libation. He might even have accorded Dace a wee tot of Old Crow. This time Uncle R was sitting at the boy's side with his free arm slung across his shoulders.

No wonder Dace had come looking for his Uncle R's kids. Uncle R was family as he remembered it; family as it was in the days when he was young and life was good. If he'd been estranged from his own children it would be natural for him to dream of forging a bond with the only family he had left. He'd wanted to be clean and sober before he presented himself. According to Dandy, he'd been drunk until the day he died. So much for that idea.

I heard the rustle of paper.

"Well, this is a kick in the pants," Aaron said.

I looked up to find him examining the final document, which was backed in blue. "Is that his will?"

"Indeed."

"What's the date? Dandy said it was July 8."

"That's it," he said.

"So not sewn into the lining of his sleeping bag after all?"

"Nope. Are these the three witnesses you mentioned?"

He flipped the pages and held out the final page so I could see the printed names and signatures: Pearl White, Daniel D. Singer, and Felix Beider.

I realized that "Dandy" was the shorthand version of Daniel D. Dan D. "I never heard their last names except Pearl's, and I wasn't sure that was correct. Dandy referred to her as Miss Pearly White, but I thought it might have been a play on words."

Aaron returned to the first page. "Not a word about the disposition of his remains, but his kids might expect to have a say in the matter. He's got all three listed, but there's only one address and that's his son, Ethan's. Nothing for the two girls, so maybe he didn't know where they were living."

He turned to the second page and I saw his gaze zigzag down the lines of print. His mouth turned down in an expression that suggested surprise. "The guy was frosted. Says here, 'I have intentionally omitted to provide in this will for my son, Ethan, or for my daughters, Ellen and Anna, whose loathing and disdain are irreparable and who have repudiated our relationship and severed all ties.'"

I said, "Dandy told me about that. It must have been quite a blowup."

"Well, this is helpful," Aaron went on. "Says, 'Be it known that I own no real property, have no debts, and have no assets other than the monies deposited in my savings account and the incidental personal effects in my safe deposit box. It is my desire that the executor of my estate should notify my children of my death and deliver the gifts I've set aside for them.'"

"If he's disinherited his kids, does it mean his money goes right back to the state? That would be a pisser," I said.

"Oh, no. He made sure he had all his ducks in a row. For starters, he's set it up so the executor and sole beneficiary are the same."

"Meaning what? Is that a good thing or bad?"

"It's not a problem one way or the other. I think the tricky issue lies elsewhere."

He pushed the document across the table and I leaned forward so I could read the name listed in two different places on the same page.

I said, "Oh."

Because the name was mine.

11

I don't remember the drive home. I kept my emotions on hold, unable to accept what I'd been confronted with in black and white. Before Aaron and I left the bank, the teller made one copy of his inventory sheet for me and a second to be kept in the safe deposit box. She also made a copy of Dace's will, along with copies of the other paperwork, which she returned to the safe deposit box. Aaron received one packet and I was given the other. Since I was named executor of the estate, she also handed me the original of the will to be submitted to the superior court clerk when it was entered into probate. I intended to contact an attorney as soon as possible because I already knew I was in over my head. I needed legal guidance and I needed help understanding the full impact of this strange turn of events. This was like winning the lottery without buying a ticket. Half a million bucks? Unreal.

Out on the street, Aaron and I shook hands. I have no idea why. There was simply the sense that some agreement had been reached and we'd sealed the bargain with that age-old gesture, denoting courtliness and nonaggression.

He said, "At a totally mundane level, I still have Dace's sleeping bag. Looks like that belongs to you along with every-thing else. You want me to hang on to it?"

"No, thanks. I can tell you right now I won't be crawling into that thing no matter how many times it's been cleaned."

Once on my street, I parked, locked the car, passed through the squeaky gate, and went around to the back patio. I let myself in, dropped my shoulder bag on the counter, and sat down at my desk. I opened the file drawer and took out the folder where I kept the photocopy of my parents' marriage license application. I knew what I'd find, but I needed to see it again nonetheless.

Four years previously, a piece of my personal history had surfaced unexpectedly. In the course of an investigation, a woman I was interviewing made a remark about the name Kinsey, wondering aloud if I was related to the Kinsey family up in Lompoc, an hour north of Santa Teresa. I dismissed the idea, but something about the comment bothered me. I'd finally gone down to the courthouse, where I searched public records and came up with the information my parents had supplied on the application for their marriage license, which listed my father's date and place of birth, my mother's date and place of birth, and the names of both sets of parents.

And there it was.

My mother, whose maiden name was Kinsey, was born in Lompoc, California. I was indeed a member of the Kinsey family, despite the fact that there had been no contact (that I knew of) in the years since my parents' death. At the time, I'd paid for a copy of the form, which I'd placed in my files. Now I looked at it with new eyes. My paternal grandfather—my father's father—was Quillen Millhone. My grandmother's maiden name was Rebecca Dace. Their only son, my father, was Terrence Randall Millhone, who went by the name Randy. He listed his place of birth as Bakersfield, California, which I'd forgotten. Terrence Dace's full name was Randall Terrence Dace. The two given names had probably been recycled through the family in variations from one generation to the next, going back who knows how far. If Rebecca Dace had brothers, it would explain how the surname Dace remained in play.

Why hadn't I made the connection when I first heard the

name? It's not as though Dace was a common name like Smith or Jones. The truth was, I'd been raised thinking of myself as an orphan. My Aunt Gin, for reasons of her own, had neatly sidestepped any talk of our family history. While she was intimately acquainted with the facts, she felt no compulsion to advise me of my antecedents. When assorted Kinsey relatives appeared in my life, I reacted as though my world were being invaded by aliens. I was unaccustomed to cousins and aunts, and I chafed at their overtures, which were motivated by goodwill. The existence of my maternal grandmother, Cornelia Straith LaGrand Kinsey, was a shock and not one I received with grace. Over the past couple of years, I'd adjusted (more or less), but I wasn't entirely reconciled to any of it.

In my defense, when I'd first clapped eyes on the John Doe, cold and gray and still as stone on a gurney in the coroner's office, I'd had no reason in the world to believe the man was in any way related to me. Now, for all practical purposes, he belonged to me, and I was charged with the responsibility of overseeing the distribution of his assets, which apparently consisted entirely of cash, left entirely to me. Why did this seem so wrong? There was no mention in the will itself as to what he'd wanted done with his remains. I'd make arrangements for his funeral, but his children might want a part in that decision. Despite their rejection of him and his subsequent repudiation of them, he was still their father, and the issue was by no means settled. Whether his death did or did not change the emotional climate in their hearts, it was still my job to carry the news to them and to offer an olive branch. Surely, his kids must have felt relieved when they learned of his innocence. Whatever the nature of their estrangement, at least the specter of their father as a sexual predator and cold-blooded killer had been laid to rest.

The other question that bore consideration was this: if R. T. Dace and I were related, which appeared to be the case, then what was the connection? While it was only speculation on my part, the answer seemed obvious. Dace had come to Santa Teresa because he'd heard that his favorite "Uncle R" had moved here with his family. He'd heard the news of his uncle's death, but he'd still thought he might contact surviving family members. The slip of paper in his pocket didn't refer to the personhood of Millhone, the private investigator. It was Mill-

hone, the private citizen. The only conclusion that made sense
was that Dace's favorite "Uncle R" was my father, Randy
Millhone. Terrence Randall Millhone and Randall Terrence
Dace were related by blood, though I had no way of knowing
if their relationship was actually that of uncle to nephew or
something more convoluted. If I was correct in tracing a line
to my grandmother Rebecca Dace, then Terrence was most
likely my cousin somewhere along that branch.

This is what stopped me in my tracks. If I was right, then
the four black-and-white photographs of Dace's "Uncle R"
were the only pictures of my father I'd ever seen. I shut the
door on that painful notion, which I'd deal with once I had the
snapshots in hand. Right now, they were tucked away in Dace's
safe deposit box along with the other documents I could lay
claim to once I sorted through legal matters.

I pulled out the telephone book and looked in the yellow
pages under "Attorneys." In the subcategory "Wills, Trusts
and Estate Planning," there were twenty-one lawyers listed
and I'd never heard of one. It wasn't quite noon, so I picked up
the phone and called Lonnie Kingman, my attorney of record.
He's my go-to guy at the first sign of legal troubles, which have
cropped up more than once in the course of my career. For a
period of three years, we'd shared office space, in that he'd
accorded me the use of his conference room for business purposes after I left California Fidelity Insurance.

Eventually, his firm had outgrown the space he was in and
he'd bought an office building on lower State Street into which
he'd moved some two years before. I realized with embarrassment that I'd never even stepped foot in the place. Maybe
I should have considered that good news because it meant I
hadn't been arrested, jailed, or legally threatened of late. Instead, I was forced, once again, to acknowledge the gaps in my
upbringing. Aunt Gin hadn't fostered feelings of connected-
ness and I hadn't had occasion to develop them on my own.
Maybe it was time to at least *pretend* to be a nicer person than
I knew I was. I dialed Lonnie's office number.

When the receptionist picked up, I identified myself and
asked to speak to Lonnie. I didn't recognize the receptionist's
name. She told me he was out of the country and wasn't expected back until the following week.

"What about John Ives? Is he in?"

"No, ma'am, he's not. Mr. Ives has left the firm and opened offices of his own. I can give you his number if you'd like."

"Martin Cheltenham?"

"He moved to Los Angeles . . ."

"Who's left?"

"I can put you through to Mr. Zimmerman."

"What's his specialty?"

"Personal injury."

"Do you have anyone who handles estate law? Wills, dead people? Anything like that?"

"Burke Benjamin."

"Fine. I'll take him."

"Her."

"Right. Could you put me through?"

"She's not here at the moment but I expect her back after lunch. Shall I set up an appointment?"

"Please. I'm a friend and longtime client of Lonnie's and I can be there at one o'clock if she's available."

"Looks like it to me. I'll make a note of it."

"Thanks so much."

I spelled my name for her. She asked for my phone number and I dutifully recited it. I thought she might ask for a credit card number, like a restaurant hedging against no-shows, but she let it go at that.

I used the time before my appointment to get out my index cards and transfer information from the photocopies of the paperwork in Dace's safe deposit box: California driver's license, which included his then address; his social security number; and his son's street address in Bakersfield. There was no phone number that I could find. There were other incidental bits and pieces I consigned to index cards, which were easier to carry with me than an eight-by-eleven folder. I created a file for him, into which I tucked the photocopies. It looked like there would be much more to follow before I was through with him.

The three-story building Lonnie'd bought on lower State Street was the original home of the Spring Fresh Ice Cream Company, which had operated from 1907 until it went into bankruptcy proceedings in 1931. The name Spring Fresh and the year 1907 were carved in Gothic-style lettering in the gray stone lintel above the entrance. For twenty-four years, the ground floor was occupied by the Spring Fresh Ice Cream Emporium, after which the space was taken over by a series of food-related businesses—a luncheonette, a candy store, a soda fountain, and a tea shop—while the two stories above it were let as offices. I learned all of this because a plaque mounted to the right of the front door sketched the building's metamorphosis, including its designation as a historical landmark.

When I pushed through the glass doors into the lobby, I could see that the walls had been taken back to the bare brick. The city had doubtless required Lonnie to do some serious earthquake retrofitting, but the contemporary infrastructure—steel girders and supports—had been hidden in the walls. I suspected that the materials I was looking at, while old, had been rescued from a teardown elsewhere in town. The ceiling had been removed and an atrium now extended from the ground floor to a lofty third-floor dome. Light poured in through the curved glass with brass ribs, which resembled a giant umbrella overhead.

The second and third stories opened onto the atrium, ringed with circular wrought iron balustrades. A continuous stretch of offices was visible on each floor. Below, the reception area was so large that it dwarfed the sixty-inch glass table in the center with its collection of antique milk canisters and churns. Instead of art, the walls were hung with old black-and-white photographs of Santa Teresa in the early part of the century. Two gentlemen in bowler hats and three-piece suits posed in front of the building with a mule-drawn milk wagon at the curb. In the photo taken just after the 1926 earthquake, the buildings on either side had been reduced to rubble while the Spring Fresh headquarters had escaped with only minor damage.

The marble floor was white tile with a pattern of black insets; probably new but mimicking the original. I will swear to you that the air smelled like vanilla ice cream. I checked the directory and located the office number for Burke Benjamin, 201, which I assumed was on the second level. An ancient-looking cage elevator with polished brass doors was still in operation. I entered, slid the retractable metal gate shut, pressed the brass 2 button, and went up. My ascent was slow and curiously entertaining as the facing walls, just outside the cage, had been plastered with a collage of vintage Spring Fresh posters and circulars.

When I stepped off the elevator on the second floor, the receptionist looked up and smiled pleasantly. She was a woman in her fifties with unrepentantly gray hair and a gray sweaterdress that looked handknit. Far from washing the color from her complexion, the overall palette generated a vibrant aura, which was both striking and soft.

The name placard on the desk indicated that the receptionist was Hester Maddox. "I'm Hester. You must be Kinsey."

"I am. Nice meeting you," I replied as we shook hands across her desk.

Hester glanced at the old-fashioned wall clock. "Ms. Benjamin should be here shortly. Why don't you have a seat? Can I get you anything? Water or coffee?"

"I'm fine, thanks."

I settled on a camelback sofa upholstered in a caramel velvet that looked good enough to lick. On the small brass-and-glass coffee table in front of me there were copies of *Forbes* magazine, the *ABA Journal*, the *New York Times*, the *Wall Street Journal*, five law-related publications, and three issues of *People* magazine, a guilty pleasure of mine. I skipped the issue devoted to Mike Tyson's latest difficulties and bypassed the lengthy coverage on caring for aging parents and the painful decisions attendant thereon. Given my orphan status, the problem wasn't one I'd have to face. Henry and his sibs might be octogenarians and nonagenarians, but they had always been self-sufficient, and if one of them suffered a medical malfunction, the others would rally with unfailing support.

I picked up the October 10, 1988, issue and turned to the story about Jersey Girl Patti Scialfa replacing actress Julianne Phillips in Bruce Springsteen's heart. The article detailed the development of the romance, which surfaced a scant three years after Springsteen and Julianne Phillips were married. The story moved from Patti Scialfa's early career to her current state of bliss and ended with gushings of the "they were clearly meant for each other" variety. Oh yeah, right. Like that marriage would last.

I heard the elevator doors open and looked up as a curly-haired adolescent boy emerged in bicycle shorts and running shoes. He had no helmet that I could see and I wondered if his mother knew. His shirt was plastered to his back with sweat and his blond hair was a mass of dripping ringlets. As he passed, he glanced at me. "Are you Kinsey?"

"That's right."

"Burke Benjamin," she said. She wiped her right palm on her pants and then held it out. As soon as we shook hands, she moved on, saying, "Come with me."

I set the magazine aside and followed. She held open her office door for me and then closed it behind me.

"Have a seat. I'll be right with you."

I chose one of her two leather-upholstered visitor's chairs, thinking she'd excuse herself and retire to the ladies' room to shower. Instead, she opened her bottom desk drawer and pulled out a dark red terry-cloth bath towel. She kicked off her running shoes, peeled off her gym socks, and crossed her arms so she could pull her soggy T-shirt over her head. Shirt dispensed with, she peeled out of her bra and bike shorts. "Hester says you're a friend of Lonnie's."

"I am," I said, eyes averted. She wore thong underpants. This is a sight that doesn't inspire confidence when consulting an attorney in the matter of half a million bucks.

She was completely nonchalant as she toweled sweat from her neck and underarms. She wadded up the damp shirt and tossed it in her bottom desk drawer, simultaneously taking out a clean bra, which she hooked into place, followed by a white T-shirt that she slipped over her head. She removed a neat navy blue skirt from a hanger and zipped herself into it, then slipped on heels without hose. From another drawer, she pulled out a hair dryer that was apparently permanently plugged in. She bent from the waist and blew her hair dry with a protracted blast of hot air that riffled papers on her desk. By the time she returned the dryer to the drawer, she looked completely put together and her manner was properly professional, including the ringlets, which offset her no-nonsense air.

"What can I do for you?"

"I find myself in a peculiar situation and I need help."

"Well, you came to the right place. What's up?"

I removed Dace's will from my shoulder bag and passed it across the desk to her.

The document was only four pages long. She took her time, leafing back and forth through the pages until she grasped the whole of it. She placed the document on the desk in front of her. "Nice. I take it the two of you were close."

"We're related, but I never met the man," I said.

"Well, I guess that pretty much eliminates any claim by his three kids that you exercised 'undue influence' over dear old Dad," she said. "What's the nature of your relationship?"

"I'm guessing we're second cousins, though I haven't had that confirmed. I know my grandparents' names, but aside from that I know nothing about my father's side of the family. This has come as a complete surprise."

I gave her an abbreviated version of the story, which sounded just as preposterous in summary as it would have if I'd stopped to spell it out. I gave her a thumbnail account of his conviction for felony murder and his subsequent exoneration, the $600,000 settlement, and his falling-out with his kids. Fortunately, Burke Benjamin was smart and she'd doubtless been exposed to stories just as bizarre. Toward the wrap-up, I said, "I don't know what happened when Dace last saw his kids. According to Dandy, who was one of the three witnesses to the will, Dace showed up at Ethan's door shortly after he got out of prison. He thought he could make amends, but he was stonewalled."

"So he got his back up and disinherited all three of them?"

"That's what he told Dandy. Again, I don't know them and I have no idea what the family dynamic was."

"He was a Santa Teresa resident?"

"As I understand it, yes. He lived in Bakersfield for years before he went to prison. After his aborted reunion with his kids, he headed to Santa Teresa in hopes of finding me. Apparently, he loved it here. He told Dandy this was it. He had no intention of living anywhere else."

"Homeless though he was," she said.

"Homeless though he was," I said back to her with a smile.

"Which would make the Santa Teresa Courthouse the proper place of probate administration," she said. She picked up the will again and glanced at the last two pages. "I see an address for Ethan Dace. What about the other two kids?"

"I don't have contact numbers for them. I've been thinking I'd be smart to drive to Bakersfield to deliver the news in person. I'm hoping Ethan can put me in touch with Ellen and Anna."

"I'd put that item at the top of the list. You're required to give proper legal notice to the children. That's essential. They can be served by mail or by personal delivery with the notice of hearing. In fact, I'd send the full package—the notice and the petition for probate with all attachments, including the will."

"Even if I'm sole beneficiary?"

"Especially if you're sole beneficiary. The will states he's deliberately omitting his three kids, but that's subject to challenge. The notice gives them the opportunity to attend the hearing and assert their rights, should they choose to do so. You'll also have to publish the notice of petition to administer estate in the *Santa Teresa Dispatch*. That's something you can mail to the legal publication department of the paper. Even though he states he has no debts, the notice of petition will advise any other interested parties that they can serve the representative of the estate with a written request of special notice when the inventory, appraisement, and petition for final distribution are filed."

I held up a hand. "You mentioned a hearing."

"Good point. Let me back up and talk you through this. Where's the body currently?"

"The coroner's office."

"Have him moved to a mortuary and they'll provide you with six to ten copies of the death certificate so you can wind up his affairs. You'll also have to notify the Social Security Administration, but that's not pressing at this point. You'll want to go over to the superior court and pick up a couple of forms, the first of which is a petition, which asks two things: to have the will entered into probate and for a representative to be appointed. You, in this case, since that's what Dace specified in his will."

"The guy didn't do me any favors," I said. "What else are we talking here?"

She shrugged. "He says he has no other assets aside from the settlement money, but you'd be smart to verify that instead of taking his word for it. He might have community-property interest in stocks or bonds or some other item of value he's forgotten about."

"I'm assuming that was all divvied up when he got his divorce. I know the house he owned in joint tenancy with his wife was quitclaimed over to her."

"Take a look at the divorce agreement. For all you know, the decree could require Dace to provide for his three children in his estate plan. Better yet, you might call his divorce attorney, who'd be a particularly good source of information. Income tax returns are another good place to look."

"Speaking of which, am I going to have to pay income taxes on this money?"

"Nope. You're clear on that score. Federal estate tax exemption was raised to six hundred thousand dollars just last year. That's one more reason to make sure he has no other assets that might boost the estate over the six-hundred-thousand-dollar threshold. California inheritance taxes were repealed in 1982 by voter initiative."

"Well, hallelujah."

"I'm not done yet," she said. "You need to look for retirement accounts—IRAs and the like—and life insurance policies, though those proceeds, if any, would be paid to the beneficiaries identified in the policy itself."

"You think his kids will come after me?"

"Are you kidding? Why wouldn't they? Not only did he disinherit them, but he left all his money to someone he never met. Plus, he was homeless in the last stage of his life, which suggests instability. Those kids have nothing to lose. There's no bequest to them—at least not as far as I can see—so any no-contest clause would be out the window. Then you have the witnesses . . ."

I said, "Oh, man. Will they have to show up in court? I should warn you, the three aren't exemplary citizens."

"You know them?"

"I do. They're currently residents of Harbor House and at least one of them has an issue with alcohol."

"All we need are two witnesses anyway, which gives us a one-drunk margin. The will is self-proving. When the witnesses signed, not only did they declare Dace was of sound mind and memory and not acting under duress, menace, fraud, or undue influence, but that the facts were true and correct under penalty of perjury. It helps that this was signed, sealed, and delivered, so to speak, before you were pulled into the equation."

"This already sounds too complicated," I said. "Can't I hire you to take care of it?"

"Absolutely. The clerical work isn't the issue here. Where you're going to need representation is in the event that these kids show up in court with a phalanx of attorneys. Now, that would be fun." She opened a desk drawer and took out two printed sheets stapled together in one corner. "Here's a couple of pages of instructions you can keep for ready reference. It's a lot to take in and you've probably blanked out half of what I've said."

I glanced at the pages she gave me, but all of it seemed to be gibberish. "I must be having a mental breakdown. None of this makes sense."

She stood and peered across the desk. "Oh. That's the Spanish version."

She held out a hand and I returned the pages. She substituted the English-language version, which I couldn't bring myself to read.

"How soon will you be driving to Bakersfield?" she asked.

"I'd like to go tomorrow morning."

"Why don't I meet you at the Superior Court Clerk's office at eight o'clock? We can get this process under way and then you can hit the road."

"Great. That sounds good," I said. "Do I pay as we go or will you bill me?"

She waved the issue aside. "Don't worry about it. I'll bill you. You're a friend of Lonnie's and that's good enough for me."

12

I did as Burke Benjamin had suggested and stopped by the records department at the courthouse after I left her office. I paid the fee for the proper forms, which I would complete and return to the Superior Court Clerk's office next door when I submitted the original of Dace's will. I went back to my office and scrutinized the petition as though studying for a test. The format was straightforward, providing a number of boxes that could be marked with Xs or left blank according to the dictates of any given case. I flipped the page over and saw that there was another full set of questions on the back that I'd get to in due course. I rolled the first page into my typewriter and spent far more time than necessary making sure the paper was properly aligned.

When faced with a tedious questionnaire, which is essentially what this was, the only remedy is to tackle the job one line at a time. In the top box, I typed in my name and address. I typed in Dace's full name. Put an X in the box indicating the petition was for Probate of Will and for Letters Testamentary. I could see now that this was closer to a multiple-choice test where the answers had to be debated one by one to decide which seemed closest to the facts. I'd been taught to tackle the easy answers first and then go back to the tougher ones. I patiently X'd my way down the page until I reached the question about the estimated value of the estate. I wasn't sure what to say. I typed in the sum in Dace's savings account. Under "real property," I typed "none," which might or might not be correct. When I reached the bottom of the page, I scarcely had the heart to plow on, but I forced myself to persevere. I did pause at the line that read, "Proposed executor is named in the will and consents to act."

I thought, really, "consents"? I had a choice here? It hadn't occurred to me that I could abdicate my responsibilities as representative of the estate, but there was actually a box I could mark if I decided to refuse. The idea was tempting, but what justification could I supply? There were no boxes to be marked declaring that I was insane, incompetent, or stupid. I couldn't picture simply piping up in court, telling the probate judge I didn't feel like doing it, but thanks so much. That half a million bucks was going to end up someplace and I had to accept the fact that it was my job to escort it through the system.

I completed the form, removed the document from the typewriter, made a copy, and then made four copies of Dace's will on my handy-dandy copy machine. I then put the paperwork in a manila envelope, which I slid into my shoulder bag. A copy of the inventory form and copies of the papers that had been in the safe deposit box I tucked into a file folder, which I'd be taking with me. I was already thinking ahead to the trip, for which I'd have to allot two days. The drive was roughly two and a half hours. If I took care of clerical matters first thing in the morning, I could probably leave by nine. Once in Bakersfield, I'd track down Ethan at the address his father had noted in the will and hope he'd be willing to put me in touch with his sisters. I knew nothing of the family, but if Evelyn Dace still harbored hostile feelings about her ex, it would be smart to avoid her altogether. The provisions of the will wouldn't affect her in any event, and I was praying she'd keep her distance.

I stowed my Smith-Corona in the trunk and then drove home, taking my emotional temperature, which was only slightly elevated in anticipation of events to come. I was certain my anxiety could be soothed if Henry offered me a batch of cinnamon rolls or an eight-by-eight pan of chocolate-chunk brownies. All in all, I felt good. I like having a mission. I like being on the move. The actual balance in Dace's bank account was funny money as far as I was concerned. I wasn't going to think about it until the details were sorted out.

I parked and I was making my way through the squeaky gate when I stopped in my tracks.

Was I out of my tiny mind? The implications of the situation descended like a hundred-pound weight. I had a brief vision of myself knocking on Ethan's door. *Hi, you don't know me, but I'm a very,* very, *distant relative. Your father cut you out of his will and left everything to me.*

This was not going to go well. Dace's kids knew nothing of me and I knew precious little about them. In one stroke, Dace had relieved them of a sizable inheritance and placed the burden on me. Why would they be pleasant or courteous or even civil when I was delivering such bad news? They'd be pissed as hell. Maybe notifying Ethan by mail was a better approach. If he or his sisters wanted to contest the terms of the will, he could contact me through his attorney. That would save me driving 150 miles to get the shit kicked out of me. I didn't want to deal with their rage or their indignation. If the three of them were indifferent to news of their father's death, I didn't want to deal with that either. Dace had made a mess of his life, but he'd tried to make amends. Drink and drugs aside, he'd been dealt a bad hand. It was time for someone to give the poor guy a break.

Just then, Henry came striding around the corner of the building with a bucket of water and a folded newspaper under one arm, narrowly avoiding bumping into me. I yelped as water sloshed out of the bucket and down the front of my all-purpose dress. I don't know which of us was more surprised.

He put the bucket down. "Sorry. I'm so sorry, but I had no idea you'd be standing there."

"Don't worry about it," I said. I'd thought to reassure him, but I must have telegraphed something of my upset and confusion because his look changed from surprise to concern. He reached out and touched my arm. "What's the matter?"

"Nothing. I'm fine. It's been a hell of a day."

"You look like you lost your best friend."

"Worse. It's much worse. I don't even know where to begin."

"I've got time."

"No, really. You're in the middle of something. I don't want to interrupt."

"Washing windows. I haven't even started yet. What's worse than losing a friend?"

"Someone left me half a million bucks. Give or take," I added in the interest of being accurate.

"The bastard. That's terrible!"

He expected me to laugh, but all I could do was moan. There have been occasions when his kindness has caused me to burst into tears. I couldn't even manage that. He set the bucket and the newspaper on the walk and took me by the arm. He steered me toward the back patio, where he sat me down in an Adirondack chair. I propped my elbows on my knees and hung my head, wondering if I was going to throw up or faint.

He grabbed a lightweight aluminum lawn chair and swung it over close to mine. "What in the world is going on?"

I pressed my fingers against my eyes. "You won't believe this. *I* don't believe it."

"I'm not sure I will either, but give it a try."

"Remember the guy in the morgue with my name in his pocket?"

"Of course. The one who died on the beach."

"Turns out we're related—probably by way of my Grandmother Dace. He came here in hopes of finding a distant family member and it turns out I'm it. Not only that, but he was on the fritz with his kids so he left all his money to me, which means I'll have to drive to Bakersfield and spring the news on them. Half a million bucks and I'd never even met the man."

"Where'd he get the money? You said he was homeless."

"Homeless, but not broke. Big difference. He spent twelve years in prison for a crime he didn't commit. Once he was exonerated, he sued the state."

"For half a million dollars?"

"For twelve million. The *settlement* was six hundred thousand dollars. After a few minor withdrawals, there's five hundred and ninety-five thousand, three hundred and fifty dollars left."

"No strings attached?"

"Are you kidding me? It's all strings. He also named me executor of the estate so I now gotta jump through legal hoops.

And what am I supposed to do about a funeral? The guy has to have a decent burial. What if his kids won't step up to the plate? I'll have to take care of that on top of everything else. I don't get it. How did I end up babysitting a dead guy?"

He slapped his knees decisively and got up. "I have the solution. You come with me. This calls for a pan of brownies."

And that's when I burst into tears.

As soon as the brownies were cool enough, I ate half the pan and then stayed through supper. Henry plied me with comfort foods: homemade chicken noodle soup and homemade dinner rolls slathered with butter and strawberry jam. Weeping deadens your sense of taste and smell, so I had to suck it up and compose myself. For dessert—as a reward for cleaning my plate—I had two more brownies, which left him with two. Through the meal, we argued about the trip, which I was now thoroughly opposed to. It felt good to focus on a plan over which I had some control.

Henry thought my original instinct was correct. "Dace's children are probably already feeling put upon and betrayed," he said. "What good could possibly come of their learning about his death through a notice in the paper or a letter in the mail?"

"Better than hearing it from me," I said. "How am I going to explain they've been disinherited? If I show up on Ethan's doorstep with *that* news, he'll think I'm there to gloat."

"You'll do fine. You're articulate. Open a dialogue. Tell them how you got caught up in this. You know about the last few months of Terrence Dace's life. His children should have the information."

"I don't know anything about the last few months of his life. I'm only going on what I've been told."

"Matters not. You said Dace made a point about the executor of his will delivering the news."

I was shaking my head in despair. "I can't do it. Truly. They're bound to react badly. It's like begging to be abused. First they find out he died and then they find out he's screwed 'em over in death the way he screwed 'em in life."

"You don't know that for a fact."

"What, that he screwed 'em over in life? Look at it from their perspective. God knows what they went through during his arrest, trial, and sentencing. They must have been mortified. After that, Mom divorces him and he goes to prison, presumably for life. He put them through the wringer."

"But he didn't commit a crime. He was falsely accused. The legal system was at fault. The judge, the lawyers, and police made a terrible mistake. You'd think his kids would be thrilled to find out he was telling the truth."

"Not so. From what Dandy tells me, the visit was a bust."

"Do you think he told his kids how much money he had?"

"Beats me. Dandy and Pearl suspected he had money, but apparently he never revealed how much. I don't want to be the one who drops that bomb on them. Once the kids find out I'm sole beneficiary, no telling what they'll do."

Henry shook his head. "You're just trying to save your own skin."

"Of course I am! Wouldn't you do the same?"

"That's neither here nor there. Tell them what happened. Lay the whole story out the same way you told me. It's not your fault they severed the relationship. It's not your fault he named you in his will."

"You think they'll take such a charitable view?"

"Well, no, not likely, but it's better if you take the high road and handle this one-on-one."

I put my head down on the table and groaned.

"Kinsey, the money isn't theirs. It was never theirs. Their father had the right to do anything he wanted with it."

"What if they feel entitled to it? They're his natural heirs. Why wouldn't they feel they had a right to it?"

"In that case, it becomes a legal issue and they'll have to hire an attorney."

I thought about it briefly. "I guess if they raise a huge stink, I could offer to divide the money among the three of them."

"In no way! Absolutely not. If he'd wanted them to have the money, he'd have set it up that way. He named you executor because he trusted you to carry out his wishes, which are plainly stated."

I reached out and grabbed his arm. "I just had a great idea! You can come with me. You're good at things like this. You're diplomatic and I'm not. I'll make a botch of it. If you're with me, I'll have an ally."

"Nope. No can do. I've got William to contend with. Someone has to get him to his physical therapy appointments."

"He can take a cab. He's already said he would."

"You're forgetting Ed. I can't very well go off and leave the little guy. We're in the bonding process. He'd feel betrayed."

"You think a cat can feel betrayed?"

"Of course. Why would he not? He might not understand the concept as such, but he'd certainly be crushed if I abandoned him after finally winning his trust."

"William could look after him, couldn't he? He's just as much a part of Ed's life as you are."

"He most certainly is not!"

"Well, nearly. I mean, Ed *knows* William. It's not like you'd be leaving a stranger in charge."

"Why don't you look at it another way? There's a big chunk of your history buried in Bakersfield. You're actually related to these people. I'm not sure how, but that's a question worth pursuing. Think of yourself as a diplomat. You're a delegate from your branch of the family reaching out to theirs. I grant you the introductions might be awkward, but as long as you're going, you can fill in some gaps in your family tree. Actually, Dace did you a good turn. This is a rare opportunity, a chance to integrate. Forget the emotional content and play it straight."

I stared at the floor. "I wish I had your confidence."

"You'll be fine."

I left Henry's at 9:00 that night and made a quick trip to the nearest service station to put gas in the car. On the way home, I stopped by the bank and pulled cash from an ATM. I was in bed by ten. I didn't sleep well, but then I didn't expect to sleep well. I woke at 2:30 and again at 4:00. The next time I opened my eyes it was 5:15 and I decided to call it quits. I got up, made the bed, and pulled on my sweats. I started a load of laundry and left it to churn while I did my three-mile jog. The run was the last thing in the world I wanted to do, but I knew it was the right stress-busting move. When I returned thirty minutes later, I shifted the damp clothes into the dryer and then took my shower.

By the time I'd dressed and eaten my cereal, I was feeling better. Talking through the problem with Henry had helped me put it in perspective. I was making things too complicated. The trip to Bakersfield was a necessary element in my responsibilities as executor of Dace's estate. It was a mistake to overthink the task. I had no clue what kind of reception I'd get. The best tack was to go with an open heart and deal with whatever came to pass. Looking back, I can't believe I was able to say this to myself with a straight face.

My clothes were still warm from the dryer as I packed my duffel. I was eager to hit the road, but I had matters to tend to first. When the Santa Teresa County Clerk-Recorder's Office opened at 8:00, Burke Benjamin and I were the only two people in line. I presented myself, paperwork in hand, paid the fees, filed the petition for probate, and submitted the original of Dace's will. I could have strung out the process, waiting to file until I returned from Bakersfield, but I knew I'd reached the point of no return and I liked the sense that forward motion was inevitable. The clerk assigned a case number and gave me a court date that fell in the middle of December, which meant I had ample time to take care of the busywork. Burke made sure I had certified copies of all the necessary documents. At her suggestion, I picked up forms to fill out for the notice I'd need to have published in the *Santa Teresa Dispatch*. Burke said she'd cover anything that came up in my absence.

I made a quick stop at the office to pick up the mail. I sat down at my desk and took care of a detail or two. Mostly, I tidied up so if I ran off the road and died, my survivors would think my desk was always neat. At 9:00, I put in a call to Mr. Sharonson at Wynington-Blake Mortuary, asking him to retrieve R. T. Dace's body from the coroner's office and move him to the funeral home. I could tell Mr. Sharonson was on the verge of rolling out condolences, but I pretended I had another call coming in on my one-line phone and thus made short work of it.

Before I hit the road, I stopped at the house to let Henry know I was on my way. He was out somewhere, but he'd left a hinged wicker picnic basket on my doorstep. I lifted the flap and saw that he'd packed me a sandwich, an apple, some potato chips, and six chocolate chip cookies. He'd also tucked in a map of Bakersfield. Ed, the cat, had contributed a parting gift as well. He'd caught and killed a mole, graciously leaving me the head, which he'd licked clean of fur right down to the bone. I was on the road by 9:30.

The die, as they say, was cast.

13

PETE WOLINSKY

June 1988, Four Months Earlier

Friday morning, June 17, a lengthy typewritten report arrived in the mail, postmarked Reno, Nevada. The report itself was dated June 15, 1988, and covered the surveillance on Mary Lee Bryce during her stay at the conference hotel over the Memorial Day weekend. The bill attached was for three thousand dollars plus change. The cash expenditures and credit card charges were neatly itemized with all the relevant receipts attached. Pete ran the total himself and found it to be correct. The PI hadn't fudged by a penny, which Pete found hard to believe.

Pete hadn't wanted to do the legwork himself because he didn't have the money to fly to Reno. He'd canceled the second set of round-trip plane tickets he'd paid for, though he realized he'd forgotten to turn them in for his refund, which the travel agent assured him would be forthcoming. He had no intention of shelling out any of the twenty-five hundred bucks Willard had paid. Once the cash was safely tucked away, Pete contacted Con Dolan, now retired from the STPD and always up for a chat. He mentioned needing to sub out a job and Dolan had said he'd get back to him with a contact name shortly. Once Dolan passed along the contact numbers, Pete made the call and laid out his problem. While the fellow didn't seem wild about the work, he agreed to do it, quoting what Pete considered an exorbitant fee. Pete asked the PI to include an invoice when the work was done and he submitted his report. As this was a matter between two professionals, a verbal agreement was sufficient.

Pete laid the report on his desk, pressing the pages flat, and then leaned close enough for the typeface to come into focus. His eyesight was getting worse. The last time he'd seen an optometrist, he was told he might be helped by corrective surgery, but the procedure sounded risky to him and the expense made the option unlikely. He followed the lines of print with his finger so he wouldn't lose his place.

The report came as a surprise. There was no indication whatever that Mary Lee Bryce was spending time with Dr. Linton Reed for romantic purposes or any other kind. Apparently, they attended most of the same symposia and were both present for many of the papers being presented. She was in the audience for the one given by Dr. Reed, but she didn't appear to hang on his every word. The two never sat together and barely even spoke. They shared no meals, didn't meet for drinks, and their rooms were not only on different floors, but at opposite ends of the hotel. When their paths did cross, they maintained the appearance of civility, but that was about it. The Nevada PI had even snapped photos in which Mary Lee Bryce and Dr. Reed were both in the same frame, their body language attesting to their mutual disinterest if not mutual disdain. This didn't constitute proof of any kind, but it was telling.

What surfaced instead was the fact that Mary Lee Bryce met twice with a reporter named Owen Pensky, who worked for the *Reno Gazette-Journal*. She and Pensky had met in the hotel bar Thursday night, heads bent together briefly over drinks. The second assignation was a late supper on Sunday after the official conference sessions were wrapped up for the day. The two were apparently engaged in a lively discussion, and while there were no displays of affection, their interest in each other was clear. Pete studied the series of black-and-white photographs of the two, candid shots that were surprisingly clear given the use of a telephoto lens, which often distorted images or rendered them grainy.

Even more titillating were the additional documents attached. Secondary sources revealed that Mary Lee Bryce, whose maiden name was Jacobs, was a classmate of Pensky's at Reno High School, the two having graduated in the class of 1973. Included with the written report were photocopies of the relevant pages of the yearbook, showing the two at various school activities. Mary Lee Jacobs and Owen Pensky were both members of the debate team and both worked for the school paper, which was called *The Red and Blue*. While it wasn't clear that they were boyfriend and girlfriend, they had many interests in common. How many times had Pete heard tales of high school classmates reconnecting at reunions years after having parted company? Nothing more potent than old fantasies suddenly given new life.

The Nevada investigator had done some extracurricular digging into Pensky's background and turned up newspaper accounts of a scandal of major proportions. Two years before, Owen Pensky had been working for the *New York Times* as a feature writer. He'd already made quite a reputation for himself when he was accused of lifting passages from the work of another journalist. The charge of plagiarism gave rise to an investigation that uncovered evidence that Pensky was also guilty of inventing sources for certain features he'd published. Every article he'd ever written became suspect. He'd been fired and he'd left New York in disgrace. After ten months scrambling for employment, he'd finally managed to pick up work at one of the Reno papers, a low point for a fellow who'd been everybody's darling such a short time before.

Pete sat back and thought about this unexpected turn of events, wondering what to make of it. It wasn't necessarily the case that Mary Lee Bryce and Owen Pensky were having an affair. Maybe this was just a matter of two old friends catching up while the one was in town for professional reasons. Whatever the truth, there had to be a way to play it for maximum effect. The first move was to spread the facts over more than one document. No point in turning over everything at once. It would be a kindness to let Willard digest the discovery by degrees. Pete went through the photographs and selected two from the Reno High School yearbook, the *RaWaNe*.

As a senior, Mary Lee Jacobs was petite, a redhead with pale brows and an expression that suggested perpetual anxiety. Owen Pensky looked like the typical high school dork— black-rim glasses, bad haircut, his neck barely big enough to hold up his head. In some ways, Mary Lee Bryce and Owen

Pensky seemed well suited for each other since both projected insecurity. Pete himself had been an outcast in his teen years, so he didn't fault either one in that regard. He couldn't help but wonder if Pensky was dishonest by nature or if he'd taken up cheating to compensate for a lack of self-confidence.

Odd that Mary Lee had ended up married to a man whose coloring was so much like her own. She and Willard were close enough in appearance to be brother and sister instead of husband and wife. Pete wondered how Willard's unfortunate accident had factored into the overall equation. The wreck that killed his best friend and resulted in the loss of his own leg dated back to his youth, which meant he was already on crutches when he and Mary Lee first met. Some women were drawn to the physically impaired; witness his own wife's attraction to him.

He swiveled his chair and scooted closer to a rolling typewriter table and removed the cover from his manual Remington Streamliner. He'd bought the machine in 1950, and aside from a few minor repairs, it had served him handily ever since. He opened his desk drawer and removed two sheets of stationery and placed a carbon between them, then rolled them into the carriage and began the laborious job of retyping the report on his own letterhead. He made minor adjustments so the language would sound more like his own.

Despite his two-fingered-typing technique, he was fast and accurate. Even so, the job took him the better part of an hour. The Nevada investigator was very detail oriented and he spared nothing in his passion for spelling out the minutia. This allowed Pete to pick and choose his facts while he converted the report to his own personal style. By judicious editing, he could easily fashion a follow-up report and charge for that as well.

The relationship between Mary Lee Bryce and this Pensky fellow certainly cried out for further study. If he could talk Willard into extending their agreement, he could submit a second round of paperwork without actually having to do anything. The report itself offered no interpretation or speculation about the nature of the relationship. Pete liked the neutral tone, which seemed crisp and professional, one he might have adopted himself if he'd elected to do the work. He'd offer Willard a verbal summary first in which he'd set the stage. Properly prepared, Willard would be eager to authorize additional surveillance.

Pete took the finished report, made a copy for his files, and attached the photocopies of both sets of round-trip tickets with the relevant adjustments made to reflect how thoroughly he'd done his work. The Nevada PI had spent four nights at the same convention hotel where Mary Lee Bryce had been. Pete made a copy of the bill, whited out the other fellow's name and credit card information, typed his own into the blank, and photocopied the bill for a second time. He leaned close to the page, inspecting the results, and decided it would be fine and dandy for his purposes. Willard would be too busy hyperventilating over the contents to pay attention to expenses. Generously, Pete discounted his fees by twenty percent, which he noted at the bottom of the page.

He tucked the paperwork in the half-filled banker's box and shoved it in the kneehole under his desk. He put a call through to Willard. Pete had scarcely identified himself when Willard jumped on him with both feet.

"You want to tell me what's going on?" he snapped. "I should have heard from you weeks ago. As much money as I paid, I expected you to be prompt."

"Now, let's just hold on a minute, son. I'm not some pal of yours, doing you a personal favor. You hired me to do a job and I went far above and beyond. Your tone is a hair accusatory for a man who'll benefit mightily from my being such a thoroughgoing professional. Most investigators would be content to leave well enough alone. I went the extra mile. Let's not even talk about the twenty percent discount I accorded you in appreciation for your business. I guess none of what I uncovered is of interest."

He could picture Willard's eyelids turning a brighter shade of pink. Willard probably wasn't accustomed to being backed into a corner and it took him a few seconds to collect himself.

"I didn't say I wasn't interested," he murmured.

"You sounded pretty hot under the collar if you want my take on it."

"I'm sorry. I've been a wreck waiting to hear from you. That's all I was trying to say."

"You like, I can drop my report in the mail to you without further ado. You might find it more instructive if I go over it in person, but that's entirely your choice."

"'Instructive' meaning what?"

"There's reality and then there's facts. I'm saying there's a difference that I'd be happy to clarify. I should point out you could have called me at any point during these past two weeks and I'd have told you the same thing. I had the information in hand. What's taken the additional time is the verification supplied by an out-of-state colleague purely as a courtesy to me. Do you want to take a look at it or not?"

"Of course. I'm sorry if I spoke out of turn. Mary Lee came home jumpier than I've ever seen her. I tried talking to her, but she shut me down. I have no idea what's going on."

"The good news is I'm now in a position to fill in some blanks. I won't say my report's definitive, but it's a start. I can stop by later this afternoon."

"That won't work. She's been leaving the lab early, practically barricading herself in the bedroom to make phone calls. You'd have to be here by three and you can't stay long."

"Might make more sense if we conduct our business off-site. Why don't I pick you up and we'll go somewhere else?"

"What if she comes home while I'm out?"

"Leave her a note. Tell her you're having coffee with a friend and don't specify the gender. Want my opinion, you'd benefit from creating an air of mystery around yourself. She's doubtless taking you for granted and that won't help your cause."

Pete picked up Willard at the prearranged spot, a block and a half from the Bryces' apartment. He liked the cloak-and-dagger aspects of the meeting. He'd wanted to put Willard in the proper frame of mind, talking him through the findings before he surrendered the written account. Willard was having none of it, already impatient at having had to wait this long. He held out his hand, snapping his fingers twice as though Pete were a dog. Pete had no choice but to pass him the manila envelope.

He drove south on the 101 while Willard removed the report and read it. Pete was uncomfortably aware of Willard's mounting distress. He took the off-ramp at the bird refuge, where he pulled into the abbreviated parking strip twenty-five feet from the water's edge. As a goodwill gesture, he'd picked up a bag of assorted doughnuts and two oversize cups of coffee he hoped would pacify Willard's angst. He experienced a twinge of guilt when Willard saw the photographs, almost as though he'd betrayed the man himself.

Once Pete shut down the engine, they sat in the car. Pete was quiet, looking out at the saltwater lagoon where a passel of ducks squatted on the muddy shore. Certain times of the year, the lagoon threw off an aroma of rotten eggs. Pete didn't know how any of the nearby businesses could survive. Across from the parking lot, there was a restaurant, an athletic facility, and a bar called CC's, the Caliente Café, where the off-duty cops hung out. Today the odor wasn't too bad. The lagoon smelled faintly dank with a secondary aroma of soggy vegetation and bird doo-doo.

Willard held the papers loosely in his lap. "This is embarrassing."

"I wouldn't take that attitude. At least you know your instincts were good. Only difference is Dr. Reed's not the one you should be worried about. From the information I managed to dig up, this is a former high school classmate. Fellow named Owen Pensky."

Willard's expression was a curious mix of perplexity and gloom.

Pete said, "I don't mean to suggest a course of action. That's your decision. I will say if it was me, I'd push this. Right now you really don't know what's going on."

"Why's she even talking to the guy? I don't understand."

"That's because you don't have all the information. If I might make a recommendation, your next move would be to put a tap on the line."

"Are you talking about tapping our home *phone*?"

"Well, if she's calling him on her work phone, that's a tricky proposition. I'm not sure how I'd get into the lab to put a bug on that line. Simpler and more sensible to monitor her calls from home. That might tell us where to go next."

"I don't like it."

"I understand," Pete said. "The connection with this Pensky fellow may be entirely innocent. High school buddy lives in Reno? No big deal. She knows she'll be in town for this conference so she sets up a meeting to say howdy and catch up on old times. I suspect there might be something more, but we're not going to know unless I'm authorized to act."

"Shit."

"No need to assume the worst. There's probably more to it than meets the eye, but from what I observed, I don't believe it's anything of a romantic nature."

"What is it then?" Willard sorted through the pages a second time and then studied the copies of the black-and-white photos from the high school yearbook. His complexion, ruddy by nature, now looked like he'd spent too much time under a heat lamp.

"I wouldn't want to speculate. She ever mention this Pensky fellow?"

"No."

"She might have looked him up when she got to Reno, on the off chance he was still in town. Old high school chum, a classmate. Nothing wrong with that."

"But look how intense they are."

"Fellow might have marital issues. Had you thought of that? She calls him to say hi, letting him know she's in town, he might have jumped at the idea of having a confidante."

"*Is* he married?"

"Records check is next on my list if you decide to proceed. I didn't have a chance to go over to the Washoe County courthouse while I was there. Enough going on at the hotel that I felt my time was better spent on the premises."

"What am I supposed to do now?"

"Up to you," Pete said. "Phone calls in the bedroom with the door shut? I don't like the sound of that." He paused to shake his head. "Easiest solution is to install a bug."

"Stop saying that. I don't like spying on her. It's not right."

"It's a little late to fret when you have a guy like me chasing all the way to Reno to take photographs. What's the point of stopping short when it might all be easily explained?"

Willard sank into a brooding silence.

Pete had to suppress his impatience. Here he was spoon-feeding the fellow, coaxing him toward the obvious conclusion. Nothing as persuasive as a self-generated decision even if it was Pete nudging him in the right direction. Let Willard think he'd come up with it on his own. Pete grew uneasy, wondering if he'd pushed the man too hard. "Believe me, I understand where you're coming from. You love your wife, so it's natural to want to maintain trust. At the same time, I can think of other explanations for what seems troublesome."

"Such as what?"

"Suppose he had personal problems. Might have had a setback of some kind in his career. Fellow's a journalist, so it might be worthwhile to check that out."

"What's involved in a phone bug? I mean, assuming I agree."

"Simple matter of installing a device in the handset before she gets home. I can put a voice-activated tape recorder on remote; close by, but not actually in the apartment. You don't want her to come across a piece of hardware while she's cleaning house. I can also plant a pen mike. Looks like a ballpoint pen, but it's capable of transmitting sound for short distances."

"What will that accomplish?"

"Remains to be seen. My suggestion is we run audio a few days and see what we pick up. This whole business might not have anything to do with you."

Willard turned and stared out of the car window. "Okay."

"Good man," Pete said. He continued to sit in silence.

Willard looked over at him. "So is that it?"

"There's the matter of another advance. Soon as I have that in hand, I'll go to work. Any more contact between the two and I'll head back to Reno and do deep background on him."

Which is how Pete ended up two days later in Colgate, wearing a coverall while pretending to weed the flower border under Willard's bedroom window. He avoided yard work as a rule. Here, it wasn't unpleasant, but it seemed undignified to be crawling around the building on his hands and knees. This was the second late afternoon he'd weeded. Day One had produced nothing. He'd started his labors in the central courtyard, uncertain where he'd pick up the best reception. Several residents had noticed him and nodded in acknowledgment though none had stopped to chat. They seemed pleased that someone was actually being paid to tidy up.

In addition to the phone bug, he'd supplied Willard with a pen mike and suggested he place it in the bedroom, preferably on the floor near the bedside table where the phone sat. There was an off chance Mary Lee might notice it, but if she was intent on shenanigans, she probably wouldn't be that observant.

Day Two, Pete picked up a most enlightening fragment of conversation. Mary Lee was home by 4:00. Pete had advised Willard to run an errand, giving her the opportunity to make a call, which is exactly what she did. Pete heard a lilting melody of numbers being punched, long-distance judging by the length. Sure enough, when a fellow on the other end picked up, all she said was, "It's me. I don't have much time, so let's make this quick. What's happening on your end?"

"Nothing. I told you my hands are tied. What about the charts? Did you find them?"

"Not yet. I know where they are. I just can't get to them. I'm trying to track the one guy down but it's tough. Can't you use the information I already gave you?"

She said something else Pete missed. He pressed a hand against his earphone.

Pensky's response was muffled. ". . . here says one could be a fluke. You need a pattern."

"Owen, I know that! How do you think I spotted it in the first place? The pattern's there. What I don't have is proof. Meantime, I'm walking on eggshells . . ."

Something, something Pete missed.

"You think Linton suspects?" Pensky asked.

"I hope not. You don't understand how ruthless he is. It's fine as long as I'm in the lab, but I can't get anywhere near the clinic."

"Why not?"

"The lab's in Southwick Hall. The clinic's in the Health Sciences Building."

"Why are the charts kept there?"

"Because that's where the subjects are seen for follow-up."

"You can't just go over and ask?"

"Oh, right. Talk about a red flag," she said.

"You gotta give me something or I can't help. I told you that to begin with."

Exasperated, she said, "Shit. I'll think about it. Maybe I can come up with some excuse."

"Listen, I went back over my notes last night and came

across that business about the paper you wrote. Plagiarism's serious damn business. Look what happened to me."

"I figured you'd appreciate the finer points," she said drily.

"So can't you use that?"

"To do what? The journal was published in Germany. I wouldn't have known about it myself if someone hadn't sent it to me."

"That was a happy coincidence."

"Not at all. The friend who saw the article knew the subject was close to what I was working on at the time. He had no idea Linton lifted it from me. The department chair sure didn't want to hear my side of it. Linton was teacher's pet and could do no wrong."

"Too bad."

"'Too bad' is right. What he's doing here is worse. With the grant he got, he can't afford to fail."

"He's covered his butt by now, don't you think?"

"Nuhn-uhn. He has no clue I'm onto him. Otherwise, he'd have found a way to get rid of me before now. I mentioned his ripping me off because it's indicative of his . . ."

Pete missed the word. Distracted, he looked up and caught sight of Willard returning to the apartment. How long had he been gone? Fifteen minutes tops? Not long enough to accomplish anything. Willard gave him the high sign, but Pete was too busy listening to respond.

"Hey, I understand. I'm just tapping on the wall to see if I can find a way in. What about his computer?"

"I have his password, but that's it so far."

"His *password*? Good girl. How'd you find it?"

"It was written on a piece of paper in his desk drawer. How's that for clever?"

"But if you haven't actually gone into his database, what makes you so sure he's cooking?"

"Because I saw the printout before he shredded it."

"What's that other term you used?"

"Dry-labbing it. Don't get sidetracked," she said.

Pete missed Pensky's response. He pressed his hand against the ear bud and closed his eyes as though that might improve his hearing. Had he used the word "trial"? Must be clinical trials if they were talking about medical charts.

"Listen, Owen. I'm working ten-hour days. I don't have a lot of time to play Sherlock Holmes. I can only do so much."

"What about the incident at Arkansas?"

"No good. Hearsay. The girl who told me says he skirted disaster by going away for a 'much-needed rest.' After that he disappeared and reappeared somewhere else. She talked to Dr. Stupak twice, but he wouldn't pursue the matter for fear it would negatively impact his career."

"Stupak's career?"

"Not Stupak's, Linton's. These guys are always circling the wagons. Any hint of trouble, they close ranks. Shit. Gotta go. Bye."

The line went dead though he was still tuned into her end by way of the pen mike. Pete heard a door open and a muffled exchange. Mary Lee said, "Wrong number."

A few seconds later, the door shut and there was silence. She and Willard must have moved into the living room.

What he'd been listening to wasn't romance. It appeared Mary Lee and this fellow were in cahoots, but what was the object of the exercise? Linton Reed, obviously, but in what context? Pete swapped out the tapes, inserting a blank on the off chance another call might transpire while he was gone. Once he was back at his desk, he put the recording into his player and listened to it twice. At first, he was annoyed he couldn't make heads or tails of it. Clearly, Mary Lee Bryce and Owen Pensky were trying to get the goods on Linton Reed, and if Pete hoped to profit, he needed to know what he was talking about. Faulty information was useless. "Glucotace" was the word he'd missed. He deciphered it on the third go-round and figured it must be a medical condition, maybe a test of some kind. There'd also been mention of cooking numbers, which must be what it sounded like. You cook numbers, you're slanting the results. That's why Linton's getting the big grant put so much at stake. He worried the subject, turning it this way and that. As far as he could tell, there was only one interpretation. Linton Reed had been falsifying data. He wasn't sure how Mary Lee picked up on it, but she'd known him in the past and apparently she'd been an early victim of his shady manipulations.

At 5:00, he gave up, locked the office, and headed for home. He was just pulling into his garage when he had a flash. He'd been thinking he couldn't move forward until he filled in the blanks, and how was he to do that when he didn't have a clue? What occurred to him was that all he had to do was go over to the medical library at St. Terry's and have somebody look it up. Linton Reed was vulnerable. Pete had no idea how, but he knew Owen Pensky and Mary Lee Bryce were closing in on him. Judging from their phone chat, the good Dr. Reed hadn't quite caught on yet. Pete would be doing him a personal service by alerting him to the danger. There might even be a way to head off trouble, which was bound to be worth something to a bright young fellow with a rich wife and his whole life ahead of him.

14

The route from Santa Teresa to Bakersfield isn't complicated, but there aren't any shortcuts. I could drive north on the 101 and head east on Highway 58, which meandered a bit but would finally put me out on the 99 a few miles north of Bakersfield. Plan B was to drive south and cut over to Interstate 5 on the 126. It was going to take me two and a half hours either way.

I went south, in part to avoid passing the town of Lompoc, where my Kinsey relatives were entrenched. My grudge against my mother's side of the family was predicated on the fact that they were only an hour away and never once made contact in the three decades following my parents' death when I was five. I'd enjoyed feeling righteous and I'd taken great satisfaction in my sense of injury. Unfortunately, the conclusions I'd drawn and the assumptions I'd made were dead wrong. I'd taken the Kinseys to task only to find out there was far more to the story than I'd known, and while I was willing to admit my error, I didn't like to be *reminded* of it.

I wasn't sure why it hadn't occurred to me to hold my father's family to the same strict accounting. Where had they been all these years? As it turned out, they'd been in Bakersfield, which seemed curiously remote. Geographically, it was only 150 miles away, but located in an area of the state through which I seldom traveled. Somehow that afforded them a pass in the matter of my resentment. Contributing to the difference in my attitude was the fact that my rage had begun to bore me, and my long whiny tale of woe had become tedious even to my own ears. As much fun as I'd had being irate, the drama had become repetitive. I could probably still wring sympathy from a stranger, but the recital had taken on a certain rote quality that lacked energy and conviction.

I tuned into the moment at hand. The sky was a washed-out blue, contrails like chalk marks beginning and ending for no apparent reason. Sunlight caught the telephone wires and turned them silver, linking them from pole to pole like strands of spider silk. Just shy of the Perdido city limits, I left the 101 and took the 126 east. Now, instead of having the Pacific Ocean to my right, the countryside was awash with orchards and mobile homes.

Along the horizon lay a range of low hills of the sort that hikers would disdain. At intervals, signs announced FRUIT STANDS 100 YARDS! Most were closed for the season. The road was heavily traveled with pickup trucks, dump trucks, panel trucks, and semis. I passed a tree farm that resembled a portable forest of palms. Quonset huts served as nurseries. Fields were covered in opaque plastic like an agricultural frost.

I reached the junction of 126 and Highway 5 and headed north, driving through miles of flat farmland. The snow-capped mountains in the distance seemed so incongruous they might as well have been pasted on. Kern County is about the size of New Jersey, give or take a few square miles. Bakersfield is the county seat, the largest of the inland cities, and the ninth-largest city in the state. Los Angeles is 110 miles to the south; Fresno, 110 miles to the north. This part of the state lies in California's central valley, blessed by good weather much of the year. Once upon a time, millions of acres of wetlands graced the area, but much of the water was diverted for irrigation purposes, creating a rich agricultural region where cotton and grapes flourish.

I cruised into town at 11:45, taking the off-ramp from Highway 99 onto California Avenue. I was hungry by then and ready to stretch my legs. With the first break in traffic, I pulled over to the curb and studied the map Henry had so graciously provided. Beale Park was in easy range. I took surface streets as far as Oleander Avenue and parked on a stretch between Dracena and Palm. The park itself was probably five acres all told, featuring old trees, large swatches of grass, a playground, and picnic tables. More to the point, there was a public restroom, which was clean and in perfect working order. I went back to the car and hauled out my picnic basket, which I set on a table in the shade of an oak.

After lunch, I tossed my napkin, crumpled waxed paper, and the apple core into the nearest trash can. I returned to the car and cruised the area until I spotted a one-story Thrifty Lodge that looked about my speed. According to the motel marquee, the rooms were cheap ($24.99 per night) and came with color TV and a free continental breakfast. There were no burglar bars on the windows, which I took as a positive sign. By that time it was 1:15 and I figured I could drop off my bags and do some reconnoitering. I checked in, collected the key, and headed down the outside walk with my duffel in hand.

I unlocked the door and flipped on the light. The interior was dank. On the beige wall-to-wall carpet there was a ghostly foot path from the bed into the bathroom. A small secondary side road ran from the bed as far as the television set. I did a quick circuit. The heating and air-conditioning system, if you want to call it that, was a narrow unit installed just under the windowsill, with seven options in the way of temperature control. Heat: off or on. Cold: off or on. Fan: on, off, or auto. I tried to calculate the number of possible combinations, but it was way beyond my rudimentary math skills. The bathroom was clean enough and the motel had provided me two bars of soap, neatly sealed in paper. One was slightly larger than the other and was intended for the shower. I unwrapped the smaller one, standing at the sink. The chrome fixtures were pitted and the cold-water knob squeaked in protest when I paused to wash my hands. I felt a tap on my head and looked up to find water dripping slowly from a ceiling fixture. I unloaded my toiletries from the duffel—shampoo, conditioner, deodorant, toothbrush and toothpaste—and lined everything up on the vanity. True to form, there were no other amenities provided, so I was happy I'd brought my own. I tried the wall-mounted dryer and smelled burning hair.

I was getting a bit long in the tooth to stay in places like this. When you're young and intent on proving how nonmate-

rialistic you are, a bare-bones motel room is a prize. *After all,
you say to yourself, I'll only be here at night and why do I care
about the room when I'm sound asleep?* At my age, there
ought to be more to life than feeling virtuous about how many
pennies I was managing to pinch. I could see how the shadowy
notion of half a million bucks might alter my perception. Since
the money was only nominally mine, I was loath to fritter it
away on high-class imaginary digs. What bothered me was the
suspicion that when I crawled into bed that night, the sheets
would feel *moist*.

I sat down on the side of the bed and checked the bed table
drawer, hauling out a tattered copy of the telephone book. I was
hoping to spot Ellen or Anna Dace, even Evelyn, the ex-wife. I
went to the Ds and discovered a chunk of pages missing, the
very ones I was hoping to consult. I took out my city map and
opened it to the full. The address I had for Ethan, which Dace
had noted in his will, was on Myrtle Street. I checked the list
of street names, found Myrtle, and traced the coordinates from
section 13 on the vertical and G on the horizontal. I'd focus on
the house numbers once I reached the neighborhood. My guess
was that Dace's two daughters had refused to give their father
contact information, which is why he'd mentioned them by
name without including phone numbers or home addresses.

I put a call through to Henry, letting him know the name
and number of my motel in case he needed to get in touch. All
was quiet on the home front, so we chatted briefly and let it go
at that.

I retrieved my car and circled back to Truxtun, one of the
main arteries through town. I found Myrtle and scanned the
house numbers as I crept by at half speed. When I finally spotted the correct address, I pulled over to the curb. The house
.was dark and there was a For Rent sign on a wooden stake
pounded into the lawn. I killed the engine, got out, and walked
up the short concrete drive. What had once served as a two-car
garage was now walled in and stuccoed over, probably in
order to create additional interior space. There was a window
built into the center, so I cupped my hands around my eyes and
took a peep. Not surprisingly, the room I was looking into was
empty.

I knocked at the front door without result. It was locked, so
I went around to the rear of the house, where a "spacious back

patio" consisted of a six-foot undulating hard-plastic overhang supported by six metal poles. A window on the right was boarded over. I tried the back door and was delighted to discover that it was unlocked. I offered a couple of tentative yoo-hoos. "Hello? Anybody home?"

When I received no reply, I treated myself to a tour of the place. The interior looked like it had been gutted in advance of a demolition. Doorknobs were missing, switch plates had been removed, and the wall-to-wall carpeting had been pulled up, leaving the concrete floors spotted with patches of black mastic. The kitchen cabinets were scuffed and the backsplash at the kitchen sink was some kind of wallboard, scored to look like ceramic tile. There were no lightbulbs in any of the overhead fixtures. Maybe Ethan was the kind of tenant who believed his rent entitled him to anything that wasn't nailed down, including the toilet seat, which was nowhere in evidence. The laundry room was edged in black mold that crept along the seams like grout. Leaking water had loosened the hinges on the bathroom vanity, and the rust streaking from the faucets looked like the run of mascara on a weeping woman's face. All the rooms smelled of mildew, animal dander, and pee.

"Any information I can offer you about the place?"

I shrieked and whipped around, clutching my chest to prevent my heart from tearing through my shirt. "Shit!"

I stared at the man who'd shortened my life by years.

He was in his early thirties, with a cresting wave of dark hair cutting across his forehead. His eyes were dark and his eyebrows were thick, while his mustache and beard appeared to be a recent undertaking that, so far, wasn't a success. He wore an oversize black shirt that hung down over his jeans in a style that was meant to disguise his weight. I put him a good thirty pounds over the line, though it didn't really look bad on him. I was going to tell him so and decided I'd best not. Men sometimes mistake a compliment for an invitation to become better acquainted.

His smile was apologetic, his teeth white, but cluttered. "Sorry. I didn't mean to scare you. I saw you go around the side of the house as I was driving up. I figured you noticed the For Rent sign and wanted to check it out." He'd smoked a cigarette at some point in the past fifteen minutes.

"Actually, I'm looking for Ethan Dace."

"Too late. He pulled up stakes a week ago. At least from what the neighbors say."

"How long did he live here?"

"I don't know. Eighteen months? Might have been less."

"I take it he left without giving notice."

"He also left owing two months' rent. Are you a bill collector?"

I shook my head. "I'm here on a personal matter. His father died. I figured someone should let him know."

"Why you?"

"We're distantly related."

"How distant?"

"Second cousins, once or twice removed. That's a guess on my part. I've never understood the distinctions."

"I take it you never met Ethan."

"I've never had the occasion."

"You're in for a disappointment. I'm not saying the guy's a bum, but he's a lousy tenant. He was a slow pay and sometimes he couldn't bring himself to pay at all, which I was supposed to tolerate on account of he's such a talented guy. If I came knocking on his door to collect, he'd pony up, but it always seemed to take him by surprise. I was about to evict him anyway, so he saved me the paperwork. Get a deadbeat in a rental and it's damn near impossible to get 'em out."

"You know where he went?"

"Most likely back to his wife. This is the third or fourth time she's kicked him out. Bugged her no end that he wouldn't get a job. Able-bodied white male and all he does is sit around and play his guitar. Time to time, he collects unemployment, but that doesn't go on forever. Problem is, with him gone, she's stuck shelling out a bundle for child care. She's got one in school and two were enrolled in what they call 'pre-kindergarten' to the tune of two hundred bucks a week. Per kid. She's better off with him on the premises. What the hell else is he doing with his days?"

"Why'd you rent to him if you knew he didn't have a job?"

"I felt sorry for the guy."

"What line of work is he in?"

"Musician, which I don't think of as a 'line of work.' It's more like goofing off, accompanied by a musical instrument. He has this band, Perforated Bowel—or something equally profound. He's lead singer and doubles on guitar. The other two play keyboard and drums, respectively. They have gigs in town couple of weekends a month. That's the claim at any rate, for what it's worth."

"Is he any good?"

"Don't know. I never heard him play. He says he's booked into the Brandywine, but I haven't checked it out. With him gone, it's no concern of mine."

"You know his wife's name?"

"It's on his application. Heitzerman, Heidelman. Heidie-something. I can't remember how it's spelled and I might have got it wrong. First name's Mamie. Like in Eisenhower. House is in her name. I called her, hoping she'd be kind enough to pay his back rent. No such luck. Chick's smarter than I thought."

"Wonder why she didn't take his name when they married."

"She probably didn't like the family association. I guess you heard what happened to his dad."

"The business in 1974?"

"Was it that long ago?"

"That's the year he went to prison."

"I'd have said, five, six years. You're talking fourteen."

"Time flies," I remarked. I gestured toward the empty house. "Was Ethan the one who stole the doorknobs?"

"The doorknobs are gone?"

"Some of them. Did he strip the carpeting?"

"I did that. He kept his dogs locked up while he was out and they tore the place apart. Only two of 'em, but they must have egged each other on. Get rid of the smell of dog pee, I'd have to burn the place down. You smell that or is it just me?"

"Place stinks."

"Appreciate the confirmation. He talked me out of a pet deposit. I must've been smokin' crack that day. You're not a local?"

"I'm not. I drove up from Santa Teresa this morning."

"What'd he die of, the old guy?"

I didn't see any reason to tell this guy the whole of it so I shrugged. "I don't know the details. Just the broad strokes."

"The broad strokes being what?"

"Probably a heart attack," I said. "I'd like to talk to Ethan's sisters as long as I'm in town. Ellen and Anna. Are they still around?"

"The younger one for sure. Anna's the wild child. She does manis and pedis in some dump of a salon. The other girl, I never met."

"'Manis and pedis'—meaning manicures and pedicures?"

"Whoa! You are really *sharp*."

I ignored the sarcasm. "Do you know how I can reach them?"

"What's your stake in this?"

"What makes you ask?"

"I can't believe you drove all the way up here for something you could've done by phone."

"I didn't have Ethan's number. Besides, if I'd called I'd have missed him by a week, right? I thought it would be a kindness if they heard it from me instead of reading about it in the paper."

"You're a good Samaritan."

"Some would call it that."

"Any rate, you don't want to rent the place, it's time I locked up."

"I appreciate the information about Ethan's wife. I'll see if I can track her down." I held a hand out. "My name's Kinsey Millhone."

"They call me 'Big Rat.' And don't ask. Long story and it really doesn't have a point."

We shook hands.

"If I run into Ethan, I'll tell him you're in town," he said.

"He won't know who I am. I didn't find out about him until yesterday."

"You expect to be here overnight?"

"Unless I catch up with him today."

"I run into him, I'll let you know. Where you staying?"

I didn't think it was any of his business, so of course I lied.

"Don't know yet. I haven't found a motel. What would you suggest?"

"Padre Hotel. It's been around for years. Used to be high-class. Now it's so-so, but location's good. Close to downtown."

"What happened to Evelyn Dace?"

"She married someone else. Some guy from her church. I have a friend rents a little place above their garage."

He slipped his wallet from his back pocket and removed a business card that he held out. "Tell you what. I get back to the office, I'll look up Dace's application and get you his wife's name. Probably a phone number listed as well. Might save you some time. Give me a call in an hour or so and I'll try to help you out."

"Thanks." I glanced down at the card, noting that his last name was Rizzo. I was betting his nickname, Big Rat, originated from the film *Midnight Cowboy*, twenty years before. Dustin Hoffman played the part of Ratso Rizzo.

Big Rat said, "I don't guess he's coming into money now his old man's croaked?"

"None as far as I know, but it never hurts to ask."

"Amen to that."

I sat in my car for a moment, making a quick note about the club where Ethan played on weekends and an approximation of his wife's last name. I watched as Big Rat locked the front door and climbed into his truck, which he'd parked at an angle in the foreshortened driveway. He backed out and swung wide, giving me a jaunty wave as he disappeared down the street. His red Nissan pickup with yellow flames custom-painted along the bed was as conspicuous as my car, which served as one more reminder to dump the Mustang and find something else.

I got back on Truxtun and turned right, trolling in an eastward direction. I confess I was having trouble getting the hang of how the streets were laid out. Some were numbered and some of them had names. The ones I was passing were lettered, as in E, F, G, H, and Eye, the latter probably spelled out so the I wouldn't be mistaken for the number one. Truxtun and California Streets seemed to be parallel, but other streets were a-kilter, as though the whole geographical plain had taken a forty-five-degree turn. I was looking for the Beale Memorial Library, which according to my map was no more than half an inch away.

Once I spotted it, I parked in the lot to the left of the structure and headed for the entrance. The exterior was handsome, buff colored, with a band of desert rose along the roofline. The building was new with a plaque on the side indicating that it had been dedicated only six months before, April 30, 1988. A time capsule had been sealed in the foundation to be opened in April of 2038. It might be worth a trip back just to see what

was buried there. I'd be pushing eighty-eight years old and
ready for a touch of excitement, assuming it didn't prove too
much.

The interior was spacious and smelled of new commercial
carpeting. The ceiling was high and the light was generous. I
couldn't even guess at the square footage or the number of
books the building housed, but the patrons had to have been
thrilled with the facility. I asked a woman sitting at the information desk where I might find old city directories, and she
suggested the Jack Maguire Local History Room on the second floor. I bypassed the elevator and trotted up the stairs. The
door to the local history room was locked and empty from
what I could see through the glass. I spotted a woman in a
wheelchair working at a desk in the room next door.

"Is there any way I can get in there? I'd like to check city
directories from a few years back."

"You might ask Verlynn at the reference desk. She has a
key." She pointed to a desk halfway across the vast carpeted
expanse.

I crossed and waited my turn. When Verlynn was free, I
explained what I wanted and she followed me back to the history room with her key in hand.

She unlocked the door and opened it, flipping on the overhead lights. "The volumes you want are on that wall straight
ahead. We have city directories going back to 1899 and telephone books from about 1940. Those shelves over there you'll
find yearbooks from elementary, junior high, and high schools
in the area. Not every year is represented. We depend on our
patrons for donations. Will you be okay on your own?"

"I'll be fine. Thanks."

"Let me know when you've finished and I'll lock up."

"I'll do that."

I already knew where Dace had lived before his incarcera-
tion. I'd picked up that address from the expired California
driver's license in his safe deposit box. What I was interested
in were two other sets of addresses. I hoped to track back in
time to the point where Dace interacted with his beloved Uncle
R. The dates on the backs of the two black-and-white photographs I'd seen were September 1941 and June 4, 1945. Something else occurred to me. My parents were married in 1935,
which meant my mother might well have been with him on

trips to Bakersfield. What if she was the one who'd taken the two photographs? The notion sent a chill down my spine.

I was also looking for any Millhones in the area at that time, and for Quillen and his wife, Rebecca, in particular. If my father grew up in Bakersfield, there might be other family members still in town. I pulled the Polk and the Haines directories for 1942, 1943, and 1946. The 1941 city directory was probably published early in the year, which meant that by fall of 1941, the information might be six months out of date. The same was true of the photo taken in June of 1945. People move. They die. Couples get divorced. The constant shift in status and location far outstrips any attempt to report.

The Polk Company has been publishing city directories since 1878, beginning with a simple alphabetical listing of the residents of any given town. In 1916, the directory was expanded to include both an alphabetical listing of residents and an alphabetical listing of street addresses, with names of the occupants included. The Haines directory, also known as a crisscross, is a mechanical reversal of the information in the phone book, its listings ordered by street names and by telephone numbers in sequence, beginning with the area code, then moving on to the exchange. If you have a street address and you want to know who lives there, you can consult either publication. If you have a phone number but no clue whom it belongs to, you start a search with the Haines and work backward to the name and address of the person to whom the number has been assigned. There are a certain percentage of unlisted numbers, but in the main you can uncover more than you'd imagine.

In addition to the six directories I had, I pulled both the Polk and the Haines for the calendar year 1972 to see if any of the names carried over. I toted all eight volumes to the closest table and sat down. I loved having the room to myself. It was quiet and smelled of old paper. The windows were clean and the light spilling in had a peaceful quality. I reached into my shoulder bag and found my index cards. I removed the rubber band and shuffled through them until I found the address I'd cribbed from Dace's driver's license. I picked up the 1942 Polk and began a finger walk through the pages.

Moving from page to page, I uncoupled my emotions, like a string of railroad cars I was leaving behind while the engine chugged on. This was about numbers and street names, which meant nothing to me. I simply recorded the information as I came across it. Later, I would attach sights and sounds to each location as I discovered it.

There were two Dace families. The first, Sterling Dace (Clara): util wkr, PG&E, (h) 4619 Paradise. The second was Randall J Dace (Glenda): srvc rep, PG&E, at 745 Daisy Lane. I was guessing these were Dace's parents. If so, it looked like he'd moved into the family home at some point after his mom and dad had passed away. I circled the address in my notes and then picked up the names, occupations, and addresses of the nearby neighbors. I wasn't sure what the relationship was between Randall and Sterling. Brothers? Cousins? Maybe father and son. I turned to the Ms and found Quillen Millhone (Rebecca): winch trk oprtr, Keller Ent (h) 4602 Choaker Road.

I pulled the 1946 Polk directory from the stack and placed my hand on the cover as though swearing an oath. I worked my way through the oversize pages and found the same two listings for Randall and Sterling Dace at the same respective addresses.

I backtracked to the Ms and again found Quillen Millhone. I could find no other Millhones. Again, I made a note of the neighbors on either side of the Choaker Road address on the off chance there might be someone still living who remembered them. A quick study of the city map showed Choaker Road off Panama Lane, which was too far out of town to worry about at this point. I'd confirmed that the Daces and my grandparents were contemporaries. I'd seen both sets of names in the years 1943 and 1946. All were present and accounted for.

I checked the 1972 Polk and found R. Terrence Dace. Evelyn was there as well (her name tucked next to his inside parentheses), followed by his occupation, tree trmr, and the street and house number, 745 Daisy Lane. I noted the names and addresses of neighbors on either side. There was a David Brandle at 743, a Lorelei Brandle at 743, and a Penrose and Melissa Pilcher at 747. No Millhones. I returned the books to the shelves. On a hunch, I moved forward in time to the current telephone book in hopes of finding the last names Pilcher or Brandle, wondering if Dace's neighbor lady was still living. There was an L. Brandle at another address, though I didn't expect the two were a match. There was no sign of Mr. and

Mrs. Pilcher. In that same phone book, I flipped through the residential listings to the Hs, searching for Ethan's wife. I ran a finger down the page: Heiman, Heimendinger, Heimluck, Hein, Heindle, Heinemann, Heining, Heinrich, Heintz, Heiser, Heisermann. The name after the surname Heisermann was Mamie, complete with a street address in the 5600 block of Laurel Canyon Drive. That was the best news I'd had all day. I made a note of the phone number, though I didn't intend to call first. In my business, it's better to tackle certain interviews without warning the subject in advance. Metaphorically speaking, you can sometimes catch people with their pants down around their ankles.

15

I stood on Ethan's front porch and rang the bell. Mentally, I amended that to *Mamie's* front porch, as the house was in her name. This place was a big improvement over the one he'd been renting. No doubt, his budget was limited. A wife who kicks her hubby out for idleness is usually not that eager to pay for his idleness somewhere else. A banged-up white Toyota was parked in the drive. As I passed, I peered in, making a note of the car seats, toys, board books, Happy Meal boxes, and cracker crumbs, which suggested he used the vehicle to tote the children from place to place, as why would he not?

This was a neighborhood of tract homes probably built in the past ten years. All of the exteriors were peach-colored stucco and the roofs were the standard red tile. It was clear the occupants took pride in their properties. The backyards I could see through a succession of wire fences sported evidence of young children: a chunky-looking plastic sliding board, a tricycle, two Big Wheels, a wading pool, and a one-room playhouse also made of plastic, complete with shutters and window boxes.

Ethan answered the door with a girl-child on his right hip and a boy-child crowded against his left leg. He said, "Yo!" as a form of greeting.

"Hi, are you Ethan Dace?"

"That's me." His expression changed from pleasant to cautious.

"I'm Kinsey Millhone," I said, holding out my hand.

Obligingly, he shifted the baby so we could shake hands. His manner was pleasant, but it was clear my name meant nothing to him. The Millhones must not have occupied a prominent place in the family lore. He said, "If you're here trying to sell me something, I'm afraid I can't help. Sign says no soliciting."

He gestured toward a stenciled notice to the right of the front door.

"I can see that," I said. "I'm here for something else."

"You better make it quick. Baby needs a diaper change."

"I drove up from Santa Teresa this morning with bad news about your dad. Would it be all right if I came in?"

He stared at me briefly, his expression opaque. "Might as well."

He moved aside, allowing me to step into the living room. He closed the door behind me. "These are my kids. Two of 'em, at any rate. I got another girl in first grade."

The little boy was staring at me, trying to make up his mind if I was of interest.

The baby's age was indeterminate. He looked down at her, jiggling her in a manner that made her smile. She had four teeth the size of freshwater pearls. "This is Bethany. We call her 'Binky,' and this is Scott. Amanda's still at school, though she should be home shortly. A neighbor picks her up."

"How old is the little one?"

"Ten months. Scott's three and a half, in case you're about to ask."

From somewhere in the back, two big Doberman pinschers trotted into the living room side by side and checked me out. Lean and muscular and black, with caramel-colored trim, they flanked me, giving me the sniff test, which I hoped I would not flunk. I wondered if there were traces of Ed, the cat, on my jeans. Ethan didn't issue a warning, so I assumed there was no danger of an attack.

"Do the dogs have names?"

"Blackie and Smokie. The kids came up with those," he said. "Have a seat."

He was handsome in a low-key way; dark straight hair. One lock fell forward across his forehead and the rest of it he wore shoulder length. On most men, this style is not flattering, but fellows will persist. He was otherwise clean-shaven with straight brows and green eyes. He carried the baby to one of a pair of brown leather couches separated by a big blond-wood coffee table. He laid her on her back and picked up a disposable diaper from a wicker basket at his feet. Binky arched her back and turned one shoulder, intent on rolling over. I figured babies must be like turtles; when they're on their backs, they're always working to right themselves. There was a doorknob resting between couch cushions. Ethan handed it to the baby. She held it by the shaft like a lollipop and gnawed on it, sufficiently distracted that he was able to proceed with the diaper change. If Big Rat wanted his doorknobs back, he was going to have to come over here and wrestle with Binky, who was clearly attached.

She had perfect baby looks, like something you'd see in a print ad for baby food. Her brother was also blessed with prettiness; big dark eyes, curly dark hair, luscious coloring. He returned to a small table and chairs, arranged to the right of the kitchen door. He was in the middle of a scribbly piece of art, using a red marker pen.

Ethan was decked out in jeans, desert boots, and a white long-sleeve waffle-pattern shirt with a button placket that suggested thermal underwear. I watched him tape a clean diaper into place, after which he made a neat bundle of the urine-soaked specimen he'd just removed. This he placed on the coffee table, where it sat like a big white plastic turd. He lifted Binky and stood her upright against the table. I watched her sidle around the edge, banging on the top intermittently with her doorknob when it wasn't in her mouth. Maybe she was teething and the metal felt good on her gums.

He leaned toward me with his elbows on his knees, returning to the subject at hand. "By bad news, I'm assuming my father passed away."

"He did. Last week. I'm sorry to have to spring it on you."

"I can't say I'm surprised," he said. "What happened?"

"He was found in his sleeping bag at the beach. He probably died of a heart attack. The coroner's investigator is still hoping to track down his medical records."

Scott piped up and said, "Daddy, you didn't give us any lunch yet." Not whining or lodging a complaint, simply stating a fact.

Ethan said, "Shit. Hang on a sec."

He got up and crossed the room, disappearing through a doorway. I caught a glimpse of a run of upper kitchen cabinets with the doors ajar. One of the drawers under the kitchen counter extended by six inches as well. I've noticed there's a whole class of people who can pass an open cabinet door or drawer without reaching out to close it. I am not one.

I took advantage of Ethan's absence to do a survey. The wall-to-wall carpeting was beige. The walls were also beige except for the multicolored crayon marks. There was a corner fireplace constructed out of white-painted brick, and a big picture window looking out to the street. A bicycle was propped against the wall near the front door. The rest of the home furnishings consisted of two toy boxes, a stationary exercise bike, a high chair, a stroller, and a television set. Someone had assembled a series of bins for the children's belongings, each neatly labeled. So far everything seemed to be strewn on the floor. The house smelled of doggie breath.

The pile of clothes to my right was a distraction. I'm a neatnik and it was hard to sit there without starting to fold little T-shirts and onesies and child-size blue jeans with elastic in the waist. This is not proper behavior for a hard-boiled private eye, especially on an occasion such as this, telling a perfect stranger he'd been disinherited. I was already anxious about the conversation coming up and I had to put my hands between my knees to keep from matching stray socks.

I could hear Ethan banging and thumping in the kitchen. Blackie and Smokie were currently on the floor having a pretend doggie wrestling match, mouths open while they worried at each other with their teeth. Scott flung himself into the fray, landing on one of the pair, which put them into an ecstasy of squirms and fake growls.

"Leave the dogs alone," Ethan called idly from the other room.

Scott rolled off and returned to his seat at the little table. Moments later, Ethan appeared with two small plastic plates that each held half a peanut butter and jelly sandwich. He put the plates down and Scott began to eat, holding the sandwich in his left hand so he could color with his right. There was a coffee can of marker pens he was using one by one. Most lay uncapped on the table in front of him.

"Hey, Binkers, you want lunch?"

The baby dropped to her hands and knees and made a bee-line from the coffee table to the lunch plates, crawling with speed and assurance. She looked like a wind-up toy, hands and knees moving with mechanical efficiency. Scott pushed her plate closer to the edge of the table. She pulled herself up on fat baby legs, grabbed the half sandwich, and banged it on the table. Then she stuck it in her mouth.

"Sorry about that," Ethan said as he returned to his seat. "Nice of you to drive all this way. Were you a friend of his?"

I shook my head. "A relative. Rebecca Dace was my grandmother. She was married to Quillen Millhone. I believe their son, Randy Millhone, was your father's favorite uncle."

His face was blank, unclouded by recognition. "You lost me there. *Who's* this?"

"My father's name was Randy Millhone. Uncle R."

"Oh, sure, sure. Uncle R. I remember hearing about him."

"I don't know if my father was actually your father's uncle. The title might have been used to simplify the blood tie."

"So *we're* related? The two of us?"

"It looks that way. My guess is we're cousins, but I'm not sure what kind. First, second, once removed."

He cracked his knuckles and his right knee jumped a couple of times. This was the first hint I'd had that he was anxious about the subject. I could see the neck of a guitar resting against the back of the couch behind him. He reached over, picked it up, and tucked it in against him as though prepared to play. His action had the same air as a man reaching for a pack of cigarettes.

"I like your guitar," I remarked.

"It's a 1968 Martin D-35. Guy let me take it out on loan to see if I like it. Three thousand bucks, I better like it," he said. "I didn't mean to interrupt. Your dad grew up here, is that it?"

"That's right. At some point, he moved to Santa Teresa. He and my mother married in 1935 and I was born fifteen years later."

"That must have been a surprise."

"A good one, I hope. When I was five, both were killed in a car wreck, so I was raised by a maiden aunt, my mother's sister. I didn't know anything about my father's side of the family until recently." I wanted to kick myself for babbling on and on. What was it to him?

I noticed we'd hopped right over the fact of his father's death and I wasn't sure if that was good news or bad. At least we were having what passed for a conversation, though the small talk was making me tense. He seemed happy enough to have me sitting there with the subject matter wandering this way and that. Maybe he appreciated the company, being hemmed in all day with the little ones. He focused on his guitar, idly approximating various chords; not actually playing them, but positioning his fingers on the frets, his gaze fixed on his hands. The pads of his fingers made a faint metallic sound as he moved them across the strings. While he wasn't being rude, it was like trying to have a conversation with someone filling in a crossword puzzle. He caught my look and smiled briefly. "Sorry. I didn't mean to cut you off. You were talking about your father."

"I was explaining why I knew so little about my Bakersfield kin."

"How'd you hook up with my dad?"

"We never met. The first I heard of him he was in the morgue as a John Doe. My name and number were on a slip of paper in his pocket, and the coroner's office called, thinking I might know who he was."

"And you turn out to be related? That's a hell of a coincidence, isn't it?"

"Not really. I'm told he came to Santa Teresa to look for me."

"Because of his prior relationship with your father," he said, as though assembling the facts.

"Exactly."

"Are you the only Millhone in Santa Teresa?"

"That's right. I'm actually a private investigator, so he might have found me in the phone book."

"No fooling. Well, ain't that a kick in the pants. I never met a real private detective before."

"This is me," I said, raising my hand.

He turned his attention to his guitar, trying a chord or two. In a whispery falsetto, he put together two lines of a song he was apparently composing extemporaneously. *"When your daddy dies, it should come as no surprise . . ."* He stopped and tried the line again. *"When your daddy dies, you have to realize . . ."* He shook his head, holding the guitar against him like a shield.

I said, "When did you last see your father?"

"September. A year ago, I forget the date. I heard a knock at the door and nearly fell over when I saw who it was. You knew he went to prison?"

"Someone told me about it."

"Man was a loser, big time. What're you going to do?" The latter wasn't meant as a question. It was verbal filler.

"I can see why you were shocked when he showed up. Did he tell you why he was released?"

"Said his new lawyer punched all kinds of holes in the case and insisted they submit blood and semen for DNA testing. No match on any of it, so they had to let him go."

"He was a very lucky man finding someone who'd go to bat for him."

"Yeah, right. Want my take on it?"

"Sure."

"Just because they let him out doesn't mean he was innocent."

I blinked. The statement was the last thing in the world I expected to hear from him. "That's an odd point of view."

"Why? You think guilty people don't get away with murder?"

"On occasion, of course they do, but he was exonerated. There wasn't any evidence that tied him to the crime."

"Except Cates, the other guy."

"Herman Cates knew he was dying and he admitted he'd implicated your father just because he could. His accomplice was someone else altogether."

"So I heard," he said in that tone that screamed of disbelief. "At any rate, I appreciate your going to so much trouble for someone you never met."

"I thought it was the least I could do . . ." I was going to add "under the circumstances" but I stopped where I was. Ethan must have picked up on the missing words.

"How so?"

"I understand the two of you quarreled."

"Says who?"

"A friend of his in Santa Teresa."

"I wouldn't call it a quarrel. More like a tiff."

"He told his friend there was an ugly scene."

"What was I supposed to do? The guy was drunk. So what else is new? Things might have got nasty, but you know how it is. Everybody calms down and life goes on."

"You weren't in touch with him afterward?"

"Wasn't possible. The man lives on the street and he doesn't have a phone. We didn't even know for sure where he was headed when he left."

"Were you aware he'd come into money?"

"Well, yeah. That's what he said. We didn't talk about it, but I got the gist. He said he filed a lawsuit."

"He sued the state . . ."

"Right, right. Because his name was cleared. I remember now." There was a pause while he plucked the D string and adjusted the tuning. He addressed his next question to the machine heads. "He die with a will or without?"

"With."

"What happened to the money? I hope you're not going to tell me he blew it."

"No, no. It's still in the bank."

He smiled briefly. "That's a relief. Man's a bum. Never did anything right in his life. So what's the process in a situation like this?"

"Process?"

"What happens next? Are there forms to fill out?"

I experienced a momentary jolt and I could feel the heat rise in my face. I'd just caught a flash of how this looked from his perspective. Now that I'd delivered the bad news, he thought I'd be telling him about the money he was coming into. He and his sisters. His asking what was to happen next was procedural. He hadn't brought up the subject sooner because he didn't want to sound greedy. Maybe he thought I'd been beating around the bush out of delicacy. Given the news of his father's death, he didn't want to leap on the pecuniary matters without first giving the impression of filial respect.

"He named me executor of his estate."

"You?"

I shrugged.

Ethan thought about that briefly. "Well, I guess the job's largely clerical, isn't it? Filing papers and stuff like that?"

"Pretty much," I said. "The will's been entered into probate."

"Whatever that means," he said, and then focused on me fully for the first time. "You act like there's a problem?"

"Well."

Annoyed, he said, "Would you quit fumbling around and just get on with it?"

I stared at the floor and then shook my head. "I don't know how else to say this, Ethan. He cut you out of the will. All three of you."

He stared at me. "You're kidding me."

I shook my head.

"Son of a bitch. All this, because we had a falling-out? I don't believe it. Is that why you brought it up? That business about the 'quarrel'?" He used his fingers to enclose the last word in digital quote marks, implying that it was my claim and not necessarily the truth.

"I'm sure it must seem harsh."

"Harsh? It's ridiculous. I don't know what you heard, but it's bullshit."

"I'm telling you what he said; the story as he relayed it to his friends. He said you slammed the door in his face. I don't know if he was speaking literally or figuratively."

"And for that, we were disinherited? A few cross words and he dumps us? That's not right. That can't be right."

I dropped my gaze and waited. It was natural for him to vent and I needed to give him the space.

"Hey. I'm talking to you."

I met his eyes.

"You want to hear what went on the last time we spoke? Fine. This is the truth and I got witnesses. I'd come over here to pick up the kids. I was living somewhere else temporarily. My wife was standing right there, so you can ask her if you want. He arrives on my doorstep so drunk he can hardly stand. He's selling me some hard-luck story about half a million bucks and how he never did nothing wrong . . . he's been falsely imprisoned . . . big boo-hoo. Like I could give a shit. He's begging my forgiveness, wanting to give me this lovey-dovey hug and stuff. He actually thinks he's coming into my house so he can get to know my wife and kids. He smells like a sewer, like he puked on himself. There's no way I'd let him in. With my kids home? I told him to get the hell out and not to call until he was clean and sober for a month, which he must not have managed since I never heard from him again."

"Did he see your sisters that same visit?"

"Of course. You probably know that already since you bought his version, hook, line, and sinker. He said he wanted to talk to them, and like an idiot I told him where Anna worked. He showed up drunk there as well and made a horse's ass of himself. Anna was so pissed at me she didn't talk to me for a month. Now we get cut from the will, like we did something to him instead of the other way around."

"Ethan, honestly, I'm not blaming you for anything."

"Why would you? You're not the butt of the joke. Tell you what. As far as I'm concerned? The guy was dead when he went to Soledad. I wrote him off the day he left and so did Ellen and Anna. Screw him. I don't want his money. He can shove it up his dead ass."

I thought it wise to keep any further comments to myself. Anything I said was the equivalent of tossing gasoline on a bonfire.

Ethan stared at me. "So is that it? Are we done now?"

Hesitantly, I said, "There are some personal items he wanted you to have. They're still in his safe deposit box, which I won't have access to until the hearing in December. I can send them to you when the time comes."

"*Personal* items?"

"He wrote and illustrated a folio for each of you. California edible plants and wildflowers." My face was feeling warm again because it all sounded so lame.

"Like a little coloring book? I can hardly wait. Meanwhile, where'd the money go? I forgot to ask. He give it away? Donate it to a worthy cause so he could look good at our expense?"

"He left it to me."

"Say what?"

"He left me the money."

"*All* of it?"

Nodding assent would have been redundant. He could see the admission written on my face.

Behind me, the front door opened and the oldest of the children came in, with an enormous backpack. She had dark eyes and long dark hair that might have been neatly brushed when she left for school that morning. Now some strands had separated while the others were in a tangle. I was so grateful for the distraction, I wanted to kiss the child, though I'd forgotten her name.

"Hey, Amanda," Ethan said with a glance at her.

"Hey, Daddy."

"School go okay?"

"Fine."

"You want a snack, you can get yourself some cookies, but share with Scottie and the Bink, okay?"

"'Kay."

She disappeared into the kitchen and returned a moment later with the box of cookies. She got out a Fig Newton and held it in her teeth while she sat down at the children's table, opened her backpack, and took out her homework. Binky used the table leg to pull herself up so she could bang on Amanda's paper with the flat of her hand. She slid it back and forth rapidly.

"Daddy, Binky's tearing my paper."

"She's not doing anything."

"She's messed it up and now I'll get a bad grade."

Ethan didn't really seem to be listening, but Scott got up and put his arms around Binky's waist from behind. He lifted her off her feet and carried her across the room in our direction. I was afraid he'd throw his back out, but maybe at his age he was so limber that picking up half his body weight had no effect. He propped her against the coffee table and went back to his work. She held on, momentarily diverted by the uncapped blue marker pen she'd snagged in passing.

I was struck by Ethan's management style, which was competent but disengaged. Granted, neither of the dogs had barked, slobbered, or jumped on me, and none of the kids had cried, screamed, or shrieked. I already liked the lot of them better than I liked most.

Meanwhile, I noticed the marker pen was dyeing Binky's lips and tongue the color of blueberries. Surely, the manufacturer made a point of using nontoxic inks, since the pens were made for kids.

I glanced at Ethan. "Is she okay with that?"

He reached over and took the pen. I expected a howl to go up, but she'd fixed her attention on the doorknob.

I removed the manila envelope from my shoulder bag. "These are copies of the will and a couple of forms I filled out. There's a hearing in December if you want to challenge the terms of the will."

Ethan had his head in his hands, slowly shaking it back and forth. "This is too much. Man, I don't believe it."

I placed the manila envelope on the table. "There's something else as long as I'm here."

Ethan looked over at me with a pained expression. "What?"

"I wondered what you wanted done with his remains?"

"His *remains*? You mean his corpse? You can't be serious. I don't give a shit!"

"I thought you might want a voice in decisions about his funeral. I delayed making arrangements until I talked to you."

"You can do anything you want. Just don't think I'm paying you one red cent."

"Don't you want to talk to Ellen and Anna first?"

"And drop the same bomb on them? That sounds like a fun idea."

"If you'll tell me how to get in touch, I can explain it all to them."

"I'm not telling you where they are. Why should I help you? You're the red-hot detective. You figure it out."

"My business card is in the envelope . . ."

"Lady, would you quit going on and on about this? I mean, give me a break. This is insulting enough as it is."

"I appreciate your time," I murmured as I got up.

Binky was already grabbing for the manila envelope, which she tried to stuff into her mouth without much success. She looked down at it, as though sizing it up for another approach.

He snatched it away from her and sailed it in my direction.

"Take the damn thing." This time, the baby's face crumpled and she howled.

I left the envelope on the floor where it landed. "I'm at the Thrifty Lodge if you need to reach me."

"I don't. Just get the hell out of here and watch the dogs don't escape."

16

I stood on the porch, waiting for the flop sweat to cool before I headed down the steps. I had to congratulate myself on my efficiency. Here it was only 3:10 and I'd already had my ass handed to me on a plate. Ordinarily, I'd have sat in the car out front, taking notes while the conversation was still fresh in my mind. Instead, I fired up the Mustang and drove half a block, waiting until I'd turned the corner before I pulled over to the curb. I took a deep breath and exhaled. That had most certainly not gone well. I reran the conversation, considering alternative responses, but I couldn't come up with any that might have served me better than the ones I'd voiced at the time. I'd hoped to persuade Ethan to give me Anna's contact information, but that was out of the question now. I recited a string of cuss words, calling up some of the really nasty four-letter jobs that trip so refreshingly off the tongue. Didn't seem to help.

I couldn't think what else to do with myself, so I went back to my motel. This was my second mistake in as many moves. The Thrifty Lodge, while thrifty, was a sorry piece of work. When I pulled in, mine was the only car in the lot. Maybe word had gone out on the motel underground that something was afoot. Why wasn't anyone else staying there, unless they knew something I didn't? I unlocked the door and stepped into my room. I'd neglected to leave a light on for myself, and even at this hour of the day the room was shadowy. Some of the gloom I attributed to the fact that the drapes were closed, blocking what was otherwise an outstanding view of the parking lot. I crossed to the big window and pulled the drapery cord dangling to the right. I gave a mighty tug, but the drapes refused to budge.

I went into the bathroom, flipped on the light, and stared at myself in the mirror. Why did I feel so guilty? Why was I chiding myself when there wasn't a good way to deliver the news I'd been called upon to "share"? I'd known I was doomed to failure before I made the drive to Bakersfield. Ethan couldn't admit he was in any way responsible for the pain and distress he'd caused his father, and he wasn't prepared to own up to the part he'd played in the changing of the will. I understood his rage. After years of humiliation, he'd suffered this final insult. During that last visit, his father had talked about the money, and while Ethan probably told himself he didn't care, the idea must have lingered at the back of his mind in the same way it had in mine. You can't anticipate a windfall like that without fantasizing what you'd do with it and what a difference it would make. Even with the money divided three ways, he was still looking at something close to two hundred thousand bucks. I could understand that, but I was puzzled by the cynicism he'd expressed about his father's release from prison. Apparently, regardless of the reality, he still believed his father was implicated in the girl's abduction and murder.

Whatever the underlying attitude, I was going to suffer a repeat of the same scene two more times, with Ellen and again with Anna. I assumed Ethan would slap them with the bad news the first chance he got, but I couldn't be sure of it. I had the option of notifying both by mail, but I still harbored the notion that I could soften the blow if I talked to them in person. Not that I'd done such a sterling job to date. Still, I figured as long as I'd traveled 150 miles, I might as well try. With luck, I wouldn't see the three of them again in my lifetime.

I left the bathroom and rounded up my shoulder bag, which I'd tossed on the bed. I checked the outside pockets and found Big Rat's business card. I picked up the handset and dialed. Three rings . . . four. His machine kicked in.

"This is Big Rat. You know what to do."

I waited for the beep and said, "Hi, Mr. Rizzo. This is Kinsey Millhone. We spoke earlier. I did manage to find Ethan at his wife's house and we talked a short time ago. Could you give me the name of the salon where Anna works? I think I better touch base with her as well. My number is . . ."

I looked down at the phone. Usually there's a circle in the dialing wheel, with the phone number of the motel, as well as the extension, which is a variation on the room number. I said, "Hang on a second . . ."

I scanned the room. The furnishings included a desk and a chest of drawers on the far side of the room, but both were bare. I opened the bed table drawer. There was a phone book, but it seemed absurd to take the time to look up the Thrifty Lodge in the yellow pages. No packet of Thrifty Lodge matches, no scratch pad, no promotional pen sporting the pertinent address and phone number. What was I thinking? There was no way the Thrifty Lodge management would pay for advertising gimmicks. Housekeeping hadn't even bothered to put a wrapper around the plastic bathroom "glass" in a nod to sanitation.

"Skip the number. I'm at the Thrifty Lodge. I guess you'll have to look it up. I'd appreciate a call."

I hung up. Now what?

I thought I'd better hang around for a while in hopes that he'd call back. I opened my duffel and retrieved the Dick Francis novel I was reading. I stretched out on the bed and found my place. I reached over and turned on the bed table lamp, which had been equipped with a forty-watt bulb. I could barely see the page. I leaned sideways, holding the paperback elevated at an angle. This was ridiculous. If I couldn't see to read now, what was I going to do at bedtime, which was my favorite time to curl up with a book?

I turned off the light, licked my fingertips, and unscrewed the bulb. I slid my room key into my pocket and locked the door behind me with the lightbulb in hand. When I reached the office, the midtwenties desk clerk was on the phone. He wore jeans, a white polyester dress shirt, suspenders, and a bow tie. When he spotted me, he held up a finger, indicating he'd be with me as soon as he was done. From his half of the conversation, I was guessing the matter was personal, so I leaned my elbows on the counter and listened to every word. In fewer than twenty seconds, he'd managed to terminate the call.

"Yes, ma'am," he said as he turned to me.

I held up the bulb. "Is there any way I can exchange this for a hundred-watt?"

"Let me check."

He disappeared into the back office and emerged moments later with a replacement. "This is a sixty. It's the best I can do. Management calculated we could save twenty-five dollars a year using forties."

"Oh wow. Good news."

I returned to my room and as I let myself in, I caught sight of the phone on the bedside table. The incoming-message light blinked its merry dot of red. I figured it was Big Rat with the information I needed, so I settled on the edge of the bed and made sure I had a pen and a fresh index card at the ready before I picked up the handset and pressed 0. A really nice automated lady told me that I had one message. "First message," said she.

It was Henry, sounding distressed. "Kinsey, it's Henry. I've been trying to reach you, but I haven't wanted to leave a message because I don't want to worry you unnecessarily. I have bad news about your friend Felix. He's in the hospital in critical condition. If you'll give me a call, I'll tell you as much as I know."

The call must have come in during the few minutes I was gone.

I punched in the Santa Teresa area code and Henry's number. The line was busy. I waited a minute and dialed again. Still busy. I schooled myself to be patient, giving him sufficient time to complete the call he was on. The third time I tried, the number rang twice and he picked up.

"Henry, it's me, Kinsey. What's going on?"

"Well, I'm so glad to hear your voice. I'm sorry for the scare, but I thought I should let you know as soon as I could. Dandy showed up at noon. He was looking for you, of course, but I told him you were out of town. He said Pearl left a message for him at the shelter. She was calling from St. Terry's emergency room. Felix had been picked up by ambulance and he was already on his way to surgery by the time Dandy got back to her."

"What happened?"

"He was jumped by a bunch of thugs and beaten half to death."

I closed my eyes, picturing the Boggarts laying into Felix with fists and kicks. "How badly is he hurt?"

I reached over and turned on the lamp, forgetting the bulb was lying on the bed beside me.

"His skull was fractured and they broke both his legs. Damage to his kidneys and spleen, probably brain damage as well. This happened outside the bicycle-rental place on lower State Street. Luckily, the owner put a stop to it, but not fast enough."

"That sounds bad." This had to be retaliation for Felix and Pearl's tearing apart the Boggarts' camp. Still, it seemed harsh. I angled the sixty-watt bulb into the socket and turned it gingerly so the threads would catch. Light bloomed.

Henry went on. "Dandy was on his way to the hospital, so I offered him a ride. Harbor House had given him a bus pass, but it seemed absurd for him to try getting there by public transportation."

"Where's Pearl?"

"She's still at the hospital as far as I know. She keeps saying this is all her fault. That's about as much as anyone can get out of her. She's close to collapse."

"He's going to be okay, though, isn't he?"

"The doctors won't say. It's one of those wait-and-see situations. At least for the next few hours."

"This is awful. I feel sick." I flashed on a quick succession of images. Most of them involving Pearl. Felix did whatever she did, but he wasn't the instigator. I'd known better myself, even at the time, and I hadn't raised enough of a fuss to head her off. It was a dumb idea and I'd gone along with it, which made me as guilty as she was. Why so savage a response to what amounted to a load of mischief? "Did someone call the police?"

"Pearl intends to file charges, but so far she's been sticking close to Felix's side. She says she knows who they are."

"Did she actually see the attack?"

"No, but she swears it's those bums who live at a hobo camp near the bird refuge."

"She can't swear to something she didn't witness firsthand."

"You'd have to talk to her about that. Meanwhile, they have Felix in a medically induced coma, hoping the swelling in his brain will subside. That's the crux of it for now."

"Have you seen him?"

"They don't allow visitors in ICU. I was able to peer in briefly, but there wasn't much to see. Pearl's claiming he's her brother, so she's been with him since he came out of the recovery room. Dandy and I hung out for a while and then I came home. Between calls, I left that message for you but didn't expect to hear back so soon."

"I had to make a run to the office and I saw the light blinking as soon as I walked in. Can I do anything from here?"

"No, no. Everything's under control, but it's been crazy as you might imagine. What about you? How's it going so far?"

"Not good. I talked to Ethan and told him about the will. He was upset, which came as no big surprise. I'll give you a full report as soon as I get home."

"Which is when?"

"I'd hoped to talk to his sister, but now I think I'd be better off hitting the road. I can do more good there than I can stuck here."

"I don't like the idea of your heading into rush-hour traffic."

"I should be fine as soon as I clear town. I don't anticipate much congestion on the 5."

"Well, don't do anything foolish. It sounds like you've already had a long, hard day."

"All the more reason to get home," I said. "The motel I'm in is such a dump, I've had to repent all my miserly ways. I want my own bed. I want to be there lending moral support. Did Rosie get home?"

"Not yet. Her plane gets in at five o'clock. The same United flight William was on. I'll pick her up while he's having his last PT appointment of the week. Once I drop her off, I'll head back to St. Terry's. You want me to turn on the porch lights for you?"

"Please."

"Will do, and if there's anything new, I'll leave a note on your door."

"Thanks. I'll see you in a few."

"You drive carefully."

"I will."

I hung up, grabbed the duffel, and toted it into the bathroom. I tossed in the shampoo bottle, the conditioner, and my deodorant. I paused to brush my teeth and then packed my toothbrush and toothpaste. I set aside thoughts of Felix, knowing I'd have plenty of time to process that development once I was on the road.

I flipped off the light and then picked up my jacket and shoulder bag. I reached the door and took a last look around, making sure I hadn't forgotten anything. Checking out wouldn't take long, especially since I didn't intend to argue about a refund. I thought about returning the sixty-watt bulb to the office but decided it would be my gift to the next guest.

The telephone rang.

With one hand on the doorknob, I stared at the instrument. Probably Big Rat. I'd just spoken with Henry and Big Rat was the only other person who knew I was here . . . except for Ethan, of course, and I couldn't believe he'd call. Might be the desk clerk calling to say he'd found me a hundred-watt bulb, but that was hardly late-breaking news. What difference would it make? By bedtime, I'd be gone.

Two rings.

Why answer the phone? If I'd been a little quicker through the door, I'd have been gone anyway. I was a heartbeat away from hearing the Mustang grumble to life. I knew how the road would feel under my wheels. If I'd been a dog, I'd be anticipating the wind in my ears, my head hanging out the window.

Third ring. I picked up. "Hello?"

"Hey, Kinsey. This is Big Rat. I just got in. Glad to hear you found Ethan. How'd he take the news about his dad?"

"I wouldn't say he's heartbroken."

"Sometimes takes a while to sink in. I know it was like that with my dad," he said. "You asked about Anna?"

"I did, but something's come up and I need to get home. I was on my way to the office to check out when I heard the phone."

"Good I caught you before you left. Name of the salon is Hair and Nails Ahoy! With an exclamation point. I don't have the street address, but it's on Chester down around Nineteenth. Sign's in the shape of an anchor."

"Thanks. I appreciate this. It looks like I'll have to make another trip if I want to talk to her . . ."

"Why not stop by and chat with her on your way out of town? Salon's open until six, so she'll be there for sure."

I was silent. The pull to Santa Teresa was so intense, I thought I'd be sucked out the door.

"You there?"

"I'm here. I'll think about it," I said. "But the situation at home is an emergency."

"Up to you," he said, and the phone went dead.

I set my duffel on the floor and paused to tally up my mental and physical states. Ethan's combativeness had taken its toll, but the impact hadn't really hit me until now when I thought I was safe. This must be what a prizefighter feels like after leaving the ring. During the bout, you're too busy dancing and feinting and dodging blows, trying to anticipate your opponent's next move. Now that I was back in the locker room, so to speak, I could assess my psychic injuries. I was exhausted. I felt bruised. There was an ache between my shoulder blades. My neck muscles were tight, and a tension headache was squeezing my skull like a bathing cap two sizes too small. Add to that the news about Felix, and my energy was at a low ebb. I put a hand against my forehead as Aunt Gin had always done when she was checking for a fever. She wasn't sympathetic to illness, so the gesture was usually the prelude to her telling me to suck it up. Which was exactly the counsel I now gave myself. I'd driven 150 miles to take care of business and I wasn't done yet. What could I do for Felix except to stand in the hall outside his room and fret? A thirty-minute delay wouldn't make a difference.

I trotted up to the office as intended and turned in my key. I returned to the car, threw my duffel into the backseat, and slid under the steering wheel. I pulled out of the parking lot and headed east. At Chester I turned right, watching the numbered streets drop from Twenty-second to Nineteenth. The salon wasn't hard to spot. Right-hand side, halfway down the block. There was even a nice long stretch of curb out front.

At 4:00, I was seated in the reception area at Hair and Nails Ahoy! It was fortunate for me the salon took walk-ins and Anna was the only manicurist. She was currently with a client. I didn't want a manicure, but when the receptionist asked what she could do for me, it seemed easier to book an appointment than to stop and explain. While I waited, I leafed through a three-ring binder filled with photographs showing a variety of hairstyles. Most were clipped from magazines and none looked right for me. Why pay a salon when you can take care of it yourself at home?

Of the two hairdressers I could see, one was clipping a gentleman's hair and the other worked on a woman customer, painting strands of hair laid out on a band of aluminum foil. A third customer came in and another stylist appeared from somewhere in the back. I watched the woman take her seat while the stylist assembled her tools. She flapped out a cape that she placed backward over the woman's clothing to avoid showering her with clippings. The gentleman got up, left a tip, and stopped at the front desk long enough to pay for his cut. Anna moved the client from her workstation to an empty one close by. The woman sat down and placed her newly painted nails in the maw of a tiny cave where a violet light bathed her fingertips, apparently to speed the drying process. I glanced at my watch and saw that ten minutes had passed. I was itchy to be on my way, but resigned to completing the task I'd set for myself.

17

Anna crossed to the desk and checked the appointment book, then gestured that I was next up. I set the binder aside and took a seat at her rolling table. I'm ignorant about the dictates of beauty salon etiquette. I murmured a greeting without introducing myself. Anna neither offered her name nor asked for mine. The tabletop immediately in front of me was padded with fresh white towels. I extended my hands, palm down, while she leaned and peered at my fingernails.

"Where do you get your nails done?"

"I've never had a manicure."

I expected a comment but her expression was neutral. Nail technician's creed: A nail professional makes no judgments. Nor does a nail professional criticize those who've come to her for help. If my nails had been in order, why would I need her?

"Nails would be nice if you took better care of them. I'll give you some sample products before you leave," she said. "You want straight across or shaped?"

"What do you think?"

"Shaped. Slender fingers, it looks better."

I peered more closely at my fingertips, trying to see them as she did. Okay, a bit ragged here and there, but my nails were clean and I didn't bite them, which surely counted in my favor.

To her right, there was a miniature Lucite rack where bottles of nail polish were perched in the equivalent of stadium seating. Every known color was represented, from dark funereal hues to fire-engine reds. The pinks ran from a neutral beige to a fuchsia shade I didn't like at all. "You know what color you want?" she asked.

"I don't wear polish."

"I'll buff them. I'm short on time anyway. This is my busy day. You're lucky Lucy managed to slot you in."

She opened the shallow drawer in front of her and took out an emery board. She picked up my left hand as if it were an inanimate object, one of a pair of gloves. She filed and shaped the nails on that hand and then placed it on the table while she got up and crossed to the sink and filled a shallow plastic basin with warm soapy water. She sat down again and placed the fingers of my left hand in the water with my hand resting on the shallow lip of the reservoir. While the left hand soaked, she addressed the nails of my right hand, which she filed and shaped to match my left.

I wanted to initiate a conversation, but I wasn't sure where to start. There's something intimate about having someone tend to your body parts; haircuts, massages, bikini waxes, the latter no more than a rumor as far as I was concerned. When you're in the hands of an expert, you give yourself up to the process. Since she seemed fully focused on my hands, I was free to study her.

She was blessed with a sulky prettiness—dark brows, long dark hair that she wore pulled up in a topknot, caught in the jaws of a big plastic clip. A few loose strands framed her face. Her skin was flawless. She had a row of tiny gold rings in a line along one ear. The holes were pierced so closely together, it looked as if she'd taken a length of spiral binding and threaded it through her ear. She wore jeans and a cotton T-shirt with a deep V in front. Boobs.

When she finally spoke, she addressed her remarks to my fingertips. "I know who you are, so you don't have to pussyfoot around."

"I take it your brother called."

"Are you kidding? The minute you were out the door. He was like totally pissed off, which I shouldn't have to tell you."

She removed my left hand from the soapy water and placed

it on the towel in front of her, patting it dry like a lettuce leaf. She moved the basin over and set my right hand to soak while she squirted a milky solution across the cuticles of my left.

I said, "I'm sorry I upset him. That wasn't my intent. I wish I'd done a better job of it."

"Don't mind him. He's a drama queen. How'd you find out where I worked?"

"His landlord."

"Big Rat. High school, he was a class ahead of Ethan's. I once dated the guy if you can believe that."

"Somehow I can't picture it."

"That makes two of us. I was sixteen and thought he was a man about town." She lapsed into silence, intent on her work.

"I guess you know about your dad's will," I ventured.

"We all know. Big powwow an hour ago. I thought the phone lines would catch fire."

"Does your mother know?"

"She knows everything. Why do you ask?"

"I was wondering how she felt about your father's death."

"She said 'Good riddance,' if that's a clue. Mamie's the one you better watch. Even Mom has a hard time with her. Talk about butting heads. Those two go at it." She took out a little pair of scissors and nipped at my cuticles, dead skin piling up in the tiny space between blades. "Mamie's Ethan's wife, in case you haven't heard."

"I didn't meet her, but I know her name. She was off at work."

"The woman's a powerhouse."

"How so?"

"She's a code-enforcement officer for the city. Property maintenance, zoning violations, abandoned vehicles, you name it. File a complaint and she kicks ass until the problem goes away. Too bad she wasn't around when Dad was doing his 'thang.' She'd have whipped him into shape."

"I take it your mother wasn't good at that."

"Mamie's the kind who gets up in your face. Mom wheedles and manipulates. She specializes in guilt trips." She was silent for a moment and then looked up. It was the first time she met my eyes and I was startled at the bright blue of her gaze. "So now you've talked to Ethan, why come to me?"

"I left the paperwork with him, but I couldn't be sure he'd pass it along to you and Ellen. Look, I understand this is difficult . . ."

"No, it's not. You know how much Daddy cared? He drank himself to death. That's what he thought about us. We were last in line. He put my mother through hell. Not that she doesn't deserve half the blame."

She took a buffer from the drawer and began to shine my nails, intent on her task.

"If you want a say in your father's funeral arrangements, this is your chance. You have any requests?"

Smiling slightly, she said, "Make sure he's thoroughly dead before you bury him. We don't want him coming back unannounced. As much as he drank, he probably pickled himself, which should save on embalming fees."

I was at a loss about where to take the conversation next, so I said nothing. I watched her work. The silence didn't seem to bother her.

Once she finished buffing, she opened a big jar of cream and rubbed a glob between her hands. She took my hand and began to massage my fingers and my palm, moving up my forearm. "Ethan says you never met Daddy. He says you never even laid eyes on him 'til he was dead."

"That's true. I had no idea we were related."

"And you got all the money. Lucky you."

"I had no say in that."

"I'm sure not. My old man was a shit."

"He wasn't all bad. His friends speak well of him. They were impressed with his smarts. Wasn't he working on a degree in landscape design?"

"Eons ago when we were little kids. He was good about taking us on hikes and teaching us nature stuff. That always frosted Mom's ass." She looked toward the salon door, checking the client who had just walked in. As though I'd pressed, she went on. "We worshiped the ground he walked on. She's the family saint and didn't like the competition."

"He put together a folio for each of you that he illustrated himself."

"Sorry to interrupt, but I got a client just came in and she doesn't like to wait. She's a regular and she tips well. Job you do, I bet you don't have to worry about things like that."

"Am I supposed to pay here or at the desk?"

"Pay her," she said, glancing at the receptionist.

Since she'd just mentioned a tip, I thought I'd better be generous. I took a ten out of my wallet and slipped it under the towel. That seemed to soften her attitude.

"If you want, Ellen and I can meet you later for a drink," she said as I got up.

I made a face meant to convey regret. "I wish I could, but I'm due home and I've checked out of my motel."

"You can't find another room?"

"I could, but I have to get back."

She seemed aghast, which I'm sure was an act. "So this is it? You pass on the papers and refuse to explain? Ethan's saying things like 'probate.' I don't even know what that is."

"This is news to me as well. I'm learning as I go. You should have an attorney explain how the system works. That way, if you need legal advice—"

"So now we have to pay a *lawyer*? Are you nuts? You waltz in here telling us we're disinherited and now we're supposed to hire a legal expert? Where's the money coming from?"

"I'm just suggesting you get an opinion from someone who's not already in the thick of things the way I am. Call Legal Aid and see if they can help. I don't think you should look to me for guidance when it may not be what's best for you. Why don't you talk to Ellen and see what she says?"

"Why is that my job? You're the one who knows everything, so *you* explain."

I closed my eyes, working to detach myself from the urge to fall on her forearm and bite all the way down to the bone. "Fine. If you'll give me a phone number, I'll be happy to talk to her."

"You won't talk to her to her face? What kind of shit is that?"

"I don't know where she is."

She stared at me for a moment and then gave a half shrug. "We could meet you at the Brandywine. By eight, her kids will be down for the night and Hank can babysit."

I didn't think this was the time to correct her notion that a father has to "babysit" his children when half the responsibility is his by definition.

"Where's the Brandywine?"

"On Ming, you moron! Check the phone book."

We exchanged a few more pertinent details, and by the time I closed the salon door behind me, she had taken out a pack of sanitized instruments for the client who'd taken my place. At the desk, I was told the manicure was fifteen bucks and I kicked myself for not paying first and calculating the tip from that.

I was uneasy about meeting at the bar where Ethan's band played on weekends, but Anna assured me the scene wouldn't heat up until well after 10:00. In the meantime, she said the bartenders there knew her and we could talk without being hustled by a bunch of cheesy numbnuts (her words, not mine).

I left the salon and found a gas station, thinking to take advantage of the lull to top off my tank. While the attendant cleaned my windshield and checked the air in my tires, I loaded up on quarters and closed myself in a phone booth located near the ladies' room.

I figured by now, Henry had fetched Rosie from the airport, dropped her off at the tavern, and returned to St. Terry's. I had no idea how to find him. He'd be in range of the ICU, but I doubted they accepted long-distance calls, and the nursing staff certainly wouldn't interrupt their work long enough to send out a runner. I dropped a couple of coins in the slot and dialed his home number. Sure enough, his machine picked up and I left a message indicating that my plans had changed. I told him not to look for me at all that night. Even if my meeting with Ellen ended at 9:00, by some miracle, I didn't want to embark on a two-and-a-half-hour drive. I paid for my gas and then I cruised the downtown area looking for a motel. I passed a McDonald's and circled back. While 5:30 wasn't exactly supper time, I paused long enough to scarf down a Quarter Pounder with Cheese, accessorized with fries and a Coke. I was nearly cross-eyed with carbs and fat grams when I wadded up the wrapping from my QP and tucked it in the french fry box. Once back on Truxtun, already my favorite street in Bakersfield, I spotted a Holiday Inn. It looked like a palace compared to the Thrifty Lodge. Since at that point I'd denounced thrift, the rates seemed entirely reasonable.

As soon as I reached my room, I stripped down and took a

shower, emerging from the bathroom fifteen minutes later with clean hair and a pure heart. I stretched out on the bed, thinking to close my eyes for twenty minutes while I worried about Felix. I had no idea what was going on. All I knew was the Boggarts had attacked him in retaliation for the raid on the camp. I woke with a start an hour and forty-five minutes later and had to scramble to throw on my clothes, retrieve the Mustang from the parking lot, and reach the Brandywine by 8:00.

The club was largely deserted at that hour, as Anna had predicted. I paused inside the door to get my bearings. Two bartenders were setting up, moving bottles and stemware, dumping ice from a plastic bucket into one of the wells. A waitress stood at one end of the bar, leaning on her elbows while she chatted with the two. The music from the jukebox played at a muted level. I picked up a portion of the sound track from *Dirty Dancing*, which I thought might bode well. The raucous thumping numbers would come later when I was gone . . . I hoped.

Since there was no sign of Anna, I sat down at a table in view of the front door. The main room was half dark and smelled of beer. The air-conditioning was turned up in anticipation of the crowd. Behind me and to my left, I could see the raised dais where the band would play. I'd make a point of being gone by the time Ethan arrived. I could hear billiard balls crack into one another smartly, and assumed there was a pool table in the back room.

I finally spotted Anna. She'd changed clothes. For her Friday-night attire, she'd selected a form-fitting red leather miniskirt, a glittering red sequined tank top, and four-inch heels. Her demeanor had undergone a transformation as well. Gone was the industrious shopgirl with her cuticle expertise. She was in hunting mode and dressed for the kill. Her eyes were lined in black and her lipstick was the same hot red shade as her nails. Her hair was still secured by a clip but arranged in a French roll instead of a tuft on top. She'd added long, dangle earrings that bobbed and sparkled as she moved. There was no sign of anyone with her.

When she slid into the seat across the table, she was accompanied by a subtle cloud of perfume. She made eye contact with one of the bartenders who knew what she was drinking without being told. A moment later, a waitress appeared with a martini on a tray. Three olives were submerged in the depths and the glass was frosted with a thin sheath of ice.

Anna glanced at me. "What are you drinking?"

"Chardonnay."

The waitress made a note before she turned and walked away.

Anna picked up her glass. "End of a long week. Excuse me if I don't wait."

"I thought Ellen would be with you."

"In a bit. Hank, too. His stepmom lives six doors down and she said she'd watch the kids. So what's the plan? Staying over?"

"I have a room at the Holiday Inn."

"Good for you," she said.

"Is this where you spend your Friday nights?"

"Saturday nights, too. I date a guy who plays keyboard in Ethan's band."

"Is that how you met?"

"Other way around. I talked Ethan into hiring him when another guy dropped out. Where're you from?" she asked, switching the subject as if the answer had slipped her mind. Ethan had probably unloaded anything and everything I'd said about myself.

"Santa Teresa."

"Nice. How's the club scene?"

"There isn't one."

"Bummer." She took a sip of her martini, holding the glass by the rim. Her nails looked great and I checked mine by way of comparison. With me, she'd used a nail buffer instead of polish, but my nails still had a high shine, as though she'd coated them with clear polish. I remembered her remark about my slender fingers and arranged them on the table in what I hoped was an artful pose.

She moved a cocktail napkin closer and set the stemmed glass in the center with care. I wondered if she already had a buzz on. "Ethan says you're a private detective."

"This is true."

She speared the top of an olive with a long red nail and held it up like a lollipop. "So what's it take to get a job like that?" She closed her lips around the olive and chewed.

"Long apprenticeship. You work for a licensed PI until you've put in the hours you need."

"Which is how many?"

"Six thousand. If you work a forty-hour week, fifty weeks a year, you're talking three years."

"Bet you need a college degree."

"I don't have one. I attended a couple of semesters of community college, but I didn't graduate."

"I never went at all. I'm the baby in the family. By the time it was my turn, Daddy was in prison and the money was gone."

"What money?"

"From the house. Mom sold it when she married Gilbert and moved into his. They've built a new one. Three thousand square feet and a three-car garage. Looks just like Tara, from *Gone with the Wind*."

I said, "What about Ethan? Did he go to college?"

"Nah. He had the chance, but he was busy with his career. You know what I got? A big fat zero. I mean, I get that Daddy left us nothing, but isn't there some way you could borrow against the estate? I'd pay you back for sure."

"At this point, the money isn't mine."

"At least Ellen has a husband," she said, apropos of nothing.

"How many kids?"

Anna held up three fingers. "Same as my brother," she said. "Remember that English writer, Virginia Somebody?" She snapped her fingers. "Woolf."

"I've heard of her, but I've never read her work."

"I was in this book club for a couple months? We read a novel by her about a day in the life of this lady who gives a party. *Mrs. Dalloway*'s the title of it. Like who gives a shit. Anyway, she committed suicide—the writer, not the hostess—and you know how she offed herself?"

"No clue," I said, wondering where she was going with this.

"Loaded her coat pockets with big rocks and walked into a river. Sank to the bottom and she drowned. Over and out. I figure kids are like that. Get pregnant, you might as well fill your pockets with stones."

The waitress appeared with my white wine, which was mercifully bad, a bonus under the circumstances, since I considered this work and I didn't want to drink too much.

Anna caught the waitress's attention. "We'll run a tab."

"Sure thing."

Anna propped her chin on one hand, giving me the big blue eyes. "Is Santa Teresa expensive? I mean, for someone like me who rents?"

"Actually, it is. A lot of people opt for Colgate just north of us or Winterset to the south."

"So how much for a studio, something small like that?"

"Six hundred a month."

"For a studio? You're shittin' me."

I shrugged. "That's the going rate."

"Are you, like, in the snooty part of town?"

"I'm down by the beach."

"Six hundred bucks a month is a lot of money. How much do you make?"

"Enough. Are you thinking about a move?"

"Well, I sure don't want to hang out in a town like this. Spend the rest of my life in Bakersfield? Get serious. I'm twenty-six years old. I got a dead-end job and I bunk in with the dog in my sister's spare room. No bathroom back there, so I have to trek all the way down the hall. Two hundred a month and I help around the house. She makes out big time on that deal, I'm telling you."

"I can see why you'd want a change."

"If I could ever catch a break. You know what gets me? Even if I want to move to, like, Santa Teresa or someplace nice? I don't know a soul and I wouldn't have a place to stay while I was looking for work. First and last month's rent? Forget about it. There's no way."

"Maybe you should save some cash."

"On my salary? Good luck," she said. She laid the big blue eyes on me. "I don't suppose you know anyone who'd put me up."

"Not off hand."

"It'd just be temporary and I could pay *some*. Not a lot, but I'd be happy to pitch in."

"If I hear of anything, I'll let you know."

I was hoping we'd exhausted the subject, but she had simply paused to sip her drink.

"So what time do you head for home?"

"I'm not sure. Depends on when I get up. Early."

"Because I was thinking I could snag a ride. As long as you're going anyway, I could keep you company."

"What about work? Aren't you supposed to give two weeks' notice?"

"I make minimum wage. What do I owe them?"

"Seems like a courtesy," I said.

"Oh, yeah, right. Easy for you to say. So how about it?"

"How about what?"

"Me bumming a ride. Crap you've laid on us, I'm entitled to *something*, don't you think?"

I stared at her. For the life of me, I couldn't think of a response.

18

As I looked away from her, I saw a couple standing in the entrance, where they'd paused to scan the room. "Is that Ellen and Hank?"

Since Anna and I were the only customers in the place, Hank had no trouble spotting us, and he was quick to raise a hand in greeting. Anna waved him over to the table like he might inadvertently sit somewhere else.

He was tall, slim, and clean-shaven with a buzz cut of light brown hair. He held out his hand, saying, "Hank Wagner."

"Kinsey Millhone," I said.

When I shook hands with him, he knew enough to provide me with a firm grip. He wore jeans and an olive green T-shirt that fit like it was tailored to size. He would have been perfect on a billboard for Marine recruits. Beside him, Ellen was petite. Her hair was blond and thick, layered so it hugged her head. Her bangs were cut straight across and fell below her brows, like a knit hat pulled low against the cold. Despite having three kids, she showed no signs of childbearing. She was small and slender and would probably always carry herself like a sixth-grade girl, shoulders slightly rounded, jeans hanging on her hips. Ballet-style flats, no socks. I turned to her and extended my hand. "Kinsey. You're Ellen?"

I got the limp hand. I saw her mouth move, but her smile

was distracted and she wouldn't meet my eyes. At first I thought she was pissed off, but I realized she was so shy she could barely raise her voice. Hank headed for the bar to buy drinks while she sat down and fussed with her purse, arranging the long straps over the top chair rail. It must have felt odd not to have to worry about bottles, diapers, and baby wipes, not to mention plastic baggies filled with crackers.

Hank appeared moments later with a beer for himself and a margarita for her. Ten minutes went by, during which we were engaged in idle chat. Anna and Ellen went off to the ladies' room, leaving me alone with Hank. He was pleasant, though he didn't volunteer anything, perhaps at a loss about where to begin. All he knew about me was I'd snatched five hundred thousand dollars out of the family coffers. Given that I interview people for a living, I was happy to break the ice. "What sort of work do you do?"

"Electrician. My dad owns the company. I have a brother works for him, too."

"Nice," I said, picturing a tool belt and a voltage meter. "How'd you and Ellen meet?"

"She was waiting tables at Wool Growers. Have you been there?"

"I've been in town one day so I haven't seen much."

"It's a Basque restaurant on Nineteenth. You ought to try it if you have a chance. Food's good and there's lots of it. After my mom died, we'd go in for dinner couple of nights a week, my dad and brother and me."

"Ellen waited tables? She seems too shy for a job like that."

"She did fine. Around strangers she gets all tongue-tied and weird. She'll loosen up in a bit. Took me a while to get to know her myself. We dated two years and been married six."

"Anna mentioned she lives with you."

"Yes, ma'am. I actually met Anna first. She used to do my mom's nails when she worked at the other salon. Before Nails Ahoy!"

"How long has she been staying with you?"

"She said it would be three weeks, but it's been like a year and a half."

"That's a bit of an imposition, isn't it?"

"Some. House is small. She's quiet. I'll say that for her. Stays up late and sleeps late, so we have to keep the kids out from underfoot. She's supposed to help out with room and board, but that didn't last long. She paid maybe two months. Since then she hasn't given us a cent. She buys too many clothes to pitch in, I guess."

"Well, that's too bad."

He shrugged. "I let Ellen handle it. She asks about the money and Anna's all like, 'Sure, no problem.' By the time the subject comes up again, another month's gone by."

"Why don't you kick her out?"

"Not my place. Ellen knows she should ask her to leave, but she can't bring herself to do it. She says Anna's family, which I can understand, but still and all."

"Do the three of them get along? Ethan and his sisters?"

He shrugged. "As long as Ellen does what they want. They yap about how she's always her dad's favorite and poor them. It's bull, but they've said it so often she believes it herself. She's afraid to stand up to them because she doesn't want anybody mad at her. I believe one reason her dad took her out of the will along with the other two is he knew if he left her anything, Ethan and Anna would talk her into giving it to them."

"Makes me happy I'm an only child."

"Too bad she's not."

The waitress appeared with a small tray, on which she'd placed two shot glasses of tequila and another margarita that she set in front of Ellen's empty chair. When Anna and Ellen returned from the ladies' room, I watched Ellen toss back the first shot without blinking an eye. She sat down, picked up her margarita, and took two swallows of the icy lime slush before she set it down again. I kept an eye on her. Tequila can make a mean drunk. I've seen grown men break chairs and punch through walls. I didn't think she'd turn combative, but it was clear she liked getting right down to it. Watching her drink was like watching roses bloom by way of time-lapse photography. After one drink, her reticence faded and she seemed to open up. After two drinks, she was outgoing, sunny, and willing to talk about anything. My guess was by drink three, she'd wilt, and by the fourth, she'd fall apart.

Hank and Anna went off to play pool, and I shifted my chair so I could talk to Ellen without raising my voice. The bar was still quiet, though a handful of patrons had begun to wander in. As much as I dreaded introducing the subject of Dace,

I figured I might as well get it over with. I didn't think it was necessary to go back over the fact that I'd never met the man. Ethan and Anna would have hammered that point home.

In a situation like this, I don't like to manipulate unless all else has failed. I don't mind shaping the conversation, but I prefer to create an atmosphere wherein people can speak their minds instead of saying what they think I want to hear. Small talk has the virtue of being indirect, carving out a space within a space where anything can occur. I did feel I should prime the pump. I caught her eye. "Anna says you had a big family powwow. You have any questions?"

"Not especially. You know . . ." The sentence trailed off. I doubted she was going anywhere with the phrase.

"I wanted to make sure you knew about the hearing in December. This is Santa Teresa probate court, and the purpose is to give you the opportunity to challenge the terms of his will if that's what you decide to do."

"I don't care about that. Ethan and Anna might, but I don't." No eye contact, but she'd managed two consecutive sentences, which I took as a good sign.

"I've told both of them it would be smart to consult with an attorney before you make a decision."

She picked up the second shot glass and tossed that down, then flicked me a look. Her eyes were the same blue as Anna's, but not as large. The net effect was that she seemed sincere where I knew now for a fact Anna was blowing smoke up my skirt.

Daintily, she touched at the corners of her mouth. "You know what bothers me? My dad never got to meet my kids. This last time when he showed up? Hank and I were in Yosemite on a camping trip. We got home Sunday night and Daddy'd come and gone, so I only heard about it after. Ethan spit on him. Did he tell you that?"

I shook my head. "I knew there was a tiff."

"He spit right in Daddy's face. He told me about it like he was proud of himself. Anna treated Daddy like shit. She treats all guys like shit, but she got in the habit with him."

"What's all the hostility about?"

"Ethan's protective of Mom and Anna goes along. They both think anything bad in life is Daddy's fault."

"How does your mother feel?"

"She hates his guts. She won't admit it, but it's true."

"Anna says she's remarried. What's your stepdad like?"

"Gilbert built her this big new house. You'd think she'd be happy, but she's not."

"That's too bad. Wonder what the problem is?"

"It didn't work out like she expected. Gilbert has money and she thought he was the answer to her prayers."

"So what went wrong?"

"Nothing in particular. She expected life would be better and it's still the same."

"Had she known him long?"

"I guess. They met at church. After Daddy went to prison, she and Gilbert left that church and joined this other one. She said people were talking behind her back."

"You like him?"

"He's good with my kids."

"What's the rest of it?"

"He's a pantywaist."

I laughed because the word was so unexpected. "What about your dad? What was he like?"

"You know what? He was just the sweetest man. Even when he was drunk, he didn't turn mean or spiteful or anything like that. I know he lost control over his drinking, especially at the end. Maybe I should be mad at him, but I'm not. After he got hurt, he was in a lot of pain. You knew he had a bad fall?"

"Someone mentioned it."

"He should've known better than to drink while he was taking all those pills, but that's what he did. I miss him."

"When did you see him last?"

She downed the last of her margarita, set that glass aside, and picked up the second, from which she took a sip. There was nothing in her manner that suggested she was wasted, but I could feel sorrow rising through her bones. "In jail, before they moved him to Soledad. Mom didn't want us to go. She said he'd be embarrassed. Ethan and Anna didn't really want to see him anyway, but I did. I knew once he left here he'd be too far away, and how would I get there? I'd just turned fifteen and I didn't have my driver's license. I knew I couldn't count on her. She wouldn't even discuss taking me."

"How did you manage it?"

"I looked up his attorney in the yellow pages. I called and

asked if he'd get me in. I don't know how he did it. There must be rules about how old you have to be."

"Attorneys are good at sweet talk."

"This one was. Daddy had the shakes. He was on the wagon because he didn't have much choice. You hear all the time that inmates have access to anything they want . . . alcohol and dope . . . but Daddy kept his distance from the other guys. He was afraid of them. Mom told us at Soledad, he got all the alcohol he wanted. I don't know how he managed it, but that's her claim."

"What'd you talk about?"

"Nothing. Stupid stuff. Whatever you say when you're fifteen and your dad's been convicted of murdering a girl the same age as you. I wasn't allowed to stay long."

"That must have been hard on you. All of it."

"You know what? In my own mind, I was sure he was innocent. Even back then when everybody else thought he was guilty as sin."

"Good you had a chance to see him sober."

"He felt good about himself. He quit on his own . . . no help from anyone. Okay, so maybe he drank at Soledad, but who wouldn't? And then once he got out, he probably had a drink to celebrate."

"If it's any comfort, his friends said he went into a program and at least made a pass at straightening up his act. Maybe he didn't do it soon enough. It's hard to know."

"Was he alone when he died?"

"He was alone when he was found, so I'd say so, yes."

For a moment, she was quiet, and I had no idea what was going on in her head.

Finally, she said, "You may not know this, but Daddy was a big guy. Six feet tall and nearly three hundred pounds before the booze got to him. In jail, it was like he shrank. The whole time I was there, I could see his hands shake. I wish I hadn't seen that. He acted like it was the DTs, but it wasn't. He was scared to death and his nerves were shot."

"Jail's a scary place if you're not used to it."

"Hank told me this story once. He said when he was growing up, the family had this big old Great Dane. He said Rupert was really smart, but he had the soul of a little dog and never understood how big he was. When they'd take him to the vet,

Rupert would just be shaking from head to toe, convinced the vet was going to put him down. All these routine appointments and Rupert would be cowering. Big old hulking dog, quaking in his boots. Hank said it was comical. They tried not to laugh, but they couldn't help themselves because the dog was self-conscious. You know what I mean? Like he was ashamed. Like he knew something was ridiculous and he wasn't sure if it was him. They never could convince him he was safe. Then when he was twelve he got sick and sure enough they took him to the vet and sure enough the vet said he'd have to put him down. Hank said what was so odd was the dog made this crooning sound, like the thing he dreaded all these years was right there and it wasn't so bad. Because instead of laughing at him, everyone was hugging and kissing him, saying how much they loved him, and that's when he closed his eyes." She was silent for a moment. "If I'd been there, I could have held Daddy's hand."

I ended up in the other room watching Anna play pool. With her in her red leather miniskirt and her red sequined tank top, most of the spectators were more interested in her butt than her bank shots. Her opponent might as well have been her twin, a woman roughly the same age and the same build. Her coloring was different. Where Anna was dark, this girl had red hair in a long braid that was wrapped around her head like a crown. She wore a snug black dress, cut midthigh, with a low square neckline. I'd seen her come in, arriving with a guy who looked like a biker: overweight, balding, with a thick handlebar mustache and a tiny gold ring in one ear. The judgment was unfounded and probably inaccurate. I'm sure there are countless slim, handsome bikers rumbling down our highways. For all I knew, this man was a renowned neurosurgeon for whom buxom redheads were a means of relaxation after countless hours in an operating theater. She played with a single-mindedness I admired and eventually Anna went down in defeat. By then, she'd switched from martinis to Champagne, which probably affected her coordination, as she drained each flute like it was apple juice. The beefy guy took her place and she and I ended up on the sidelines, idly looking on while play continued.

"You know that woman?" I asked.

"That's Markie. She's in here all the time."

"What's she do for a living?"

"Not what you think. She's an aesthetician."

"Ah," I said, though I wasn't entirely certain what that meant. Hooker seemed like a better fit, but what did I know?

I'm not sure why I stayed. I was tired and the bad wine was making my head ache. The bar had filled to capacity and the noise level was almost unbearable. Cigarette smoke had tinted the air with a milky pallor. Hank and Ellen joined us just long enough to say their good-byes, not wanting to impose on his stepmother's generosity. Ellen leaned into Hank like the floor was aslant, and the last I saw of her, one leg gave way as though she'd stepped into a hole. Hank had to steady her while she righted herself. Chances were, I wouldn't see either one of them again.

It occurred to me that since I'd be hitting the road first thing the next morning, this might be my last chance to pump Anna for information. Mercifully, she'd dropped the subject of her hitching a ride with me. I had no reason to believe she was reconciled to her father's fiduciary rebuke, but that was another subject she hadn't mentioned in the last hour.

I watched her empty her Champagne flute. A waitress passed and she held up the glass and waggled it to signal the woman that she needed a refill. If her Champagne was on a par with the low-grade Chardonnay I'd been served, she'd be nursing a world-class hangover come morning—not that it was any business of mine. Of the three Dace kids, Ellen was the only one who seemed to care about her dad. The other two I'd written off as stonyhearted.

At least Anna was speaking to me. I had no chance of getting through to Ethan. He was implacable, unwilling to concede even the smallest point in his father's favor. I wondered if my cousins saw me as just as stubborn and unreasonable with regard to family matters. Being righteous and opinionated reduces everything to black and white; much easier to deal with than all the shades in between.

With Ethan, only one small issue remained and I figured I might as well tackle it. I turned to Anna. "Can I ask a question?"

"In exchange for what?"

"Knock it off and be nice."

"Make it quick," she said.

"Ethan made a remark that puzzled me. I don't remember now how he phrased it, but I got the impression he wasn't convinced his father was innocent. Does he think Dace was somehow involved in that young girl's death?"

"How should I know what he thinks? Why don't you ask him?"

"Oh, come on. As pissed off as he is, I can hardly go back and quiz him about an offhand comment."

"I don't want to talk about this stuff."

"Why?"

"Because it's boring."

"Do *you* believe your dad had something to do with that girl's death?"

"What difference does it make?"

"The difference between believing he did or didn't commit a cold-blooded murder. Seems like that would count for something, but apparently it doesn't."

The waitress reappeared with a fresh glass of Champagne on a tray. Anna took it and made an imaginary toast. "Cheers."

I touched the edge of her glass with mine.

Then she said, "You know what your problem is? You think it's all cut and dried. Just because he got out doesn't mean he's innocent."

"That's what Ethan said! Exactly."

"A consensus of opinion at long last," she said.

"Weren't you relieved when he was exonerated? Didn't that mean anything to you? He came here thinking you'd be happy. Ellen says your brother spit in his face and you treated him like shit."

"You are really tedious, you know that?"

"We all have our little failings. Stick to the subject."

"Which is what?"

"Do you think he was guilty?"

"Maybe." She thought about it and shrugged. "Probably."

"He was home. Your mother testified in his behalf."

"She was trying to protect him."

"From what? He didn't do anything."

"Then where was he?"

"Home with her."

Anna shook her head. "He was there early in the evening but then he went out. He didn't come home again until after two. How do we know he wasn't off with Herman Cates?"

"There wasn't any evidence linking him to the crime."

"No evidence was *found*. That doesn't mean it wasn't there."

"Cates recanted. He admitted he lied. Your father had nothing to do with Karen Coffey's death."

"Talk is cheap, as I'm sure you know."

"I don't understand where this is coming from."

"He was convicted by a jury of his peers. She did what she could for him, but it wasn't enough."

"The newspaper account said a neighbor was there."

Anna's gesture was dismissive. "Mrs. Brandle. She's a busybody. Mom says she doesn't know what she's talking about. Anyway, I shouldn't have said anything. Mom did what she had to do. She'd be in trouble if the truth ever came out."

"Were you home that night?"

She shook her head. "Ellen and I were at our cousin's house. She had a pajama party for her birthday and we both went."

"What about Ethan?"

"He was off with the high school marching band at a regional competition. I don't know where the festival was held. I was twelve and I didn't pay attention to those things. I remember he left on the bus with the other kids and he was gone until Sunday afternoon."

"How can you be so convinced your dad was guilty when none of you really know if he was home or not? What's your opinion based on?"

"What she told us, okay?"

"Are you telling me your mother lied about it?"

"Would you just drop it?"

I stared at her. "Your mother perjured herself?"

She looked away from me, her face shutting down. I didn't think I could coax anything more out of her if I tackled the subject head on.

"Let's drop the word 'perjury,'" I said. "The statute of limitations has probably run out on that in any event, so it's not an issue. I'm curious how you found out she was covering for him. It must have been after the trial."

She looked off across the room.

"Giving me the time frame doesn't threaten your mother at all."

"Why do you want to know?"

"I'm just curious. Was it two years later? Five?"

"I don't see why it matters."

I shut my mouth. I could see her weigh the question, looking for the booby trap.

"Is that true what you said about the statute of limitations?"

"Sure. I don't know how long it would run, but it's been, what, fifteen years? Nobody's going to go after her at this late date."

"It was after Dad called Ethan to say he was out. He told Ethan he sued the state and got a settlement and that's what he wanted to come talk to us about."

I said, "Really. She never said anything before then?"

"I can see you're trying to make something of it, but it's all beside the point. The man was a drunk. First, last, and always. We deserved better than we got."

Her eyes strayed to a point behind me and she said, "Crap. Look what the cat dragged in."

19

I turned toward the archway that separated the billiard room from the lounge. Big Rat was making his way through the crowd, beer held aloft as he pardoned and excused himself, moving in our direction. I glanced back and realized that Anna had taken off. I caught a glimpse of her red sequined top as she headed toward the exit and wondered how she'd managed to move so fast. Meanwhile, Big Rat was all smiles. Like Anna, he was in hunting mode, having changed into a black sport coat with a black shirt under it. The silver tie added a jaunty note, like a gangster on the prowl.

He followed my gaze, saying, "Where's she off to?"

"Who knows?"

"Sorry to break up your little tête-à-tête, though I gotta say she didn't look all that happy with you."

"How did you know where I was?"

"I didn't. I swung by the Thrifty Lodge earlier. I thought with you new to Bakersfield, I might show you around, introduce you to the Brandywine if nothing else. Your car wasn't in the motel parking lot, so I was leaving you a note when the desk clerk told me you'd checked out. I remembered you said something about a family emergency, so I figured you'd left town. I'm thinking, what the heck, I might as well give this place a try since I was coming here anyway. I walk in and there you are. How cool is that? Can I buy you a drink?"

"Don't think so, but thanks. It's just about my bedtime."

"One drink. Come on. Are you having Chardonnay or Sauvignon Blanc?" He caught my look and laughed. "You didn't think I knew about white wine, am I right?"

"Ask if they have anything better than the stuff they've been pouring. Failing that, I'll have ice water."

"Be right back."

I watched him edge his way through the crowd, and for a moment I flirted with the idea of pulling a disappearing act. Seemed rude when he'd actually been a help to me, telling me where Anna worked. While I waited for his return, I went over Anna's comments. She hadn't actually admitted her mother had perjured herself at Dace's trial, but that was the conclusion I'd reached and it was one she hadn't refuted. No wonder two of the three kids were so belligerent. In effect, Evelyn had hung her husband out to dry. No alibi in their minds was equivalent to guilty. Perjury is a criminal offense and I couldn't see why she'd admit to it unless it was true. She'd be opening herself to prosecution unless the statute of limitations had run out, which I didn't have a clue about despite my reassurances to Anna. In point of fact, even if she'd lied, it wouldn't have a bearing on the legalities of the situation. All three principals were dead—Herman Cates; his accomplice; and Terrence Dace, the man he'd falsely accused. Dace's conviction had been overturned, but Evelyn's sly admission carried more weight in the eyes of his children than the court's reversal. The claim bothered me. The timing bothered me as well. Why would she suddenly 'fess up? That's what I couldn't understand. She hadn't flat-out accused him of anything. She'd simply opened a door, fanning a small ember of suspicion in the minds of his kids. At this late date, I doubted there was any way to determine the truth.

Above the background noise, which was gradually subsiding, I heard a smattering of applause and then a male vocalist. I thought it was the jukebox, but Big Rat reappeared at that moment and handed me a fresh glass of white wine. "There's Ethan."

"You're kidding me."

I moved to the doorway and checked the raised dais where

the band must have been setting up while the pool match was going on. Ethan sat on a wooden stool in a pool of light, head bent over his guitar. A hush settled and then he began to sing. He wore the same outfit I'd seen him in at home—jeans, desert boots, a long-sleeve white T-shirt with a placket down the front that he'd unbuttoned partway. He looked utterly unlike the man I'd talked to earlier. His vocalizing transformed him from an ordinary mortal to someone from another realm. I blinked, trying to reconcile this image with the man I'd seen only hours before. His voice was mellow; his manner, relaxed. What struck me was the soul shining through his song. Maybe it was technique or maybe he had a natural sense of showmanship. He seemed oblivious, so absorbed in the music he might as well have been alone in the room.

I checked the crowd and saw the same rapt attention. He seemed totally out of place in such a common setting and, at the same time, he seemed completely at home. It dawned on me that these people were here for him. The lounge was packed with avid fans, loyal followers who came specifically to hear him perform. I'd seen this before, this otherworldliness, and it had taken me years to sort the truth from the illusion.

My second husband, Daniel Wade, was a musician. The first time I saw him, he was playing piano in a bar in downtown Santa Teresa. It was late. The air was smoky in the same way it was smoky here. I don't even remember now why I was there or whether I was in the company of someone else. Daniel, with his cloud of curly golden hair, leaned over the keys like an alchemist. He played like an angel. His talent was magic, the philosopher's stone that promised to turn base metal into gold. I saw him through a haze of longing. I fell in love, not with the man, but with a mirage. Watching him play, I'd assumed he was as remarkable a person as his music implied. I wanted to believe. I projected onto him qualities he didn't possess, qualities that only *appeared* to emanate from somewhere deep inside. I don't know that he was aware of the effect he had, so I can't accuse him of trickery or deception. He was accustomed to admiration and it may not have occurred to him that his skill obscured the reality of who he was. I thought I was seeing the truth about Daniel when it was really only a reflection cast up along the wall.

And now, here was Ethan Dace, whose metamorphosis had changed my very perception of him. There was something compelling in his voice; sorrow and wisdom and hope. What was he doing in Bakersfield? I couldn't imagine him rising to fame and fortune in so unlikely a place, but clearly no one in a position to help had recognized his talent and offered him a break.

Big Rat materialized at my side, saying, "Dude can sing. The guy's like a rock star. I'm impressed."

"Me, too."

"Where the hell's this coming from? He's a douche bag."

"Apparently, he's not. Or maybe you can be a douche bag and talented at the same time."

I stayed for the entire set. I'd expected the band to be amateurish: loud and discordant, running off covers of popular songs done better by the recording artist. Instead, they played what I had to guess were original numbers with blues and jazz undertones. At some point, Big Rat peeled off, and 11:00 came and went and I realized this was way too late for me. The waitress passed and I caught her attention, making the universal gesture for the check.

She nodded and proceeded to the bar. The band took a break and the temporary vacuum was suddenly filled with loud talk and boisterous laughter. Instead of feeling magical, it was only a bar again; badly lighted and smelling rank. The waitress returned and handed me a bifold of leather with a cash register slip hanging out like a tongue. I moved to the nearest table where the light was better. I opened the folder and looked at the list of charges that ran all the way down the page. The total was $346.75.

"Wait, wait. This isn't mine. I had two glasses of wine."

"Anna said you were running a tab."

"Me?"

"Wasn't that your party?"

"We came in together, but I wouldn't call it my 'party.'"

"Is now. Everybody else is gone."

I looked at the check again. "This has to be a mistake."

"Nope. Don't think so." She peered over my shoulder, using her pen to refer to each item in turn. "Two beers. Those were Hank's. He's a cute guy, isn't he? Ellen had three margaritas and two shots of tequila."

"I counted two margaritas."

"Are you going to argue with me over every little thing? She ordered the third one while you were in the other room, watching Anna play pool. Now see here? Anna ordered two martinis and this is where she switched to Champagne."

"For two hundred and ninety bucks? How many glasses did she drink?"

"She ordered a bottle. She likes Dom Pérignon. She wanted the '82, but I talked her out of it."

"I can't believe they did this to me."

"Guess you don't know them very well. I could have told you straight off if you'd asked me nice."

I fumbled in my shoulder bag and came up with my wallet and took out my American Express card.

"We don't take AmEx. Visa or MasterCard."

I pulled out a second card, this one Visa.

She studied it briefly. "You have a photo ID?"

I experienced the miracle of self-control as I opened my wallet and held it up so my driver's license was clearly visible.

"No offense. Boss requires us to check. I'll be right back."

"You are too kind," I said, but she was already heading for the bar, where I saw her pass the check and my credit card to the closest bartender. Moments later, she returned with a copy of the cash register receipt and the charge slip, complete with carbons, bearing the numbers she'd swiped. She held out the pen.

For a moment, I struggled, trying to determine the amount of a tip. It wasn't like she'd served us food.

"The pay here is really crummy," she reported conversationally. "We pool our tips and split with the bartenders, which doesn't leave much. Most of us can barely make ends meet. And I've got two kids."

I ran the tip up another five percent, making it an even ten. It wasn't until I was going out the door that I chanced to look back. In the far room, the redhead Anna had been playing pool with was leaning up against the wall and Ethan was using his index finger to trace a line along the low square of her dress. By some uncanny intuition, he glanced in my direction and saw that I was watching him. I made my exit before he had a chance to react.

• • •

At 2:35 A.M., I sat straight up in bed. I pushed the covers back and padded across the room to the desk chair where I'd flung my shoulder bag. As is true in so many motel rooms, the glaring lights from the parking lot threw all the surfaces into high relief. I picked up my bag and dug into one of the outside pockets, feeling for my index cards. I removed the rubber band and sorted through as though preparing for a magic trick. Pick a card, any card. I flicked on the desk lamp, pulled out the chair, and settled uneasily into the leather upholstered seat, which was chilly from the air-conditioning. While I'm frugal in my use of California water, I keep a motel room at arctic temperatures. The Holiday Inn had graciously accorded me an extra blanket that I'd pulled down from the closet shelf in its clear plastic bag.

I'd gone to sleep in my usual T-shirt and underwear, blanket and spread pulled up almost over my head. Now I was aware of the cold. I returned to the bed, propped two fat pillows against the headboard, and slipped under the covers again. In checking the 1942 Polk, I'd found two Dace families: Sterling and Clara, who lived at 4619 Paradise Road; and Randall J. and Glenda, living at 745 Daisy Lane. In the 1972 Polk, I'd found R. Terrence and Evelyn, also at 745 Daisy Lane, and I'd speculated that the couple had moved into his parents' house at some point during the intervening years. I'd also noted the names and addresses of neighbors on either side. The Pilchers, who'd lived next door to Terrence and Evelyn Dace in 1972, had since disappeared. On the other side, at 743, Lorelei Brandle was no longer in evidence, but there was an L. Brandle on Ralston. I looked up the name for the second time in the current phone book and this time I made a note of the phone number. I turned off the light and burrowed under the covers.

I woke again at 6:00, disoriented. Still in Bakersfield. Just my luck. I'd have given anything to have been at home in my own bed. I lay there in a funk. Since I didn't intend to jog, I had time to go through my mental checklist again. By and large, I'd taken care of business. The only remaining question had nothing to do with my responsibilities as executor of the estate. I wanted to know what Evelyn Dace was up to. A man's honor was at stake and that troubled me. I realized I'd been hoping for a way to rehabilitate Dace's reputation in the eyes of his kids, but two of the three were unreceptive and I hadn't been able to budge them. While, technically, this was unpaid work, that half a million dollars did suggest a different point of view. In some respects, this was the highest-paid job I'd ever undertaken and I decided I might as well satisfy myself in the bargain.

I ate breakfast in the hotel coffee shop, opting for orange juice, cold cereal, buttered rye toast, and three cups of coffee. Once in my room again, I checked my notes. It was by then 8:35, which seemed early but not indecent for a Saturday-morning call. I picked up the handset and dialed an outside line, then punched in the phone number for the L. Brandle listed on Ralston Street. I was about equally torn between wanting to succeed and wanting to fail. Chances were I was on the wrong track and this L. Brandle was in no way related to the Brandle who'd lived next door to Terrence and Evelyn Dace. If that were the case, my job in Bakersfield was done and I could go home.

The number rang three times and then a woman picked up. "Hello?"

"Oh, hi. May I speak to Mrs. Brandle?"

There was a moment of quiet and I couldn't help but burble on as though adding information would change the facts. "I'm calling because I'm trying to locate a Lorelei Brandle, who lived on Daisy Lane in the early seventies."

The woman said, "She can't come to the phone right now. May I ask who's calling?"

"Really? This *is* the Lorelei Brandle who lived next door to Evelyn and Terrence Dace?"

"She doesn't go by the name Lorelei. She's been 'Lolly' since the age of two."

"Sorry."

"She moved here from Daisy Lane six years ago. Evelyn Dace remarried. I believe she's still in Bakersfield, but I have no idea where."

"Would there be any way I might speak with Lolly?"

There was a pause. "I'm sorry. I don't believe I caught your name."

"Kinsey Millhone. Terrence Dace died this past week. He's the—"

"I know who Terrence is, dear. Everyone in town knows him. If you don't mind my asking, what's this have to do with Lolly?"

"It gets complicated, but basically I'm distantly related to Mr. Dace and I've been talking with some of the surviving family members. A question has come up about his where-abouts the night Karen Coffey was kidnapped and I thought Lorelei . . . Lolly . . . might help us out."

"Just one moment."

I heard her clunk the handset down on a tabletop. There was a long interval of silence. Eventually she picked up again.

"I just went to check on her. She hasn't been well."

"I'm sorry to hear that. I drove up from Santa Teresa yes-terday and I should head back before long. I was hoping to speak to her sometime soon. Are you her caregiver?"

"I'm her cousin, Alice."

"I'll keep my visit as brief as possible. I only need a few minutes of her time."

"Ordinarily I wouldn't do this, Miss . . ."

"Millhone."

She lowered her voice. "No one in the family's been to visit Lolly in the past five years. She's eighty-six years old and she's depressed. Frankly, I think a visit would lift her spirits regard-less of the subject."

"Was that who you were talking to just now?"

"Yes, it was. She seems to like the idea or I wouldn't have permitted you to pursue the subject. What time were you thinking?"

"Shortly. Actually, right now."

Her silence made me think she was going to turn me down, but she said, "I suppose that would do."

"Thanks. I really appreciate your help. I'm at the Holiday Inn near the Convention Center downtown. I'm looking at a Ralston Street address, but I don't know where that is."

"We're on the east side of the Union Cemetery. Ralston runs two blocks between South Owens Street and MLK Bou-levard."

"Uh, could you give me directions?"

"Of course. We're only ten blocks away."

I made a note of her instructions, not even bothering to

check the map because it wasn't that complicated. I returned the handset to its cradle and the phone rang again. "Hello?"

A woman said, "May I speak to Kinsey Millhone?"

"This is she."

"This is Mamie. Ethan's wife. I'm glad I caught you. I was afraid you'd be gone by now. How are you doing?"

"I'm fine. How about yourself?"

"I'm well," she said.

There was half a beat of quiet, which I didn't want to fill with chat.

Smoothly, she said, "I know you and Ethan had a long talk yesterday and we're confused about where you come into the picture. You told him Terrence was your favorite uncle, but Evelyn says he didn't have any nieces or nephews."

"Ethan misunderstood. My father was *Terrence's* favorite uncle. I have photographs of the two of them taken years ago."

"Your father," she said blankly.

"Randy Millhone. His mother—my paternal grandmother—was Rebecca Dace."

"I can't say that means much."

"My father was born in Bakersfield. His family and the Daces were close once upon a time. Does the name Millhone ring a bell?"

"I'd have to ask Evelyn. It's not a name anyone's mentioned to me. You said something about photographs, but I'm not sure what those would tell us. I suppose Evelyn could take a look and see if she recognizes anyone."

"Unfortunately, the photos are still in Terrence's safe deposit box, which I won't have access to until after the probate hearing. I wish I could be more specific about the family connections."

"So do I," she said. "I mean, I'm not saying there's anything fishy going on, but it would be helpful if you had proof of your identity. Otherwise, it seems odd you show up out of a clear blue sky and announce you're inheriting. Can you document any of this?"

"I gave Ethan a copy of his father's will."

"I'm talking about you. How do we know you're who you say you are?"

"I can show you my driver's license and a photostat of my

private investigator's license. Turn the question around and tell me how you'd prove who you are. It's easier said than done."

"I suppose."

"Is there something in particular that bothers you or just the situation in general?"

"A little bit of both. I've gone over the papers you left and I'm confused about a number of things. We think we should get together today since this might be our only chance."

I paused, instantly resistant as I sensed my trip home drifting further away. The last thing in the world I wanted to do was meet Ethan's code-enforcer wife, but I thought I should at least *pretend* to cooperate. "I'm willing to meet you, but how will that help? I suggested Ethan get legal counsel. That way his attorney and mine could handle any questions that arise. I don't want to turn this into a personal argument with him."

"When I said 'we,' I wasn't talking about him. I was referring to myself."

"Ah."

"A conversation might help us sort ourselves out."

"Look, I'll be happy to explain how I got roped into this. What I don't want to discuss are the actual terms of the will."

"Oh? And why is that?"

"Because those are legal issues. I'm not a lawyer and as far as I know, you're not either."

"No, I'm not," she said. "So what do you suggest? I have this morning open."

I went through a quick debate. As far as I knew, she had no legal standing in the matter and I was reluctant to subject myself to another interrogation. At the same time, she seemed to wield considerable influence in the family, which meant that winning her over might defuse the situation. I did think it was preferable to meet face-to-face. "I'm due back in Santa Teresa midafternoon," I said.

"If we're going to meet, it might be smart to have Evelyn on hand. She knows the family history better than either one of us," Mamie said.

"I don't want to complicate matters."

"It would be a way to avoid going through this again with her if it comes to that. With Evelyn present, she could ask questions that might not occur to me. I'm sure she'd appreciate the opportunity to express her views."

"You think she can be objective about this?"

"Probably not, but the two of us can't either, so what's the difference?"

I'll admit I was curious about Dace's ex-wife, whose unseen presence had hovered in the background since I'd first come across her name in the divorce decree and the quitclaim in his safe deposit box. "All right. I suppose that makes sense. I have an appointment coming up, but it shouldn't take long. Can we make it ten o'clock?"

"That should work."

"Fine. I'll meet you in the lobby and we can take it from there."

"Wonderful," she said.

On impulse, I said, "I saw Ethan at the Brandywine last night."

She said, "Really."

I was certain someone had already told her as much.

"It was Anna's idea," I said. "She brought Ellen and Hank along so I'd have a chance to meet them as well. I was actually there long enough to hear Ethan play. He's very talented."

"You sound surprised."

"I guess I am. Hard to believe he hasn't come to the attention of someone in the music business."

"I'm sure he'd love nothing more, except now he's got three little kids and where would they be if his career took off?"

I experienced a quick flash of Binky gnawing on her doorknob. If Ethan left, her baby heart would break. "That would be very tough."

"Yes, it would. My opinion, if he was so hell-bent on success, he should have pursued it before he made babies."

"Probably so."

Mamie and I went through polite fare-thee-wells. I hung up, wishing I hadn't agreed to meet. It wasn't a conversation I was looking forward to. My curiosity about the ex–Mrs. Dace was the only draw.

On my way to Ralston Street, I took a ten-minute detour, stopping at a Walgreens drugstore just long enough to buy a Whitman's Sampler, which I didn't think they were even making anymore. These were the Russell Stover deluxe candies . . .

coconut, chocolate-covered cherries, nougats . . . all the kinds I hate. The box had a bird and a basket of flowers on the front that looked like it had been stitched in needlepoint. I could have purchased the sugarfree candy, but why bother? For $6.99, I also picked up a bouquet of daisies, Alstroemeria, and some fluffy green stuff, all wrapped in cellophane.

I got back in the car and rolled down the windows. This was mid-October and the day was sunny. The humidity must have been low because while the temperature posted on the bank marquee I'd passed said it was eighty-five degrees, the air had an autumn feel to it, as though scented with the hint of burning leaves. There was little evidence that the trees were changing colors. From the flora and fauna I could see, the evergreens outnumbered deciduous species by three to one. Beyond a variety of palms, I recognized manzanita, junipers, California bay, and the coast live oak.

The house on Ralston was plain: a dark green one-story box with a modest yard, enclosed by a picket fence. The place would have benefited from the services of a handyman. The front gate sagged to the point where I had to lift it off the sidewalk before it would swing open. The wooden porch steps needed a coat of paint. I wasn't sure what to expect of Cousin Alice. She'd sounded like a young woman, but telephone voices can be deceptive. I rang the bell. A flat metal mailbox was affixed to the wall near the front door. The printed calling card visible in a small slot read ALICE HILDRETH FIX.

The woman who came to the door appeared to be in her seventies. I suspected she was wearing a wig because her blond hair was too thick and glossy to be her own. She wore it in what in my day was referred to as a flip: shoulder length, with the ends turned up perkily. She wore a yellow crewneck sweater and a gray tweed skirt, knee-high hose, and penny loafers. I wouldn't have guessed about the knee-highs, except that she'd rolled both down around her ankles to ease her circulation.

"Hi, I'm Kinsey," I said. "And you're Alice?"

She opened the storm door. "I am. Lolly's mother and mine were sisters. Are those for her?"

"Oh, sorry," I said, handing her the bouquet. I held out the candy box. "These are for her as well."

She took both, saying, "Very nice. Won't you come in?"

"Thanks. I really appreciate your letting me stop by."

"Lolly's in the backyard," she said. "I'll introduce you, but I should warn you, ten minutes from now she won't remember who you are. She suffers dementia and she's easily confused."

I felt my heart sink, wishing she'd mentioned this on the phone. My optimism faded as I followed her through the house. I'd be asking Lolly about events that occurred some sixteen years before. It hadn't seemed like such a stretch when I came up with the plan. Now I wondered if there was any point.

20

PETE WOLINSKY

July 1988, Three Months Earlier

On Saturday, Pete drove over to Santa Teresa Hospital and had a long chat with the medical librarians, doing what he thought of as due diligence. He explained that he was a freelance journalist, working on an article about Glucotace. He said another writer had passed along preliminary notes, but Pete couldn't make heads nor tails of his handwriting, so he wasn't sure how the term was used, only that he was expected to cover the subject, which would run as a two-part series.

These two women presided over thousands of medical texts and professional journals. They also had computer resources Pete couldn't have accessed for love or money. Apparently, no one ever asked for assistance because they were soon falling all over themselves, getting him what he needed. They sat him down at a table and provided him with medical literature from which he made copious notes. He wasn't entirely clear on some of the language or the medical terms—doctors had to fancy everything up with Latin—but the gist of it began to sink in as he read. Turned out Glucotace was an oral hypoglycemic medication, manufactured by a Swiss company called Paxton-Pfeiffer. The drug had been pulled off the market in 1969, after reports of users suffering serious and sometimes fatal side effects, among them blurred vision, anemia and other blood disorders, headaches, hepatic porphyria, stomach pain, nerve damage caused by excessive levels of porphyrin in the liver, hepatitis, hives, itching, skin rash, and skin eruptions. Pete shook his head. Last thing in the world a diabetic needed was another load of grief.

He moved on. Two recent abstracts suggested that the drug was going into Phase II clinical trials for off-label use in combination with certain first-generation sulphonylureas in the treatment of alcohol and nicotine addiction. One of the librarians returned to his table with additional information, providing him with an abstract of a proposal submitted to the National Institute of Alcohol Abuse and Alcoholism, which was part of the NIH, the National Institutes of Health. The randomized, double-blind study was intended to develop behavioral and drug-relapse prevention for individuals dependent on both nicotine and alcohol using a combination of Acamprosate, Naltrexone, and Glucotace.

According to the abstract: "The aim of this study is to compare the effect of cognitive therapy in adjunct of three different pharmacotherapies."

The sponsor was Paxton-Pfeiffer in collaboration with the Santa Teresa Research Institute at the University of California Santa Teresa. The start date, September 1987. Estimated study completion date, September 1989. Estimated enrollment, 40. "This study is currently recruiting participants," it said. Principal investigator: Linton Reed, M.D., Ph.D. Pete made a note of the eleven-digit clinical-trials government identifier number and then sat and thought about what he'd learned. The subject was still perplexing, but no longer opaque.

When he went back to the main desk and inquired about a Dr. Stupak, first name unknown, they rustled up a Viktor Stupak in an AMA publication that listed his graduation from medical school, his subsequent internship and residency, and various appointments, leading up to his current position as chief of Surgical Oncology, Arkansas Christian Cancer Center, which was affiliated with Arkansas Christian College in Conway, Arkansas.

Out of curiosity, he had them track down a photograph and bio of Linton Reed, which allowed him to trace his educational history as well. Reed had done his undergraduate work at Florida State. He remembered now that Willard had mentioned Florida State as the place where Linton and Mary Lee had met. After Florida State, Reed had been accepted at Duke, where he picked up his Ph.D. and M.D. in successive years. He then completed an internship and began his surgical residency at the very Arkansas Christian Cancer Center where Viktor Stupak, M.D., was currently ensconced. Linton Reed had been there a scant six months. After an unexplained gap, his career history picked up again when he was awarded a two-year fellowship by the National Science Foundation. Pete considered putting a call through to Dr. Stupak but didn't think he'd have much luck. These medical types could be a close-mouthed lot.

Pete paid for copies of the documents he thought relevant and put them into a file folder. When he returned to his car, he put the folder into one of the boxes he was taking home. First chance he had, he'd consolidate all the paperwork, organizing the files for easy access. Pete spent way too much time hunting down documents he should have had at his fingertips.

First thing Monday morning, Pete called the UCST Health Sciences Building. He'd picked up the number from Willard, who was blissfully ignorant of what was going on behind the scenes. Dr. Linton Reed wasn't important enough to have a secretary of his own. The gal Pete talked to was the gatekeeper for the whole medical facility and took her job much too seriously. She mentioned her name in a clipped fashion when she picked up his call, but Pete missed it. After that, she did everything possible to thwart and obstruct his desire for a meeting. First she claimed Dr. Reed was in his clinic office only two days a week, on Tuesdays and Thursdays. When Pete pressed for an appointment the next day, she wanted to know the nature of his business, suggesting it might be something she could help him with, thus saving the oh-so-important Dr. Linton Reed the bother of having to deal with the likes of him.

"This is strictly personal," Pete said.

"Personal" was a word that apparently had no place in this woman's vocabulary.

She said, "I understand you may feel that way, but the fact remains that Dr. Reed is tied up this week. The next possible appointment is on Thursday, the twenty-eighth."

"Let me tell you something, Miss . . . What was your name again?"

"Greta Sobel."

"What you should be aware of, Miss Sobel, is that my proposal to Dr. Reed is not only personal, it's date sensitive. He's not going to appreciate your making my life difficult. All I need is twenty minutes of his time, so you can either work me in tomorrow or he's going to know how uncooperative you've been."

"There's no reason to take that tone."

"Apparently there is, given your attitude."

"If you'll give me your name and number, I'll check with Dr. Reed and get back to you."

"How about you figure it out right now or I'll come over there myself and tell him what's going on."

Silence. "Just one moment."

She put him on hold. He suspected she was giving herself a little breathing room to get her temper under control. She clicked back in. "One o'clock."

He said, "Thank you," but she'd hung up on him by then.

Tuesday morning, he cruised by his office, circling the block once. He spotted his landlady's car parked in the adjacent lot and continued on his way. He drove down to the beach, following Cabana Boulevard as far as the bird refuge. He had ways to make good use of his time. Before he got out of the car, he adjusted his scarf to keep the chill off his neck. He opened his trunk and unlocked the briefcase where he kept his Glock, which he slid into the pocket of his sport coat. He extracted his gun-cleaning kit from behind the boxes of books and old files that he was gradually moving from his office to his garage at home. In the event his landlady served an eviction notice, he'd be able to clear the premises in short order.

He carried the kit and yesterday's newspaper to a picnic table, where he spread the first section across the crude wood surface. He set out a tin of CLP, his cleaning rags, Q-tips, a barrel brush, a cleaning rod, and an old toothbrush and then removed the Smith & Wesson Escort from his shoulder holster and Glock 17 from his coat pocket.

He worked on the Escort first, pulling the slide back to assure himself the chamber was empty. He popped out the magazine, sighted down the barrel, aimed, and dry-fired at one of the ducks, which took no interest in him whatever. He field-stripped the gun, removing the recoil spring and the barrel from the frame. He wiped down the parts, eliminating any excess lubrication, then took a dry brush and cleaned all the surfaces. He'd done it so many times, he probably could have done it by feel. His mind wandered first to Dr. Reed; then to Willard; and then to his own wife, Ruthie, the love of his life. For their fortieth anniversary, coming up the following year, he wanted to surprise her with a river cruise, which was why he'd picked up the brochure from the travel agent. This was something she'd always wanted to do. He liked the idea himself, gliding down a river in Germany. He imagined the quiet, the sumpy smell of inland waterways, excursions to nearby points of interest. He pictured villages, stretches of empty countryside, the occasional larger town where they might venture out to see the sights. His hope was to do it in style— maybe not first class, which they couldn't afford, but not on the cheap by a long shot.

He set the Escort aside and went to work on the Glock.

With his office rent in arrears, he knew the money would be better spent catching up, but he was already so far behind he couldn't see the point. He'd met Ruthie when she was a month shy of nursing school, an accelerated course she'd enrolled in after she got her AA degree. He'd finished his own education with no clear sense of what he wanted to do with his life. He'd tried a little bit of everything before he got a job doing repos for a small collection agency. Eventually, he apprenticed as a private investigator and for a while, he felt he was where he belonged. Things hadn't quite panned out as he'd hoped. Lately, the work had dried up almost completely, leaving him scrambling to survive.

He looked up. One of the on-ramp bums was standing on the path watching him. This was a big fellow he'd seen countless times; red baseball cap, red flannel shirt, jeans, and what looked like new boots tough enough to kick a man to death. He knew people who resented the homeless and wanted them chased off the grassy areas where they loitered from day to day. His policy was live and let live.

Pete said, "Can I help you, son?"

Fellow put his hands in his pockets. He wasn't bad-looking, but he carried himself with the menacing posture of a thug. Pete gave him credit for persistence. He himself wouldn't be able to tolerate a life of begging on off-ramps, or anywhere else for that matter.

"My dad had a gun looked like that."

"Lot of semiautomatics look similar."

"What's yours?"

"Glock 17."

"Is it new?"

"New to me. The 17 came out in 1982. I didn't acquire this one until recently."

"How much does a gun like that cost?"

It crossed Pete's mind that the fellow's interest might be more than idle. With a gun in his possession, other methods of picking up pay would certainly be available.

Pete said, "More money than I got now, I can tell you that for a fact. Important thing is to handle a weapon like this with the respect it deserves. Safety comes first."

"You ever kill anyone?"

"I have not. How about yourself?"

"Not me, but my dad was in the army and he killed a bunch. Messed with his head."

"I'd imagine so."

Pete let the conversation lapse. After a minute, he looked up. "Anything else on your mind?"

He met the panhandler's gaze and the fellow shook his head in the negative, saying, "Take care."

"You, too."

The bum backed up a few steps and then moved off, heading toward the scrub. Pete had heard there was a hobo camp up there somewhere, but he'd never seen it himself.

When he finished cleaning and reassembling the Glock, he tidied up his rags and brushes, crumpling the newsprint into a wad that he tossed into the public trash container. He holstered his pocket pistol and returned his cleaning kit to the trunk. He pulled out a bag of birdseed and took a seat on the wooden bench. He wasn't crazy about the ducks. Ducks were stupid and the geese could turn hostile if you didn't watch your step, not that he begrudged any of them their place in the greater scheme of things. To his way of thinking, pigeons were the perfect birds; each intricately marked, gray and white with touches of iridescence.

The minute he opened his bag of seed, a high-pitched shriek would cut the air, a shrill announcement to any bird within range that there were treats in store. He liked that about birds, their willingness to share. He broadcast seeds in the area around him. He left a trail of seeds across the shoulders of his sport coat. The birds descended in a cloud, their wings batting and fluttering. They settled on him as though he were a tree, talons digging into the sleeves of his coat. They clustered on his lap, some flapping off and then on again. They ate from his outstretched hand. They pecked at the seeds he sprinkled in his hair. If children passed while the birds were feeding, they'd stare at Pete transfixed, recognizing the special magic known only to persons of a certain type. To the children, he must look like a scarecrow; tall and rangy and lean, crooked teeth, crooked smile, and fingers as long as sticks. He attracted birds from across the lagoon as though the wind had blown them into a darkened spiral, whirling around his head before they alighted.

Fondly, he shooed them away, smiling to himself. He folded over the neck of the bag of birdseed and secured it with a rubber band. He glanced at his watch. The lunch hour was coming up and he'd promised Ruthie he'd be home. She'd been doing private-duty nursing, working as needed, which seemed to be all the time, but she was off today.

Home again in the kitchen, he felt at peace. She made grilled cheese sandwiches and tomato soup. He sat down at the kitchen table, watching her flip the two sandwiches until both sides were brown. She was unusually quiet as she ladled soup into two bowls, removed the sandwiches to a cutting board, and sliced them on the diagonal before she slid them onto the plates. It wasn't until she sat down that she glanced at him with what he thought was a touch of guilt.

She was looking worn. Her complexion was still clear, but her coloring had faded and a series of fine lines now radiated from the outer corners of her eyes. Her jawline had softened and now looked more touchable. Her beautiful long blond-gray hair was pulled back into a knot at the nape of her neck.

"You had a phone call," she said. "A man named Barnaby from Ajax Financial Recovery."

"Collection agency," Pete said. "The guy's been bugging me for weeks. I can't think why he'd call here when I just sent off a check. I told him it was in the mail, but he wouldn't back off. He's the kind of fellow can't admit he made a mistake."

"He said the account had been turned over to him because payment was overdue by six months. With late fees and charges, the total's six hundred dollars."

"Well, then it's lucky I took care of it before they jacked up the total again. Ask me, it's a hell of a way to earn a living, harassing folks over something like that."

She studied his face carefully. "If you had problems you'd let me know, wouldn't you?"

"Absolutely, I would. Happily, that's not the case. In fact, business is looking up. I've got an appointment at one o'clock that I think might net me a handsome chunk of change."

"But you know you can tell me, right? If there's a problem?"

"When have I not? That was the deal we made, how many years ago? Coming up on forty by my count." He stretched out his hand on the table and she laced her fingers into his. "Speaking of which, I've got a surprise. I wasn't going to tell you, but it occurred to me I better give you fair warning."

He removed the brochure from his jacket pocket and placed it on the table, elaborating as he went. He showed her the route along the Danube, pointing out some of the stops on the itinerary: Budapest, Vienna, Passau. He was honest about not having the entire sum set aside, but he was getting there, he said. She didn't seem as excited as he'd hoped, but the idea might take some getting used to. They'd never traveled abroad. Europe was just a rumor as far as they were concerned. They had passports, which they were careful to keep renewed, but they'd never had occasion to use them. Her spirits seemed to pick up as he told her about the accommodations. He had ways of making it seem real; not an extravagance but something they deserved after forty years of being happily married and careful about the money they spent. They finished lunch. He cleared the table and made quick work of the dishes. By the time he left for his run to Colgate, she was her usual sunny self again and he felt better. No point in being depressed when there was so much to look forward to.

• • •

The meeting with Linton Reed started off on a bad note. Pete reached the university in ample time, but he was forced to drive around the campus in search of the Health Sciences Building, which he hadn't spotted on the map he'd picked up at the campus information center. He pulled a ticket from the dispenser and circled the lot until he found a parking space. On reaching the clinic's administrative offices, he made a point of asking to have his parking ticket validated. In the event the conversation didn't go well, he didn't want to get stuck paying the campus parking fees. The department secretary didn't approve of his being there, but she didn't have the nerve to refuse to validate his ticket. She pasted three stickers to the back. He took a sly satisfaction from her dislike of him, which she could barely conceal.

To retaliate, Pete was made to wait thirty-five minutes before he was escorted down the hall and allowed into His Holy Presence. The good doctor was handsome: smooth cheeks, clear blue eyes, fleshy lips, and a nose with a slight upward tilt to it. His was the kind of face most would trust. Dr. Reed's first glimpse of Pete had generated a nearly imperceptible flicker of surprise in the good doctor's eyes. Pete caught it. He always caught that look.

Linton Reed observed him with clinical detachment and Pete could see his mental processes at work. Dr. Reed had doubtless read about Pete's disorder in medical texts, but this might have been the first real live instance he'd come across. Naturally, that would make Pete a curiosity. Dr. Reed said, "Which of your parents suffered from Marfan syndrome?"

"My father," Pete said. He felt an instant dislike for the young man, who apparently thought his being a doctor entitled him to probe Pete's genetic history when the two had only just been introduced. Marfan was an autosomal dominant condition, which meant that a defective gene from only one parent was needed to pass the disease on. It also meant that each child of an affected parent has a fifty-fifty chance of inheriting the defective gene. It annoyed Pete that in his "doctor" role, Linton Reed had adopted a deeper tone of voice. This was meant to underscore his authority, conveying the rights vested in him as a medical wizard entitled to pry into everybody else's private business.

The good doctor probably hoped to open up a whole discussion of Pete's condition, but Pete had something else on his mind. Linton Reed was a charmer and fully accustomed to exercising his personal magnetism. He was a sheepdog at heart. He looked harmless, but he couldn't resist herding his fellow man. He'd been born with an unerring instinct for bending others to his will. Pete had had a dog like that once, a border collie named Shep who just couldn't help himself. Take a walk in the woods with friends and Shep would dash ahead and behind, keeping everyone together whether they wanted that or not. The urge was inbred and the implication was always that the dog knew better than you did.

Pete loathed the man sitting across the desk from him. He remembered prigs like him in grade school, smart, but soft from sitting on their big fat superior white asses while kids like Pete rose to the challenge of the bullies. Linton—shit, even his name was prissy—would dissolve in tears while Pete fought down to the bitter end. His nose might be bloody and his shirt torn, the back of his pants streaked with dirt and grass stains, but the other guy always backed off first. His opponents took to coming after him with chains and stones, at which point he was sometimes forced to concede. Anything short of that, Pete was fearless.

Dr. Reed adjusted his watchband, not checking the face, which would have been rude, but making his point nonetheless.

"Ms. Sobel mentioned you had a personal matter to discuss."

"I'm here to do you a favor."

The set smile appeared. "And what might that be?"

Pete opened the folder he'd brought with him and placed it on the desk. He wet his index finger and turned a page or two. "It's come to my attention that you're in a bit of a sticky situation."

"Oh?"

"This is in regard to the Phase II clinical trials involving a drug called Glucotace. I confess I don't understand all the nitty-gritty details, but according to my sources, the drug was originally intended for diabetics until it was taken off the market for what turned out to be, in some instances, fatal side effects. Your current hypothesis is that in combination with Acamprosate and another drug . . ."

"Naltrexone, which is in common use. Studies have shown it mitigates the craving for alcohol."

Pete held up a piece of paper. "I'm aware of that. It says so right here. Your theory is those two drugs plus Glucotace might prove effective in the treatment of nicotine and alcohol addiction."

"Statistics show alcoholic smokers are more prone to severe nicotine dependence than are nonalcoholics with higher smoking rates." Dr. Reed's tone was bemused and slightly professorial, as though Pete might benefit from enlightenment. "We're just beginning to address the relationship."

"And we appreciate your attention to the matter," Pete said. "With regard to Glucotace, your observation was that patients in treatment for alcohol dependence often develop a craving for sweets, which naturally plays havoc with their insulin levels. Your idea was to control glucose as a means of minimizing the peaks and valleys. Use of Glucotace, in this instance, would be classified as off-label."

The doctor smiled. "And you know this how? I'm just curious."

"Get an NIH grant and much of this is public record. The rest I picked up on my own. Success here would go a long way toward boosting your career. Comes to publishing, you're already ahead of the curve. How many papers in this year alone? Forty-seven by my count. You're a busy boy."

"Some of those were coauthored."

"Duly noted. I made a copy of the list."

Linton Reed's face remained blank. No herding behavior here. "I don't understand where you're going with this."

"You want the long version or the short?"

Dr. Reed's eyes were dead. "Keep it short."

"There's been some suggestion you're cooking your data."

"Pardon?"

"The clinical trial. You're manipulating the numbers, making them look better than they are; something I gather you've done in the past. There was that business in Arkansas, which I grant you was a problem of a different sort."

"You don't know what you're talking about."

"I may not know the whole of it, but I know enough. Whatever's going on is of no interest to me personally, but I gather it's of the utmost importance to you. You have that pretty little bride of yours, new home the in-laws bought you, nice car."

"Leave my private life out of this."

"Just pointing out how much you have to lose. Good job, all those high-class friends. This comes to light and you can kiss all that good-bye."

"This conversation is over."

"Conversation's over, but your jeopardy is not. I have an idea how you might sidestep disgrace. I'd be happy to spell it out if you're interested."

The good doctor's voice dropped into the manly range that must have served him so well in other circumstances. "If you don't leave my office this minute, I'll call security."

Pete stood and took out a business card that he placed on the desk. "I'd give it some thought. You've got a lot at stake and you can't afford to get caught out. Even the *accusation* of trimming, founded or unfounded, would open up a can of worms, especially in light of your previous infractions."

"Get out of here."

"Call if you want to chat, buddy. I'm here for you."

Linton Reed was already reaching for the phone, prepared to summon the troops. Pete left in as unhurried a manner as he could muster, refusing to admit the doctor had struck fear in him with the threat of campus gendarmes. The secretary studiously avoided looking at him as he passed, which was fine with him.

He returned to his car and when he pulled up to the exit gate, he noticed the kiosk was empty and the parking attendant was nowhere to be seen. Pete waited a moment, then got out of the car and walked around the rear until he reached the kiosk window. He peered over the sill, reached in, and activated the mechanism that raised the gate. Then he got back in his car and pulled out. The validated ticket he stuffed in the glove compartment in case he had some future use for it.

Pete headed for home. He'd planted the seed and now he'd leave it to Dr. Reed to follow the thread to its logical conclusion. Give him a week and he'd cave. What struck Pete as weird was he didn't feel that good about the deal. There was something depressing about the whole thing. Linton Reed was a bad egg. He was a man who cut corners and to date he'd managed to tap-dance out of harm's way, using his considerable charm and his good looks. The encounter should have given Pete the satisfaction for a job well done. In truth, he was weary beyond belief.

Maybe it was time to retire. Ruthie made excellent money and it wouldn't be a problem getting by on what she earned. Essentially, that's what they'd been doing for the past eighteen months. The house was paid for and their expenses were minimal. She must know how broke he was. She could probably see through Pete's pie-in-the-sky claim of imminent financial gain. She knew him better than he knew himself, and what he loved about her was she'd never dream of calling him on his shit. She was protective of him. She made it possible for him to save face. In the meantime, it crossed his mind that if the good doctor never called him, it might be reason to rejoice. They'd find a way to survive. If the good doctor didn't call, he'd take it as a sign and he'd hang up his spurs.

At the office first thing the next morning, his phone rang. He nearly let the call go to the answering machine, but for once he picked up.

Linton Reed said, "What do you want?"

"Whatever you think it's worth."

"I'm not going to *pay* you. Why would I do that? You're way off. You don't know the first thing."

"You don't want to pay, we have nothing to discuss."

"Whatever you think you have on me, you're dead wrong. What you're attempting is extortion. I'll call the FBI."

Pete felt something sour rise in his throat. "I'm not talking about money to keep quiet. I'm talking about making the threat evaporate. You got a problem. I got a plan."

"For which I pay."

"Everybody pays for services. That's how business is done."

"How do I know you won't come back for more?"

"Because once I neutralize the danger, that's the end of it."

"What are you, a hit man?"

"What's the matter with you? I don't hurt people for any

reason. I'd never do such a thing. Any rate, I don't think this is something we should discuss on the phone. Why don't we find a place to meet? That way, we can pursue the matter in private and see if we can reach an agreement."

There was a long silence and Pete waited it out.

Finally, tersely, the good doctor said, "Where?"

21

I followed Alice as she crossed the back porch and went down the wooden stairs. Lolly sat in a shady spot under a cottonwood tree on one of two metal lawn chairs. These were duplicates of the ones I remembered from the scrim of yard in the trailer park where I'd lived with Aunt Gin; metal back and seat, supported by a continuous bend of U-shaped tubing, which gave the chairs some bounce. The finish here was chalky from sun exposure, but the chairs were otherwise in great shape. Between the two, there was a metal table resting on three legs.

The larger part of the backyard was given over to a vegetable garden, densely planted and still producing: cherry tomatoes, peppers, eggplants, and two kinds of squash. The beds were bordered with dark green kale and bright orange marigolds. The roses along the fence had been pruned to short, blunt sticks.

Alice said, "Lolly, this is Kinsey. She's a friend of Terrence and Evelyn Dace. They lived next door to you and David on Daisy Lane. Do you remember them?"

"Oh, yes. It's so nice to see you again," she said, and then looked at her cousin, waiting for the next cue.

Alice said, "I'm going to bring you some lemonade. You

can tell Kinsey about the garden." And then to me, "Lolly designed the beds when she first came to live with me and now we work awfully hard to keep them in shape. I'll be right back."

She returned to the house, leaving me alone with Lolly, who looked every bit of her eighty-six years; big-boned and gaunt with wide shoulders and a wide, sloping bosom that disappeared at her waist. Her eyes were buried in soft folds. The dress she wore was cotton with an old-fashioned faded floral print in blues and pinks. She wore opaque beige stockings and sandals with thick straps. She had a colander in her lap and she was shelling peas, though the results were a jumble of torn and broken pods with the occasional spill of bright green. Once in a while she looked down, puzzled by the sight, but unable to correct for the error in play. Her expression was probably one she'd settled on for most occasions: pleasant, but with a fixed quality, like someone traveling in a foreign country, unacquainted with the language and therefore hoping to avoid conversation.

She flicked an anxious look toward the back door and then leaned close. "Who is that woman?"

"Your cousin, Alice. Your mother and hers were sisters."

Lolly's expression was anxious. "Alice is young. That woman's old. She moved into my house and now she's bossing me around. What right does she have to give orders?"

I felt myself detach from reality for a quick reassessment. My neighbor Gus had fallen into the hands of an unscrupulous caregiver who operated in this same manner, discounting complaints and suggesting psychological problems where there were none. If Gus told anyone how mistreated he was, the listener's natural inclination was to write him off as a mental case. For all I knew, Lolly was telling me the truth. At the same time, if Alice was indeed a stranger taking advantage of an elderly woman, she wouldn't have allowed me to see Lolly in the first place, would she have?

"I just met her," I said. "I called and asked if I could visit and she agreed."

"I've never seen her before in my life. Have you?"

"Not until just now," I said. "Do you remember Terrence and Evelyn Dace?"

"Of course. Are you a friend of Evelyn's?"

"No, but I talked to her children, Ethan—"

"Ellen and Anna," she said, filling in the family tree.

I was thinking, good, we're back on track. "Do you remember the name Karen Coffey?"

"Oh, yes. She went missing in February and they found her days later stuffed in that culvert, not two miles from Daisy Lane. She'd been raped and strangled with a cord. I felt so bad for the family. They were members of my church."

"You have a good memory."

"Do I?" she asked, and then, hesitantly, "Have you seen my daughter, Mary?"

"I don't know Mary. I wish I did," I said. "Were you at Terrence and Evelyn's house the night Karen Coffey disappeared?"

"I was. David and I went next door at six o'clock for a pot-luck supper. I brought a three-bean salad and homemade rolls. Evelyn made that casserole she does with cauliflower, sour cream, and grated cheese. I've asked for the recipe four times, but she won't give it to me, which I told David is just typical of her."

"Did you have a pleasant evening?"

"We did. The pastor of our church and his wife were there. We had supper and then talked about raising money for the new Sunday-school building."

"David's your husband?"

"Yes, but you know he went out some time ago and hasn't come back since. He'll be upset if he hears that woman's been bossing me around. Do you know who she is?"

"I believe she's your cousin, Alice."

"The visiting nurse said the same thing, but I know Alice and that's not her."

"Do you remember where Terrence was that night?"

"At the house with the rest of us. The pastor's wife brought meatloaf, which I thought was too dry—though please don't repeat what I said. When Terrence went to the store for ice cream, the pastor halted the discussion, thinking he might have something to add when he got back. Evelyn told him vanilla and he bought peppermint. Was she upset? Oh, my stars. That woman can throw a fit. Are you a friend of hers?"

"I haven't met her," I said. "What's she like?"

"Crazy as a loon." She crossed her eyes, stuck her tongue out the side of her mouth, and made a circle with her index finger at her temple.

"Lolly, can you tell me who's president of the United States?"

She leaned forward and put a finger to her lips. "I didn't vote for him. Don't tell."

"What's his name again?"

"Richard Nixon."

I stayed long enough for half a glass of lemonade and some inconsequential chat. I kept a discreet eye on my watch and at 9:45 I excused myself, saying I had to get back to the hotel in order to check out. I thanked Lolly for her time. I thanked Alice for allowing me to come. When she accompanied me back through the house to the front door, I saw no sign of the flowers or the box of candy I'd brought. I hoped Lolly got something out of the deal. Did I trust her recollection? I most certainly did.

I crossed the lobby of the Holiday Inn on my way to the elevators. I'd planned to check out before Mamie and Evelyn arrived, but it occurred to me I should hang on to my room so I could put a call through to Henry prior to my departure. I had just enough time now to pack my belongings and get myself centered before the meeting. I could also use the opportunity to make a few quick notes.

A woman called out, "Kinsey?"

I knew the minute I turned around I was looking at Ethan's wife. Mamie wasn't fat by any means, but she was solid. She was taller than I and a good forty pounds heavier. Dark eyes, dark hair skinned back and held with a clip at the nape of her neck. Her face was full, tanned as though she spent all of her waking hours outdoors. She was packed into a pair of black slacks and a crisp white blouse, the shirttail out and belted at the waist. She wore big silver hoop earrings and she carried the manila envelope I'd left behind with Ethan. I knew it was the same because in one corner, I could still see the imprint of Binky's wee front teeth.

Behind Mamie, seated on the couch, was Evelyn Dace, whose expression I can only describe as sorrowful. She wore a lightweight tweed suit, wren brown, with a white polyester blouse under the jacket topped by a big softly draped bow.

Mamie was holding her hand out. "Mamie Heisermann." Her voice was of the booming type.

I shook hands with her obligingly, murmuring exactly what one does in situations of the kind.

"Let me introduce you to Evelyn," she said. "I hope you don't mind our coming early."

"Not at all," I said, though I did mind. The move was meant to catch me off guard, which it had. In the meantime, I couldn't help but think that Ethan and Mamie were as unlikely a married couple as any I'd seen. She carried herself with authority. He seemed both self-involved and clueless about others' perception of him. I was impressed by his stage persona, but not with the man himself. I wondered if Mamie had any idea how he behaved when he was out of her sight. Surely, any woman married to a musician has some inkling of what goes on.

I tagged Evelyn Dace at roughly her ex-husband's age, which I knew was fifty-three at the time of his death. Her eyes were blue, but not the same bright shade as Anna's. The orbs of her eyes seemed sunken, defined by shadow. She kept her smile modest, as though the hardships in life had robbed her of humor and hope.

We shook hands. Anna had told me Mamie and Evelyn didn't get along, so the two must have set aside their hostilities in order to present a united front. I might have felt flattered, but I realized a better interpretation was that the two had now merged their antagonisms, the better to focus them on me.

Mamie said, "I talked to the manager and he says we can use the conference room as long as we're out by noon."

I thought, *Two hours? Shit!* "No problem. I'm on my way home, so I don't have long. I'd like to be on the road by eleven."

"So you said on the phone. I hope you're not thinking to cut the discussion short. What if we haven't reached an agreement?"

"About what?"

"Well, I can see you're already being argumentative."

"Let's just see how it goes," I said, not wanting to engage. We might end up in a fight but it didn't have to start right *now*.

She led the way down a short side corridor off the lobby in a section of the hotel set aside for trade shows and conventions of a modest sort. The room we entered could have accommodated fifty people, but not many more. Windows ran the length of the room. The carpet was dark blue and the walls were faced with a neutral fabric meant to deaden sound. I could imagine a meeting in progress; coffee carafes arranged on the sideboard with trays of sweet rolls, doughnuts, and other pastries. Maybe a fruit platter if management wanted to make a show of healthy choices. The big conference table would be furnished with a scratch pad and ballpoint pen at each place. There'd be pitchers of ice water with plastic cups stacked nearby. I truly wished I were going to that meeting instead of the one pending.

This table was bare and the room was empty except for a whiteboard with an instant-erase marker pen. Someone had drawn a "Kilroy Was Here" cartoon in the center. We arranged ourselves at one end of the conference table, Mamie at the head. I took the seat to her right so I was facing the door. Evelyn sat across from me. With the glare from the window at my back, she probably couldn't see my facial features.

I glanced at Mamie. "Where do you want to start?"

She removed a copy of the will from the manila envelope, leafing through the pages like a prosecuting attorney approaching the witness stand. Some of the faux friendliness had faded and we were getting down to brass tacks. "I have to say we're perplexed. Evelyn and I were talking on the way over and she reminded me that before Terrence went to prison, he drew up a will that was nothing like this one." She fixed her brown eyes on mine.

"He rewrote his will after he arrived in Santa Teresa. The date's probably on there someplace. This was after he and Ethan quarreled and he left Bakersfield. It must have been a hell of a fight if this was the end result. Ethan said you were there. You want to talk about what went on?"

"The less said about that the better," Mamie remarked, her expression chaste.

"Terrence was drunk," Evelyn said. "No big surprise. He was always drunk."

"Oh, sorry. I didn't realize you were there or I'd have asked your impression."

"I'm telling you what I heard."

I turned my attention to Mamie. "Anna says Ethan spit in his father's face. Is that true?"

"That was uncalled for. I told Ethan he was way out of line on that score. Even so, I don't believe it warranted this level of retaliation."

Evelyn jumped in. "I'm in total agreement with Mamie. We can't understand why you've been given a role in such an intimate family affair. How in the world did you end up executor of the estate? My husband's death is distressing enough without this blow on top of it."

"Ex-husband," Mamie said.

"I was as surprised as anybody else," I replied.

"I'll just bet you were," Evelyn said, cutting me short.

Mamie gave Evelyn a warning look.

"Well, I don't see why we should shilly-shally around," Evelyn said, bristling.

"And I don't see why I should sit by while you turn this into a big stinking fight," Mamie snapped back.

"If you like I can go through the chain of events," I said.

Mamie's gaze flicked to mine. "Please."

"First of all, you know who Rebecca Dace was?"

Evelyn spoke up. "She was Terrence's aunt. Her brother Randall was Terrence's father. She had another brother named Sterling, but he died some years ago."

"Rebecca Dace married my grandfather Quillen Millhone. He and Rebecca had one child, my father, Terrence Randall Millhone. From what I've been able to piece together, he was Terrence's favorite uncle."

"Which doesn't answer my question," Evelyn said. "Why did you inherit all that money with such a flimsy blood tie? You're barely related to us at all. It just doesn't seem right."

"I'll tell you as much as I know," I said, and repeated my account, which I rendered in excruciating detail, hoping to dispense with any questions she might pose.

When I finished, both women stared at me.

Mamie shook her head slightly, checking the last page of

the will to make sure she hadn't missed anything. "What about these witnesses? We don't recognize the names."

"Those were friends of his."

Evelyn said, "Well, I'm happy he had friends. That wasn't always the case. I'm sure you understand why we'd be skeptical."

"You want to tell me what's on your mind?"

Evelyn reached for the will and checked the pages as Mamie had. "Well, who is this Mr. Singer? Have you any idea?"

"He and Terrence met at a homeless shelter. I didn't make the man's acquaintance until last week."

"What about Ms. White and Mr. Beider?"

"I met them at the same time," I said. "Dan Singer told me the three of them witnessed the will at Terrence's request. It was all straightforward and aboveboard."

"They're homeless?" Mamie asked. Her tone put them in the same low company as pedophiles.

"Yes."

She blinked. "Do they have mental health issues?"

"Not that I observed."

"What about problems with substance abuse?"

I thought, *Oops.* "I've only known them a week," I said, as though that ruled out my opinion.

Evelyn's turn. "But you can see why we'd question the signatures if these three *misfits* were drunk or mentally impaired."

"Actually, I think only two witnesses are required, so I'm willing to concede one of them."

Mamie stared at me. "Is that a joke?"

"Sorry. I didn't mean to be flip. If you want to challenge their competence, you'll have to hire an attorney and take them into court. There's no point in our discussing the issue since none of us are qualified mental health professionals. As far as I know," I added, having eliminated our law degrees in the earlier conversation.

A little knot appeared between Mamie's brows but her tone remained mild. "All this talk about attorneys. Is that really what you want?"

"All I want is to avoid turning this into a personal debate."

Evelyn said, "But why bring attorneys into it? We'll end up paying them the lion's share and how will any of us benefit?"

"This is not something we can settle among the three of us. This is awkward—"

"It's not a matter of *awkwardness*. It's a question of what's right. Terrence was angry," Evelyn said.

"Okay, fine. That's true as far as it goes."

Sounding slightly more conciliatory, she went on. "I'm not blaming him, I'm only pointing out that if he'd had a chance to calm down, he might have reversed himself."

"But he didn't. In point of fact, what we're left with is what's spelled out in that document," I said.

"Here's what you don't seem to grasp," Mamie said. "Terrence loved his children. You've been drawn into a drama that goes back many years. I don't think you appreciate the hardships they endured. I don't know how Evelyn managed to hold her head up." Mamie glanced at Evelyn as she said this and Evelyn managed to look especially stricken.

"Look, I can understand how difficult it must have been. That doesn't change anything."

Evelyn said, "You know he offered them the money. Are you aware of that?"

"I'm assuming that's why he came to Bakersfield," I said.

"That's exactly right. The minute he had the settlement in hand, he called Ethan, saying he wanted to make amends. He talked about dividing the money equally among the three children to compensate them for their suffering."

"You keep referring to them as children when they're fully grown adults," I said.

She dropped her gaze. "I suppose I'll always think of them as children. Do you have any of your own?"

"I don't."

"Then it might be hard for you to fathom how a mother feels."

"Off topic," Mamie warned.

Evelyn gave her a hard look and turned back to me. "What I'm getting at is I may not know how the law works, but in my mind, and Terrence's as well, his talking to them about splitting the money was the same as a verbal contract."

Mamie said, "Evelyn, I'm not sure you're helping matters. I'm guessing Kinsey's already spoken to an attorney since she's brought it up so many times."

"I'm just telling her how I see the problem. Terrence wanted to do right by them, which is why he came back."

Mamie flicked a look at me. "She might have a point."

"Thank you," Evelyn said tartly, and then turned to me. "Surely, you don't believe the terms are fair. After what they went through? Terrence felt rejected and he rejected them in response, but it's not unreasonable to imagine him regretting his haste. It's unfortunate he died before he had a chance to undo the harm. Doesn't that seem reasonable to you?"

I indicated the papers. "The will is dated July 8, 1988. He and Ethan quarreled in September, ten months before. That's hardly acting in haste. He had time to think about what he was doing both before and afterward."

Evelyn went on as though I hadn't said a word. "You have no idea how much that money would mean to them. This could be a life-changing event," she said. There was a small tremor in her voice that I thought was entirely manufactured.

"I'm not here to negotiate. I made that clear to Mamie on the phone."

"Hear me out . . . as a courtesy if nothing else." She kept her eyes on me as though waiting for my permission to continue.

I gestured her on.

"As executor of the estate, you're in a position to tip the balance, don't you think?"

"No."

"Then how do you see your role?"

"It's not a *role*. As executor, it's my job."

"Your job, then."

"I'm responsible for seeing that his assets are distributed according to the provisions in the will. I can't just make these things up. I have to answer to the court."

"But once this is settled, you do have a say in what happens from that point on."

"If the judge decides the will's in order, I'll see that Terrence's wishes are carried out. That's the only power I have."

"But isn't this a conflict of interest? You admit you had no relationship with Terrence and yet you've managed to insert yourself between the man and his own offspring. Why can't you give them a chance to accomplish something in life?"

"Let's not go on with this. Please believe me when I tell you it's not up to me."

"That's not true," Evelyn said. "All that money's going to end up in your pocket, isn't it?"

"In theory, I suppose."

"What I'm suggesting is that once the money's yours, you can do anything you want with it. Isn't that correct?"

I raised a hand. "I want to talk about something else."

Evelyn said, "I haven't finished making my point. I'm not saying you shouldn't have a share, but think about this. If you divided it four ways, you'd each come out with about a hundred and fifty thousand apiece, which seems equitable."

I was shaking my head, irritated that she was pressing the point.

Mamie interceded. "Would you let Kinsey have a turn? You've talked long enough." She turned to me. "What were you going to say?"

I loved how cranky she was. I said, "I'd like to back up a bit if you don't mind. Here's what I don't get. All this posturing aside, why weren't Ethan and Anna more charitable when Terrence was exonerated? I know Ellen was out of town when he arrived, but Ethan and Anna both still believe he killed Karen Coffey. Even with all the evidence that came to light. Why weren't they happy? Why didn't they rejoice? That's the crux of the problem, isn't it? Not that they believed he was guilty, but that they refused to believe he was innocent."

"You'd have to ask them. I wouldn't presume to speak for them. After all, they're adults—as you so aptly pointed out."

I said, "Can we stick to the point? Terrence cut them out of the will because they mistreated him, yes?"

"I grant you their behavior was unfortunate, but let's not make matters worse," she said.

"That's not where I'm going with this. Do you know why they quarreled?"

"Because Terrence was drunk," she said.

"No. They quarreled because you insinuated he'd actually had a hand in that girl's death."

Mamie waved that aside. "That's ridiculous. Evelyn did no such thing."

"Yes, she did." I looked at Evelyn. "If you hadn't poisoned

the well, your 'children' might have been receptive to their
father's overtures. They might have accepted the fact that he
was cleared of wrongdoing. If the visit had been a good one,
he'd have left them everything, so this is really more about you
than it is about me."

Evelyn lowered her gaze. Color was creeping up her neck,
which I considered a thrilling sight. She said, "I don't think
you understand the relationship they had. They worshiped
him. He was a hero to them. When this hideous crime came to
light, they were devastated. I wanted them to realize that he
wasn't quite the innocent victim he portrayed himself."

"You think he killed her?"

"I think he had the means, the motive, and the opportunity."

"What are you talking about? This isn't a television drama."

"Karen was Ethan's friend. She'd been to the house more
than once."

"So what?"

"I could see Terrence took a shine to her. I never had any
proof, but I wasn't at all shocked when the police came to the
door and asked to speak to him. He looked terrible. His skin
was gray. He was sweating and his hands shook. That's not the
demeanor of an innocent man."

Mamie looked at her mother-in-law with disbelief. "Are
you serious? He shook and turned gray anytime a drink was
overdue."

Evelyn was still focused on me. "I don't know where in the
world you got the idea I turned the children against him. I'd
never do such a thing," she said.

"I heard it from Anna. She told me last night."

"Told you what?" Mamie asked, annoyed at being out of
the loop.

"Nothing," Evelyn said.

This was beginning to feel like politics, consisting as it did
almost entirely of finger-pointing and accusations.

I turned to Mamie. "Anna told me the day her father called
to say he'd been released, Evelyn confessed that she lied on the
witness stand. She said he went out that night and was gone
until the wee hours."

Mamie looked at Evelyn with dismay. "You did that?"

I said, "Oh, yes, indeed. She also told the three of them not to mention it to anyone for fear she'd be charged with perjury, which is a criminal act. Ask Ethan. He'll tell you the same thing. Ellen, too."

Mamie was staring at her mother-in-law. "I don't believe it. You said he was there at the house when he wasn't?"

I wagged a finger, correcting her. "It was the other way around. She told the truth on the witness stand and lied about it later."

"But why would she do that? She'd have to be nuts."

Evelyn leaned toward me. "You don't know what you're talking about. Were you there?"

"Of course I wasn't, but I'll tell you who was. An hour ago I talked to Lolly Brandle."

Mamie wrinkled her nose in confusion. "Who?"

"The woman who lived next door to Evelyn and Terrence back then. She was at the Daces' house the night Karen Coffey disappeared. She says Terrence was home the entire evening except for a brief trip to the store to pick up ice cream."

Evelyn's tone was prim. "You can hardly credit her account. She has dementia."

"She may not remember what happened yesterday, but she remembers that night, right down to the flavor of the ice cream he went out to buy. Here's a question for you, Evelyn. Who was the president of the United States at that time?"

"I have no idea. How is that relevant?"

"Because Lolly knows. I asked her the same thing and her memory is as clear as a bell. Richard Nixon."

"I can see you're determined to take her word over mine," she said. "I've been to visit her twice. She has no idea who I am and I've known her twenty-five years. Besides which, how do you know she isn't lying for reasons of her own?"

"Because the pastor of your church was also there with his wife. I'd be happy to track them down, and I'll bet you they'll back Lolly Brandle. Are you going to call them liars as well?"

"I did not commit a crime."

"I know you didn't. You told Ethan and Ellen and Anna you lied on the stand when you actually told the truth in court. Later, you insinuated that Terrence went out that night and had a hand in that girl's death. You didn't accuse him outright. You undercut his credibility and you did such a fine job of it that

Ethan and Anna were completely alienated from their dad. And still are, for that matter."

"Accuse me of anything you like. You have no proof and there's nothing you can do about it even if you did."

"You got me on that one. At least Mamie knows now and we'll see what she does with it."

22

The meeting faltered to a close and we parted company. Verbal clashes seldom come to a satisfying end. They peter out in weak retorts that leave you wishing you'd been as clever in the moment as you are in reviewing the conversation later. I hadn't scored even one decisive point and none of us had altered our positions in the slightest. I was glad I'd met Evelyn because I had a better sense now of who she was and how she operated.

Poor Dace. I'd formed a ragged picture of his life, joining fragments like a reel of film spliced together with all the big scenes missing. The story line was there but the point was lost. The meaning of life (assuming there is one . . .) is the glue we use to join events, trying to fill the cracks in hopes the whole of it will make sense. Beginning, middle, and end don't always add up to much, and, in his case, only an odd note of melancholia remained.

I went up to my room and packed. I took the elevator down and presented myself at the front desk with my duffel in hand. I signed the credit card receipt and returned my key. It wasn't until I was crossing the parking lot that I saw Ethan Dace appear on the far side of the Mustang. He'd parked his banged-up white Toyota in the slot to the left of mine. At first I thought he'd crouched between the two cars to keep himself out of view, but maybe he'd only bent to tie his shoelace. I was on the verge of asking how he'd figured out where I was, but we all knew by then that my Grabber Blue Mustang was better than a flashing neon sign.

Casually, he turned and opened his passenger-side door. He tossed something onto the front seat before he slammed the door again and turned to face me. He tilted his head in the direction of the hotel entrance. "What was that about?"

"What was what about?"

"I saw my wife and mom leave just now. You call a meeting?"

"That was Mamie's idea. She had questions about the will. It was a waste of time in my opinion, but I wanted to show what a good sport I am."

"What else did you talk about?"

"That was it," I said. Then the light dawned. "Oh, now I'm getting it. You think I summoned Mamie and your mom so I could tattle on you."

"Nothing to tattle. I was talking to a friend."

"My mistake. It looked like you were flirting with that redheaded hottie. Anna's friend, isn't she? I didn't catch her name."

"That's none of your business."

"Fear not, good sir. My lips are sealed. Now if you'll step away from my car door, I'd like to get in."

For some reason, that set him off. He rose up on the balls of his feet, leaning toward me while he jabbed a finger in my face. The fact that he didn't raise his voice made the underlying anger more sinister than the threat that followed. "You want to make trouble? I'll make trouble for you and don't think I won't."

"What did you have in mind?"

"I'll sue. Me and my sisters will sue your ass, you get that?"

"I do. Thanks so much. Is there anything else?"

"You better lawyer up. That's all I'm saying."

"I have an attorney."

"I'll bet you do. I bet you hired one the second you found out about the money because you knew what kind of hole you'd dug for yourself. My dad was a drunk, which you seem to know all about. So maybe you talked him into cutting us off so you could step into the breach."

"Let's not talk about this, okay? You want to hire an attorney, you can go right ahead. I told you to do that the first time we spoke. You have a copy of the will. You have the hearing date, and you can do anything you like."

He turned without another word and moved around the back of his car to the driver's seat. He got in and slammed the door.

It took him two tries to get his car started, but then he peeled out with a chirp.

Anna was right. The guy was a drama queen.

I unlocked the Mustang, tossed my duffel into the backseat and my shoulder bag in the front. I got in, started the car, and pulled out of the slot. Such was the thrilling climax of my twenty-four-hour sojourn in Bakersfield.

By 11:52, I was driving west on California Street toward the southbound on-ramp to State Route 99. There were two more delays coming up but I didn't know that yet, so I was excited about getting home. Bakersfield had been a bust. In the main, I'd accomplished my goals, but in doing so, I'd stirred up a nest of hornets. Two of Dace's three kids were hopeless. I couldn't convince them their father had been dealt a bad hand. As far as Ethan and Anna were concerned, his leaving me the money had only fanned the resentment they'd carried for years. How else could it have turned out? Of course they were angry. Of course they responded with more of the same.

There were other elements in play. It would be disingenuous to claim I was above caring about $595,350. I'd never been close to that much money in my life, and while it wasn't really mine, it was certainly a subject worthy of consideration. Briefly, I fantasized about what would happen if I disregarded the terms of the will and divided the inheritance equally among the three. How far might that go toward healing the rift? Nowhere. Ethan and Anna would blow their portion and then expect Ellen to fork over hers until that was gone as well. Ellen would agree because she felt guilty about the two of them, an attitude they'd fostered in her over the years.

I toyed with the idea of handing over *part* of the money—say, $100,000 divided three ways instead of the half a million plus. The flaw there was that if I thought they were entitled to a *little* bit of money, why not the whole amount? Either it was all right or all wrong. Acting in opposition to Dace's wishes was clearly wrong, regardless of Ethan's threats or Evelyn's maneuvering. Money aside, from their point of view the crux of the problem was Dace's love affair with hooch and his refusal to give it up. In his children's eyes, he'd died preferring alcohol to them.

Driving south on the 99, I hadn't even cleared the city limits when I caught sight of the highway sign for the Panama Lane off-ramp. The name jumped out at me because I'd seen it in my paper search for Choaker Road, where the Millhones had lived in the early forties. When I'd consulted the city map, the address was too far off the beaten path to worry about; at the time, Ethan Dace was uppermost on my mind. Now I was in range of the house where my father had lived and the question was this: did I care enough to delay my trip home?

Nah, not so much. The Millhones were long gone, and getting back to Santa Teresa mattered more to me than exploring sites of historical family significance. I was curious, but going five miles out of my way seemed irksome when all I wanted was to put distance between me and Bakersfield. On the other hand (I was always thinking in terms of this "other hand" horseshit . . .), who knew if I'd ever be here again? Henry would ask what I'd learned and I didn't fancy telling him I'd jettisoned the search. He wouldn't chide me, but I'd be chiding myself for not taking advantage of the occasion while I could.

I signaled my intention, took the off-ramp, and pulled over to the side of the road at the first decent opportunity. I was annoyed. Why couldn't I go back to being an orphan like I'd been all my life? Had I ever once complained about it? No, I had not. I'd taken a certain peevish pride in being without close family. Now my lone-wolf status had been taken away and I resented the loss, even if it had always been entirely delusional on my part. As it turned out, I was embroiled in the same dysfunctional mess as everyone else I knew.

I opened the oversize map, which was thirty-six inches by fifty and printed on slick, heavy-duty paper that was awkward to unfold. Once I wrestled it into submission, I ran my eye down the page and traced Panama Lane both east and west. The delicate lace of intersecting streets defined a succession of neighborhoods. This must have been farmland once upon a time, perhaps much of it still was. The burgeoning city spread out in all directions as the inhabitants multiplied.

Through the windshield I was looking at the same flat landscape that characterized the entire area, which was pockmarked with housing developments that finally gave way to open fields. Choaker Road was farther east, close to the north-south axis of Cottonwood Road.

As I drove, I kept an eye on the passing street signs. Having committed myself, I could picture my spotting the old homestead. Perhaps I'd park and get out. I might knock on the door to ask the current occupant if I could make a quick tour of the rooms. It was possible the present owner had bought the house from someone who knew when it was built or how many hands it had passed through. I slowed in anticipation of my turn and took a left, checking house numbers as I proceeded from 4800 down to the 4600 block with a mounting sense of dismay. There was no 4602. The entire neighborhood was gone. I pulled over to the curb.

Where the Millhone house had once stood there was a settlement of condominiums; identical six-story stucco structures, arranged in a staunch grid spread over twenty-five or thirty acres. The few trees I saw were young and newly planted. The streets that branched off of Choaker Road had been named after New England states—Maine, Vermont, New Hampshire, Connecticut, Massachusetts, and Rhode Island. If the colony continued to expand, the Eastern Seaboard might be called into play, starting with New Jersey and running all the way down to Florida.

I pulled away from the curb and proceeded along Choaker until I reached a set of ornamental gates. I turned in and cruised the roads that ran between the monolithic buildings. There wasn't much to see since they were all identical. My grandparents' house had been erased, as had the houses on either side—as had the homes extending for six or eight city blocks in every direction. Even the soil had been excavated and carted away, so any relics—arrowheads, sun-bleached bones, the caps from old soda bottles—were gone now as well. I could take a metal detector and scan the surrounding area for two square miles without turning up so much as an old spoon.

This is your reward for denial, I thought. You decide you don't care and the family home vanishes. The irony wasn't lost on me. The Universe was having a little tee-hee at my expense. Whereas the Kinsey branch of the family was chockablock with cousins, aunts, and uncles, even an ancient living grand-mother, the Millhones had disappeared. As further punishment, I was now saddled with a cluster of second or third cousins related to me tangentially through Rebecca Dace, and I was far better acquainted with that bunch than I wanted to be. I'd also inherited the family corpse, a dead guy whose last rites had fallen to me. The only upside I could see was that the Daces made my mother's side of the family look like bastions of mental health.

I headed back to the 99 and took up my southbound journey. Forty miles outside of Bakersfield, I checked my watch. It was 12:45 and I was starving. I hadn't bothered to eat anything before I left the hotel. I'd been more interested in getting the journey under way than in feeding my face. How foolhardy was that? I'd never make it to Santa Teresa without something to eat. I wouldn't arrive until midafternoon and by then I'd be gnawing my own arm. I pulled my shoulder bag closer and fumbled through the interior, but all I came up with was a sugarfree breath mint of no known nutritional value. At that very moment, I realized I'd forgotten to call Henry to advise him of my estimated arrival time. That did it.

I started scanning for highway signs, looking for the closest rest stop. Of particular interest was the crossed knife and fork, the universal symbol for fatty foodstuffs. Coming up on the Tejon Pass, I took the Frazier Mountain Park Road where the Flying J promised numerous forms of relief: weighing scales, a pump dump, liquid propane, diesel fuel, a travel store, and overnight RV accommodations. The parking area was expansive, probably three hundred spaces, only a small number of which were taken. Most important of all was the Denny's restaurant rising up in splendor.

I parked two aisles away from the entrance, locked the Mustang, and went in. I availed myself of the facilities and then found an empty booth. A kindly waitress brought me water, a menu, and silverware. Since I'd eaten breakfast a scant four hours before, I skipped that section of the menu and looked at the garish photographs of burgers. Most were alarmingly large; double-meat patties with cheese and all manner of folderol piled up in a bun. Feeling virtuous, I opted for a salad, knowing that before I left I could hoof it over to the minimart and stock up on candy bars.

When I paid my check, I asked the cashier to make change for a five-dollar bill. I'd seen a pay phone outside the service station and I was headed in that direction when a middle-aged man approached from the parking lot and tagged me by the arm.

"Is that your Mustang?"

I turned to him with surprise. "It is."

"I thought so. I saw you pull in. My wife and I had a booth by the window and she's the one who called it to my attention. We were just having a closer look."

"I take it you're a fan."

"Yes'sum, but that's not why I came looking for you. Are you aware you have a flat tire?"

"You're kidding. Flat as in dead flat or low on air?"

"Come on and I'll show you. I worried you might not notice it. You get back on the road and first thing you know, you'd be riding on the rim."

He turned and headed toward the rows of parked cars and I quick-stepped to catch up.

"Where're you coming from?" he asked.

"Bakersfield. I'm on my way to Santa Teresa."

We passed through to the second aisle. His wife was standing by the Mustang and she sent me an apologetic smile, as though she felt responsible for the problem I'd been dealt.

He said, "I'm Ron Swingler, by the way, and this is my wife, Gilda."

"Kinsey Millhone," I said as we shook hands all around. "I appreciate your taking the time to let me know about this."

They shared a similar body type, round through the middle with truncated extremities. Easy to see how their shared lifestyle and eating habits had created the symmetry.

"What about you? Where are you from?" I asked.

"Texas. This is our honeymoon. We've been married two days."

There went that keenly observed conclusion.

Then I caught sight of my left rear tire. "Well, dang. That *is* flat."

"Look here." He pointed to a round metal circle the size of a pencil eraser between the sidewall and the hubcap with its tiny silver horse in the center. "Looks like a roofing nail, which is technically called a clout nail. Short shank with that wide flat head? I put myself through college working as a roofer. This is the type we used to fasten shingles or roofing felt. Nail like that isn't but about that long," he said, showing me with his thumb and index finger. "Pull it out, you'll probably see a ring or screw shank."

"Weird spot for a nail. How you think it got there?"

"My opinion, you're looking at an act of vandalism. Somebody had to hammer this little fellow through your sidewall. You must have been parked in a bad neighborhood."

"I guess I was," I said. I thought about Ethan appearing between the two cars, his tossing something ever so casually into the front seat of his Toyota.

Ron Swingler said, "You want, I can swap that out for you, as long as your spare's in good shape."

"Thanks, but I can talk to someone at the service station. I don't want to hold you up."

Gilda spoke up, saying, "He doesn't mind. Why don't you let him give you a hand?"

"It won't take fifteen minutes. Probably less," he said.

I thought about it briefly. These were good people and I suspected the more I protested, the more they'd insist. Maybe their kindness would offset Ethan's malevolence to some extent. "Actually, I could use the help if you're sure you don't mind."

"My pleasure," he said. "Why don't you and Gilda wait in the RV and I'll come get you when I'm done."

Which is what we did. Their motor home was parked one aisle behind the one I was in. Gilda unlocked the door to the RV and stepped in ahead of me, then turned back and held open the door.

"You want coffee?"

"I'm fine. I'm hoping to get home without making another stop. Coffee would go right through me," I said.

The interior was snug: two bench seats with a table between, a tiny galley-style kitchen, and a bed that seemed to fill the front end. I wasn't sure what we were going to talk about, but that wasn't a problem because she had plenty on her mind. As we took our seats, she said, "Let me ask you something. Do you have kids or grandkids?"

I shook my head. "I'm afraid not."

"Listen to this and tell me what you think. Ron has a

granddaughter, Ava, who's seven years old. She's all into figure skating, which she practices twenty-two hours a week. Her
mom and dad—this is Ron's son and daughter-in-law—are
spending nine thousand dollars a year on lessons and competi-
tions. Does that sound right to you?"

"I guess the discipline might be good for her."

"I don't know what to think. Seven years old and that's all
she does. Doesn't read. Doesn't play with Barbie dolls. She
hardly ever goes outside, for Pete's sake, and that's all I cared
about when I was her age. There's something off about that."

"I hear you," I said.

"What's her mother thinking is what I want to know."

She went on in this vein long after my interest waned. I
tuned her out, making polite mouth noises while I checked the
wall clock behind her. I could tell she was processing the idea
of keeping her mouth shut, which is generally a smart move
though I've never mastered it myself.

When her husband finally opened the door and told me the
spare was in place, I thanked both of them profusely. I didn't
want to bolt when he'd just done me such a service, so we chatted for a bit. I expressed my gratitude again and he waved
aside my thanks. I knew better than to offer him money. He
was clearly a man who enjoyed being of service to women in
distress.

We finally affected our farewells and I continued on to the
pay phone, where I piled change on the metal shelf, inserted
coins, and dialed Henry's number.

He picked up on the third ring. "This is Henry."

"Hey, Henry. It's Kinsey. Sorry I didn't have a chance to
call you earlier."

"Where the heck are you? I thought you were on your way
home."

"I am but I had a flat." I filled him in on my stop for lunch,
wondering how far I might have gotten driving on a tire with
a nail driven into it. No point in worrying about it now, so I
moved on. "How's Felix doing?"

"Not well. He developed a clot on his brain, so they had to
go in and operate. Now it looks like he's fighting some sort of
secondary infection, which is more bad news."

"Is he going to make it?"

"Hard to know. William swears he's on his way out."

"William thinks everybody's half dead. What do the doctors say?"

"They don't seem optimistic. It's not what they say; it's the look in their eyes," he said. "I'll be glad to have you home. What time do you think you'll get in?"

I checked my watch again. It was now 2:22. "Not for another couple of hours."

"Why don't you plan on having supper here? You'll be tired and you'll need a glass of Chardonnay."

"Sounds good."

We were winding up the conversation and I was close to hanging up when he said, "Oh! I almost forgot. Your friend Dietz is on his way down from Carson City. He says he should be here by six, so I invited him for dinner, too."

I could feel myself squint. "Dietz? What's he want?"

"I guess there's a problem with that job referral."

"*Job* referral?"

"That's what he said. I figured you'd know what he was talking about."

"I have no idea."

"You can ask him yourself when he gets here," he said.

And with that, he hung up.

23

Naturally, the rest of the trip was uneventful and the miles flew out behind me at warp speed. Just when I longed for a delay (a minor car wreck, perhaps, or a sudden bout of the runs that would have me getting off the highway at every other exit lest I mess my underpants), there was no such luck in store. Feeling crabby and out of sorts, I brooded about Ethan Dace hammering a nail into my tire and then, as if I wasn't sufficiently annoyed, I took a little trip down memory lane, summing up my relationship with the aforementioned Robert Dietz.

I'd met him five years before, in May of 1983, when I found myself on the hit list of a small-time Nevada punk named Tyrone Patty, who'd been charged with attempted murder in the shooting of a liquor store clerk. He'd fled to Santa Teresa and I was assigned the task of tracking him down, which I did. He was sent back to Nevada, where he was tried, convicted, and thrown into prison. From that point on, his life had spiraled out of control and he held four of us personally accountable: me; the Carson City DA; the judge who'd sentenced him; and Lee Galishoff, the public defender who'd represented him. Never mind that Tyrone Patty was a persistent felon long before we entered the picture. Like many whose poor choices have led them astray, he accepted no responsibility as long as he had someone else to blame.

Once out of prison, he'd gone right out and murdered three more hapless victims—also our fault, no doubt—but while still in prison, he'd put out feelers for a contract killer to whack the four of us. Galishoff had gotten wind of it and called, urging me to hire a bodyguard, which I thought was absurd. Who can afford a bodyguard twenty-four hours a day? Was he nuts? He'd suggested Robert Dietz, a PI who specialized in personal protection. I'd recognized the name because I'd put a call through to him the year before when I needed a quick job done and it made no sense for me to travel all the way to Carson City.

Galishoff gave me his number again and I jotted it down with no real intention of contacting him. I'd just picked up a new job and I was on my way to the Mojave Desert. I didn't take the threat seriously until someone ran my VW off the road and into a ditch. I ended up in the hospital and that's when I called Dietz. He agreed to escort me back to Santa Teresa. In that same phone call, he told me the judge had been gunned down in front of his own home despite the presence of the police.

Dietz showed up in my hospital room and drove me home in his little red Porsche. Once the jeopardy passed and life returned to normal, if Dietz and I ended up in the sack, that was really nobody's business. What followed was a three-month live-in relationship, at which point Dietz took off for Germany, where he was under contract to the military to conduct antiterrorist training. I was miffed by his departure, but what choice did I have?

He'd said, "I can't stay."

I'd said, "I know. I want you to go. I just don't want you to leave me."

We connected again in January of 1986 after an absence of two years, four months, and ten days. That visit bled over into March, a period during which he had knee-replacement surgery and I agreed to drive him back to Nevada. By the time we parted company, I'd spent two weeks at his place in Carson City playing nursemaid, a role in which I have never been known to shine. I'd driven a rental car from there to Nota Lake, picking up an investigation that would have been his to handle if he hadn't been laid low. I hadn't seen him since.

I'm not an on-again, off-again kind of girl, and Dietz wasn't good at staying put, so emotionally we were always at odds. To be fair about it, neither one of us was suited for a long-term commitment. Dietz was afflicted with wanderlust and I was chronically self-protective, having been married and divorced twice.

Here's how it seems to work in my life: Usually when you say good-bye to a friend, it's a casual matter because it doesn't occur to you that you might not see that certain someone again. It's an *à bientôt* kind of thing . . . a term I remember from my high school French class. These are the few phrases I committed to memory even though I never got better than a C on a test.

> *À bientôt* . . . see you soon.
> *À plus tard* . . . see you later.
> *À demain* . . . see you tomorrow.
> *À tout à l'heure* . . . see you in a while.

When it comes to partings, the French are ever the optimists. My outlook is bleak. While my attention is fixed on the totally wrenching boo-hoo of an impending separation, the French language conveys hope and expectation, the happy assumption that in a short period of time, they'll be *bonjour*ing each other all over again. My lifelong "good-bye" experiences lean toward finality and pain. My parents died. My aunt died. My first husband died. I'm dead set (as it were . . .) against having a pet because the risk of loss would soar into the stratosphere and I've got troubles enough as it is.

After our last parting, I'd set Dietz out on the curb, metaphorically speaking, in hopes the alley fairies would come along and cart him away. It's not that I never thought of him, but by and large, people in my life knew better than to mention his name. Now here he was again and I couldn't figure out what was going on.

I pulled up in front of my studio apartment at 4:25. I grabbed my shoulder bag and duffel, locked my car, and made my way through the squeaky gate and around to my front door. I left my Smith-Corona in the trunk of my car, intending to take it into the office with me first thing Monday morning. There was no sign of Henry, but the backyard smelled of pot roast and freshly baked bread, both of which he does to perfection. I let myself in and carried my duffel up the spiral stairs to the loft. I'd been telling myself Dietz's arrival didn't matter one way or the other, but I postponed my official appearance at Henry's door until I'd slipped into a change of clothes. I stuck to my standard outfit: black turtleneck, blue jeans, and boots. I didn't want it to look like I was trying too hard. I skipped the makeup, which I seldom wore in any event. I did floss and brush my teeth, and then stared at myself in the bathroom mirror.

In novels, the protagonist is forever doing this because it affords the author an opportunity to describe the character's physical traits. That ploy won't work here because I always look exactly like myself. This can be discouraging. Sometimes when I'm standing in a supermarket checkout line, I'll spot the cover of a tabloid magazine plastered with candid photos of well-known actresses the paparazzi have caught off guard. What a shock it is to see legendary beauties looking washed-out and furtive, with matted hair, puffy lids, and splotchy complexions; flaws made all the more alarming for the images we carry of them, creamy-skinned and doe-eyed with tresses artfully tousled and sprayed to a hard shine. My looks fall somewhere between the two extremes, but closer to the puffy end. To my credit, I don't misrepresent my basic attributes with a lot of gunk. Anyone who's startled to see *me* looking splotchy hasn't been paying attention.

It was 4:55 when I knocked on Henry's back door. I was feeling more curious about Dietz than uneasy, which shows you what a moron I am. Dietz wasn't due for an hour and I was grateful for a brief interlude alone with Henry so I could fill him in on my trip to Bakersfield.

Henry let me in. He'd already opened a bottle of Chardonnay, resting now in a cooler on the kitchen counter. I grant you it was a teeny tiny bit early for a glass of wine, but how could I refuse the half a glass when he handed it to me? He poured himself a tot of Black Jack over ice and we sat down at the kitchen table.

One of Henry's many endearing qualities is his interest in matters that are of interest to me. He has remarkable recall of my past attitudes and behaviors, and he doesn't hesitate to bring inconsistencies to my attention. He's also free with his opinions even if they don't coincide with mine, which is an irritating trait but one that I've come to appreciate.

He had two freshly baked loaves of bread sitting on a towel on his kitchen counter, and his oven was exuding enough mild heat and roasting aromas to make the room feel cozy. I knew he'd serve a salad and something simple for dessert. Of particular interest on this occasion was the presence of the cat, who had apparently taken possession of Henry and everything related to him. Ed had been in residence only briefly when I'd taken off for Bakersfield. I could still hardly believe I'd been there so short a time when it felt like I'd been gone for so long.

I said, "Tell me about Felix. How's he doing?"

Henry waggled his outstretched hand in a gesture that indicated not so good. "After supper, we can go over to St. Terry's, if you like. He's unconscious, so you can't actually visit but you could look in on him. The nurses are kind, but I don't like being underfoot. As one nurse put it, ICU doesn't lend itself to looky-loos."

"No improvement at all?"

"They've been pumping him with antibiotics, which I gather hasn't done much good. In a situation like this, things tend to go from bad to worse. I don't mean to sound so pessimistic, but there's no point in mincing words."

"How's Pearl holding up?"

"She's currently off on a bender from what I hear. Your friend Dandy as well."

"You can't be serious."

"Oh, yes. I was at the hospital last night and Pearl was conspicuously absent. She'd been at his bedside, as faithful as a hound, whenever she was allowed. Suddenly, no sign of her, so I stopped by the shelter as soon as I left the hospital. I couldn't get a word out of Ken, the guy at the desk, but one of the residents heard me ask about her and he took me aside, which is when others chimed in."

"Are they holed up someplace?"

"Someone suggested a sports bar in the area. I don't know the name."

"Dandy mentioned the place. They play darts there on weekends if they're sober enough."

"I doubt they're playing darts. I'd have looked for them myself, but I don't have the patience."

Throughout this exchange, Ed was sitting in Henry's rocking chair, following the conversation solemnly with his oval eyes, the one blue, the other green. He was short-haired and white, with a patch of black over the right side of his face and touches of black and caramel on the left. His ears stood straight up, triangles lined with pink and edged in black. His stub of a tail looked like a black-and-tan powder puff. Henry regarded him with a doting expression, which the cat seemed to think was entirely his due.

I nodded at the cat. "How's he been? Looks like he's settled in and made himself at home."

"He's a very good boy. He's caught everything from mice to moles. Two lizards yesterday and one today."

"I hope no birds or bunnies."

"Of course not. We had a chat about that and I explained his limitations. He comes when he's called and doesn't play in the street."

"I thought Japanese bobtails were supposed to be talkative. He hasn't uttered a peep."

"He only speaks up when he has something to say."

"Is it okay if we discuss him like this when he's sitting right there?"

"He likes being the center of attention. He's even taught me a trick. Watch this." Henry picked up a wad of yarn the size of a golf ball. Ed was instantly interested, and when Henry tossed it across the kitchen, Ed streaked after it, brought it back, and dropped it at Henry's feet. Both Henry and Ed seemed extremely pleased with themselves. Ed watched Henry for a bit to see if they'd play again.

I said, "This is weird. Like you just had a baby and all we're going to do from here on out is sit and stare at the little tyke and admire everything he does."

"Don't be churlish," he said. "Tell me about your trip."

This I did while I set the table and Henry put together a rustic apple tart, rolling out a round of pie dough that he covered with pared apple slices, butter, sugar, and cinnamon. He seemed to recognize that I was still trying to settle on an attitude about my newly discovered cousins, so we didn't pursue the subject beyond the basic information. Meanwhile, Ed curled up in the rocker and closed his eyes, though his ears continued to twitch like rotating antennae.

"So what's with Dietz? I can't believe he called after all this time."

"He put in a fair amount of effort looking for you. He said he tried you at your office and tried you at home. He left messages both places, but when he didn't hear back he called me, asking if I knew where you were. I said Bakersfield, but you'd be back this afternoon. He said he was on his way and then he hung up."

"No explanation?"

"He doesn't strike me as a man who explains himself."

"Good point."

Henry opened the refrigerator door and took a bag of fresh salad mix from the crisper drawer. "I wonder if you'd give these a rinse. The package says 'ready to eat' but that's a relative term. Lettuce spinner's in there."

He indicated the corner cabinet that was outfitted with a lazy Susan so that cooking items could be stored in otherwise dead space. I opened the cabinet and removed the spinner, took out the perforated inner bowl, dumped the loose lettuces in, and ran water over the greens. I popped the bowl back into the spinner and pulled the cord, which made the inner bowl rotate at high speed, excess water flung off by the centrifugal force. The rapidly retracting cord snapped back and caught me in the hand. Wow, shit, hurt, ow.

I was happy for the distraction. Henry had mentioned an estimated 6:00 arrival time for Dietz, whom I knew to be punctual. I stole a quick glance at my watch. It was only 5:20, so I figured I was still in the safety zone. I couldn't imagine why a job referral would warrant a trip to Santa Teresa. Maybe he meant to refer *me* for a job. I knew I hadn't sent any business his way. When the knock came at Henry's aluminum screen door, the sound barely registered, so I was startled when Henry opened the door and I heard Dietz's voice.

In the first glimpse I had of him, I knew something major had gone down in his life. As usual his hair was shorn close, but the medium gray had now turned almost entirely white. Something in the change suggested he'd been hit with an emotional blast, like a flash fire that leaves singed hair where your eyebrows had once been. I blinked and saw him restored to himself, looking as he always had. The white was the natural progression of a graying process already under way. His nose was long and sharp, humped at the bridge where a fan of lines ran upward intersecting the horizontal lines that traced his forehead. It was the gray eyes and the deep tan that made his face arresting, along with the occasional lopsided smile.

He wasn't a big man, maybe five foot ten. He was light-framed, narrow through the shoulders, with a wiry strength as opposed to brawn. In the past, he'd worked out with weights and he'd run six miles a day, except for the stretch when his bad knee proved too painful. He'd apparently recovered from the knee surgery with no lingering effects. At least he had no limp that I could see. He looked tired, but then maybe we all look tired as the years mount up. He wore the same boots, faded blue jeans, and the same tweed jacket I'd first seen him in, complete with a black turtleneck. I put a self-conscious hand to my own black turtleneck, wondering if anyone would notice the match.

He'd taken me in with a glance. I was the same as I'd always been, but I wondered if he saw a difference. I caught Henry's gaze flicking from me to Dietz and back. He seemed to hold himself in suspension, removing his personhood while Dietz and I sorted ourselves out.

I said, "How was the trip?"

"Good. Fast. Can't believe I didn't get a ticket." His tone was pleasant, but he didn't meet my eyes. What was that about?

"You still have the Porsche? I expected to hear your car rumbling from half a block away."

"Still here. I thought about a new one, but mine's only ten years old."

Henry said, "How about a drink? Black Jack on the rocks?"

Dietz smiled. "Good memory."

"Have a seat," Henry said.

"Just let me freshen up."

"Sure thing. Bathroom's that way."

Dietz left. Henry and I exchanged a look, wondering what had prompted the nine-hour drive. There wasn't time to discuss the matter, so we went about our business, leaving it up to Dietz to explain himself. His usual style was to jump right in.

By the time he emerged from the bathroom, a scant four minutes had passed. Henry had dropped ice cubes into a high-ball glass and poured whiskey neat. "Water?"

"Perfect as is. Thanks."

Dietz sat down. As though coaxed, Ed jumped down from the rocker and jumped up into Dietz's lap. He did this without appearing to crouch and spring. He seemed to levitate. Four paws on the floor . . . airborne, straight up . . . four paws in Dietz's lap, as neat as you please. Ed studied Dietz at close range, the two eye to eye. Dietz ran an idle hand along the cat's head and the cat arched against his palm. Dietz scratched behind one ear. Daintily, Ed curled up in his lap, prepared to nap with his head on his paws. Henry took note of Ed's vote of approval. I had to suppress the urge to roll my eyes. A conspiracy of men and Ed was leading the charge. What had I ever done to him?

We chatted while we ate, skipping from topic to topic, avoiding anything significant. The longer this went on, the more tense I felt. I didn't know if Dietz was delaying so he could talk to me alone or if he was setting the stage for a show-down. I thought it was better to have Henry on hand while I heard him out. I felt guilty, but I didn't know what I'd done. Dessert out of the way, Henry inquired whether either of us wanted coffee. I declined and Dietz shook his head in the negative as well.

I looked at Dietz. "So what's up?"

The smile he turned on me was set and I could see now how angry he was. Not a hot anger, but the cold flat kind that's all the more dangerous because it's been driven underground.

"I was hoping you'd tell me," he said. "You recommended me to a guy who turned out to be a deadbeat. I did the work and submitted a report. That was June 15. No response. I billed again July and he called, which was nice of him. He claimed the client was a slow pay and if he didn't get the money that week, he'd pay me himself and collect from the client after the fact. Sounded good to me, so I waited. Still nothing. I bill again in August and the mail bounces back. Big block letters: 'Return to Sender.' I try calling and the number's a disconnect. I can't get through to you, so here I am."

He stared at me and I stared back.

"I have no idea what you're talking about," I said.

"Wolinsky. Pete. The PI."

"Well, it's no wonder you never heard from him. He's dead."

"Since when?"

"August 25. He was shot during a robbery attempt and died at the scene."

"Would've been nice if you'd let me know."

I squinted. "Why would I do that?"

"Because you gave him my name and he subbed out a job to me."

"I didn't give Pete your name."

"Yes, you did. That was the first thing he said."

"He said *I* sent you? When was this?"

"May. A week before Memorial Day. He said he ran into you downtown and asked if you knew a Nevada PI. You suggested me."

"I haven't talked to Pete in years. I'd never give him your name or number for any reason at all. The man's a scumbag."

"He said he worked with you at Byrd-Shine."

"He did not! He *never* worked at Byrd-Shine. I had nothing to do with giving him your number."

"Well, if you didn't send him, who did?"

"How would I know?"

"I only agreed because of you. I wouldn't have taken the job otherwise."

"Have you been listening to anything I said? He might have *claimed* I referred him, but that doesn't make it true."

"How'd he hear about me, then?"

"Maybe another PI in town."

"You're the only one I know."

I lowered my voice, feigning calm. "I have not talked to Pete since Morley Shine died and that was five years ago. I ran into him at the funeral, where he was trolling for business." In the midst of my protest, I felt a spark of recall and held up a hand. "Uh-oh. Wait."

Dietz said, "What."

"I just remembered. I got a call from Con Dolan, who said someone needed a Nevada PI. He asked for your phone number and I gave it to him. This was months ago. I told him I had no idea if you were still in business, but he was free to try. It didn't occur to me to ask what it was about. I knew you liked Con and he liked you, so it all seemed okay."

"That's probably it, then. My dumb luck."

"I'm sorry. Honestly, if I'd known it was Pete, I wouldn't have said a word."

Henry got up and poured me another glass of wine. Dietz had already reached for the bottle of Black Jack that was sitting in the middle of the table. He topped off his glass and when Henry held out his tumbler, Dietz filled that as well. The silence was dense.

I couldn't quite meet his eye. "How much does he owe you?"

"Three thousand dollars and change."

Another silence accumulated while I pondered the sum. Three thousand dollars would have seemed like a lot prior to my windfall of five hundred grand. All a matter of perspective, isn't it? "For doing what?"

"Surveillance."

"Who's the client?"

"Some young fellow here in town suspected his wife was having an affair with an old flame. This guy's wife and her old boyfriend both now work at the same research firm. The two were flying to Reno for a conference and I guess hubby wanted to know if they were up to no good."

"Were they?"

"Not that I saw. The two didn't interact at all. She met with an old high school buddy and they put their heads together on two occasions, but there was nothing romantic going on. I sent Pete my report and an itemized expense account with all of the receipts attached. This was four full days' work and I invoiced him accordingly."

"You want his office address?"

"I have it already. That's where I sent my bill. I'll take a run over there on Monday and see what's what. Maybe his partner can fill me in."

"I don't think Pete had a partner."

"Of course he did. Able, as in Able and Wolinsky."

"That's probably a ruse on his part to net a favorable position in the phone book."

"Shit," Dietz said.

"I still have his unlisted home phone in an old address book. I don't remember the number offhand, but I know where he lives."

"Never mind. Not your problem," he said.

"Of course it is. I should have asked Con what was going on and then cleared it with you before I passed your number along."

Dietz said, "Wouldn't have made any difference. If I'd known the request came from Con, I'd have agreed. Besides which, Pete sounded legit when I talked to him."

"'Legit' is a relative term," I said.

Henry slapped his knees and stood up. "Well, now that you've settled the matter, I'm off to bed. You kids can thumb-lock the door and pull it shut behind you when you leave. Take all the time you want."

Dietz set the cat on the floor and got to his feet. Across the front of his jeans there was a ghostly cat outlined in newly shed white hair. "I better be on my way. I'm at the Edgewater, scheduled for late arrival, but why risk them giving my room away?"

He extended a hand to Henry and the two men shook hands. "Thanks for supper. I owe you one."

Henry said, "Good seeing you again. As long as you've come all this way, I hope you're staying a while."

Dietz made no response.

Our good-nights were superficial, not even accompanied by a perfunctory handshake or a neutral buss on the cheek. I was sorry he'd driven nine hours to chew me out when I could have set him straight on the phone. I was about to suggest that he submit his bill to the probate court, assuming Pete Wolinsky'd died with a will, but I was certain the idea would occur to him without my piping up. At this point, it seemed best to leave well enough alone. I'd already done him a disservice without even meaning to.

He waited until I'd unlocked my door and I was safely inside before he returned to the street. I heard him pass through the squeaky gate and moments later, I heard his Porsche grumble to life. The sound faded as he drove off. I looked at my watch. It wasn't even 9:00. Despite the long, hard day I'd endured, one more question remained. I picked up my jacket, my shoulder bag, and my car keys, locked the door behind me, and headed out again. I had Felix on my mind.

24

When I reached the Santa Teresa Hospital, visiting hours had wound to a close, but there was still foot traffic in and out. The Intensive Care Unit was quiet. I passed the empty waiting room. Even with the corridor lights dimmed, the business of life and death went on behind the scenes. This was the time for clerical work; charts to be caught up, supplies ordered, reports prepared for the shift change. There was no one in the hall. At the nurses' station, I inquired about Felix. A young Hispanic woman in blue scrubs got up from a rolling office chair and indicated that I was to follow. "Where'd Pearl disappear to?" she asked over her shoulder.

"Don't know. I'll have to look into it," I said.

She had me wait in the hall while she slipped into Felix's room and pushed the curtain aside, sliding it along the track above his bed. She stood on the far side and watched him as I did. Felix lay in a pool of light, attached to machinery that monitored and recorded his progress for good or for ill. Blood pressure, respiration, pulse. His head was heavily swaddled in white, both legs in casts. There was none of the usual in-patient detritus in range. No bed table. No flowers, no get-well cards propped up, no bucket of ice, and no oversize plastic cup with a flexible drinking straw. Life-sustaining fluids dripped into him from the clear bag that hung from the IV pole beside him and waste fluids trickled into a container out of sight under his bed. His sheets were snowy; the light in the rest of the room was subdued.

Poor Felix. The big Boggart, who'd stumbled into the camp while Pearl and Felix were trashing it, must have known she was the instigator. Felix responded to life in the moment, ill equipped to form a long-range plan and act on it. I could picture their desire to retaliate against Pearl, but why him? And why so savagely? Surely not for sport. Maybe this was better revenge from their perspective than attacking her directly.

Where I stood, no sound reached me. Felix didn't move. Even the rise and fall of his breathing was difficult to discern. He was alive. He was safe. He was warm. He didn't seem to be in pain. Sleep was all that remained to him. So much of the "stuff" of life was already gone, leaving him undisturbed. Maybe he would swim into consciousness again or maybe the gods would set him adrift. I kissed the tip of my index finger and pressed it to the glass. I'd come back the next day. Maybe by then, he'd be surfacing from his long sleep.

Sunday morning, by all rights, I should have slept in. Instead, I woke at 6:00 and while I didn't stir from my bed, I lay under the weight of my quilt and savored the warmth. The Plexiglas skylight above my bed showed a half dome of blue. I'd slept with my windows open to the full, and the morning air wafting in was scented with seaweed and burning leaves. Dietz was less than a mile away. He was one of those people who needs very little sleep. In the time we'd spent together, he was typically up until two, down for four hours, and up again at six. Sundays in particular, he took a long time over coffee, reading the paper section by section, even the parts I skipped.

I pushed the covers back, got up, and then turned and made the bed like a good girl. Live alone and you have two choices— be a tidy bun or a slob. I brushed my teeth, showered, and threw on the clothes I'd worn the night before. I drove to the Edgewater Hotel and left my Mustang in the hands of a parking valet. I went through the entrance to the hotel, crossed the lobby, and moved along the wide corridor with its stretches of Oriental carpets over high-gloss Saltillo tiles. To my left, windows looked out onto an enclosed patio. Ficus trees, potted palms, and birds of paradise, like stiffly crested orange cranes, were arranged throughout, separating seating areas and providing the illusion of privacy. I spotted Dietz at a table against the stretch of windows that looked out toward the ocean. He was in jeans and a gray fleece shirt with a zippered placket and long sleeves that he'd pushed up. The paper was spread across the tabletop, one edge anchored by a coffee carafe. He wore round wire-rim glasses.

The hostess moved as though to greet me. I pointed at Dietz, indicating that I'd be sitting with him. She held up a menu that I waved off. Dietz looked up as I approached. He moved a hefty section of the *Los Angeles Times* from the nearest chair and I sat down. I could see now that my initial take had been correct. He looked tired and the gray in his hair had given way to white. He put his hand on the table, palm up, and gave me that crooked smile of his.

I placed my hand in his. "What happened to you?"

"Naomi died."

"Of what?"

"Cancer. It wasn't easy, but it was mercifully brief. Six weeks from diagnosis to the end. The boys were there and so was I."

"When was this?"

"May 10. I got back to Carson City on the fifteenth and four days later, the call from Pete Wolinsky came in. If you'll pardon the hocus-pocus sentiment, it felt like a sign. There's no question I'd have done the work . . . anything to distract myself . . . but there was something in the idea it was coming from you. Naomi always said I used work to avoid being close, a claim I hotly denied until the truth of it came home."

"Where are the boys at this point?"

"Nick's in San Francisco, working for a brokerage firm. He graduated from Santa Cruz with a degree in accounting. Naomi steered him toward finance and it seems to agree with him. Graham got his degree this past December. He hung around with Nick for a while and then took off. He's footloose and fancy-free, for the time being at any rate."

"Sounds like you."

"He is like me. Nick was always more like Naomi. Her coloring, her temperament."

"She got married, didn't she?"

"Two years ago. He's the one I feel for. Poor bastard. Marriage was a good one from everything I heard. He'd lost his first wife to cancer and he thought he'd survived the worst of it. Then Naomi got sick and now he's right back where he was."

"What about you?"

"She was my touchstone—another revelation in the wake of her death. Whatever happened, I knew she'd be there. I couldn't live with the woman, but we had those two boys and she was part of my life. I probably only saw her every three or four years. I'm off balance. They say it's like that when you lose a toe. You take for granted you can walk just fine. You've been doing it all your life without giving it a second thought. Suddenly your gait goes wobbly."

He signaled the waitress and I saw her moving toward the table with a fresh carafe of coffee. Dietz got up and retrieved a coffee cup and silverware setup from the table next to us. It was a nice way of creating emotional space so I could absorb what he'd said. I'd never met Naomi. I'd seen photographs of her and I'd been startled by how beautiful she was. She and Dietz had been apart longer than they'd been a couple. They'd lived together for a time, but she'd refused to marry him. Or maybe he'd never asked.

He returned to the table and sat down.

I said, "The minute you walked into Henry's kitchen, I knew something was wrong. I could see it in your face."

"Surprised the hell out of me. This is what's so weird. We were never in love. There was some kind of chemistry I wouldn't even classify as sexual. It was more fundamental than that. Ours was a bad mix of personalities. We drove each other nuts. Happiest day of my life was when I left her the last time. Then she died and the bottom dropped out."

"I'm sorry."

"Being angry with you was a relief."

"Easier than grief."

"Right," he said. "Look, I know you were mad that I left."

"Don't project. I wasn't *that* mad," I said.

"Could have fooled me. Times I thought about you, I didn't have the nerve to call. I figured you'd cut me down and rightly so. After a while, the absence just seemed to compound itself. When Pete didn't pay me I figured it was your revenge."

"Too subtle. If I take revenge, it'll have my name written all over it."

"So now what?"

"I could use some breakfast. I'm starving," I said.

Dietz joined me in an orgy of bacon and eggs and all the accompaniments. It was a meal that never ceased to satisfy. I was still munching on a piece of buttered rye toast when he returned to the subject that had brought him to town.

"So here's what bothers me," he said. "Pete hires me to do a job and next thing you know he's dead. What's that about?"

"Well, it wasn't *quite* like that," I said. "You did the work when, the last weekend in May? The robbery went down in August."

"I know, but I keep thinking the two might be linked. This isn't a gig you see much these days. One spouse spying on the other? We live in the land of no-fault divorce, so it struck me as odd."

"Why'd you take the job?"

"It sounded like fun. I can't remember the last time I was asked to skulk around a hotel taking pictures with a telephoto lens. I did a damn fine job of it even if I say so myself. Then the guy who hired me gets shot to death and I don't like it so much."

"Just because one event follows another doesn't mean the first *caused* the second," I said.

"I get that and I hope you're right, but as long as I'm here I'd like to satisfy myself."

"Tell me about the surveillance again. When you talked about it last night I was feeling so defensive I didn't hear a word you said."

"I was tailing a woman named Mary Lee Bryce and her boss, a doctor named Dr. Linton Reed. Both work at a local research institute. Apparently, they knew each other years ago and were involved in a romance of some kind. I have no idea if it was serious or not. The point is, her current husband was worried about the two of them in Reno staying in the same hotel."

"Why'd they go to Reno?"

"They attended a conference over the long holiday weekend."

"And was she having an affair with him?"

"Not that I picked up on. The two barely spoke."

"Might be camouflage."

"I considered that. They ignore one another in public and bang away in private. Problem is they had no personal contact at all. I'd be willing to swear to it."

"Didn't you say she met with an old high school friend?"

"Now, see, you *were* listening," he said with a smile. "You're right. A fellow named Owen Pensky, an investigative journalist. I ran a background check on him. Big scandal in his past."

"What kind?"

"He was fired from the *New York Times* for plagiarizing someone else's work."

"What was he doing in Reno?"

"He lives there. He picked up a job at one of the Reno papers."

"You think her relationship with him was business or personal?"

"I have no idea. She and Pensky met twice, but I couldn't get audio. Place was too heavily populated. If I'd known in advance where they were meeting, I'd have planted a bug. I guarantee they didn't go to his room or hers."

"But she *could* have been having an affair with him."

"If so, the two of them did a flawless job of keeping it under wraps."

"How did you frame it in your report?"

"I was careful. I drew no inferences and I didn't offer my unsolicited opinion. Nice neutral language not meant to inflame."

"What are the ethics in a situation like this? With Pete dead, can you talk to her husband about whether the bill was paid?"

"I'll have to. I doubt the wife has any idea Pete hired me to keep an eye on her. I tip her off and the situation could turn ugly."

"I still don't see what this has to do with Pete's death. Feels like a fishing expedition."

"Sure it is, but why not? Somebody owes me."

"Pete could have collected and just not paid you."

"In which case, I'm probably out of luck. Meanwhile, I

don't like thinking the guy got killed because of me. If there's no link, then fine. If I manage to collect my money, it's better yet."

"You have a plan?"

"I'm hoping I can talk Pete's wife into letting us have a look at his accounts. Meanwhile, what's on your plate?"

"I have to get the Mustang over to the service station. Some asshole drove a roofing nail into my sidewall tire," I said. "What about you?"

"I thought I'd pay Con Dolan a visit and see what he knows. Maybe the cops have a suspect in sight, or one already in jail. If so, I'll quit worrying the job was in any way linked to his departure from the planet Earth."

"You know where Con lives?"

"I do and it shouldn't take me long. After that, if you're free, I'll treat you to dinner at Emile's."

"Sounds good. You want me to check with Henry?"

"We'll save that for another occasion."

"How long will you be here?"

"Don't know yet," he said.

After breakfast, we reclaimed our respective vehicles from the parking valet and then he set off for Con Dolan's house while I continued on to the nearest gas station, where I dropped off my tire. The service bays were closed, but the two mechanics would be in Monday morning, and the fellow manning the pumps said he'd have one of them get on it first thing. He'd call when the tire had been fixed and was ready to be picked up. In the interim, the spare tire, while not optimal, was sufficient to get me around.

That issue out of the way, the job I assigned myself was to round up Dandy and Pearl, who by all accounts were using Felix's precarious medical state as one more excuse to misbehave. I was reasonably certain the sports bar where they played darts on weekends was one called the Dugout I'd seen on Milagro, a block and a half past the minimart where I'd bought the three packs of cigarettes a lifetime ago.

I found street parking around the corner from the Dugout and hoofed my way back. A judiciously placed waste container had done double duty as a trash can and as a barf receptacle for a patron who'd almost managed to reach it.

The place was open, of course. Ten in the morning on a

Sunday was the same as church to some folks. As this was the Pacific time zone, football games being broadcast from the Midwest and the East Coast would soon be underway. The bar itself looked like every other sports bar you've ever seen. Booths, free-standing tables and chairs, six big-screen television sets mounted at intervals, each tuned to a different sporting event. The bar itself extended the length of the room on the left-hand side, with stools lined up smartly, most of them occupied. A second room was furnished with foosball tables and pool tables. I caught a glimpse at the rear of a series of dartboards, but no one was throwing at that hour. Twelve men at the bar turned to look at me as I walked in and then went back to their drinks.

The bartender ambled in my direction. He was a middle-aged man, short and stocky, wearing chinos and a vintage jersey of some vague hockey-like sort. He placed a cocktail napkin on the bar in front of me. I said, "I'm looking for Pearl."

"Too late. Her and Dandy came in yesterday, kicking up a fuss. Now they're eighty-sixed."

Being eighty-sixed was the drunkard's equivalent of being barred for life, though most bar owners would eventually relent.

"You know where they went?"

"Shape they were in, it wasn't Harbor House. Curfew's at seven. Last I saw 'em it was two A.M."

"They were here all that time?"

"They went out for a while and then came back in. Spreading the joy, I guess."

"What kind of trouble did they make?"

Mockingly, he put a hand to his chin. He twiddled his fingers and looked skyward, as though trying to remember and calculate. "Well, let's see. Second time they showed up, they started knocking back shots. Dandy's not a maudlin drunk like she is, but he gets in everyone's face. He's a guy who wants to engage in long, rambling chats. Folks don't want to deal with that. The two of 'em tried throwing darts but neither one could see straight. Pearl fell over backward and busted up a chair and then he weighed in and broke a second one for good luck. She got sick and then he fell down. I should have called the cops at that point, but I got too big a heart."

"I heard they were on a bender."

"I can testify to that. Here's the deal: I like Pearl. I wish her the best and I mean that. Who knows what put me where I am and put her on the street? Call it the Fickle Finger of Fate, but she's wanking on about how everything's so unfair. I got no patience for that. Like I said to her, I didn't invent the game and I didn't make the rules. Maybe it all stinks and I'm sorry as hell, but I got a bar to run."

"She's a tough one," I said, hoping to defuse his irritation and sidestep an argument.

"She says she's down on her luck but luck's got nothing to do with it. She makes choices the same as I do. I don't know if she's lazy or stupid or mentally ill, and I don't care. Point is, I got fifteen employees dependent on me, but how the hell can I run a business when Pearl and her ilk come in here and puke all over the place?"

I shook my head, saying, "I hear you" in what I hoped was a sympathetic tone. In truth, I was more interested in their current whereabouts than a history of their bad behavior.

"Fact is, my taxes pay for her room and board and her medical care. You ever think about that? And you know what? My wife got sick and ended up in St. Terry's for ten days. You want to know how much that cost me? Ninety thousand bucks. I kid you not. I'll be paying that off until I'm ninety myself. Pearl gets sick? It's not gonna cost her a dime. They got *programs.* Shelter and clothing and three meals a day. I should be so unfortunate. Point is, I'm done with her and I'm done with her friend. Tell you something else and this makes no sense: Dandy's a smart guy. His father taught math at the high school. You ever hear about that?"

"Actually, I did."

"Dandy could have made something of himself, you know? He decides to take the low road, why does that obligate me?"

I made a few more mouth noises and then excused myself. Raise the subject of the homeless and everybody has a strong opinion. Fifty percent of the local citizens are sympathetic and the other fifty are pissed as hell. Does the problem get solved? No, it does not.

I retrieved my car and headed back down Milagro toward the beach, hanging a right when I reached the small side street where Harbor House was located. Again, I parked the car, hoofed the half block, and went in. The common room was largely empty, but there they were, Pearl and Dandy sprawled on adjacent couches, both of them dead to the world. She had her jacket pulled over her head but her body type was distinct. I couldn't miss the bulk of her, swaddled in fake leather. Dandy reclined in an upholstered chair, hands clasped across his lap, his legs extended in front of him. He was slack mouthed and snoring. The air around them smelled of fruitcake.

I found a chair and watched for a while, wondering at the life they led. I couldn't handle it myself. I don't have the discipline. I might manage to be idle for half a day and then I'd be back in my routine: getting up at six, jogging my three miles, going into the office, walking up to Rosie's for a bite to eat. Doing nothing makes me itch. I don't have the temperament or the strength of character.

After a few moments, Pearl roused herself and sat up. Her face was high-blood-pressure pink, her hair as stiff and dry as straw. She'd bleached it blond once upon a time and what was left had worked its way down to the tips. In the wake of her drinking binge, I could tell that many of her elementary body parts were in full mutiny. I didn't feel sorry for her, but I could identify to some extent. She must have felt she'd been stricken with a tropical disease, some hideous malady she'd done nothing to deserve. I could see her looking inward, perhaps measuring her nausea level on a scale of one to ten. I would have pegged her at a six and rising.

"How're you feeling?" I asked.

She said, "Man, oh man."

She ran a hand across her face and peered at me as though the light hurt her eyes. "Where'd you come from?"

"Back from Bakersfield."

"How'd it go?"

"Not that well. What about you?"

"I think I picked up that stomach bug that's going around."

"It's a bad one from what I hear."

She held a hand up. "Hang on a sec." She pushed herself to her feet. She pressed two fingers against her lips and walked with great purpose toward the ladies' room, speeding up as she got closer. Even with the door closed, I could hear the misery. Such are the charms of drink. Dandy would be lucky if he managed to sleep for a while, letting his body metabolize the excess alcohol in his poor beleaguered system.

Pearl was moving slowly when she returned. I could tell she'd splashed some water on her face and I was hoping she'd had a chance to rinse her mouth. She eased herself back down on the couch by degrees as though her back had gone out on her.

"Word has it, you and Dandy got eighty-sixed from the Dugout," I said, mildly.

"Won't last. You know why?"

"I'd love to hear your analysis."

"Guy's got a big heart. Besides, he likes me."

"He'd have to."

"Anyway, what'd we do to him? Hey, so once in a while we mess up, but who don't? . . . doesn't," she said. She slid a pained look in my direction and I imagined I was the only thing standing between her and another round of sleep. "You stop by for some reason in particular?" she asked.

"Just wondering where you were. Last night I went over to St. Terry's to see Felix."

"Bummer," she said. "I been there for hours. Anyone tell you that?"

"I heard you were faithful as a hound."

"You got that right. You don't happen to have any Vicodin."

I shook my head in the negative.

"Percocet?"

"Fresh out," I said.

I heard the phone ringing at the desk behind me. Someone picked up and when I glanced over my shoulder, I saw a volunteer standing with her palm across the mouthpiece. "Pearl?"

She held up the handset by way of summons.

"What'd I tell you?" she said, struggling to her feet again.

"Guy owes me an apology big time. I don't know if I'm accepting it or not. I don't like abuse, especially when I didn't do nothing to him."

"Well, good luck," I said. "Show the guy some mercy."

Pearl said, "Ha."

Meanwhile, Dandy had pulled himself upright. Maybe our conversation had reached him in the depths of his inebriated state. As much as he'd had to drink, he wouldn't be sober for another two days. If Pearl's condition was a harbinger, he'd be in a hurt locker the size of hers.

From the direction of the desk, I heard Pearl's voice rise.

"DO NOT SAY THAT. Don't you say that to me, you son of a bitch!"

There was a silence and Pearl's voice rose. "Shut your trap! That is not TRUE! You're a lying sack of shit."

Another silence while someone on the other end had a few more things to say.

Pearl's response was to the point. "Hey! You say that again, I'll come down there and punch you in the face!"

She listened briefly, and then slammed down the handset. "That's bullshit. What kind of bullshit is that?"

She headed toward us at a lumbering pace, still in too much pain to move with any speed. She was sweating and her skin had turned blotchy in the wake of her rage. Dandy pushed himself to his feet. "What's up?" he asked.

"I'll tell you what's up. You want to know what's up? That asshole's telling me Felix died."

"I saw him last night," I said.

"Yeah, well, he died an hour ago. How could he do that when I loved the guy? Hey. You know what? Hey . . ."

Her voice broke. Whatever she meant to add, a howl went up instead. The sound was sufficient to freeze everyone in place and then send half the residents scurrying to her aid as though her hand had been caught in the blades of a fan.

25

Here's how hard-hearted I am: I was irritated by Pearl's wailing. It seemed pumped up, artificial, overdone. My response was to disconnect, as though I were pulling a plug out of a wall socket. I couldn't react to the news of Felix's death because her excess had shut me down. It was as though she'd preempted any honest feelings generated by his passing. At the same time, I wondered if Pearl was the normal one and I was too psychologically stunted to experience sorrow. This didn't seem like the proper moment to sort out questions of such complexity, but the idea had occurred to me on previous occasions—this sense that I was somehow out of step with the rest of humankind. Maybe I'd seen too much. Maybe I'd been exposed to matters so coarse and wrenching, I was no longer capable of feeling pain. I could almost picture myself in a therapist's office, gingerly picking my way across this mine-field. Was I nuts?

Nah, I was almost sure it was Pearl. If I were *that* screwed up, I wouldn't be capable of reflecting on the point, would I?

So, there I stood while she collapsed on the couch in what looked like a parody of grief. Granted, it's not my job to judge how others process emotions, but I gave her a 2.5 out of 10 on the basis of her phoniness. Dandy made no move to comfort her. I wasn't sure if he felt equally alienated or he was simply helpless in the face of female histrionics. I didn't doubt Pearl loved Felix. I just thought she was cranking up the theatrics so she could command center stage. I crossed my arms and kept my gaze on the floor, knowing my body language testified to my state of mind, which was cranky and withdrawn. I could have sworn Pearl was aware of my disconnect because she took to thrashing about like a kid in the throes of a temper tantrum, determined to get a rise out of Mom.

Someone brought her a glass of water. Someone wet a paper towel and gently dabbed her face. I wanted to slap the shit out of her but somehow managed to restrain myself. This went on for longer than was absolutely necessary to make her point clear. Two of the residents helped her to her feet and she was led from the room like an athlete injured on the playing field. The others stood by in respectful silence while I mentally crossed my eyes. Dandy and I exchanged a look, but I couldn't read the content.

I said, "What in the world happened while I was off in Bakersfield? I know those guys beat the shit out of Felix, but what precipitated the attack? Did he and Pearl find some way to add insult to injury?"

"Not that I know. Pearl mostly stayed here, worried they'd come after her. Felix didn't seem concerned. I don't think the notion that actions have consequences meant anything to him. He did what he did and then forgot about it. That boy wasn't blessed with much in the way of common sense."

"What have the police done about the Boggarts?"

"Asked around, I'm sure. Filled out paperwork. I know they talked to the fellow who called 911, but he won't help. Sorry it happened and so forth, but he's not sticking his neck out for a bum who gets in a brawl with three other bums."

"Meanwhile, you and Pearl go off on a toot," I said. "What was that about? You'd think the last thing you'd want to do is get shitfaced."

Sheepishly, he said, "Feels good sometimes, you know? When bad things go down, you want to cut loose. Get loaded and forget. Better than feeling sad or mad or depressed."

"Are you okay now? You don't look good."

"Naw, I'm not feeling so hot. I need to find me a spot where I can curl up and sleep."

"You'll keep an eye on Pearl?"

"Oh sure. Gotta look after my pal."

"You go off on another bender and I'll wring your neck," I said with all the compassion I could muster, which was none.

Then I repressed the urge to hug the man, primarily because he had what looked like a streak of spit-up down the front of his shabby sport coat. I patted him on the arm. The gesture was weak but it was the best I could do.

On my way out, the volunteer at the desk beckoned to me. I checked behind me to make sure she meant the gesture for me. I paused at the desk. She said, "Are you related to Terrence Dace?"

"Yes."

"The one he made executor of his estate?"

"That's me. I'm Kinsey."

"Belva," she said. "The reason I ask is I came across some mail for him and thought you should have it."

"Well, thanks. That's good of you."

She turned and picked up a couple of bank statements in windowed envelopes and a fourteen-by-twenty mailing pouch. The package was thick, and when she passed it across the counter to me, I was surprised by the weight. The label was self-addressed in the printing I'd come to recognize. The postmark was June 29, 1988.

"I appreciate this," I said. I pulled out a business card and placed it on the desk for her. "If anything else comes in, would you let me know?"

"Of course. I'll leave a note for the other volunteers in case there's something more."

I thanked her and carried the bulky package to my car. The package was so plastered over with clear tape that I couldn't make any headway. I'd have to wait and open it later to see what he'd shipped to himself months before he died. I sat for a while. No point in consigning Felix's death to an index card. I wasn't sure what time he'd died or what the attending physician had listed as the cause of death. I didn't even know how old he was. All I knew for a certainty was he'd never get his braces off and that seemed too sad for words. I turned the key in the ignition and headed toward the bike shop at the foot of State Street. I turned into a side street just shy of the intersection and found a parking place. I locked my car and walked around the corner to the bicycle-rental shop.

The weekend art show was in progress: paintings, ceramics, and assorted crafts displayed in a line of booths laid out alongside the walk. Some vendors had erected lightweight tents to display homemade articles of clothing, wind chimes, lawn ornaments, jewelry, and whirligigs. Given that it was Sunday afternoon and the sun was out, the beach beyond was littered with people—screaming children, joggers with dogs, and prone lasses who'd loosened the tops of their bikinis to avoid the tan lines. The restaurants along the boulevard had flung their doors open, and those establishments with outside seating were filled to capacity.

The bicycle-rental shop was doing a lively business as well, especially with their pedal surreys, which were always popular with kids. I went in. In addition to bike rentals, the shop sold surfboards, bathing suits, T-shirts, shorts, ball caps, sunglasses, sunscreen, and accessories. I looked for someone in charge and settled on a fellow in his sixties who stood at the cash register, ringing up a sale. His Hawaiian shirt was one of those with washed-out colors, shades of pale blue with a design of palm fronds picked out in white. He was balding and wore a pair of reading glasses on top of his head. He sported a wedding ring and a wristwatch that looked sturdy enough to flush down a toilet without losing time.

I moved to the counter and waited my turn. When he'd finished with the customer, he looked at me expectantly.

I held out my hand. "Kinsey Millhone," I said. "Are you the owner?"

My introducing myself put me in a category with traveling salesmen and promoters hoping to post a flyer, advertising a little theater production no one wanted to attend.

After a slight hesitation, he shook my hand. "I own the place, yes. Last name's Puckett. What can I do for you?"

"I'm a friend of the young man who got beat up out front."

His smile dimmed. "You're talking about Felix. How's he doing?"

"Not that well. He died a little while ago."

He held up a hand. "Hold it. Before you get into your spiel, I know what you want and I can't help. Those goons kicked the shit out of him and I'm sorry he died, but I'm not going to go down to the station to look at mug shots. I know who they are. I see 'em down here all the time. What's it to you?"

"I didn't know Felix well, but I feel bad."

"Me, too. Who wouldn't? He was a good kid, but that doesn't change the facts. I'm sick to death of the homeless population. If they're not hitting up the tourists for change, they're passed out between buildings or parked on public benches, talking to themselves. I don't begrudge a guy a place to sleep. What gets my goat is every night I got someone peeing on my front step. It smells like a urinal out there. I got some gal takes a dump out by my fence every single night. What kind of person does that?"

"Maybe she's mentally ill."

"Then maybe she should be put away somewhere. Worst thing ever happened was Reagan closing down all the loony bins back in the seventies—"

I cut him off. "Let's not get into the politics, okay? I understand your complaints, but I'm not here to debate. I'd like to talk about Felix, not the rest of this stuff."

"Point taken. The kid was never disrespectful, so I don't mean to tar him with the same brush. Homeless in general, I got no beef with as long as they lay off what's mine. Town's filled with weepy-minded liberals—"

"Hey!"

"Sorry. I didn't mean to go off again," he said. "Comes down to identifying the assholes who throttled him, I got nothing to say. That big goon gets picked up, what's the system gonna do with him? Run him through the courts and spit him out the other end."

"But why should those guys get away with murder?" I asked. "Homeless or not, those are bad men."

"I agree," he said. "Let me tell you something. I knew Felix a lot longer than you did. First time he showed up was six or eight years back. He couldn't have been more than sixteen years old. He asked for a couple of bucks and I turned him down. I said I needed work done and was he willing or not? He said yes, so I let him sweep up. He'd break down boxes, take out trash, and stuff like that. In exchange, I'd buy him dinner. Nothing fancy, but it wasn't fast food. Sometimes I'd slip him a ten to see him through until his disability check came in. After a while, I guess he lost interest or found some other way to make ends meet. I'm sorry about what happened to him."

"But you still won't look at mug shots."

"No, I will not. You know what I'd get in return? That two-bit gangster and his cronies would come in here looking for me. Punch my lights out, smash my plate-glass windows, pull merchandise off the racks, and stuff it down their pants. Where does that leave me?"

"Would you at least think about it?"

"No, because nothing's going to change. Not you, not me, not that kid's death. I get your point. You'd like to do what you can. Me, too, for that matter, but I won't put myself in harm's way. I got a wife and kids and they come first. You might think I'm a coward, but I'm not."

"I understand. I just can't think what else to do for him."

"I appreciate the sentiment. This is nothing against you or Felix. I know my limits. That's all I'm trying to say."

I took out a business card and placed it on the counter. "If anything else comes up, could you give me a call?"

"No, but I wish you luck."

When I returned to the studio, I passed Dietz's red Porsche parked half a block away. Either he hadn't found Con Dolan at home or information had been in short supply. There was a parking place on the far side of the street, so I made a U-turn and pulled into it. I grabbed my shoulder bag and the mailing pouch, locked my car, crossed the street, and let myself in through the gate.

When I reached the back patio I stopped dead. Henry sat in one of the two Adirondack chairs. Anna Dace had settled in the other. Her dark hair was pulled up on top of her head and held in place with a series of silver clips. Boots, jeans, a denim jacket, under which she wore a low-cut T-shirt. All well and good. It was the oversize suitcase beside her that caught my attention. I also took note of Ed the cat, who was curled up in her lap sleeping like a baby.

I held Dace's package against my chest like body armor as I stared at her. "How did you get here?"

"A Greyhound bus."

"I thought you didn't have a dime."

"I had to borrow the money from Ellen. If you'd given me a ride like you said, I wouldn't have had to bother her."

"I never said I'd give you a ride."

"You sure as shit didn't say no." She glanced at Henry. "Excuse the trash talk, but I'm sure you can see my point."

He had the good grace not to comment one way or the other. He ventured a smile at me. "Your father's side of the family. This is nice."

I was still focused on her. "You can't stay with me."

"Who asked you? I got a place to stay."

Henry said, "It's no trouble. I have a spare bedroom. We were just going in to get her settled. I thought you'd enjoy having her close by so the two of you could get to know each other."

"Did you come up with that plan or did she?"

Henry blinked. "I don't quite remember now. I thought I did."

"I have work to do," I said.

I hadn't given Dietz a key, but he must have hung on to the one he had made when he was last in town. The apartment was unlocked and the door stood ajar, leaving a plank of October sunshine lying on my floor. I had to stand in the doorway for a moment to regain my self-control. I couldn't blame Henry. How was he to know how manipulative she was?

I put the package on my desk.

Dietz was sitting on my couch, bare feet propped on the coffee table while he worked his way through my copy of the Sunday *Los Angeles Times*. This was the very paper he had open across the breakfast table when I'd found him at the Edgewater earlier. He'd put on a fresh pot of coffee and his empty cup was resting within reach. "You're upset."

"No, I'm not."

"You *look* upset."

"I don't want to talk about it," I said. "It has nothing to do with you."

"Imagine my relief."

I tossed my shoulder bag onto one of the kitchen stools and settled on the couch beside him. "I should've let you finish reading the paper while you had the chance," I said.

He smiled. "I can do this all day. I like the bits and pieces buried at the back. I check the personals columns and study the car ads. You never know when you might come across the deal of the century."

"What did Con say?"

"He wasn't home. Neighbor said he and Stacy Oliphant went off to Cabo for a couple of weeks. Sport fishing, I gather. We'll chat with the homicide detectives tomorrow and hope they have information to trade. Your old boyfriend still assigned to the crimes against persons unit?"

"Who, Jonah? He was never a *boyfriend*. He was a guy I dated when his wife wasn't jerking him around."

"Really. I don't think I knew about him. I was talking about the other one. Curly-haired fellow whose dad has all the dough."

"Doesn't ring a bell," I said, though I knew perfectly well he was referring to Cheney Phillips.

I wasn't sure how he could contemplate the subject of my so-called love life. If I'd known he'd been involved with two other women, I'd have been too insecure to mention either one. In my opinion, this was exactly the sort of issue that lengthy and frequent separations bring to the fore. I didn't want to "share." I was an only child and I still tend to cling to the notion of "what's mine is mine." Actually, Deitz was an only child as well, but he'd gone to the other extreme. Where I was possessive, he was laissez-faire, a free-market kind of guy. I knew it was his coping mechanism, but I wasn't sure how it worked. Maybe he was casual about bonds because he was always out the door and always moving on. He had no interest in putting down roots. To him, life was a slide show and he was happy with the change of scene. He liked stimulation and novelty. He didn't attach emotional meaning to what I did, especially since he felt it had nothing to do with him. I don't understand how men can operate like that. Given my abandonment issues (and I confess I hate talk of that sort), I was always in danger of losing what I longed for most—stability, closeness, belonging. In my head, I knew better. Being needy is actually a way of keeping others at bay. It may seem attractive to those addicted to rescue, but the yearning can never be fulfilled and the clinging ends up driving folks away. Why would

you want someone hanging around your neck, worried you
don't care enough and asking for constant reassurance on the
point?

"I think we should do something," I said.

"Like what?"

"I don't know. Let's get out of here."

He folded the paper and put his bare feet on the floor, feeling around for his loafers. "I'm game, though I'd prefer to have
a plan."

"I'm thinking we should take a look at Pete's office. Maybe
he actually has a partner with a shitload of cash. You can collect and be on your way."

"I didn't say I was leaving."

"But you will."

"You have a bad attitude."

"I know, but it's the only one I have."

We took Dietz's car to avoid the wear and tear on my spare
tire. The drive into town was a simple matter of taking Cabana
to State and hanging a left. Pete's office was on Granita in a
building that had seen better days. We found street parking in
a small lot nearby. The neighborhood was funky. The entire
block would doubtless be bought someday soon, razed, and
replaced with a more lucrative concern: a parking garage, a
condominium complex, a hotel of a modest chain. Pete's
ground-floor office was marked A.

The agency had apparently never been graced with a sign
hanging out front. The names Able and Wolinsky were still
lettered on the plate-glass window in black and gold decals
that had largely flaked and fallen away. In the lower right-hand
corner a For Lease sign had been propped with a contact number. There was no Realtor or property manager mentioned by
name. Dietz jotted down the phone number while I peered
through the glass.

The office consisted of one large room with a closet. I was
guessing he had access to the executive restroom, located
down the hall and open to the public. His space was bare of
furniture. The closet door stood open, revealing an empty
hanging rod and a few makeshift shelves. There was a second

door in the middle of the back wall that probably opened into an interior corridor. Knowing Pete as I did, I imagined a number of hasty departures when circumstances warranted his absenting himself on short notice. As this was Sunday, the offices on either side of his were closed.

"You want to track down the property manager?" Dietz asked.

"I'd rather see if Pete's wife is available."

I remembered Pete's home address from the days when the Byrd-Shine agency was still in business. While I was accruing my training hours, I also made coffee and ran errands for the two. If Pete was late turning in a report, I'd be sent over to pick up the paperwork. The Wolinsky house was ten blocks away; a story and a half of white frame with a small recessed porch barely large enough for the two dusty white wicker chairs arranged to one side. Two sets of double windows sat one above the other. A single diamond-shaped pane to the right suggested attic space. The window frames and the trim pieces around the front door were painted dark blue. An enormous eucalyptus tree in the front yard was leaning drunkenly to one side where the edge of the porch prevented its upright growth.

I twisted the handle on the mechanical doorbell. The resultant response mimicked an alarm clock going off. Ruthie Wolinsky opened the door. I hadn't seen her for many years, but she looked much the same—tall, very slim, with long thinning hair brushed away from her face. She wore a long-sleeve white lace blouse and a long denim skirt with boots. She was easily sixty years old, and while the headband might have looked incongruous on anyone else, it was perfect for her. Her hair color had shifted from mild brown to gray with much of the original shade still in evidence. Her brows were pale over mild green eyes. Soft lines defined her elongated face with its high forehead. When she saw me, recognition flickered, but it had been far too long for her to recall my name.

"Kinsey Millhone," I said. "Pete and I were professional acquaintances years ago."

"I remember you," she said as her gaze shifted to Dietz.

"This is my colleague, Robert Dietz."

Her gaze returned to mine. "You know Pete was shot to death in August."

"I heard about that and I'm sorry." Already, I admired the straightforward manner in which she conveyed the information. No euphemisms; no attempt to soften the facts.

"Is there a problem?" she asked.

Dietz said, "I'm a Nevada PI. I did some work for Pete last May—a four-day surveillance in a Reno hotel. There's a balance outstanding on the account."

"You'll have to get in line with everyone else. Pete died without a penny to his name. His creditors are still swarming out of the woodwork."

"We're hoping to pursue another approach. One that won't involve you," I said.

She stared for a moment, making up her mind, and then held open the wooden screen door. "You're welcome to come in. I'm not liable for his debts, but I don't mind listening to what you have to say."

Dietz and I stepped into the foyer. There was a living room to our left, and she led the way to a small seating area. Dietz and I sat side by side on an upholstered settee that probably didn't get much use. I suspected she occupied cozier rooms at the back of the house.

"How are you doing?" I asked. "It must be difficult."

"I'm getting along well enough, though every other day, a new problem seems to crop up."

"Such as what?"

"People like you arriving at my door," she said. Her smile was slight and carried no rebuke. "I've stopped opening his mail. There's no point in knowing about bills when there's nothing I can do."

"What are the police telling you?"

"Not much. They were interested at first. Now other cases have taken precedence."

"No suspect?"

She shook her head. "They think he was killed with his own gun, which was missing from the scene. He took his Glock and his Smith and Wesson with him everywhere. Especially if he went out at night, he wouldn't have been without one or the other. Usually he carried both."

"Both of his guns are gone?"

"Just the Glock. His pocket pistol was returned to me. They found that in the trunk of his car. They believe there was a second gun involved, also missing. A Lieutenant Phillips is handling the case. I'm sure he could tell you more."

"You have no idea why he was out that night?"

"He was an insomniac, so he was out many nights, roaming the streets. There was nothing unusual about that night, at least as far as I know."

"No business dealings that might have gone sour?"

"He mentioned a job coming up and he was optimistic about his prospects. I have no idea what came of it."

"What about friends? Was there anyone he might have confided in?"

"You knew Pete. He was a loner. He didn't have friends or confidants."

Dietz said, "Were you aware he was in financial straits?"

"I suspected as much, though his affairs are in much worse shape than I thought. He'd let his life insurance lapse. He had nothing in savings, his checking account was in overdraft, and his credit cards were maxed out. I knew he had problems, but I had no idea of the magnitude. When we got married, we swore we'd be honest with one another, but his pride sometimes got in the way. The house is paid for, but both our names are on the deed. I haven't talked to an attorney but I'm hoping I won't have to sell or take out a mortgage to satisfy his creditors."

"Did he leave a will?"

"I haven't found one so far. That was the sort of thing he postponed. In his mind, there was always time."

"What about assets?" Dietz said. "I'm not asking from self-interest. I'm wondering if there's anything you might've overlooked."

"I'm surprised he hadn't filed for bankruptcy. I have two accounts in my name that he had no access to or he might have gone through those as well. It was easy come, easy go with him."

"A free spirit," I suggested.

"Not free, from my perspective," she said, tartly.

I noted the flash of heat with a feeling of relief. She was keeping her anger in check, but it was there.

She went on, her gaze fixed on the floor. "Two months ago he told me he was setting money aside for our anniversary. Next year would have been our fortieth and he wanted us to go on a river cruise. I didn't take him seriously, but I was hoping he'd managed to tuck a little something away. If I could lay hands on anything, I could at least pay the noisiest of his creditors."

"You haven't found anything?"

She shook her head. "I've turned this house upside down and there's nothing except for the twenty-two dollars' worth of coins he tossed in a jar."

"No investments?"

"Oh, please. No stocks, no bonds, no annuities," she said. "He drove a Ford Fairlane with over two hundred thousand miles on the odometer. The police impounded the car at the scene, but it's since been returned. I sold it for a hundred dollars and I was delighted to get that much. The new owner's picking it up later in the week. It's parked out back if you'd like to take a look. Maybe he stashed a winning lottery ticket in the glove compartment."

Her tone carried a touch of irony, but she wasn't being sarcastic or self-mocking. She must have been appalled at the position he'd left her in.

Dietz said, "What about you, do you work?"

"I'm a private-duty nurse. I make more than adequate money for my personal needs. Even if I'm forced to mortgage the house, I'll be fine, but it's not what I pictured at this stage of my life."

"I'm sorry we've had to burden you with this along with everything else," he said.

"How much did he owe you?"

"A little more than three thousand dollars."

She said, "I apologize."

"Not your fault," Dietz said.

"You mentioned another approach."

Dietz said, "A long shot. It's possible Pete hadn't been paid for the job he subbed out to me. If we can take a look at his files, we might find his account receivables and collect from the client instead of having to worry you."

"If someone owed him money, wouldn't the income count as part of his estate?"

"All I know is I did the work and I'd like to be paid."

She considered the request and then seemed to shrug. "There are files in the garage. He'd been carting home boxes a few at a time over a period of weeks. I realize now he was worried about being evicted and wanted to be prepared." She rose to her feet. "You can follow me if you like."

26

On the way through the house, she picked up a set of car keys from a kitchen drawer. We followed her across a yard that was stripped down and unadorned. The grass, already in its dormant phase, had turned a dispirited shade of brown. It was clear neither she nor Pete had made any effort outdoors. An empty bird feeder hung from a branch of a dwarf citrus tree, but there were no other signs of attention to the exterior, which seemed to have survived in spite of them. The two-car garage was a separate white-frame structure located at the rear of the property. Ruthie let us in through a side door.

The two sets of double doors that opened onto the alleyway were operated by hand, and it was clear neither had been used in years. The hinges were dark brown with rust, and cobwebs lined the crevices, like fake Halloween effects. Spiders had set up small nurseries, swaddling their eggs in gauzy tapers until time to hatch. The floor was concrete, though little of it showed. There was no room for cars given the staggering number of cardboard boxes in evidence, among other things. The space was jammed with old furniture, power tools, lamps, file cabinets, crates, broken appliances, luggage, discarded doors, and miscellaneous lawn equipment, also rusted from neglect. Dilapidated cartons were stacked ten deep and eight high, sealed with masking tape and unmarked. Some had toppled over and their contents had fallen out and been left where they landed. The air smelled of mice and dust.

"Is this everything?" Dietz asked, not quite masking the plaintiveness in his tone.

"I'm afraid not. I haven't been able to face his office, so the furniture and any remaining files will be there. I know his rent was in arrears and I don't have the nerve to contact his land-lady for fear I'll be forced to pay up. I'll give you the key if you want to go through his desk and his file cabinets."

I said, "We stopped by Pete's office earlier. The place has been cleaned out."

She seemed surprised and then recovered herself. "Well, that's one more tiresome chore I don't have to bother with. I'm still emptying closets and drawers here. I can't tell you how many trips I've made to Goodwill. Some of the items I've dropped off are an embarrassment, but I didn't want to throw them in the trash."

"What about his business records? You'll have the IRS to deal with eventually," I said.

"They'll just have to come after me," she said. "I don't have any idea what he paid in the way of state or federal taxes. I took care of property taxes and he did the rest."

"You filed jointly?"

"We did," she said. "I made sure he had my W-2s and any relevant receipts. He'd have me sign the forms, but I really never looked at them."

I didn't press the point. I wondered why she'd trust him with filing state and federal tax returns when he was so irre-sponsible, but she had problems enough and her relationship with the government wasn't any business of mine.

I said, "We'll probably be out here for a while. You want us to let you know when we're done?"

"No need. We leave the garages unlocked. If I'm lucky someone will come along and steal everything."

She handed over the car keys and left us to our task. Judg-ing from surface dust and the ribbons of ratty tape coming loose here and there, the majority of the boxes had sat un-touched for years. We left those alone and focused on the ones that were clean, intact, and closest to the door. As far as I could tell, Pete had no system. His approach was to dump cartons willy-nilly wherever he found room. Dietz hauled a couple of lawn chairs from the assortment of old furniture, which allowed us to sit in reasonable comfort while we searched.

"She's a beautiful woman," Dietz said. "She had more faith in the guy than he deserved."

"Pete was a piece of work," I said. "Homeliest man you ever laid eyes on. I have no idea what she saw in him."

"What's your take on the story about his putting money aside for a cruise?"

"Pete's belief was if you expressed your desires, they'd manifest themselves. His phrase was 'putting it out to the Universe.' I'm not sure that entailed actual savings."

We settled down to work. Most of Pete's files were unmarked. Where folders were labeled, the tag might be scratched through with a subsequent name written over it in ink. Sometimes the label was gone or had nothing to do with the contents. There was no visible order to the folders he'd shoved into a particular box. Catalogs, old letters, unpaid bills, and unopened mail would be dumped unceremoniously into the same container. This forced us to sort page by page, doing a quick read as we went along. Dietz's method was to put a stack of folders upright on his lap, pick his way through, and then return them to the box. I left the files where they were and hunched over each box, pulling out one folder at a time. Most were junk, but we didn't dare toss anything because it wasn't our job. Who knew what Ruthie might consider worth keeping?

After we'd labored an hour, I sat back. "This is pointless. We're being optimistic thinking he'd even bother with anything so organized as 'accounts receivable.' More likely, he kept his cash in an old coffee can."

"Sounds about right."

For a moment, we sat and contemplated the disorder. Dietz said, "Let's try his car. He might not have unloaded all of the boxes he'd brought."

"Like the idea," I said.

We restacked the boxes we'd searched and then angled our way across the garage, stepping over and around the jumble until we reached the door. A gate in the fence opened into the alley. Pete's Ford Fairlane was parked in a wide place probably meant to accommodate trash cans. Those were now lined up against the shrubs, lids sitting like little caps on top of bulging black trash bags. There were no cardboard boxes in the backseat and none in the trunk. We found a bag of birdseed and a gun-cleaning kit, but that was it. No accounts payable, no accounts receivable, no contracts, and no recent correspondence. Certainly no caches of money tucked away. So much for our fishing expedition, which was disappointing, but not entirely fruitless. At least we'd written off a handful of dead ends. The glove compartment was jammed. I emptied it, piling the contents on the passenger seat, but there was nothing of significance as far as I could see. Gasoline receipts and parking tickets, plus paper trash of every conceivable sort. I returned all the miscellany and used brute force to get the glove compartment closed.

At 4:00, Dietz dropped me at my place while he returned to the hotel to shower. He said he'd be back to pick me up at 7:00. In an earlier conversation, he'd mentioned Emile's for drinks and dinner, but he hadn't mentioned it since. As I got out of the car, I leaned in the window. "What's the dress code?"

"Wear what you have on."

I looked down at my filthy hands and my sooty jeans and decided against. "I look like shit."

"No, you don't. You look cute."

I watched him drive away, and I then passed through the gate and around to the rear patio, where I let myself into the studio. The first thing I did was to sit down at my desk. The bulky package Dace had mailed to himself had been sitting there since the volunteer had handed it over to me.

I pulled the mailer closer and turned it over. There was a tag at one end of the padded envelope and I tore the strip open along the length. Inside were medical charts for three patients: Terrence Dace, Charles Farmer, and a man named Sebastian Glenn. All three charts were fat with lab work, doctor's notes, and medical reports. How had Dace managed to get his hands on them?

I took the bundle upstairs with me. I stood in the loft trying to think where I might stash the contents for safekeeping. I cleared the footlocker at the near end of my bed, removing a pile of heavy sweaters to make room for it. I closed the trunk and placed the stack of sweaters on top. Maybe Dandy would have some idea what Dace had in mind.

In the meantime, I went through my usual routine: shower, shampoo, and a change of clothes. Dietz and I were doing okay and I was happy with the pace we'd set. I wasn't prepared to jump back into the relationship without getting my bearings first. For now, there was a blank space between us, packed with all of the moments that had flown by while we were apart. On prior occasions, when we'd come together after a separation, there was this same period of adjustment. Last round, I'd been cranky at first, only gradually letting down my guard. This time I was less resistant, but the chemistry was still on hold.

The phone rang as I was coming down the stairs. I picked up on the second ring to find Dietz on the line.

"Kink in the works. I just got a call from Nick. He's on his way down from San Francisco."

"What's going on?"

"He says he's taking time off work, but that's as much as I know. He called from the road and said he'd explain the rest when he gets here."

"Well, that's worrisome."

"Remains to be seen. He sounded fine."

"What time's he getting in?"

"Depends on where he was when he called. The city's a six-hour drive, so I'm guessing ten at the earliest."

"If you want to take a rain check on dinner, it's fine with me."

"Let's don't do that. Nick's a big boy. If he gets in while I'm out, he can pick up a key and make himself at home. I'll leave word for him at the desk."

"Here's another plan. Why don't I come over to the hotel and we can order room service? That way if he gets in, you'll be on the premises."

"Not a bad idea, but it's up to you."

"We can go out another night."

"You sure you don't mind?"

"Not a bit," I said.

"Great. I'll see you shortly."

I hung up, found my jacket, and shrugged myself into it. I grabbed my shoulder bag and fished out my car keys, realizing as I stepped out the door how dark and chilly it was. A trip to his hotel was a bad idea. I was tired and I really didn't feel like driving across town. I stopped in my tracks, wondering how

tacky it would be if I called and begged off. I'd spent much of
the day with him and I'd have been happy with a stretch of time
on my own. I stood there, wishing I hadn't piped up. Me and
my big mouth. I should have done us both a favor and let him
off the hook. Now, since I was already in motion, it felt easier
to proceed to my car. I unlocked the Mustang and slid under
the wheel. I sat for another brief interlude, conflicted and out
of sorts. Finally, I turned the key in the ignition and pulled
away from the curb. I'd have one glass of wine and a quick bite
to eat and then I'd come home. Nick was probably more in
need of his father's attention than I was at this point.

When Dietz answered the door he was in a fresh pair of jeans
and a collared shirt, over which he'd pulled a black cashmere
sweater. His hair was still damp from the shower and I could
smell soap and aftershave. He helped me out of my jacket and
tossed it over the arm of a chair. He'd ordered a bottle of
Champagne that was nestled in a silver ice bucket frosty with
condensation. He picked up the bottle, put a cloth over the top,
and worked the cork out with his thumbs. He held up a Champagne flute, his way of asking if he could pour me a glass.

"By all means."

The room was larger than my apartment, no big surprise.
My studio is small, which is why it suits me so well. Here the
king-size bed seemed to dominate the room with its puffy
white duvet like a heavy layer of snow. The bed frame was
topped with an ornate wrought iron crown. The walls were a
buttery yellow, the Oriental rug awash in muted colors, mild
green dominating. There was a corner fireplace with a real
wood fire, throwing out a warmth I couldn't quite feel from
where I stood. The furniture looked antique, which may or
may not have been the case.

Dietz handed me my Champagne flute and I took a sip,
experiencing the surprise on my tongue. If I drink Champagne
at all, it's the cheap stuff, which is closer to a freshly poured
glass of tonic water with harsh undertones. This was delicate,
like a mouthful of sunshine and butterflies. I watched him pour
a glass for himself.

"Have a seat," he said.

I settled on a leather-upholstered easy chair with a matching ottoman, one of two set at angles on either side of the snapping fire. The bed was stacked three deep with pillows, each covered in a faded chintz and trimmed with a thick fringe. Dietz had money. I had no idea how he'd come by it. To hear him tell it, his family was a shiftless lot of gypsies and vagabonds. His father worked the oil fields when jobs were available and otherwise spent his life crisscrossing the country in a series of dilapidated station wagons and vans. His mother rode shotgun, her bare feet propped on the dashboard while she drank beer and tossed empty cans out the window. Dietz and his grandmother occupied the backseat, playing cards or reading road maps and picking out towns with weird names. They made a point of traveling south for the winter, usually to Florida, but any place warm would do. If they couldn't afford a motel, they slept in the car. If money was *really* in short supply, they'd cruise country roads and raid kitchen gardens for something to eat. He was largely homeschooled and he had little in the way of formal education. I suspected his job history was checkered, yet he seemed at home in this opulent hotel room, which felt alien to me.

"You hungry?" he asked.

"Getting there."

"We should probably take a look at the menu. Room service is slow at this hour, so the sooner we order, the better off we'll be."

He handed me a menu while he sat down in the other leather chair with a menu of his own.

The bifold was oversize, printed on heavy card stock. I ran an eye down both pages, which were writ in an elegant hand as though a scribe had just left the premises. Shrimp cocktail was $14. Asparagus soup, $10. All of the entrees were $35 or more. Personally, I'd have preferred a peanut butter and pickle sandwich; seventy-five cents max. "A bit pricey, isn't it?"

"Don't worry about it. It's my treat. If you're feeling cheap, have a sandwich."

"Who said anything about cheap? The cheeseburger's twenty-one dollars! Two dollars more if you add bacon or avocado."

"Relax. The burgers are prime sirloin ground to order. The patties are hand-formed and cooked any way you like."

I held up my Champagne glass. "I think I'll make do with this and fix my own supper when I get home."

"Don't be silly. If you don't eat, you'll get too snockered to drive."

"I can't stay that long anyway. It would have been smarter to postpone. I'm tired."

"No, no. It was a great idea. Nick won't roll in for another couple of hours."

"What's he going to think if he gets here and I'm in your room?"

Dietz studied me quizzically. "Are you concerned about that?"

"I should have stayed at home. At least I could've put on my comfies and read a good mystery."

"You can do that here. I have two Robert Parker paperbacks in my suitcase," he said. "Is there something else going on? I'm not reading your mood."

"I don't have moods."

"What is it then?"

I was tempted to tell him about Dace and the money he'd left me, but I was still trying to come to terms with it myself. I wasn't sure why I couldn't just make my peace with my newfound riches and rejoice. "How did you get so comfortable with money? You seem at home in a place like this while I'm out of my element."

"I like what money buys. Space, mobility, leisure, freedom from anxiety."

"I've got all those things."

"No, you don't. You live like a monk."

"Don't change the subject. Where'd your money come from? I thought your father was a roustabout. Isn't that what you said? The way you talk about your youth, I assumed you were poor."

"We were dirt poor for years. As it turned out—and I wasn't aware of this at the time—my dad trained with a man named Myron Kinley. He's the guy who developed techniques for fighting oil-well fires. It was dangerous work and very lucrative, of course. My dad loved high stakes. At some point, I guess my mother put her foot down. The job was way too risky, so eventually he got out. Meantime, he'd saved up a big chunk of change that was literally burning a hole in his pocket.

When we moved from Oklahoma to Texas, he met a guy who fancied himself quite the entrepreneur. This fellow had come up with a scheme to buy oil and gas leases with an eye to flipping them, but he was short on capital. He and my dad each put up a couple of thousand bucks and started picking up expired leases. They'd pay pennies on the dollar, then turn around and resell them to oil companies that actually had the capacity to drill."

"Sounds like a great idea."

"To a point. Problem was, they fought all the time. They were both headstrong and opinionated, so they couldn't agree on anything. Eventually, they split their holdings down the middle and called it square. The other guy went broke. My dad hung on to his shares and eventually cashed in big. I didn't know anything about it until he died."

"Nice story. I like that."

The phone rang and we both turned to look at it. Seemed too early for Nick's arrival, but who else would be calling? Dietz crossed to the writing desk and picked up. "Dietz."

He listened briefly and said, "Great. Send him up." He returned the handset to the cradle. "It's Nick."

"It's good you were here and not out somewhere."

"I'm sure my being gone never crossed his mind. Kids are egocentric. Parents exist strictly for their convenience. He probably can't conceive of my having a life of my own."

I got up and set my glass on the side table. "I should go and leave the two of you to catch up."

"Stay and say hello. If he hasn't eaten, the three of us can have dinner downstairs."

"I'd love to meet him. I didn't mean I was galloping off right this minute."

When the knock came, Dietz opened the door. He and Nick grabbed each other in a big enthusiastic hug. Then Dietz put an arm across Nick's shoulders and ushered him into the room. "Someone I want you to meet," he said to Nick. "This is Kinsey." And to me, "My son, Nick."

Nick turned a dark-eyed look on me, his smile diminishing almost imperceptibly. It was clear he had no idea his father would be entertaining anyone. He was tall and lean with the same striking features I'd seen in his mother's photograph. In his faded jeans and a leather bomber jacket, he still somehow managed to look elegant. He was actually my concept of a snooty prep school kid who'd had his choice of Ivy League colleges. He was Dietz's counterpoint and (perhaps) just as appealing in his own way.

As he'd never laid eyes on me, he was already wary and unreceptive. I'd have been willing to swear there was nothing in my demeanor to suggest the nature of my relationship to his dad. It's not like I was half dressed or my hair was messed up. Neither of us had gone near the bed, so the covers were smooth. Granted we'd been intimate in the past, but we were still in neutral gear this round, so there was no charge whatsoever in the air. Something had cued him and I'd been marked as the enemy.

I smiled and held out my hand, saying, "Hi, Nick."

He said, "Hello."

We shook hands briefly and I covered nimbly for the chill wafting in my direction.

I reached for my jacket and picked up my shoulder bag. "I was just on my way out. Your dad and I are working a case together and we were comparing notes."

I have no idea why I offered this lame story, which cast the occasion in a false light. The toss-away comment, while true, sounded implausible on the face of it. I found this unnerving since I usually lie with greater finesse. Nick flicked a look at his father and his eyes then strayed to the room service menu I'd left open on the chair behind me. From there his gaze flicked to the Champagne bucket and half-filled flutes. I felt a flash of guilt, as though sharing a meal might have illicit undertones.

Meanwhile, Dietz was looking at me perplexed. "Why take off now?"

"I've got things to take care of at home," I said. "We can chat tomorrow if you have a minute."

"Sure thing," he said.

He saw me to the door. Nick's gaze remained fixed on me while I eased into the hall.

Dietz said, "You drive carefully."

"I will and thanks for the drink."

"You bet."

Over his shoulder, I gave Nick a quick, friendly wave. "Nice meeting you."

"Same here," he said.

Uhn-hun, I thought. I turned and walked down the hall, doing a little quick step to speed myself along.

Once outside, I waited for the valet to bring around the Mustang, which he handed over in exchange for a folded bill. I'd given him a five, which I thought was absurd, but I couldn't bear to be cheap with Dietz's comment still ringing in my ears. I hadn't been feeling *cheap*. Twenty-one dollars for a damn cheeseburger was robbery. I got in the car and released the handbrake, putting a gentle pressure on the accelerator. As I turned right out of the hotel driveway, I cranked the heater up full blast and still I shivered most of the way home.

In the morning, I jogged three miles and then continued with my usual routine. I had no idea what I was going to do that day, but I figured I'd better not count on Dietz. By 9:00, I was showered and dressed and drinking a second cup of coffee when the phone rang. I set the paper aside and picked up.

Dietz said, "Hey, it's me. I just talked to Pete's landlady. She'll be in the office shortly if you want to pop over there with me."

"Great. What about Nick?"

"Still asleep. I told him I had work to do this morning and we'd have lunch when I got back. You want me to pick you up?"

"Sure."

"Good. I'll see you in a few."

I was waiting out in front when Dietz pulled up. I got in the car and we exchanged courtesies, both of us behaving as though everything was fine, which I suppose it was from his perspective.

He sent me a quick, proud smile. "What'd you think of Nick?"

"Nice kid. Handsome," I said. "I see what you mean about his favoring his mom."

"Two peas in a pod."

"So what's going on with him?"

"He's got a bug up his butt about quitting his job to go

traveling. We chatted about it some, without going into any great detail. The plan seems half-baked, but I didn't want to argue the point until I heard him out."

"I thought Graham was the one with the wanderlust."

"Nick must have caught it from him, or from me for all I know. Fortunately, he's still cautious enough to want my approval before he flings himself into the abyss."

"So, he's in the market for some fatherly advice?"

"Let's hope not. I'm new at this. What do I know about parenting? This is the stuff Naomi dealt with."

"Ah, well," I said. I had nowhere to go with the subject and he didn't seem that comfortable talking about incipient fatherhood. "How'd you end up talking to Pete's landlady? You caught me by surprise on that."

"I'd made a note of the number and called first thing this morning and introduced myself. I said I was representing Pete's widow and suggested we might make a deal for the back rent."

"Somehow I was picturing a guy."

"She sounds like one. Her name's Letitia Beaudelaire. I notice she didn't invite me to call her Letty, so maybe that's reserved for tenants who're paid in full. I told her we wanted to pick up Pete's files."

"Was she receptive?"

"Actually, she was. I thought she'd put up a fuss, but she said come ahead."

"You did mention money."

"So I did. Clever me," he said.

As it turned out, the real estate company that handled Pete's lease was in the same building, one floor up. We passed the empty office again on our way to the entrance and couldn't help but notice the For Lease sign had been removed. Inside we could see a painter at work on the interior walls; drop cloths, a ladder, and all the attendant paraphernalia.

Dietz said, "Hope she's got a new tenant. That might make her receptive to a negotiation."

A woman came close on our heels as Dietz pushed open the glass door to the lobby. We entered and Dietz paused to hold the door for her. She was short and round, dressed in a business suit and spike heels, a ribbon of perfume streaming in her wake.

We crossed to the elevators and he pushed the button for the second floor. We got in, the doors closed, and the three of us rode up in silence. I watched her fumble in her purse, apparently looking for a pack of cigarettes, which she found. She shook one loose and put it between her teeth, where it tilted at a jaunty angle while she searched for a light. Her lipstick was bright red and she wore a matching shade of polish on her short blunt-cut fingernails.

When the doors opened on 2, she got off the elevator, firing up her cigarette while she walked. Smoke rose above her head and drifted back at us. Dietz paused to study the directional arrows, indicating which office numbers were to the left and which to the right. "Two-thirteen's the one we want," he said. We ended up turning left as she had.

Meanwhile, the woman had stopped in front of an office door, topped with half a panel of opaque glass.

As we caught up with her, Dietz said, "Are you Letitia?"

"I wondered when you'd figure that out. You're my nine-thirty appointment."

"I am, indeed," he said.

"I pictured you alone. Who's your friend?"

"This is Kinsey. She's a private eye like me. You two should get along fine. She's tough as nails."

Letitia removed the cigarette from her lips, appraising me with a long look as she unlocked and opened the door. She placed her bag on a desk and crossed to the window, where she opened the Venetian blinds. I was hoping she'd grace us with fresh air, but I guess she didn't want to dilute the effect of all the secondhand smoke.

The office consisted of two adjoining rooms with a short hall leading to what I was guessing was a third room with the door currently shut. It was unclear how many people the company employed. The furniture wasn't arranged to accommodate a receptionist and boss or even two equal partners. Too many chairs and not enough working space. I counted three phones, two of which were unplugged. Most of the surfaces, including the windowsills, were stacked with office supplies. Ten mismatching file cabinets had been jammed into a space better suited for eight. The last two were angled so none of the drawers would open to the full.

When Letitia removed her coat, I could see that what I'd

thought was a business suit was really a wool skirt and matching vest with big mother-of-pearl buttons down the front. The
fit was tight and I was betting she was in denial about the extra
thirty pounds she'd gained the day she reached menopause.
The skirt waist had inched up her midriff, which shortened the
hem to a coquettish three inches above her knees. The lapels
on her vest no longer met in the front, but that might have been
due to the size of her breasts, which threatened to topple her.

In her smoke-husky voice, she said to Dietz, "How'd you
get tied up with Pete Wolinsky? You know he's a deadbeat."

"That's our Pete," Dietz said, equably. "On the other hand,
his wife's a lovely woman who's now facing the mess he left."

That netted him no response.

Dietz allowed his gaze to skirt the room. "What happened
to his office furniture? Ruthie intended to have it moved to the
house."

"And I was supposed to know this how? She hasn't even
bothered to get in touch."

"A call from you might not have been out of line. She had
a lot on her mind."

"I sold his stuff for two hundred bucks and that included
that rickety rolling chair of his. I couldn't even give away that
piece-of-shit typewriter, so I tossed it in the trash."

"Too bad. That was a collector's item."

"Liar," she said.

Dietz smiled. "What about his file cabinets?"

"You're looking at 'em. I took those for my own use."

"All we're interested in is the contents. She needs his business records for tax purposes."

"It's all in boxes."

"Mind if we take a look?"

"Actually, I do mind. He died owing me a bundle. I thought
you were here to haggle over his back rent. Isn't that what you
said?"

"Words to that effect."

"Think of his files as collateral."

"In other words, if his wife wants them back she'll have to
come up with the ransom money."

"Why would she not? Somebody's gotta pay me. I got fifteen boxes of his crap."

"All worthless," Dietz said.

"Must have some value or why would you be here?"

"We thought we might take it all off your hands and save you a trip to the dump."

She stared at him, her eyes narrowing with amusement. "You'd have to have a signed authorization. Otherwise, I can't be handing over his private papers. I'm sure there's a law against that."

Dietz smiled. "Signed authorization. I'm happy you mentioned it."

He took out his wallet and removed four one-hundred-dollar bills, which he fanned out for her inspection. "These are signed by the secretary of the Treasury, James Baker. Remember him? Reagan's old chief of staff."

He held the bills up.

She made no move. She lifted the cigarette to her lips, inhaled, and let the smoke drift upward across her face. She glanced at me. "Where'd you find this guy?"

"I needed a bodyguard."

"Don't we all," she said with a bawdy laugh.

Dietz added two more hundreds. "Last chance," he said.

She reached out and removed the cash from his hand as daintily as a feral cat accepting a morsel of food.

"In there," she said, using her cigarette to point toward the room down the hall.

27

PETE WOLINSKY

August 1988, Two Months Earlier

Pete and the good doctor Reed ran into difficulties deciding where to meet. On the phone, prior to their get-together, the two had settled on a price: four thousand dollars for Pete's services, which was stunning when you considered it was an hour's work at best. Pete insisted on half up front and the balance once the job was done. He was surprised at how little argument Linton Reed put up but decided he was unaccustomed to bargaining, especially in touchy matters such as this. Pete's first thought was to ask for six, but he didn't want to push. Four was very reasonable for what the man was getting.

Pete had roughed out a plan and he was eager to test the idea. The problem was Linton didn't want to be seen with him, which meant the university was out. Too great a risk of running into someone who'd recognize Dr. Reed and wonder why he was deep in conversation with a fellow who looked like Ichabod Crane. They couldn't meet at Pete's office. He scarcely dared go there himself. The property manager had offices in the same building, and Pete was still kicking himself that he'd bought into the arrangement. They'd talked about connecting up in one of the parking lots at the beach, but again, the setting was too public and Reed had nixed the idea. Pete thought Reed was being melodramatic. He doubted the good doctor's comings and goings would interest anyone.

They finally agreed to meet on the sea wall that jutted out from the marina. Mid-August and it was late in the day. The sun had faded and the wind was blustery. Lines of spray shot up as each incoming wave crashed against the rocky barrier. This was an unpleasant place for Pete, whose bones often ached with the damp. The only virtue of the location was that the setting was so miserable that no one else was there.

Linton Reed stood with his hands jammed down in the pockets of his dark overcoat, looking out toward the islands, barely visible in the haze. "What's your proposal?"

"Couple of questions about security measures before I get into it. The lab's in Southwick Hall, is that correct?"

Linton nodded tersely.

"You have a guard in the lobby?"

Linton focused on him. "I hope you're not thinking of going into the lab."

"Just answer my questions and I'll tell you what I'm thinking when I know what's up. Guard or no guard?"

"No need for one. Electronic access only. The building and the lab both have swipe-card entry systems. Staff and employees are each assigned an ID badge with a magnetic strip and personal identification number. Every ID has an integrated circuit chip that triggers both locks. You slide the card through a reader and then punch in your code."

"You use the same swipe card to get out?"

"In this system, yes."

"What about closed-circuit TV?"

"There was talk of installing cameras but the university doesn't have the funds. In the end, we decided this is a college campus, not a bank. I've seen security stickers on certain doors, but it's just for show. Lots of signs—No Admittance; Authorized Personnel Only—none of it means anything."

"How good is the lighting?"

"Campus safety's a big deal, so there's good visibility outside, especially along the paths and in the parking lots. Inside, lights are blazing all the time."

"Lot of people work late?"

"That happens occasionally, but most of us have families. I've never seen anybody in the lab after nine. There are people going in and out just about any time of day," he said. "Now, I'd appreciate an explanation."

"Fair enough. So here's the idea. You pick a night when there's some big shindig going on that you and your wife plan to attend. You go and make sure you're conspicuous throughout. Cocktails, conversation, dinner. Everybody knows you're there. Airtight alibi. You have anything like that on the horizon?"

Linton looked off to the left and then said, "Close enough. August 24. That's a Wednesday night. There's an advisory board meeting of the local commission on alcohol and drug abuse. Dinner first and then I'll be closeted for hours with a number of medical types. There'd be no question I was present and accounted for."

"Sounds good. While you're tied up, I let myself into the lab using the Bryce woman's ID and PIN."

"Her *ID*? How do you propose to do that?"

"My worry, not yours. I figure if I wear a white lab coat and employee badge, no one will pay me any mind. Make sure I have a map and then I'm just some schmo on the premises like anybody else. I go in, I stay a while, and then I come out. Swipe-card entry systems retain an audit trail of events at the door. Anybody checks on it later, it's all set in stone—what time she went in, how long she stayed, and when she came out again."

"Then what. I don't understand. You go in the lab to do what? You don't know anything about our work."

"I don't have to know. You handle that. Sometime the day before you get on your computer and make changes to your data. Nothing outrageous. You want it to look bad but you don't want to overplay your hand. Elevate a number here and there, downgrade a few. Tamper, but not too radically. Just enough to suggest someone familiar with your work has been in there poking around."

"Why would I alter my data when that's what she's accusing me of in the first place?"

Pete offered Linton a benign smile. "Morning after this event you go into work and discover your computer's up and running. You're confused because when you left Wednesday afternoon you remember shutting it down. It looks like someone's gotten into your database and you're worried. You can't imagine what's going on so you start checking sensitive documents."

Linton stared at him. "And discover my data has been sabotaged."

"That's exactly right. Someone's falsified your statistics, inflated the test results, and who knows what else? You go straight to your boss. You're stunned. You're white-faced with shock. You have no idea what's going on, but someone's undermined your work. You know everything was fine the day before because you started a printout of what you'd done to date. You can even show him pages you printed on both days and point to the discrepancies. Someone wants to make you look bad. If you hadn't picked up on it, you'd have ended up submitting results that were way off. Doctored, if you'll forgive the pun."

"Do I mention Mary Lee?"

"You let him do that. You've complained about her before, haven't you?"

"I did when she first came to work. I had to tell him I'd been involved with her in case she started bad-mouthing me."

"Exactly. The woman's trying to damage your reputation because you resisted her attempts to rekindle the flame. You rebuffed her and now look what she's done."

Linton thought about it for a moment and then shook his head. "Don't like it. Too risky."

"That's my lookout."

"What if somebody's in the building and wants to know what you're doing?"

"Won't happen. Look like me and nobody wants to stop and chat about anything."

"But why would she give you her ID?"

"She won't know I have it."

"You can't pull it off. There's no way."

"Let's don't argue the point. Give it some thought. If you decide we have a deal, we'll meet again."

"And if I don't call you, the deal is off?"

"That's correct."

Linton stood for a moment, debating with himself.

Pete said, "Don't decide right now. Let it sit. If I can't deliver my end, I'll let you know."

Linton shook his head and backed up a step before he turned away. Pete watched as he retraced his steps, hands in his coat pockets. Wind blew spray, like a fine mist, across the breakwater, wetting the concrete so that Linton left a brief set of shoe prints in his wake.

The real hurdle Pete faced was talking Willard Bryce into playing his part, which was critical to the overall success of his scheme. Pete called Willard the next morning as soon as he calculated Mary Lee had left for work. They agreed on a time and Pete swung by and picked him up at the designated corner like a couple of spies. As with Linton Reed, Willard was a man who loved to self-dramatize. Why else go to such lengths when they were the only ones who gave a shit? Small talk back and forth on their way to the beach, where they parked and sat in the car.

Willard said, "I don't understand why we had to meet. I thought our business was done. I have your report and I've paid you everything I owe."

"I've been thinking it might be a smart move to check Mary Lee's work space. Maybe there's information to be picked up in a place she thinks is safe from prying eyes."

"Stop right now. This has gone far enough."

"Just listen to what I have to say. She feels comfortable at work, right? She's relaxed. She assumes you have no access to the lab, so she might leave stuff around. Might be notes back and forth between her and this Pensky fellow."

"You said there was nothing going on."

"I said I didn't *think* there was. I said there might be other explanations. All I'm saying now is it won't hurt to look."

"I won't do it. How the hell would I manage that? I can't ask for her ID and go off for an hour. Are you insane?"

"You don't have the stomach for it, I'll handle it myself. Here's how I see it. There'll be a couple of swipe locks—one to get into the building, the other to get into the lab. All you have to do is get me her ID and her PIN. You have any idea what that is?"

"It's 1956. She uses that for everything. The ID I can't help you with. She takes it with her when she goes to work. How else would she get in?"

"Then get it when she's not at work," Pete said, patiently. Willard was a moron. Did the man have no imagination?

"I never know when she's going in. Especially lately. It could be any hour."

"Does she sleep at night?"

"Of course she sleeps at night. What kind of question is that?"

"Where's her ID badge when she's asleep?"

"On top of the chest of drawers."

"Why don't you take it then and leave it outside your front door. I'll pick it up, go into the lab, have a look around, and then return it when I'm done. Won't take an hour and I'll put it back where I found it. All you have to do is pick it up off the welcome mat and return it to the chest of drawers. She'll never know it was gone. I'll contact you first chance I get and tell you what I found."

"When would you do this? Go into the lab."

"Haven't decided yet. I'll pick a date and let you know."

"I don't like it."

"I don't like it any more than you do. You have a better idea, I'd love to hear it."

"I don't need a better idea. I never asked for any of this in the first place."

Pete lapsed into silence. He knew from past experience that once you persuaded somebody to cross the line the first time, it didn't take much to talk 'em into doing it again. Willard wasn't nearly as scrupulous as he pretended.

Willard's face had darkened to that brooding look, triggered by his insecurities. "Actually, anything she has at work, I'd never know about."

"Exactly. And you can't go there yourself because if she woke up she'd know you were gone. Aside from that, you'd be too conspicuous thumping across campus on that one leg of yours."

For some reason, Willard laughed at that and Pete knew he'd won.

Pete's next meeting with Linton Reed took place in the parking lot at Ludlow Beach, roughly across the street from the Santa Teresa City College running track. It had taken some arguing, but the good doctor had finally agreed to the spot.

Pete arrived first and got out of his Ford Fairlane, crossing a patch of grass to one of the picnic tables. Beyond the wide expanse of lawn, the beach extended for another five or six hundred yards. Beyond, the Pacific Ocean stretched for twenty-six miles until the islands peeked up at the horizon.

By way of a prop, Pete had bought himself an oversize container of coffee, still too hot to sip. He heard a car and turned as the doctor pulled in, driving a turquoise Thunderbird. For a man worried about being seen, the car couldn't be more conspicuous. Linton locked his car and approached casually with a copy of the *Santa Teresa Dispatch* under his arm.

Pete waited until he sat down on the far side of the table, neither of them making eye contact. Linton made a show of opening the paper as though he'd arrived solely for this purpose.

"Let me know when you have a minute," Pete said.

"I'm listening."

Pete said, "Somebody's going to think we're sweet on each other. Why else would you come over to my table and sit down?"

"Don't mock me. Let's just get on with it."

"I take it we're on or you wouldn't have called again."

"What do you think?" Linton said, snappishly.

Pete noticed that he'd neatly sidestepped consent. If Pete were caught, he could honestly say he hadn't agreed to anything.

Pete said, "If we're on, I want what was promised. The map for starters."

Linton took a folded sheet of typing paper from his pocket and handed it to Pete. Pete opened it and made a quick study of the drawing Linton had done, showing the location of the building that housed the research lab in relation to the campus parking lots, some of which were designated for staff or employees only. There was apparently no restriction on vehicular ingress and egress.

Linton had marked the first point at which a card needed to be swiped. He'd also drawn the layout of the lobby with a series of directional arrows from the door to the elevators. Nice. If Pete were passing himself off as someone who knew his way around, he couldn't be blundering down the wrong hall. The lab occupied the entire second floor. Linton had also roughed out the interior offices, marking his desk, the desk where Mary Lee Bryce worked, and a few other significant landmarks.

"Looks good," Pete said. "You have the other business?"

Linton took out a thick envelope and placed it on the table without making visual reference to it. Then he got up and walked away.

Pete took the envelope and slid it into the inner pocket of his sport coat. He'd count the cash later to make sure it was all there before he tucked it away for safekeeping. Linton was right about the risk. Pete wasn't nearly as sanguine as he appeared to be. The very notion of what he had to do made the hair stand up on the back of his neck. He had no confidence the plan would work, but with the two grand in his pocket and two more on tap, what choice did he have?

He waited a day and then he called Willard and suggested the night of August 24 as the date he'd need the ID.

"Why then?"

"Middle of the week. Nothing else going on. Seems as good a date as any."

"Students will be back on campus by then."

"So what? I'm doing this at night. All you have to do is wait until she's asleep and put the ID outside the door. Nothing to it."

Willard seemed to concede the point, but he wasn't happy. Pete eased the conversation along without giving him an opportunity to protest. It wouldn't pay to argue because Pete's position was weak and he didn't want Willard to think about it too much.

Late afternoon on August 24, Pete did a dry run. He drove out to the university and used Linton's hand-drawn map to get the lay of the land. He left his car some distance from the building where the lab was housed and proceeded on foot. He knew the lab was on the second floor. Even at that hour, he could see the offices and labs marked by a stripe of brightly lighted windows that extended all the way around. It seemed odd to Pete he'd be trespassing in full view of anyone who happened by that night. With his height and his odd build, he stood out like a sore thumb wherever he went, and while he'd equipped himself with the requisite white lab coat, he didn't look like a scientist. Of course, scientists came in all shapes and sizes. Smart people could look any way they wanted and no one thought twice about it.

Satisfied with his reconnoitering, he returned to his car and threaded a course across campus, which was already chocka-block with students. Most wore shorts, flip-flops, and T-shirts, bare limbs exposed, all that young flesh in evidence. UCST was known as a party school; beer and dope, kids loitering at every turn. Occasionally he'd see a student reading a book, but that was the rare exception. Pete wondered what life would have been like with so many advantages. Didn't warrant too much thought at this point, as any options he might have had were gone by now.

He picked up a burger and fries and went back to the office. His message light was blinking, but he had no time for that. He ate at his desk with the cruise line brochure open in front of him. He'd told Ruthie he was on an all-night surveillance, so she wouldn't be expecting him until morning. He reached the portion of the brochure that detailed a cruise on the Danube and leaned in close to read, tantalized by the descriptions of the amenities. All meals were prepared on board, it said, using the finest and freshest ingredients. Complimentary wine; bottled water replenished daily in each state room. Four countries, nine excursions. "Gentle walking options," he read, which was good given his physical limitations. He still had a portion of the money Willard had paid him and with Linton's four grand added to his stash, he was almost there.

At 11:30, he left the office and drove to Willard's apartment complex. He parked on the side street, walked to the gated entrance, and stepped into the courtyard. He paused, making sure there was no one about. Assured that he was alone, he continued at a casual pace to Willard's front door, where he antici-pated finding Mary Lee's ID. There was no sign of it. He lifted the welcome mat, thinking Willard had tucked it out of sight. He took out his penlight and flashed the narrow beam around the foundation plantings. Nothing.

He walked around the side of the building and checked the Bryces' bedroom windows. Dark. No sound. No flickering to suggest the television set was on. Surely, Willard hadn't gotten his dates mixed up. Pete was at a loss. He couldn't call at this hour. Mary Lee might pick up instead of Willard and then what? Another possibility was that hubby might be waiting to make sure she was soundly sleeping before he took the badge from its usual place. If that were the case, a ringing phone would spoil everything.

He went back to the center of the courtyard and settled in a lawn chair, arms crossed, hands tucked away for warmth. The temperature had sunk into the low fifties and the air felt damp. All he could do was wait, so he waited. From time to time, he got up and returned to Willard's door, which remained a blank. What was wrong with him? Pete couldn't spend all night in the cold. At 1:30, he returned to his car, where he huddled for another hour before he fell asleep.

He woke at 6:30, stiff and desperate for a pee. The sun hadn't quite shifted into view, so he got out of the car and relieved himself behind a nearby tree. In the car again, he waited until he saw Mary Lee leave the apartment, coffee container in hand, her purse under her arm. She got in the car, fiddled with her seat belt, checked her makeup, and adjusted her travel mug in the cup holder. Pete thought he'd go insane if she didn't get out of there. She finally drove off, presumably on her way to work.

Pete was frosted. Willard, for whatever reason, had failed to deliver, and where did that put Pete? The night had come and gone and who knew when another opportunity would present itself? Linton Reed wasn't going to be happy when he heard the plan had gone awry. He left his car unlocked while he crossed the grass and entered the center courtyard. He knocked on the Bryces' door and waited.

When the door finally opened, Willard said, "What do *you* want?"

"What do you think? You want to tell me why you reneged on our agreement?"

"We don't have an agreement. I left a message on your office phone. Mary Lee's decided to quit. She's giving her two weeks' notice today. She's fed up. She says life's too short."

Pete was taken aback. "I'm sorry to hear that. I guess it's a done deal, then."

"You better believe it is and if you ever breathe one word of this business to anyone, you'll be sorry," Willard said, his voice ominously low, and then he shut the door in Pete's face.

Pete stood for a moment, trying to process the implications. Obviously, if Mary Lee quit, then Linton had no need of him. After today, all bets would be off since essentially there was no way to blame her for the data tampering. He'd been paid to go into the lab, launching a scheme that was suddenly completely irrelevant. Nothing to be done about it now. More problematic was the certainty the good doctor would insist Pete give his money back, which Pete had no intention of doing. That money was for him and Ruthie, with every nickel going toward their trip abroad. Linton had plenty more where that came from. Pete Wolinsky did not. For the moment, Pete was safe. For all Linton Reed knew, he'd done what they agreed.

Pete returned to the office and sat down at his desk. This time he pressed the play button on his answering machine. He listened to the message from Willard about Mary Lee quitting her job. There were two additional messages from Linton Reed, who neglected to identify himself, but he said roughly the same thing both times: the deal was off. In neither instance did the good doctor specify the reason for the cancellation. Pete's only option was to play dumb. He put in a call to the doctor, whose answering machine picked up. Pete left his number without mentioning his name, asking if the doctor would call at his earliest convenience. Linton must have been sitting right there, letting calls go through to his voice message, because within minutes he called back. "You owe me two grand," he said.

"And why would that be?"

"Something's happened."

"I gathered as much. You want to tell me what's going on?"

"Not on the phone."

"How about let's meet, then."

"When?"

"Ten o'clock tonight?"

"Where?"

"Bird refuge," Pete said. He depressed the plunger, cutting the connection before the doctor could argue the point.

• • •

Traffic was light when Pete arrived at the bird refuge shortly before ten. The Caliente Café was crowded, its parking lot jammed. Arriving patrons had snapped up additional slots in the strip lot across the way. Pete slowed the Fairlane to allow a pedestrian to cross in front of him. Belatedly, he registered the big panhandler's red baseball cap and red flannel shirt; fellow heading home for the night after a hard day's work. The panhandler turned and gave Pete a lingering look, which Pete ignored.

Pete hoped there'd be one last parking place, but he spotted the turquoise Thunderbird and realized Linton had beat him to the punch. Pete was forced to park on the street, which mattered not except for the psychological one-upsmanship. In a momentary nod to caution, he went around to the trunk of his car and swapped out the S&W Escort for his Glock.

The two men came together in a wide pool of shadows between two streetlamps. The path was lined with shrubs. A patchwork of rustling leaves created shifting patterns of light, adequate for conversational purposes but preventing either man a clear view of the other's face. The damp night breeze coming off the lagoon smelled sulfurous.

Linton wore the same dark wool overcoat he'd worn at their earlier meeting. Pete's sport coat was inadequate for the evening chill, and he envied the other man's comfort. He was still debating how to play the occasion, so he offered Linton the first throw, saying, "What's this about?"

"Mary Lee Bryce quit her job. Game's over."

"Nice if you'd told me before I went out to the lab."

"I left two messages on your office machine, telling you the deal was off."

"When was this?"

"Two o'clock and again at five."

"I wasn't in the office yesterday. If I'd known she quit, I wouldn't have put myself out."

"Too bad. I want my two grand back."

"No can do. I went in with her badge as agreed. You ask your computer techie and he'll show you the trail she left."

"Prove it."

"I can't prove it standing out here. You prove I didn't."

"You're a liar."

"Unlike yourself," Pete said.

"I gave you two grand for nothing and I'd like it back."

"No need to repeat yourself, son. Money's gone. You want it back, you're out of luck."

"Where is it?"

"Something came up."

"That's it? Something came up and now you keep my two grand?"

"I did my part, so, technically speaking, you owe me two more. Under the circumstances, I'm giving you a break. Let's consider it payment in full."

"For what? I told you I didn't need you. If you did it regardless, why should I be out the dough?"

Pete lifted his hands. "Hey, I'm done and I'm gone. Your money's gone as well, so how about we call it square? I don't owe you and you don't owe me. Anything I have on you stops right here."

Pete was dimly aware of the panhandler standing in a wash of darkness while the argument went on. Fellow must have decided to forgo his campsite and come have a look. In the dark, Pete couldn't make out the red cap or the red shirt, but he knew the man's size and body type and the lighter block of his face.

"Anything you *have* on me?" Linton said, shrilly. "What would that be?"

Pete kept his voice low. He was reasonably certain Linton had no idea there was a witness to their fight. "I know more than you think and I'll use it if I have to. To be honest about it, I'd prefer not."

"Are you *threatening* me?"

"I'm just pointing out you got your money's worth. With that woman gone, you can blame her for anything. She quits in a huff and before she leaves, she trashes your work. Same story plays and I came up with it. That's what you paid me for."

"What good does that do me now?"

"If you're smart you'll wipe the slate clean and dump everything you've done."

"I don't want to dump it. Why should I do that?"

"To cover your butt. Keep that data, she's got your nuts in a vice. Now she's unemployed, you think she won't come after you? She's a loose cannon. What's she got to lose? She can accuse you, point fingers—whatever the hell she wants and you're a sitting duck."

"You don't know what you're talking about."

"*I* might not, but she does. Now see here? Lookit. I'll do you one more favor. This for the same two thousand dollars you were kind enough to shell out. She's been in touch with a reporter. Are you aware of that? Journalist who has connections at the *New York Times*. Fellow's done his homework. They'll blow you out of the water."

"I don't believe a word of it."

"Fine. Then our conversation's over and I'll be on my way," Pete said, keeping his tone light.

Linton reached out and grabbed his arm, saying, "Hey! Don't turn your back on me. I'm not finished."

Irritably, Pete flung off his hand. "The hell you aren't."

"You know what? You're more dangerous than she is," Linton said. "She's righteous. You're corrupt."

"I got no interest in you. We did business and now it's done. End of story."

"What if you flap *your* big mouth?"

"To who? Nobody gives a shit. She might nail you, but I got no dog in that fight. Trouble with you is you think you're more important than you are."

"Who's the reporter? I want his name."

"Too bad."

Linton reached into his overcoat pocket and pulled out a gun, racking back the slide. Pete lifted his hands in a show of submission, but in truth he was more curious than cowed. What was this about? Linton didn't seem to know what came next. This was apparently his big move and now what? Pull a gun on a fellow, you better be prepared to shoot.

Pete dropped his gaze to the weapon. He couldn't see it clearly in the faulty light, but he was guessing it was a .45. Pete could feel the comforting bulk of his Glock in the shoulder holster under his left arm. He knew how to draw and fire a lot faster than Linton did. "Where'd you get that?" he asked.

"My father-in-law."

"Hope he shared some safety tips."

"He's out of town. I borrowed it."

"Trigger pressure's tricky if you're not used to it."

"Like this?"

Linton altered the angle of the barrel and fired once. Both men jerked instinctively at the blast. The cartridge popped up to his right like a jumping bean.

Pete could tell the good doctor was showing off, making a point about how serious he was. While Pete wasn't worried, his attention was fully focused on the man in front of him. There was something odd at work: Linton role-playing, trying on an alternate personality; tough guy, an overeducated Al Capone. Linton Reed was on unfamiliar ground but getting hyped on the power. The question was how far he'd be willing to push. Pete suspected this was the first time he'd brandished a gun and he liked the feeling it gave him. You'd think a man in his position would be fully accustomed to deference, but this was dominance of another sort.

Linton said, "What's the reporter's name?"

"What difference does it make?" Pete asked, irritably.

"I'm asking you a simple question."

"Why don't you go ask her? She's the one in cahoots with him."

Linton backed up a step and raised his arm. The weight of the weapon caused his hand to wobble ever so slightly. "I'm warning you."

"Hey, fine. You win. Guy's name is Owen Pensky for all the good it'll do you."

He thought Linton might put the gun away since his demand had been met, but the good doctor wasn't ready to concede. It was possible he didn't know how to make a graceful exit. Pete was trying to figure out how to resolve the standoff before it got out of hand. Pete was close enough that if he'd kicked upward, he might have been able to propel the gun from Linton Reed's grip, but his Marfan's made such a move impossible. Whatever he intended to do, he knew he better do it quickly before Linton had time to think. If the gun's safety was still off and Pete made a move, there was a chance Linton's trigger finger would tighten reflexively, causing the gun to fire, but Pete couldn't worry about that.

He stepped to one side, put his hands together like a club, and brought it down abruptly on Linton's outstretched hand. The blow failed to break his hold on the gun, but it did catch him by surprise. Pete swung a fist and Linton stepped aside

more quickly than Pete thought possible. Pete swung again
and missed, only this time, he stumbled into Linton and his
momentum took both men down. Pete's fall was buffered by
his landing on the other man while the doctor's fall was cush-
ioned by his heavy coat. His right hand went down, the butt of
his gun hit the pavement, and the impact jarred the gun loose.
The weapon flew off and landed on the path three feet away.
As Linton rolled over onto his side and stretched to retrieve the
gun, Pete lunged across him and knocked it out of reach.

Pete pushed himself upward. Staggering to his feet, he
pulled the Glock from his shoulder holster and aimed it
squarely at Linton's chest. "Leave it where it is."

Linton caught sight of the Glock and paused. Pete doubted
the good doctor could even identify the Glock as such, but he
must have recognized the ease with which Pete handled it. Linton pulled himself together awkwardly and stood up, brushing
at his pants.

Pete said, "Back up."

Linton stepped back a pace. Pete moved to his left, bent
down casually, and picked up the errant handgun, which he
holstered for safekeeping. His own gun he kept pointed at the
doctor. Now that Pete was in control, he felt better. He had
both guns; Linton's weapon in his holster, his own held loosely
in his right hand. He didn't want this to escalate because the
odds weren't that good for either one of them. He was older
and more experienced, but he was poorly coordinated and unaccustomed to physical exertion. Linton was the shorter of the
two—five nine to Pete's six foot two—and heavier by fifteen
pounds, his stocky build a sharp contrast to Pete's long-boned
frame.

Linton said, "Give me my gun."

"Kiss my ass. I'll mail it to you at the lab."

"Give it to me! I told you it belongs to my father-in-law. I
have to put it back."

"Not my problem."

Linton snatched at Pete's sport coat. Pete brought the butt
of his Glock down on Linton's wrist and then gave him a one-
armed push. Linton righted himself and launched a sharp two-
handed blow that knocked Pete to the ground. Still hanging on
to his gun, Pete scrambled forward and wrapped his arms
around Linton's legs, leaning into him. Then Pete took him

down. It wasn't a tackle so much as a slow toppling as Linton was thrown off balance by the weight dragging at him like a bag of sand. Inadvertently, Pete's trigger finger contracted as Linton went down. The weapon fired and the casing ejected into the dark. The shot had gone wide, but Pete's ears rang with such intensity he was rendered momentarily deaf.

Linton took advantage of the moment to punch Pete in the side of the head. Neither man was in shape for a fight, and their clumsy blows and kicks left both floundering. In reality, they fought for less than two minutes, though from Pete's perspective, the fistfight seemed to go on forever, his own responses weakening as Linton continued flailing. He managed to shove Pete away from him, then lashed out with a savage side kick to the knee.

Surprised by pain, Pete lost his grip on his gun. He heard it hit the pavement, but he was off balance and was dismayed to find himself falling into the shrubs. Grimly, he extracted himself, aware of how ridiculous the entire encounter was. He knew no good would come of it. He might not lose, but neither would he win.

Linton stepped back, as though declaring a momentary truce, which was fine with Pete. He was winded. He hurt. His lungs burned with every heave of his chest. He made a dismissive gesture and leaned forward, head hanging while he rested his hands on his knees. "Whoo. Forget it. This is nuts. I'm outta here," he said.

He righted himself and dragged a hand down his face, feeling grit and sweat. He wiped his damp hand on his pants and straightened his jacket.

Linton said, "Look what I got."

Pete didn't catch the words. His scarf was missing and he was intent on finding it. He spotted it lying on the path behind him, picked it up, and hooked it around his neck, and then turned toward the street where his car was parked. There was no shame in withdrawing from a battle that was pointless from the get-go and had already played out. That was it for him. He was bushed. It would take him days to recover as it was. He hadn't gone four feet when he heard the shots.

He looked down with astonishment. A fiery arrow of pain pierced his left side. Pete didn't see the muzzle flash because his back was turned when Linton fired. Someone looking on might have caught that quick flame of superheated incandescent gas emerging from the barrel in advance of the slug, that small penetrating missile followed by the sudden intense burst of light as gas and oxygen ignited. A pungent smell hung in the air.

Pete turned to Linton with amazement. "Why did you do that?"

He saw that Linton held the Glock, which he must have snatched from the path while Pete's attention was diverted. He shouldn't have taken his eyes off the man, but he couldn't worry about that now. He tallied his wounds, neither of which seemed devastating. Linton had shot him once in the side. A second bullet had grazed his right calf. It wasn't his injuries, but the insult that stung, the violation of the rules of fair play. He'd given up. He'd thrown in the towel. You weren't supposed to go after a guy once he'd done that.

Pete shook his head, looking down at himself and then at Linton. "Help me out here. I'm hurt."

Linton gave Pete the once-over, his glance taking in the blood seeping through his pant leg. Even to Pete, the bleeding from the wound in his side didn't amount to much.

"You'll be fine," Linton said. His tone was light, with a touch of condescension, the sort of reassurance a specialist might offer a patient with a medical condition of no real consequence.

He slipped the gun into his coat pocket and turned away, strolling toward the parking lot. His pace was measured. He wasn't hurried. There was no panic that Pete could make out, though it seemed clear he wanted to get out of the area in the event someone had heard the shots and dialed 911. Pete could conceive of Linton as a man who'd always wondered what it would feel like to shoot another man down. It must have crossed his mind, the idle thought of someone who'd never done much of anything except pull the wool over other people's eyes. It made a certain amount of sense. If Linton had been good at what he did, he wouldn't have had to cheat. The gun established his superiority, making him better than he was. It was as simple as that.

Pete felt a fine sheen of sweat break out on his face. He wasn't sure he'd be fine at all. His early outrage had drained away and he wondered what kind of trouble he was in. Just like that, his vision crowded in on him and he toppled. The arms he flung out in front of him to slow his fall were useless. When his face hit the pavement, he registered little if any pain.

Dimly, he realized he'd broken his nose. He hadn't believed the good doctor would shoot him and yet here he was, down on the asphalt, a hole in his side and a stinging gash on his calf. His leg was the least of his concerns.

When the bullet tore into him, a fragment of jacket lining had traveled into his flesh along with the slug. A large temporary cavity had bloomed and collapsed. That same slug had struck his rib cage, shattering bone before it veered off at an angle, taking a ragged zigzagging path through his descending colon. The trajectory of the lead had scarcely slowed when it nicked a far-flung tributary of his superior mesenteric artery no bigger than a piece of string, which began to pump out blood in a series of tiny spurts. Even if the bleeding had been caught, the resulting spill of fecal matter into his abdominal cavity would have overwhelmed his system soon afterward. None of this—the nomenclature, the knowledge of anatomy, or the acquaintance with the consequences of internal rupturing—was part of Pete's thinking as he puzzled the sensations besetting him. He was intimately aware of the savage and destructive tunnel the pellet had plowed as it whipsawed through his organs, but he lacked the language necessary to express his dismay. It would fall to the coroner to translate the damage into its myriad elements, reducing fierce heat and sorrow to a series of dry facts as he dictated his findings, days later, in the morgue.

Pain was a bright cloud that danced along Pete's frame, expanding until every nerve ending jangled with its flame. He wondered where the other gun had gone. He'd pulled his Glock, thinking to deter the doctor, though the sight of it might well have egged him on. He felt something press against his ribs and he wondered if the gun was under him. He closed his eyes. Mere seconds had passed when he heard the doctor's car door slam. Headlights flashed across his eyelids, receding as Linton Reed backed his turquoise Thunderbird out of the space, turned the wheel, and pulled out of the parking lot.

Pete rested. What choice did he have? All of his faculties were shutting down. He lost a moment, like nodding off and jerking awake again. When he opened his eyes, he saw boots. He angled his gaze, taking in the big fellow with his red baseball cap and his red flannel shirt. Pete longed to speak, but he couldn't seem to make himself heard. This was his chance to say Linton Reed's name, putting the blame for the shooting where it rightfully belonged. Tomorrow, when the panhandler read about his death, he could go to the police and tell them what the dying man had said.

The big man hunkered beside him. His expression was compassionate. He knew as well as Pete did that he was on his way out. He leaned closer and for a moment, the two were eye to eye. The man reached out and slid an arm under him. Pete was grateful, thinking he meant to lift him and carry him to safety. It was too late for that, and Pete knew instinctively that any jostling would waken the pain that had faded to almost nothing. The man fumbled, turning him over onto his side. Pete wanted to shriek but he didn't have the strength. He was aware of his watch sliding over his wrist. He felt the man pat his pants until he found the square of his leather wallet and slipped it from his pocket. The last conscious thought that registered was the man lifting the handgun from the holster, tucking it into the small of his back. Pete watched him amble away without a backward glance.

There was no way Pete could rouse himself. Who knew dying could take so long? He was bleeding out; heart slowing, belly filling up with blood. Not a bad way to go, he thought. He heard the beating of wings, a nearly inaudible whisper and flutter. He felt quick puffs of wind on his face, feathery grace notes. The birds had come back for him, hoping he had something to offer them when, in fact, every kindly impulse of his had fled.

28

The six hundred dollars Dietz had surrendered to Pete's land-lady netted us an additional fifteen banker's boxes, too many to fit in Dietz's little red Porsche. The expenditure should have been classified as "throwing good money after bad," as he was now out the six hundred *plus* the three thousand dollars and some odd cents he'd already been cheated. I called Henry for assistance and he obligingly backed the station wagon out of his garage and drove to Pete's former office building. We'd brought the boxes down on the elevator and stacked them at the curb. It took no time at all to load up the rear of Henry's vehicle, after which I rode home with him while Dietz followed in his car.

We all pitched in transferring the boxes from the station wagon to my living room and there they sat. Henry said he'd lend a hand examining files, but we vetoed the idea. We knew what paperwork had already passed through our hands. We also knew what we were looking for and there was no point in stopping to educate Henry on the fine points of Pete's filing system. We thanked him for his transportation services and I assured him I'd check in with him later in the day.

This left Dietz and me sitting cross-legged on my living room floor, pawing through more boxes. "I spend an inordinate amount of time doing shit like this," I remarked.

"We don't turn up something soon, I'm bagging it," he said. "No point in spending more time trying to collect for a job than I devoted to the job itself."

"You worked four days. We've been chasing your fee for one."

"True, and I'm already bored."

The first box I opened contained the contents of Pete's wastebasket, which Letitia Beaudelaire must have upended and emptied with one mighty shake. Here, in layers going back for weeks, was an accumulation of overdue notices, judgments, legal warnings, dunning letters, threats, unpaid bills, and bank statements showing countless checks returned for inadequate funds. It appeared that Pete, when he had his back pressed to the wall, would send off a bad check as a means of buying himself a few days' time. The plan always failed—how could it not?—but he was too busy putting out fires to worry about the ones that flared up again.

Dietz said, "At least he was sincere about the river cruise. Take a look at this."

He leaned forward and handed me a glossy brochure that featured a color photograph of a sleek boat on a body of water. This was not a 2,600-passenger cruise liner tracking the Norwegian fjords. This was river travel. A village was laid out along the shore, with a low rolling mountain beyond. The bell tower on the church was reflected like a shimmering mirage at the water's edge. Everything about the image was inviting, including the sight of passengers on the upper deck where a swimming pool was visible. "I could learn to live like that," I said.

"I told you money has its advantages."

"For sure. I just couldn't picture anything I wanted. Now I'm getting it," I said. "It'd be nice if he'd set aside some cash to pay for the trip. I'm sure Ruthie could use the getaway."

"You think she'd go without him?"

"Not really. I think if she had the money, she'd pay off his creditors before she did anything else."

I watched Dietz pick up a sheaf of papers. As his eyes traced the lines of print, he let out a bark of outrage. "Son of a bitch! Look at this! What the hell is he doing here?"

I took the typewritten pages and glanced at the first. "What am I looking at?"

"My report. He stole the whole damn thing. Retyped it and dicked around with the language, but essentially it's my work, with all my receipts attached. I'll bet he was reimbursed for everything, including my time. This is my original. Look at that."

I leafed through both reports, keeping the two documents side by side for comparison purposes. Pete had rewritten Dietz's account on his own letterhead, embellishing in places, altering the wording so it sounded more folksy. Attached were invoices showing two sets of round-trip tickets from Santa Teresa to Reno, trips he'd certainly never made. He'd done a clumsy job of substituting his name for Dietz's in the hotel bill, but he probably thought his client wouldn't know the difference. I couldn't think why he'd kept Dietz's original. He'd have been smarter to destroy it unless he'd hoped to lift details to fashion a follow-up report. I doubted he had any intention of paying Dietz at all and what options did Dietz have? Trying to collect in California for work done in Nevada would have been an exercise in frustration. Taking Pete to small claims court would have been time consuming, and even if Dietz had won a judgment, what was he to do with it? Pete was flat broke.

"I hope he made good use of my photographs while he was at it," he said.

He opened the manila envelope that bore his return address and removed the pictures he'd taken.

I peered over his shoulder. "That's the gal you were hired to spy on?"

"Mary Lee Bryce, right." Dietz shuffled through the prints while I looked on. "This is her when she first arrived at the hotel and this is Owen Pensky, the high school classmate she met with. Here's one of her with the boss she was supposed to be having the affair with."

"No love lost there," I remarked.

"Unless they're really good at faking it."

"I bet Pete collected up front and in cash. He wasn't the type to bill after the fact."

"Depressing, but you're probably right."

"So if Willard Bryce has already paid Pete, there's no point in asking him for the money. He'd turn you down cold."

"When you said Pete was a scumbag, I thought you were exaggerating."

"I should point out that *you* had a better motive to shoot Pete than any armed robber did. All that guy got was an empty wallet and a cheap watch."

Dietz tossed aside the manila envelope. "You know what bugs me? Here I was so worried his death was connected to the job I did. If I'd known he was ripping me off, I wouldn't have given it another thought."

"He did provide a great excuse for spending time with me."

"Well, there's that."

I checked the receipts for the two sets of plane tickets. "You think he actually paid for tickets? These are copies of copies. I wonder what happened to the originals."

"He had to pay for 'em or he wouldn't have tickets in his possession in the first place. I'm sure he didn't make two trips to Reno. Hell, he didn't even make one."

"Maybe he has a refund coming."

"Maybe he collected the money and spent it all. Who cares?"

"I'm sure Ruthie would appreciate the windfall."

"Fine. Give her the file and let her figure it out."

"Such a grouch," I said.

Dietz was dropping files back into the banker's box he'd placed in front of him. "What time is it?"

I checked my watch. "Ten fifteen. Why?"

"I told Nick I'd be back in time to take him to lunch."

"It's the middle of the morning. We have eight boxes to go!"

"Not me. I've had it."

"I don't want to do this on my own."

"Then don't. Nobody's paying you."

"Come on. Don't you have any curiosity at all about who else he might've been working for? Suppose he had half a dozen other clients who were all set to pay?"

"He didn't. That Bryce fellow was the only one."

"But suppose there was another one?"

"What if there was? If I'd done business with Pete and heard he'd been shot dead, I'd count myself lucky and lay low."

Dietz hauled himself to his feet. I extended my hand and he pulled me into an upright position.

He stepped into the kitchenette to wash his hands. Mine

were as filthy as his, but I planned to go on working, so there wasn't any point in being dainty.

He picked up his car keys, looking way too cheerful for my taste. "I'll check with you later. Why don't you plan on having dinner with us?"

"You better chat with Nick first. He may have other ideas."

"You think?"

"Dietz, so far he hasn't been here one full day. He came to talk to you about his plans and from what you've said, he hasn't even told you the whole story yet. You need to pay attention to these things."

"How complicated could it be?"

I would have laughed, but he hadn't meant to be funny. I said, "Forget about tonight. Find out what's on his mind and we'll get together some other time."

Once he was gone, I turned my attention to the remaining eight boxes, which I confess didn't have quite the same appeal. Doing a tedious chore in the company of a friend makes the labor seem less onerous. These files had been packed haphazardly without the benefit of Pete's casual organizational skills. This was the work of his landlady, who was already annoyed with his bounced checks and probably not that sorry to hear about his unhappy fate. On the other hand, I was feeling slightly more charitable about the man. He might have been a skunk, but he wasn't a malicious skunk; just someone with a tendency to deceive. Nothing wrong with a lie or two when the situation demanded it.

I sat down again and started to work. Ruthie was right about his being a pack rat. In the next box I tackled, the topmost file caught my attention. I opened the folder and had a quick look, leafing through photocopies of various articles related to a diabetes study and some to an NIH grant for a clinical trial being run out at UCST. All of it pertained to Linton Reed—the clinical trial, his educational background, his CV, and numerous scientific papers that made reference to a drug called Glucotace. I was curious about Pete's sudden passion for medical matters. When I knew him, he seldom pursued a subject unless he smelled some monetary benefit. Clearly his interest in Linton Reed went beyond any suggestion that he was in a relationship with Mary Lee Bryce. That theory had been knocked flat. I set the folder aside, placing it on top of the one that contained Dietz's surveillance notes and his photographs.

Next layer down, I came across a thick cross-section of signed contracts, surveillance logs, typed reports, and confidential client information from the old Byrd-Shine days, material Pete shouldn't have had in his possession. I couldn't imagine how he'd managed to get his hands on the files or why he'd held on to them all these years.

Tucked in one end of the same box, I found a pen mike and a handful of tape cassettes, along with his tape recorder, crude and clunky looking by today's standards. I checked the window in the lid, where I could see a cassette still in place. The Sony Walkman had been his pride and joy. I remembered running into him years before when he'd first bought it. He was excited about the technology, which he considered cutting edge. He'd given me a lengthy demonstration, crowing with delight. At this point, the device seemed ancient. New cassette recorders were half this size.

Pete had a penchant for illegal wiretaps. He was a big fan of planting mikes behind picture frames and slipping listening devices in among the potted ferns. I guess we all have our preferences. I put the tape recorder where it had been, replaced the lid on the box, and marked it with a big X. I'd chat with Ruthie and explain why I wasn't returning it. Even a decade later, Byrd-Shine business was confidential. The contents should either be shredded or permanently consigned to my care.

I did a cursory search of another five boxes before I lost heart. Dietz was right. I wasn't getting paid, so why bust my butt? I suppose I'd been hoping to find a fat manila envelope filled with spare cash, but apparently among the treasures Pete clung to, money wasn't one. It wasn't noon yet, but I was hungry. I was also grubby enough that I longed for another shower. There's something about used paper and old storage containers that leaves you feeling chalky around the edges. I trotted myself up the spiral stairs, stripped down, and started my day all over again, emerging from the hydrotherapy feeling happier. I swapped out my sooty jeans for fresh and pulled on a clean turtleneck. I knew Rosie's would be open for lunch, so I grabbed my shoulder bag and a denim jacket and headed

out. I was in the process of locking my door when I spotted
William out of the corner of my eye.

He was sitting bolt upright in an Adirondack chair, wearing
his customary three-piece suit, starched white dress shirt, and
a dark tie, carefully knotted. He had his face tilted up to absorb the October sunshine, and his hands rested on the cane
he'd propped between his highly polished wingtip shoes.

"Hey, William. What are you doing out here?"

"I came to visit Ed."

"Is he here?"

William opened his eyes and looked around. "He was a
minute ago."

We both did a quick survey, but there was no cat to be seen.

"Where's Henry? I'm assuming you've met his houseguest."

"Anna's your cousin, isn't she?"

"A cousin of sorts. She lives in Bakersfield unless she's
decided on a permanent change of residency. I take it they're
off someplace."

"A beauty-supply shop. They'll be back in a bit. You don't
care for her?"

"I don't. Thanks to her I got stuck with a huge bar bill and
then she tried bumming a ride with me. I had no intention of
driving her down here so what does she do? She takes a bus
and now she's moved in next door. Don't you think that's
pushy?"

"Very. I don't like pushy people."

"Neither do I."

I pulled over a lightweight aluminum lawn chair and sat
down next to him. "How's your back doing these days?"

"Better. I appreciate your concern. Henry's bored with the
subject and Rosie thinks I'm faking it," he said. "Actually, now
that I have you here, there's something we ought to chat
about."

"Sure. What's up?"

"I just returned from a visitation and service at Wynington-
Blake." His tone had shifted at the mention of the mortuary.

"I'm sorry. Was this for a friend of yours?"

"No, no. I never met the man. I came across his obituary
while I was waiting for my last physical therapy appointment.
Gentleman named Hardin Comstock. Ninety-six years old
and he was allotted one line. No mention of his parents or his

place of birth. Not a word about hobbies or what he'd done for a living. It's possible there was no one left to provide the information."

"Who paid for the funeral?"

"He took care of his own expenses before he passed. I admired his forethought. I think he might have hired a small band of professional mourners. There were three people there who didn't seem to know each other, let alone the man to whom they were paying their respects. Tastefully done, I must say, except for the inclusion of that unfortunate hymn, "Begone Unbelief." Never cared for that one. Rhyming the word 'wrestle' with 'vessel' strikes me as unseemly."

"Well, yeah."

"I was the only other visitor, so I felt obliged to sing along. When I came to the word 'wrestle,' I hummed instead. I couldn't help myself. I hope you don't think I was out of line."

"Well within your rights. No question. Entirely up to you," I said.

"Thank you, though that's not what I wanted to discuss."

"Ah."

"After the service, your friend Mr. Sharonson took me aside, expressing his concern that you hadn't yet met with him to discuss arrangements for your family member."

"Family member?"

"Terrence Dace."

"Oh, Dace. Oh, him. I'm sorry, I drew a blank. I was focused on Hardin Comstock and the reference threw me. I did have Dace's body transported from the coroner's office, but that's as much as I've done. I'm postponing decisions until I hear from his kids, which might get tricky. It's hard to say at this point."

"As I understand it, that's why Anna's here. To help with the arrangements."

"That's just an excuse."

William said, "Nonetheless, I'd like to offer my assistance. I have years of experience in planning the formalities. Visitation in advance and graveside services as well. A modest reception afterward would be nice."

"I appreciate the offer. Anna won't lift a finger, but when the time comes, we'll chat."

"Excellent. I understand there's a second chap."

"A *second* one? I don't think so."

"This fellow, Felix. Wasn't he a friend of yours?"

"Yes, but that doesn't mean I'll pay to *bury* him. I've got my hands full as it is."

William blinked in puzzlement. "Perhaps I'm mistaken. Terrence Dace was your cousin. Isn't that correct?"

"Something of the sort."

"As I understand it, Terrence and this Felix fellow were inseparable."

I could feel uneasiness creeping up my spine. "I wouldn't go that far. I mean, I don't think they were *close*. They were both homeless and hung out at the beach, so they knew each other, but that's about it."

"I'm sure they'd take comfort in being together now that they're . . ." William raised a finger and pointed heavenward.

I looked up, thinking he'd spotted the cat on a branch above our heads. When I caught his meaning, I made a face. "You're picturing a double feature; two for the price of one."

"If you care to think of it that way."

I put my hand across my forehead, like I was coming down with something. "Oh, man. This is all a bit much. Let me give it some thought, okay? Dace I can accept, but I knew Felix a week and a half and I don't think I'm responsible for his remains."

"If the county buries him, you know it will be a miserable affair."

"Probably."

"Good we agree on that point. I'll put together my suggestions before we meet again. I'm sure we can fashion a program satisfactory to everyone."

I abandoned the idea of Rosie's and retreated to my studio, undone by the sudden prospects of tandem funerals. During the conversation with William, I hadn't heard my phone ring, but as I closed the door behind me, I saw the message light winking on my answering machine. I turned on my desk lamp and took a seat. I pressed play and listened to my outgoing recorded greeting, wishing I didn't sound quite so adenoidal.

A young-sounding fellow said, "Hi, Kinsey. Sorry I missed you. This is Drew from the car wash. Wonder of wonders. My

friend finally paid me back, so I'm flush. Give me a call and
we'll see what we can work out."

He recited his number.

I had no idea who he was or what he was talking about.
Sounded like an anonymous drug deal gone wrong except he'd
used my first name and I don't do drugs. Okay, except for
NyQuil when I have a cold, but that's commercially marketed
and doesn't count. What car wash? What money? I listened to
the message a second time and comprehension dawned. The
guy at the car wash . . . oh, *that* guy. Drew was the one who'd
admired my Boss 429 a lifetime ago. When I'd offered to sell
the car for the five grand I paid, he expressed interest, but I
hadn't taken him seriously. I still hoped to get rid of the car,
but not just now. In order to off-load the Mustang, I'd have to
line up another vehicle, which might take weeks. You don't
just run out and buy the first car that catches your fancy. That's
how I'd acquired the Mustang and look what a dumb move
that was.

I tried Drew's number, which was busy. I left the scratch
pad in plain sight to remind myself to try him again.

I peered out of the window. William still sat in the sun, his
head back, his eyes closed, this time with Ed on his lap. The
cat stood and stared into William's face intently, perhaps mis-
taking him for dead. I was praying nobody else would die or
I'd have three funerals on my hands. To appease my jangled
sensibilities, I made myself another hot hard-boiled-egg sandwich with a line of mayonnaise so thick it looked like a slice
of cheese. The copious amounts of salt I shook onto the mayonnaise glistened like artificial snow. I knew if I'd gone to
Rosie's right then, I'd have ordered a glass of wine just to settle
my nerves. As often as I thought of Dace, I kept forgetting he
was dead. Not only dead, but related to me, and I was charged
with his care. In the "olden" days when I longed for family—
which I'd now thoroughly repented—I always pictured living
persons instead of the other kind. Now I had some of each.

I finished lunch and put a call through to the service station
to inquire about my tire. The attendant seemed surprised to
hear from me and it was clear he'd forgotten. Happily, the
mechanic in the service bay had taken care of it. I drove the
four blocks and read a comic book while the newly repaired
tire was swapped out for the spare. While the mechanic was at

it, he insisted on rotating and balancing the tires, a process I had little patience with but endured nonetheless.

When I got home, I scurried through the backyard like a thief, unlocking my door in haste. It would only be a matter of time before Anna came knocking on my door, trying to con me out of who knows what.

I settled on the sofa with a book, pausing to peek out the window now and then to see if William was still there. For a while he remained, making notes on the back of an envelope. The afternoon stretched on. When I found myself sliding down on the sofa, I pulled a quilt over me for warmth. For unpaid time off, due to lack of work, this was close to perfect. All the comforts of home and it wasn't costing me a cent. Next thing I knew, I'd drifted off to sleep.

Of course I didn't hear from Dietz. I couldn't believe he was so clueless when it came to his son. I've never even had a kid and I still had a better sense of what was going on. It was natural for Nick to be territorial. Not that there was any reason to be alarmed. Dietz and I were not an item. In the ebb and flow of our relationship, the tide was usually going out. I'd thought of Dietz as a gadabout, a freewheeling soul whose ties were few and whose life was his own. But nobody with kids can evade the commitment indefinitely. Dietz had lived as though he had no one to answer to. Naomi had stepped into the breach for him and filled the parenting role. Now that she was gone, he was "it." Apparently, he hadn't twigged to the fact that Nick and Graham would be looking to him for guidance, companionship, and spare cash. For the first time in all the years I'd known him—five by my count—I saw Dietz as a man with baggage. In the singles world, "baggage" is a dirty word, denoting ex-wives, double mortgages, spousal support, writs, liens, offspring of all ages, split vacation time, alternating holidays, family-counseling sessions, attorneys' fees, PTA conferences, private schools, college tuition, accusations, court appearances, and vicious spats on every conceivable subject, including any new relationship the offending parent was engaged in that the other parent objected to.

In my brief fling with Jonah Robb I'd had a taste of this. I was relegated to the wings, a peripheral character in the play that he and his wife/ex-wife had produced, cast, and starred in from seventh grade until the present. I'd bowed out in short order, smart enough to realize I'd never count for anything where he and Camilla were concerned. Let's not even talk about his two girls, whose names I still had trouble remembering. Courtney might have been one. This new development with Dietz didn't bode well for anyone. Nick had figured that out the first time he laid eyes on me.

It wasn't until after dark that I roused myself, brushed my teeth, doused my flattened hair with water, and ventured out. I couldn't help but check Henry's house, where I could see lights on in his kitchen, his back bedroom windows aglow as well. I should have warned him about Anna, but how did I know she'd show up unannounced?

I headed for Rosie's. I knew William would be tending bar, but I didn't think he'd raise the subject of any postlife ceremonials as long as she was nearby. Rosie has no patience for his fascination with the festive aspects of our mortality. As I pushed the door open, I spotted her sitting at one of the tables near the back, getting her nails done. Anna had brought her manicure supplies, which she'd spread across the Formica surface: buffers, emery boards, files, cuticle scissors, and bottles of nail polish. Was *that* why she and Henry had gone to the beauty-supply place? She was already taking scandalous advantage of him. Rosie's hands rested on a fresh white towel, a reservoir of warm soapy water nearby. She seemed pleased with the attention, sending me a shy smile in behalf of this lovely relative of mine.

Fine, I thought. Far be it from me to say a word. They'd all have to figure it out for themselves.

I slid into my usual back booth, which was much too close to Anna's "workstation."

She turned sulky at the sight of me. "I'm earning a living here if it's all the same to you," she said.

"What a refreshing change," said I, in response.

When Rosie's nails were done, she got up and sidled in my direction. Her garish pink polish was still drying, so she couldn't use her order pad. She blew on her nails from time to time while she dictated the dinner fare. This is what I ate through no desire of my own. *Paprikás ponty* (paprika carp, in case you hadn't heard) with a side of sweet-and-sour cabbage. Also, a dish made with onion, green peppers, tomatoes, and a tablespoon of sugar, tossed together and fried in a dollop of lard. Oh, boy. I was just cleaning sauce from my plate, using the crust of one of Henry's homemade rolls, when I looked up and saw Cheney Phillips coming in the door. He made a quick visual survey and when he spotted me sitting in the back booth he headed in my direction. Now what, I thought.

Anna had packed her equipment and she was reaching for her jacket when she caught sight of him. Cheney Phillips was, no doubt, the first Santa Teresa stud she'd clapped eyes on. She sat down again.

He slid in across from me. "Hey."

"Hey yourself. To what do I owe the pleasure?"

"No reason in particular. Your name came up in conversation today. I was in the neighborhood so I stopped by. You look good."

"Thanks. So do you." I glanced at Anna, who was looking at Cheney as though she'd like to nibble him around the edges. I was hoping he wouldn't catch sight of those blue eyes of hers, not to mention the boobs.

Rosie appeared at the table, order pad in hand. She's irresistibly drawn to attractive men, and while she's wildly flirtatious she'd never look one in the eye. She made sure her newly polished nails were handsomely displayed while she kept her gaze pinned on mine. "Your friend would care for liquid refreshment, perhaps?" Her Hungarian accent was particularly pronounced that night.

I looked at Cheney. "Are you working or do you want a drink?" I said by way of translation. There was no question about what she'd asked, but I knew she'd appreciate my intercession.

Cheney said, "Ask her if she has Dreher Bak or Kőbányai Világos."

Rosie waited patiently until I repeated his request and then said, "Is good. Preference is excellent and I'm bringing Kőbányai Világos."

I said, "Why don't you give Anna a plate of *Paprikás ponty*. I think she'd enjoy it. My treat."

Rosie said, "For the lovely Anna, is good."

As she glided away, Cheney smiled, showing a flash of white teeth. I hadn't seen him recently and I looked at him with an air of detachment. His hair was in need of a cut. He was clean-shaven and smelled of soap, which I'm always a sucker for. He wore a caramel-colored turtleneck under the sort of sport coat you want to reach out and touch. The fabric looked like suede and the color was a smoky chocolate brown. I know it's very naughty to compare one man to the next, but with Dietz lurking in the background, I couldn't help myself. If Jonah Robb had wandered in just then, I'd have found myself in range of the three men I'd slept with in the last six years. I'm not at all promiscuous. Far from it. I'm largely celibate, which is not to say I'm immune from temptation. Technically speaking, with three guys, that's only one every other year, but it still seemed alarming for someone with my old-fashioned values and a well-developed self-protective streak.

At least I could see tangible evidence of my taste in men. While the three of them looked nothing alike, they were smart guys, good souls, competent, well seasoned, and knowledgeable. All of us were involved in law enforcement to one extent or another—Cheney and Jonah more so than Dietz and me. Temperamentally, we were all compatible—competitive, but good-natured enough that we could have formed a bowling team or played a few hands of bridge, assuming any of us knew how.

Rosie reappeared and placed a paper coaster on the table, then set a freezer-chilled clear glass mug in the center. She placed a beer bottle beside the mug. "Does your friend want I should pour?"

"Tell her thanks. I'll take care of it."

"He appreciates the offer," I said to her. "He says it's kind of you to ask."

"Is no worry. Anytime is happy to be of assistance."

Cheney said, "I got that."

I watched while he tilted the bottle against the edge and filled the mug with a tawny brew.

Rosie was still waiting.

"He says he'll take you up on it sometime and thanks so much," I said.

She told me he was welcome and I passed the news along. When she'd departed for the second time, he paused long enough to sample the beer, which seemed to meet with his approval.

I said, "Bullshit aside, what brings you here?"

"I got a call from Ruth Wolinsky. She tells me you and your friend Dietz are interested in Pete's clientele."

"That's because Pete stiffed Dietz for three grand. We were hoping he had money coming in that hadn't surfaced yet. So far, no such luck. What's the story on the shooting?"

"Ballistics says there were two guns at the scene, neither of which was found."

"Ruthie told me Pete had two guns."

"He had a Glock 17 and a Smith and Wesson Escort registered in his name. The S-and-W was locked in the trunk of his car. No sign of the Glock. Ruth says he was never without the two. In his bed table drawer we found a shitload of nine-millimeter ammo that matched the slug that killed him. It looks like Pete was shot with his own gun."

"I take it you weren't referring to the S-and-W when you mentioned a second gun."

"Nope. There was one stray casing, a forty-five caliber, which suggests he and his assailant were both armed and probably struggled for control. The slug was buried in the dirt to one side of the path. All in all, four shots were fired—three from the Glock and one from the forty-five."

"With his watch and his wallet missing, you think the robber stole his gun as well?"

"Took it or tossed it. We had guys in wet suits wading the lagoon. Water's shallow for a distance of fifteen feet or so before the bottom falls away. Mud and algae are such that visibility is zilch. We also did a grid search of the surrounding terrain. Location of the two guns may be a function of how well the guy could throw, unless he took them with him."

"What about Pete's car keys?"

"In his pocket. We dusted the Fairlane inside and out, but the only prints we identified were his. The shooter might have been reluctant to add grand theft auto to his other offenses."

"Any chance Pete knew him?"

"Your guess is as good as mine. There were no eyewitnesses and no one heard the shots. Not to speak ill of the dead, but Pete was a bit of a shady character."

"No need to tell me. I notice I'm feeling more charitable, but that's because I feel sorry for his wife."

"I'm with you," he said. "So what's this I hear about you and some homeless guy? Is the last name Dace?"

"Randall Terrence Dace. Turns out we're cousins—fourth, once removed, by marriage—one of those." I decided not to mention the proximity of his youngest child. If Cheney so much as glanced in her direction, she'd gallop over and fling herself onto his lap, the better to slurp him.

"What happened to him?"

"He drank heavily for years. He was also hooked on prescription meds. When he died, he was fifty-three years old and he looked like an old man. When I saw him at the morgue I had no idea we were related. Turns out I'm his sole heir and executor of his estate."

"That ought to keep you hopping."

"Actually, it has. The man left me half a million bucks."

Casually, Cheney leaned forward. "Are you dating anyone?"

I laughed and he had the good grace to look sheepish.

"That came out wrong. No connection. I was just wondering," he said.

Robert Dietz popped to mind, but I didn't know what to make of him. Were we on again or off?

"That's a tough one," I said. "I'll have to think about it and let you know."

I watched Anna's departure without moving my head. No point in calling attention to her when Cheney had just declared himself. I kept him company for an additional half hour just in case she was lurking outside.

29

Tuesday morning, I caught my alarm clock one split second before it went off and rolled out from under the covers. The loft felt chilly and I was tempted to crawl right back in. Instead, I pulled on my sweats and laced up my running shoes before I brushed my teeth. I avoided the sight of myself in the mirror. I pulled on a knit hat, which I knew would be too hot once I got into the run. For now it did double duty: to contain my coiffeur and to muffle my ears against the damp morning air.

The three-mile jog satisfied my need for oxygen, for action, for solitude, and for a sense of accomplishment. With daylight saving time in effect until the end of the month, the tag end of my run was accompanied by a spectacular dawn. At the horizon, above the silver band of the Pacific, a wide expanse of brooding gray changed to a dark red, and from that to a matte blue. Within a minute, the atmosphere had lightened and all the rich hues were gone. Gulls rode the air currents, screeching with happiness. The wind was down and the tops of the palms scarcely moved. Slow-motion waves thundered along the sand and the surf, then receded to a hush. By the time the sun was fully up it was 7:06, and I was back in my living room, prepared for a final go-round with the remaining two boxes of Pete's crap.

Instead of getting cleaned up, I sat down and ate my cereal, put on a pot of coffee, and then washed my bowl and spoon while the coffeemaker gurgled to its conclusion. Still in sweats, I sat on the floor with my coffee cup and made quick work of the first box, which was filled with old catalogs and outdated service manuals for appliances I suspected were long gone. The contents yielded no receipts and no personal correspondence. I did come across a black-and-white newspaper photo of Pete and Ruthie on their wedding day. Saturday, September 24, 1949. They'd have been married forty years when September rolled around again.

Pete was gaunt-faced and young. His hair seemed comically thick back then and he had eyebrows to match. His shoulders protruded like the rounded metal ends of a coat hanger. The sleeves of his suit jacket were too short, so his bony wrists extended a good two inches. He did look pleased with life and more than proud to have Ruthie on his arm. She was easily as tall as he was. The dress she wore was a pale chiffon with shoulder pads and ruffles down the front. Her hair was concealed beneath a white straw hat with a broad brim, a length of white tulle serving as a band. She had a corsage pinned to her left shoulder. I looked closer and identified white roses and white carnations. The newly married couple stood on the low steps of the First United Methodist Church with a scattering of wedding guests in the background. I set the photo aside for her.

The second box contained nothing of interest. I repacked the files I'd spread on the floor and hauled fourteen boxes out to the Mustang. I kept the fifteenth, which contained the Byrd-Shine files, Pete's eavesdropping equipment, and the Bryce file, which was largely Dietz's work. I took another look at the papers Pete had photocopied, which included the proposal Linton Reed had submitted in support of his theory about Glucotace. This is what had netted him the operating funds for the study he was running. I wondered what Pete had made of it.

By the time I'd loaded the car, the trunk was full, the passenger seat was impassable, and the backseat was stacked two boxes high and four across. There wasn't much room back there to begin with and now the view out the rear window was largely blocked.

I slipped the wedding photo into my shoulder bag and then drove to Pete and Ruthie's house. I pulled around to the alleyway that ran behind the property. I could have parked in front and let the engine idle while I knocked on her door and explained what I was up to, but I wasn't *taking* Pete's possessions, I was returning them. Since he stored his boxes in the garage, I figured I should unload them there and talk to her afterward.

Pete's Ford Fairlane was no longer parked by the shrubs. I surmised, correctly as it turned out, that the new owner had put in an appearance and had made off with his new vehicle, such as it was. He'd left Pete's gun-cleaning kit and the bag of birdseed in the alley, along with a bulging plastic bag that I was guessing contained the contents of the two map pockets and the glove compartment. I toted the items as far as the side door to the garage and left them there while I moved boxes into the already overcrowded space. When I'd finished, I grabbed the kit, the birdseed, and the bag of odds and ends, and knocked on the back door.

Ruthie appeared in an old-fashioned floor-length peignoir, a filmy pale blue with pin-tucking down the bodice and a matching nightgown under it. For the first time in all the years I'd known Pete, it dawned on me he had a sex life. The notion was so embarrassing, I averted my gaze. Ruthie's hair was plaited in a long gray-and-blond braid that lay over her left shoulder. It was 9:30 by then and I'd assumed she was the sort who'd be up at the crack of dawn and ready to start her day.

When she opened the door, she said, "Oh, it's you. I couldn't imagine who was knocking at my back door. If I'd known you were coming, I'd have put on some clothes. I have the day off, so I was having a lazy morning."

"I was just dropping off the boxes we picked up from Pete's landlady. I left everything in the garage."

I held up the kit and the two bags. "His car's gone. Looks like the guy who bought it cleared out the trunk, the map pockets, and the glove compartment."

Ruthie relieved me of the items and put them on the kitchen counter. "Come in and have a cup of coffee. I could use the company."

"I'd like that, thanks."

I followed her into the kitchen. During the earlier visit, the front rooms had been tidy and I suspected the disorder here had accrued as a function of too much stuff and no clear sense of what to do with it. My guess was that for a short time after

Pete's death, she'd worked with efficiency, thinking if she kept everything shipshape, she'd stay on top of the process. Little by little, though, she'd lost control. In her shoes, I'd have called the junk man and had him haul everything away, but something of Pete's obsession with storage cartons must have been contagious. Truly, there was no way to know what he might have hidden away. Pack rats by nature are attached to the objects they accumulate—old newspapers, tires, vintage soda bottles, bobbleheads, canned goods, shot glasses, baseball caps. Pete had an issue with cardboard boxes, which he'd apparently found irresistible. I'm sometimes reluctant to toss one myself, especially if it's in pristine condition. What if you have to ship something? What would you pack it in?

As soon as we settled at the kitchen table with our coffee cups, I leaned down and removed the wedding clipping from my shoulder bag and passed it across the table. "I thought you might like to have this."

She took the picture and studied it, smiling to herself. "Nineteen forty-nine. It seems like yesterday and then I'm reminded how young we were. I swear that dress felt very stylish at the time."

"How'd you meet him?"

"I'd just completed my AA degree at City College and I was waiting to get into nursing school. I was working at the front desk at a walk-in clinic. He came in to pick up a prescription for an antibiotic in advance of some dental work. We chatted and when I got off work, he was waiting in the parking lot. He asked if I wanted to have coffee and I said sure."

"And that was that," I said.

"More or less. I was smitten with him from the first. He was sweet and unassuming and almost pathologically shy because of his Marfan's, which wasn't that severe. He had scoliosis and those long white fingers of his. His eyesight was bad, too, but none of that bothered me."

"What did your family think?"

"They were puzzled, but they didn't discourage the relationship. I'm sure they didn't think it would last. I was never interested in motherhood, and with his Marfan's, kids were out of the question because the condition's genetic and the risk is too high."

"So you didn't have to explain."

"Right, and I didn't have to justify the choice. Nobody understood what I saw in him, but I didn't care about that."

"He was a lucky man."

"I was lucky, too," she said. "I take it there was no sign of accounts receivable and no cash hidden away."

"No, though I confess I skimmed over much of it. I don't know how you'll decide what to keep and what to toss, but most of it looked like trash. No offense."

"It's the same with his belongings here. Clearly, he was secretive and it worries me to think there are items of value tucked into the nooks and crannies."

"If there's any way I can help, I'll be happy to," I said.

"I appreciate that."

"There's one issue I want to clear with you. For some reason, Pete had files that belonged to the old agency run by Ben Byrd and Morley Shine. I held on to the box because I'm uneasy at the idea of those contracts and reports in circulation. Throw files in the trash and you really never know where they'll end up."

"I wouldn't have known a box was missing, but thanks for telling me."

We chatted for a while and then I decided I'd better be on my way. I gave her one of my business cards in case she needed to get in touch. My car was still parked in the alley, so I left by way of the back door.

Before we parted company, she reached out impulsively. "I have a favor to ask. And please . . . if this is something you're not comfortable with, feel free to speak up. I'd like to have a memorial service for Pete. Not right away, but in a month or so. He didn't have close friends, but people around town knew him and I think he was well liked. He was a gentle soul and I can't imagine he had enemies. I wondered if you'd be willing to give the eulogy. You knew him better than anyone else since you worked together for so long."

I could feel the heat coming up in my face. Given my disdain for Pete, I was the last person in the world she should've asked to stand up and testify as to his sterling character. But Ruthie was good-natured and oblivious, and I felt bad at the state he'd left her in. All of this flashed through my mind before I opened my mouth.

"I don't know," I said, uneasily, and I could feel the lie

bubble up in my throat like acid indigestion. "I'm terrified of public speaking. Occasions like that trigger panic attacks. I once fainted when I was asked to read a Bible verse in Sunday school. Much as I'd love to help, I couldn't handle it."

"I understand. Just give it some thought and let me know if you change your mind. I know how much it would have meant to Pete."

"I'll think about it," I said, reciting the second lie in as many sentences. I'd already put the idea out of my mind.

She gave my hand a pat and I was on my way.

By the time I got to my car, the horror of the request had made my hands clammy. Even as accomplished a liar as I am, giving testimony about a man I'd liked so little would have been my undoing.

After I left her, I stopped by the office to make sure pipes hadn't broken and there were no pressing calls to return. I gathered bills, flyers, and catalogs from the floor where the mail had been pushed through the slot. Those I tossed onto my desk to deal with at a later time. After that, I headed for home and let myself in the gate. Once in the backyard, I saw Henry's back door was shut and his kitchen was dark. No telling what Anna had talked him into buying for her now.

Ed had left two dead lizards on my welcome mat. I unlocked the door and as I opened it, he appeared out of nowhere and strolled in ahead of me. I was about to object, but the cat seemed so interested in the place, I didn't have the heart to shoo him out.

I'd no more than closed the door when I heard a knock. I looked out the porthole and opened the door.

Anna was standing on my welcome mat, her arms crossed as though for warmth, her expression subdued; same boots and jeans, navy fleece top.

She said, "I know I shouldn't have showed up in Santa Teresa out of the blue. I would've called, but I was afraid you'd tell me not to come."

"It's your business, Anna. Do anything you want."

"I know you're mad."

"I'm not mad. I'm annoyed. I don't want you taking advantage of Henry. He's a sweetheart."

"I know that. He's a nice man."

"And you're a mooch. I know you can't help yourself. I get that. Just do not mooch off him."

"I don't intend to stay at Henry's more than a couple of days. As soon as I get a job, I'll find a place of my own."

"On your lavish minimum-wage income. Thank you for the reassurance. One reason I would have told you not to come is because you can't afford it."

"I'm here because of my dad. I'm not saying that's the only reason, but I'd like to know what happened to him. Henry told me you'd been trying to find out, so I thought maybe we could talk about it sometime. If you have a minute."

"I'll think about it."

"Anyway, I apologize for not letting you know I was on my way."

"I appreciate the apology."

She sent me a tentative smile and I didn't shut the door in her face. I said I'd see her later and waited until she was half-way back to Henry's.

The studio smelled of the coffeepot that had been sitting far too long and I realized I'd neglected to turn off the machine before I'd left. I leaned across and flipped the switch, then looked over at the answering machine. The red message light blinked merrily. I slung my shoulder bag onto the desk and pressed play. Sure enough, it was Drew again with apologies for not catching me, like it was his fault I was gone. The call had been recorded a mere ten minutes earlier, so I punched in his number and held my breath, waiting to see if I was in luck.

Two rings and he picked up.

"Is that you, Drew? This is Kinsey Millhone."

"Hey, great! I can't believe I'm actually talking to you."

We spent a few minutes congratulating ourselves on finally managing to connect and then we moved on to the subject at hand.

"We're talking about five grand, right? Because that's what I have."

"Works for me," I said. "It might take me a couple of days to find a replacement. What's your time frame?"

"The sooner the better. My brother's in town. He's the one

who had the 429 in high school. I told him about yours and he's hot to get his hands on it."

"How long will he be here?"

"A week. It's not like the deal hangs on him, but if there's a way to make this happen, it'd be great."

"I'm right in the middle of something at the moment, but first chance I get, I'll check a couple of car lots and see what's out there. No promises, but I'll do my best."

"Understood. And thanks."

The call completed, I did a quick survey to see what the cat was up to. I wasn't used to having a small animal on the premises. Ed was wholly engaged in inspecting the underside of the sofa bed. A shred of upholstery lining was hanging down, so he had to lie on his back and play with it.

I said, "What were you doing in the yard? Aren't you supposed to be inside?"

He turned his head in response to my query, looking at me briefly as though to determine if I was worthy of his attention. Apparently, I was. He came out from under the sofa, jumped up onto a kitchen stool, and then onto the counter, where he strolled to the end. He made a turn and came back, making a point of brushing up against me. In my presence, he'd never uttered a sound, but now he launched into a discourse. He pivoted and glided the other way, leaving white cat hair on the sleeve of my turtleneck.

"Oh, now you want to be friends," I said. "I saw you sitting in Anna's lap. Have you no shame?"

He sat down and made what I swear was meaningful eye contact.

"You want a bowl of milk? Is that it?"

I took out a saucer and poured a puddle of milk in the center. "This is exactly why I've never wanted a pet," I said. "It's worse than talking to myself."

Daintily, he crossed and gave the milk a sniff, and then he leveled the double-O stare with one green eye and one blue.

I sniffed it myself and sure enough, the milk was sour. He didn't seem to blame me as much as I blamed myself. When a cat comes to call, it's nice to have something to offer that isn't past its sell-by date. While I sat, Ed allowed me the incredible privilege of giving his head a scratch.

There was a tap at the door. I left Ed where he was while I looked out the porthole. There stood Dietz.

When I opened the door, he said, "Can I come in?"

Oh, sure. Like I might refuse. I stepped back. His manner was tentative and I will promise you in that split second, I knew he was leaving. In my view, it's a hell of a thing when one's intuition about a guy is solely tied to his departure. "Let me guess," I said.

"Don't guess. Let me say this my way."

"How about coffee first?"

"How about after I get this out?"

"By all means."

I kept my expression neutral. I disengaged my emotional gears. We hadn't connected at a deep level this time around. He'd been in town for three days yet here it was again. The perpetual bye-bye that seemed central to our entire relationship. I was thinking, thank god I didn't sleep with the man or I'd have been in real pain. Even so, I was already suffering the loss of him, which I covered at no small cost to myself.

Dietz said, "Nick's taken a leave of absence from work. I thought he was here to discuss the plan, but turns out it's a done deal. He wants us to travel together and get to know each other. What was I supposed to say?"

"You say yes, of course." I won't say I sounded chipper, but anyone who didn't know me well would have thought I was fine.

"It wasn't my idea," he said.

"Oh, come on. I'm not chiding you. Plan or no plan, he's your kid."

"Well, I appreciate that. I didn't think you'd take it this well."

"There you have it. Grown-up at last. So when do you go?"

"Nick's not awake yet. We settled this last night and I said I'd have to talk to you first before we hit the road."

Now, *that* hurt my feelings. There was something about the stinginess of the condition he'd laid out to his son. Yes, he'd take off with Nick. But no, he insisted on giving me my five minutes first.

I moved into the kitchenette and poured him a cup of coffee. I put the mug on the counter and pushed it in his direction.

"Thanks," he said. He took a sip, watching me over the rim of the mug. He made a face and looked down. "How long has this been sitting?"

"I don't want to make small talk."

He set the coffee cup on the counter. "You're not taking it well," he said.

"Not taking it well at all," I replied. "And I don't want a hug. That makes you feel better and makes me feel like shit."

"I'm not doing this to make you feel bad."

"But that's the effect it has on me anyway, okay? I feel like a whiny baby. I can live without the blow to my dignity."

"You want me to go through the other boxes with you?"

"Like my consolation prize? No, thanks. I did that. I returned them to Ruthie and had a nice chat about Pete, whom she adored for the better part of forty years."

"What do you want me to do?" he said. "I can't change it now. I had no idea Nick would show up. How was I to know he'd want to go off on this *field* trip?"

"You couldn't. Not your fault. It's always going to be like this. I keep thinking I'll learn to handle it, but I don't."

"Would it have been better if I never showed up at all?"

"It would be better if I didn't care one way or the other."

"But you do."

"Yes."

"Now, you see, that's nice. I like it that you care." He smiled and folded me into his arms, which of course made my face heat, my nose swell, and my eyes sting with tears.

I laughed. "Damn it. Now I'll be ugly at the same time I'm feeling stupid."

"You're not stupid. You're adorable. You make lousy coffee, but I'll try not to blame you for that."

"Quit saying nice things."

He swayed, holding me in his arms. It was like dancing in place; the first time he'd actually touched me since he'd been back. That first night, he'd declined to kiss my cheek. At that point, he was still half mad at me and I was still indignant that he'd accused me of recommending him to Pete. I could feel the whisper of sexuality rising up along my frame.

I stepped back. "Let's don't do this. It makes no sense."

"Does everything have to make sense?"

"Yes, it does and I'll tell you why. I'm the one being left behind. And I understand why and I wish you well, but I don't see any reason to put my soul on the line."

"You think my soul's not on the line?"

"I don't."

"You're mistaken about that."

"Okay, fine. I stand corrected and let's not turn this into an argument. I don't want us to leave each other with bad feelings. If you come back, we can revisit the issue."

"*When* I come back, not if."

"Don't push your luck."

He watched me for a moment and whatever he saw in my eyes must have been more eloquent than our brief exchange. "You want me to call?"

"Nope. I want you to go where the wind blows you. I want you to have an incredible adventure with your son. Anything else can wait and if I never see you again, I'll somehow manage to survive, so don't worry on my account."

"Fair enough," he said. "Although it does sound harsh."

"I'll miss you."

"Better. I'll get in touch when I can."

And that's where we left it. When the door closed behind him, I waited until I heard the low rumble of his Porsche come to life and then diminish as he drove away. I picked up the saucer and let the sour milk run down the kitchen drain. I emptied the coffeepot and washed it, washing the saucer at the same time, thus restoring order to this small life of mine. I checked Ed's reaction. "What do you have to say for yourself?"

He sat politely and we shared a long look. He blinked at me lazily and I blinked back at half speed, an exchange I later learned was called a cat kiss. When the phone rang, I pointed at Ed. "Stay."

I crossed to the desk and picked up the handset.

"Hey, Kinsey. This is Aaron Blumberg."

"Hi, Aaron. How are you?" This was me being cordial in the midst of unacknowledged heartbreak. Really, I should have been weeping my baby eyes out, but I'm made of sterner stuff.

He said, "I'm fine, thanks. I called because we have the autopsy report and lab work on Dace and I thought you might want a rundown."

"That was fast," I said. "I didn't expect to hear from you so soon."

"It's been ten days," he said. "About par for the course. Case wasn't complicated. I'll send you a copy of Dr. Palchek's notes, but you might as well get the gist of it by phone."

"Great."

"I'll give you the formal version first and then answer any questions you have. Cause of death was hepatic failure due to chronic alcoholism. Thus the jaundice. No big surprise there."

"Right."

"He was also suffering from alcoholic ketoacidosis syndrome. AKA for short. Essentially we're talking about the buildup of ketones in the blood. Ketones are a type of acid that form when the body breaks down fat for energy. Patients typically have a recent history of binge drinking, little or no food intake, and persistent vomiting. This results in a delay and decrease in insulin secretion and excess glucagon secretion. A lot of hokum here that I'll skip . . .

"Basically, all patients with severe AKA are dehydrated. Several mechanisms might be responsible, including decreased fluid intake and inhibition of antidiuretic hormone secretion by ethanol. Volume depletion is a stimulus to the sympathetic nervous system, which decreases the ability of the kidneys to excrete ketoacids and can culminate in circulatory collapse.

"My guess is if you go back and talk to his pals, they'll confirm one or more of the following symptoms. You got a pencil and paper handy?"

I picked up a pen and pulled over a scratch pad, jotting down the list as he recited it.

"Abdominal pain, agitation, confusion, an altered level of alertness. Also, let's see here . . . low blood pressure, fatigue, sometimes dizziness. Fruity breath is one key, so be sure you ask about that. Smells like acetone."

"You want verification?"

"It might satisfy any questions his cohorts have. His family might be interested as well. The bad news is, if someone had picked up on his condition and had taken him to the ER in time, he might be alive."

"Oh, man. I think I'll keep that to myself," I said. "Anything else?"

"Well, just running down the page here . . . autopsy showed

his heart was enlarged and there was also extensive kidney damage."

"Also associated with chronic alcoholism I'd imagine."

"Can be. The only thing that struck me as odd was that blood and urine came back negative for opiates and alcohol."

I was silent. "You're saying he was sober?"

"Totally."

"Are you sure? Because two of his homeless pals swear he was drunk to the end. In fact, Pearl was devastated because he swore up and down he'd quit."

"Well, there's no way to know how efficiently he metabolized alcohol, but he was clean on October 7 and probably the day before as well. He might've *behaved* like he was drunk. Kidneys start shutting down and the buildup of toxins can render you incoherent. Lethargy's another symptom that can mimic inebriation. He might have garbled his words."

I said, "I'll ask about that. I'm told he'd been going downhill for months."

"He was a short-timer. No doubt about that. All I'm saying is what *got* him wasn't the result of alcohol consumption during the two or three days prior. The time frame's a guess on my part, by the way."

"What about pain pills? I hear he was hooked on those."

"Nope. No sign of anything in his system," he said. "At any rate, if you hear something to the contrary, you let me know."

"I'll do that. And thanks."

30

I sat at my desk, wondering what to make of it. I certainly wasn't going to tell Pearl that Dace might have been saved. She had Felix's death to deal with and that was enough. She was already blaming herself for the beating that killed him. I picked up my jacket, my bag, and car keys. Ed seemed willing to follow me into the yard, but I couldn't be sure he'd behave once I was gone. I went back into my apartment and snagged Henry's house keys. I locked my door, lifted Ed, and tucked him under my arm. He purred happily, perhaps thinking we'd be going through life this way, his warm body pressed against mine. I would have kissed his sweet head, but I didn't know him that well and I was worried he'd take offense. I unlocked Henry's door and dropped him inside, a move he also accepted without complaint.

In the car again, I drove along the beach, scanning the grassy areas along the bike path for sight of Dandy or Pearl. I spotted them in their usual place, in the area under the palms, across the street from the Santa Teresa Inn. They'd set up day camp. They had their carts close by, angled against the damp breeze coming off the surf. Both purloined grocery carts were filled with blankets, pillows, and shopping bags that bulged with recyclable bottles and soda cans. There was a redemption center three blocks away and the homeless supplemented their sketchy incomes by turning in glass and plastic for whatever it netted them. Of course, they squandered the money on bad booze and cheap smokes, trusting the good folks in town would see to their room and board.

They'd spread tarps on the grass in the very spot where I'd first made their acquaintance. Dandy was stretched out on his sleeping bag and Pearl was sprawled on a blanket. A third fellow had joined them, and while I didn't get a good look at him, I wondered if he was going to be a regular now that Felix was gone. I drove past them and pulled into the public lot, where I parked and got out.

The makeshift memorial that had sprung up in the wake of Terrence Dace's death was looking forlorn. The jars of wild-flowers were still grouped together in the sand, but the water was gone and flowers themselves were wilted. The tower of carefully balanced stones had been dismantled. There was no sign of a rock sculpture for Felix, but he'd died in the hospital whereas Terrence had died on the beach. I couldn't even pre-tend to understand the unspoken rules for honoring the fallen comrades of those who had no homes.

Dandy watched me approach. Pearl ignored my arrival, except for the face she made, which expressed equal parts dis-dain and indifference. I suspected she was still miffed at me for not rushing to comfort her during her outburst at the news of Felix's demise. She paused to light a cigarette and then continued sipping from a soda can that was doubtless laced with whiskey.

I paused on the path within range of them. "Mind if I sit down?"

Dandy moved his backpack. "Make yourself at home."

He was nicely turned out: fresh shirt, a sport coat only slightly threadbare along the cuffs. As far as I could tell he hadn't been drinking. Then again, he held his liquor well and he might have been covering. At least there was no pint bottle in sight and when Pearl offered him the soda can, he declined.

As I sat down, Dandy introduced me. "This is Kinsey. She's a good friend of ours."

"They call me Plato, the preacher man," he said. He doffed an imaginary cap and his smile showed a mouth devoid of teeth. Plato was emaciated, a good sixty-five years old, with a frizzy head of gray hair and a long unkempt beard and mustache. His ears were crusty along the edges as though dusted with powdered sugar. His face had that odd red-brown hue that suggested a life spent outdoors without a proper slathering of SPF 15.

I said it was nice meeting him and he said words to the same effect.

That settled, I sat on the section of tarp Dandy'd cleared for me. The ground was damp and hard and even with a layer of plastic and a sleeping bag on top of that, I wasn't sure how to arrange myself in any semblance of ease. Nor was I clear on how I'd get to my feet again. "I have news about Dace."

Pearl said, "Whoopee doo," twirling a finger near the side of her head.

"You're annoying, you know that? I didn't have to drive down here looking for you. Are you interested or not?"

Mildly, Dandy said, "Don't mind her. I'm listening."

"Thank you," I replied. "Dace was sober when he died."

"Well, that's a load of horseshit, right there," Pearl said. "We seen him the day before and he was puking his guts out. I know you're fussy when it comes to body functions, so I won't say no more except the stuff looked like coffee grounds. You wouldn't have wanted to get anywhere near the man."

"He died of liver and kidney failure."

Dandy said, "Natural causes in other words."

"Well, natural if you take into account his heart was enlarged and half his internal organs were shot. He wasn't drunk. That's the point," I said. I turned to Pearl. "Did you talk to him that day?"

"If you want to call it that. I wouldn't say we communicated. I said, 'How's tricks?' and he mumbled something that made no sense. He was staggering all over the place, and his skin and the whites of his eyes were yellow. He might've turned into a werewolf for all I know."

"What about an odor?"

"You mean did his breath stink aside from puke? Smelled like nail polish remover, but not even Terrence was that desperate."

"That was the ketoacidosis. And don't ask me to explain. I'm just telling you what the coroner's investigator told me," I said.

Dandy opened the flap of his backpack and rooted through the interior. After a brief search, he pulled out a prescription bottle and passed it along to me.

The pill bottle was two inches high and the cap was an inch across. The vial was sealed in shrink-wrap. "What's this?"

"His pills. He told me to hang on to them."

"Why the seal?"

"So it can't be tampered with. Those are the pills that made him sick, but the clinic didn't want to hear about it. They wanted them back. Doctor even threatened to come down here after them."

"A doctor? Who's this?"

"The fellow who headed up the deal he was in."

"That seems weird," I said. I read the label. Not surprisingly, I'd never heard of the drug. "Why didn't you mention this before?"

"He said not to. I kept the bottle hid since the day he passed it on to me."

I shook the container, which rattled lightly. "And these are for what?"

"He had three different meds. One was supposed to knock down his craving for cigarettes and alcohol. Maybe not that particular pill. It could have been the other ones."

"Like Antabuse?"

"I guess."

"And he said the pills made him sick?"

"Yes, ma'am."

"But that's how Antabuse works. You have one drink and you get sick as a dog. That's the point."

Pearl cut in. "You don't need to lecture us about Antabuse. We know everything there is to know about that crud. Fact is, Terrence hadn't had a drink. You said so yourself. So now how do you explain it, Miss Smarty-Pants?"

I read the label again, rotating it in my hand as I followed the line of print. The name of the prescribing physician was Linton Reed, M.D.

Dandy's eyes were fixed on mine. "What's that look for?"

"I know this name in another context. I'm just surprised to see it here."

Dandy said, "That's from the program he signed up for last spring."

"Alcoholics Anonymous?"

Pearl made a face. "Not them. It's this other thing. FDA makes the drug companies jump through hoops before a new one gets approved. He took three pills. One was for booze jitters, but I don't think that's it."

"I take it 'booze jitters' means what it sounds like."

"Of course. Mornings, you know how bad your hands shake before you choke down those first couple of belts of hooch?"

I tried not to look quite as blank as I felt. My hands sometimes shook from anger or fear, but not from DTs.

Meanwhile, she was talking to Dandy. "I think those are the ones that kept him leveled out; preventing mood swings, I guess."

Dandy said, "Naw, now that's not what it was. Those curbed his sweet tooth. Remember he talked about all the candy he ate? He couldn't get enough and he still about passed out. Day he got kicked out of the program, they said he had to turn in his pills, as many as he had left. Terrence wasn't about to."

"Why was he kicked out?"

"He missed appointments and complained too much. He was always kicking up a fuss and wouldn't obey the rules. I'm not saying he wasn't a pain in the ass."

"Did you ever meet his doctor?" I asked. I was still trying to get my head around the fact that Linton Reed and Dace had crossed paths.

"Not me, and I hope he don't get ahold of me," Pearl said. "Terrence was in St. Terry's that time? He's so scared of the man he signed himself out."

"When was this?"

"June, I think. He left the hospital—"

"More like escaped," Dandy put in.

"That's right. He got straight on a bus to Los Angeles," she said. "He spent a month down there until he figured it was safe to come back."

"Why was he so scared of this guy?"

"Because he's the one knew Dace was telling the truth." She pointed at the pill bottle. "The day he died? When you showed up? We figured that's what you were after."

"You mind if I hang on to this?"

Dandy said, "Sure thing. Terrence knew what you did for a

living. He hoped you'd look into it proper if something happened to him."

"Nothing *happened* to him except he died," I said. "At least as far as the coroner's office is concerned."

Pearl said, "The man was fifty-three years old! He enrolled in that drug deal and went straight downhill. Don't you listen? Same thing happened to his friend Charles."

"Charles was in the same program?"

"Not both at the same time. Terrence went in later, after Charles died."

"Why didn't you tell me this before? How many times have we talked about Dace and this is the first I've heard."

"We didn't know what he died of. He said they'd claim 'natural causes,' which is what you just said. He stole those pills and I'm passing them along because he told me to," Dandy said. "You ought to look into it."

"Look into what? He'd been trashing himself for years, in prison and out. You can't do that and then turn around and express surprise at the damage you've done."

Pearl said, "Pills aren't the only thing he stole."

I looked at her with interest. "You're talking about medical charts."

"How'd you know?"

"Because I have them."

"He sent you those?"

"He sent them to himself in care of Harbor House. One of the volunteers made a point of giving me his mail."

Dandy said, "Well, I'll be. Good for him. We didn't know where all that stuff went, especially when them Boggarts walked off with his cart."

"How'd he manage to steal charts? Those are usually kept under lock and key."

Dandy smiled. "Easy. He made an appointment at the clinic. They put him in a room to take his clothes off before the doctor came in. Nurse left his chart in that slot outside the door. He waited until she left. He opened the door and made sure wasn't nobody in the hall. Then he took his chart, put it in his shirt, and walked out calm and easy as you please."

"They figured it out pretty quick, but Terrence was gone by then," Pearl said.

"He stole another couple of charts as well," Dandy said.

"Well, I know that. The man was a regular kleptomaniac," I said. "How'd he manage to steal the other two?"

Pearl laughed. "This is good. This is my favorite story. Remember he had that shirt and glasses belonged to Charles?"

"In his duffel with the picture ID," I said. "Green-and-yellow plaid."

Pearl pointed to show she approved. "So Charles was laying out at the coroner's a few days before they figured out who he was. Terrence had already took his ID. He figured nobody ever looked a homeless man in the face, so he put on the green-and-yellow-plaid shirt and glasses Charles was wearing when he had his picture took. He made an appointment in Charles's name, went into the clinic flashing the photo ID, and pulled the same thing. Stole the chart off the back of the door."

"He did it twice?"

"He did it three times, counting his. Different doctors work different days, and the nurses work different shifts. He made sure he smelt bad enough that everybody was in a hurry to get away from him."

I could feel my smile fade. "It's all in there, isn't it? Proof he got sick. Proof he told the doctor. All his lab work. Everything."

Dandy said, "Yes, ma'am."

"What do you want me to do?"

Dandy said, "I don't know, but there's bound to be some remedy, don't you think?"

"If I can figure out what it is."

I slipped the pills into my shoulder bag and struggled to my feet. I dusted off the back of my jeans and turned toward the parking lot. "I should warn you, his youngest daughter's in town. Anna. Twenty-six years old. Long dark hair, blue eyes. She's a piece of work."

Pearl piped up as I was walking away. "Hey. You have any spare Seconals?"

"I left 'em in my other jacket," I said, as though she just happened to catch me without. She rattled off a list of acceptable substitutes, Nembutals among them, but I didn't have those either. I gave her five bucks for cigarettes with strict instructions she was to share with Dandy and the preacher man. I knew it was bad form, but given her true preferences, I didn't think the sin was too great.

As I returned to my car, I glanced at my watch, surprised that it was close to 1:15. Had I eaten lunch? I thought not. I drove home. A check of the loaf of bread I had on hand showed no signs of green. After a brief search, I came up with a jar of Kraft Olive & Pimento cheese spread. I popped off the top, took out a small spatula, and made what I think of as a hand sandwich. I held a piece of bread in my left palm, slathered it with cheese spread, and then folded it in half. I snagged my shoulder bag, locked up, and dined in style as I was crossing the patio. I guess a hand sandwich could be considered fast food. Four bites.

I peered in Henry's screen door and saw him standing at the counter, unloading groceries. I tapped. He leaned over and unlatched the door so I could let myself in. He said, "Have a seat. I'm almost done."

I found myself peering down the hall. "Where's Anna?"

"Out looking for work."

"Enterprising of her. What's she have in mind?"

"I'm not sure. She went through the classified ads and circled five or six possibilities. Two were downtown, so I told her she could borrow the station wagon." He sat down. "You're not big on cousins."

"Not that one, at any rate," I said. Ed appeared and hopped up into my lap, the little suck-up. I was sure he was just as attentive to Anna behind my back. I rubbed his ears so he'd like me better than her.

Henry said, "I haven't seen you since Dietz arrived. I'm looking forward to catching up."

"Too late. He's gone again. He took off this morning with his son Nick . . ." I could tell from Henry's expression he'd forgotten Dietz had two sons.

While Henry emptied the last brown paper bag and put canned goods away, I took a few minutes to refresh his memory. That recital segued into an account of the latest developments in the drama that had begun to unfold three nights before in my argument with Dietz about Pete.

By the time Henry joined me at the table, I'd skipped from the subject of Pete Wolinsky to Aaron Blumberg's report about Dace's death. I also filled him in on the charts I now had in my possession. I reached into my shoulder bag, removed the pill bottle, and put it on the table. "Those are the pills Dace took that he swore were making him sick. Check out the doctor's name."

Henry picked up the bottle and read the label through the clear plastic wrap. "Linton Reed was Dace's doctor?"

"Looks that way."

"Doesn't that beat all?"

"I don't know if it means anything or not. Probably not."

We tossed the subject around to see what made sense. Like me, Henry was puzzled by the odd crossroads where Terrence Dace's death intersected Dietz's surveillance of Linton Reed and Mary Lee Bryce. "There almost has to be something going on there," he said.

"You think? I can't decide. It could be just what it looks like: Dr. Reed supervised Terrence Dace's participation in the drug study and he's also Mary Lee Bryce's boss. Big deal."

Henry said, "Put it that way and it doesn't seem so strange."

"Then again, according to Dandy and Pearl, Dace was scared to death of the man."

"Has anybody else confirmed all this talk of Dace going downhill?"

"Just Dandy and Pearl."

"You think they're reliable?"

"If you're asking if I believe them, I do. They may drink a lot, but they don't make things up. He must have been getting sicker or he wouldn't have died."

Henry weighed the matter. "Maybe."

I thought about that for a moment. "What's that word for things that happen at the same time?"

"Synchronicity. Eight across in a crossword puzzle two days ago," he said. "Which is an instance of synchronicity."

I laughed. "That's right."

"Carl Jung came up with it. He didn't believe in random events. He believed in a deeper underlying reality."

"And I believe in the Easter Bunny. How deep is that?" I said. "You have any cookies? I tend to think better when I'm hyped on sweets."

Henry got up and removed a cake tin from the cupboard. He placed it on the table and opened the lid. "Spice cookies. New recipe and one of my better efforts."

I ate a cookie and then said, "I mean, what if Dace was right and the pills made him sick? As Pearl points out, he was only fifty-three years old, which makes death a bit premature, don't you think?"

"I guess you could ask Dr. Reed."

"Oh, right."

"I'm serious."

"Don't think so. If he had a problem with Dace, he's not going to tell me."

"Wouldn't hurt to ask." When he saw the look I was giving him, he said, "I'm playing devil's advocate."

"I can't go hunting him down to quiz him about Dace. He doesn't know me from Adam. Even if I talked my way into his office, he could say anything . . . medical gobbledegook . . . and I wouldn't know the difference. How would I explain why I'm so interested in this stuff?"

"You could ask about the program. Tell him how much you appreciate what he tried to do for your dear departed cousin."

"Oh, please. I know I'm a good liar, but I'm not that good."

Henry held up a finger. "But as you so often say to me, you want to be good at lying, it's practice makes perfect."

"I practice," I said crossly.

"The point is, for all you know, this is a case of bungled communication. Maybe Dace misunderstood. Maybe he got the dosages mixed up. Some doctor explains what he's prescribing and half the time you tune him out. That's why the pharmacist goes over it with you a second time when you pick up the medication."

I made a noncommittal response to indicate I wasn't quite buying it until I had another cookie.

"How would I know if he's telling the truth?"

"How do you know anyone's telling the truth? You listen to what he has to say and then corroborate it with an outside source."

"I love it when you come up with a big hot plan I'm supposed to implement. You talked me into Bakersfield and look how that turned out."

"Then you'll do it?"

"Possibly."

Henry said, "Good. I'm glad that's settled."

"Anything else on your mind?" I asked. "You have that look like there's more."

"Anna. Regardless of how you feel, this is her father we're

talking about. I think she should be told what's going on. If you don't mind, I'll bring her up to speed."

"Just keep her out of my hair."

I didn't give a shit about Anna, but I had to admit he had a point in the matter of Dr. Reed. Dandy and Pearl thought he was treacherous, but that didn't make it true. The idea of calling him made my palms damp. Knowing how much I didn't want to make the call, I sat right down at my desk and went to work. Put off anything you don't want to do and the avoidance becomes only more burdensome. It took me several tries to connect with his office. I started with St. Terry's, asking someone in administration about the process by which patients with drug and alcohol problems were recommended for participation in experimental drug trials. That netted me a blank. I asked who might know and right away everyone pitched in, handing me off from person to person so as not to have to deal with me themselves.

The call was transferred from one department to another, which forced me to repeat myself. The rehearsal was doubtless good for me because by the time I'd been connected with the proper office in the Health Sciences Building at UCST, I'd told my tale so often I almost believed it myself. In point of fact, much of what I was saying was the truth, give or take. I simply embellished according to what I sensed might be persuasive to the person I was chatting with.

Within the first few words tendered by the department secretary, I was aware of her chilly manner, which didn't sit well with me. This was the first impediment I'd come up against. Her telephone greeting consisted of her identifying herself and the department in a cadence so staccato it was off-putting in itself.

I had to roll right over her, infusing my voice with a wholly manufactured warmth. I said, "Hiiiii, my name is Kinsey Millhone. I'd like to set up an appointment with Dr. Reed, if I may." I'd managed to stretch the word "hi" across two syllables and three musical notes.

There was a pause during which she marshaled her defenses, her job apparently being to ward off all who approached. "And this is in regard to what?"

"A family member died recently. This was Terrence Dace. I'm not sure if you're familiar with the name, but I believe he was enrolled in a research study of Dr. Reed's. I'd appreciate any information he'd be willing to share."

Two beats of silence before she said, "Your name again is what?"

"Kinsey Millhone, with two Ls. Terrence Dace is my cousin. The rest of the family lives in Bakersfield and they've asked me to find out what I can about his last days."

Whereas before, I'd hoped not to have to talk to Dr. Reed, I was now determined to get in to see him.

"I see," she said. "Of course, I'm not sure Dr. Reed would be at liberty to discuss a patient currently in his care."

"My cousin's dead. He's been in Jesus's care for the past two weeks."

That turned out to be a showstopper, so I went on. "I'm not asking about his *medical* problems. For heaven's sakes! That would be his own private business, wouldn't it? I want to know how he was doing . . . I guess you could say, spiritually. The family's very religious. His daughter came all the way down here out of concern. I'm sure you can imagine how upset they were when he passed so unexpectedly."

"I understand. Unfortunately, Dr. Reed won't be in the office again until Thursday and I'm not sure he has anything available. I'd have to take a look at his calendar and he's with someone at the moment."

"Thursday's fine. What time would work best for him?"

I'm sure she was panting to say that what would work best for everyone would be for me to fall in a hole and die. With palpable skepticism, she said, "It's possible he has a nine o'clock appointment open, but I'd have to check . . ."

"Perfect. Nine on Thursday. I'll be there. Thank you so much. I really appreciate your help."

I hung up, which left her in the lame-ass position of not having my contact number so she could call me back and cancel.

31

I devoted all day Wednesday to my quest for a new car so I could off-load the old. I cruised used-car lots for much of the day, my search culminating in the purchase of a 1983 Honda Accord. This was a four-passenger four-door sedan, and I bought it for the following reason: I'd been to the same lot twice and hadn't noticed it until the salesman called it to my attention. The car was boxy and plain, an unprepossessing dark blue; one owner, low mileage, with all of the service records stapled together in a manila envelope. The tires were so-so, but that didn't bother me, as they were easily replaced. I paid thirty-five hundred dollars, which meant I'd picked up an extra fifteen hundred on the deal. My stars must have been in the proper alignment, because I had money coming at me at every turn.

By the time I returned home, it was too late to worry about completing the sale of the Mustang. The DMV was closed for the day. I called Drew and suggested we meet there in the morning, but he and his brother had plans for that day, so we postponed the exchange until the following Monday morning. He'd hand me five thousand in cash, I'd sign over the pink slip, we'd turn in the paperwork to the DMV clerk, and go our separate ways. Fine with me. I had other things on my mind.

Thursday morning, I struggled into a pair of pantyhose and

then slipped on my black all-purpose dress, which I hoped would look properly funereal for my meeting with Dr. Reed. I'd jogged my three miles, of course, hoping to quash my anxieties. I had no reason to be afraid of him except that Dace had been afraid. Given our close family relationship, that was good enough for me.

Armed with my shoulder bag and car keys, I was just going out the door when the telephone rang. I didn't want to stop and chat with anyone, but I did pause long enough to hear Ruth Wolinsky say: "Kinsey, this is Ruthie. I wonder if you could stop by today at your convenience. Nothing critical, but there's something I'd like to discuss. No need to call in advance. I'm off work and I'll be here."

I locked up, already planning to swing by her house when I left the university. Ruthie's tone was new to me; a touch on edge. She didn't sound alarmed so much as puzzled. In the meantime, Henry and I hadn't had a chance to strategize about my upcoming meeting with Dr. Reed, so I was running conversational loops in my head as I drove north on the 101 and took the exit road that led to the UCST campus.

At the information booth, I told the guard where I was going. He handed me a campus map and used his pen to circle the Health Sciences Building.

"What about parking?"

"The lot's this gray area," he said. "Have your ticket validated and you won't have to pay the parking fee."

I thanked him and drove on. I hadn't been to the university for years and I was disconcerted by all the new buildings that had sprung up. Vacant lots were gone. A two-tiered parking structure had been razed and a five-story garage had gone up in its place; new dorms; a new student union building. I had my sheet map on the steering wheel, trying to get my bearings. I finally found the lot and pulled in, waiting while the dispenser buzzed and pushed a ticket through the slot. I took it and the gate arm swung up.

I grabbed the first place I spotted, then paused to check my teeth, hair, and makeup before I got out of the car. By makeup, I'm referring to the four passes with a mascara wand that had left a small black clot on one lash. I'd also applied lipstick, but that was already gone. Really, I don't get the point.

The doors to the Health Sciences Building were open. Students strolled in and out, most of them in scanty clothing—tank tops and short shorts; lots of boobs, bare arms, and flat abdomens. Footwear seemed equally divided between flip-flops and thick-soled army boots. At least a hundred bicycles had been chained to a corral of fencing outside.

Once in the building, I rounded the corner to the elevators and checked a directory posted on the wall. The only clinic was on the ground floor. As I passed the entrance, I glanced in. Several students were seated in the waiting room. I walked on, keeping track of room numbers. Several clinic doctors had offices in the same wing, strung out on either side of the corridor. I found the administrative offices, where two secretaries and three clerk-typists were hard at work.

The department secretary, Greta, was away from her desk. I'd expected to announce myself, reminding her of my name and the time of my appointment, but her chair was empty and all the other women were intent on their computers. Her appointment book was open in plain sight, but today's schedule was blank. I'd seen Dr. Reed's name on a white laminated tag mounted on the wall as I'd come down the hall. I retraced my steps.

Dr. Reed's door was open and I stepped into the anteroom. In the larger office beyond, he was seated at his desk, focused on a medical chart on which he was scribbling notes. He was left-handed, always of interest to me. I knocked on the door frame. "Dr. Reed?"

He looked up. "Yes?"

"Kinsey Millhone."

When that didn't spark a response, I said, "I'm your nine o'clock appointment."

He seemed stumped by the news. He flipped a page or two on his desk calendar and then rose to his feet. "I'm sorry. I didn't know I had anyone coming in. The secretary's usually good about telling me."

"Is this a bad time?"

"It's fine. I'm afraid I'll have to ask your name again."

I said, "Kinsey. The last name is Millhone."

We shook hands across the desk and then he gestured me into a chair. His grip was warm, quick, and firm. Nothing to complain about there. I'd taken an instant mental picture of him. Early thirties, with a full, open countenance, blue eyes, something close to a pug nose. Nice smile, good teeth, and a thick head of pale brown hair that was tinted with gold. Angled on his desk was a wedding photograph. There he stood, decked out in a tuxedo with a gorgeous young girl clinging to his arm. Judging by the sunlight, it was summer, but of course I couldn't tell if it was the one just past or one previous. I recognized the gardens at the Edgewater Hotel, which was probably where they spent their first night before embarking on their official honeymoon. I propelled them like Ken and Barbie paper dolls, first to the south of France, then to Fiji. Then I pictured them in the Swiss Alps, flying down the ski slopes in expensive matching outfits. Did it snow midsummer in the Alps? I hoped so. Otherwise, their little paper legs would get all bent and torn.

The bride was slim and blond in a strapless wedding gown as tight as swaddling and a veil that had lifted in the breeze. She, too, was all blue eyes and honey. Everything about her spoke of money, including her wedding and engagement rings, which were clearly visible—diamonds too large and too numerous to miss.

I realized Dr. Reed was waiting for me to speak. I was at a disadvantage in that I was anticipating him, but he had no idea I'd be coming in to speak with him. I gave the secretary high marks for retaliation. She'd put me in the position of having to explain myself while I was hoping she had paved the way for me by blabbing my business in advance.

"I'm sorry to catch you off guard," I said. "I had a nice long chat with your secretary Tuesday, which is when she made the appointment. She sounded like she was right on top of things . . ."

I let my voice trail off briefly and gave him an eloquent look expressing my sympathies that he was at the mercy of someone incapable of so simple a task.

His smile was perplexed and his shrug didn't amount to much. "I'm not sure what went wrong. She's usually efficient."

I said, "Ah, well. I know your time is limited so I'll tell you why I'm here."

"No rush. I have the afternoon free. What can I help you with?"

He seemed so relaxed and confident, I became curious what would happen when I mentioned Terrence Dace.

"I was hoping to talk about my cousin, who died week before last. I believe he was enrolled in a study you're running, but I'm not sure if you'll remember the name."

"There are only forty participants in this phase of the study and I know most of them well," he said. "If this is Terrence you're referring to, I should tell you how sorry I was to lose him. Aaron Blumberg called as soon as he learned he'd been under my supervision."

"I'm glad you spoke to Aaron. I was worried I'd have to start from scratch and explain everything. I know you can't discuss my cousin's health issues . . ."

"I don't know why not. Aaron said he'd already gone over autopsy and lab reports with you, so you know about as much as I do at this point."

"Well, I doubt that," I said. "I have questions, but I don't want to violate doctor-patient privilege."

"I knew Terrence primarily in my role as researcher. I wasn't actually his doctor if it comes right down to it. I can't claim we had any long heart-to-heart talks, but I know he was a smart and talented man. Take a look at this." He leaned to one side, opened his desk drawer, and removed a four-by-six-inch folio that bore Dace's characteristic printing style, neat and uniform. He handed it across the desk.

"Roadside Plants of Southern California." Like the other folios he'd done, the small hand-bound booklet was no more than sixteen pages. I smiled as I leafed through it. Some of the illustrations were done in pen and ink, and some in colored pencil; chokeberry bushes, wild cucumber, saltbush, and a plant called *Nolina parryi* identified by name. There were thirty or forty more. Each delicate drawing was accompanied by a brief description. "He gave you this?"

"I asked if I could borrow it. I don't think he meant me to have it on permanent loan. You can take it if you like."

"I would. Thanks. He left one of these to each of his children—different subjects, of course. I don't know if you're aware of this, but he was estranged from his family when he died. One of the reasons I came in was in hopes of taking away something that might soften the blow."

"I knew his personal history through his group-therapy

sessions. I think part of what motivated him was his deep shame at what went on in the past. I'm not sure how much of his struggle you were party to."

"In all honesty, we never met. I found out we were related through a complicated set of circumstances, but he was gone by then."

"He was a lost soul and I wish we'd done better by him."

"When did he enroll in the study?"

"Might have been March. He was hospitalized for acute alcohol poisoning. The social worker referred him after he'd been through detox and rehab. This was meant as long-term support."

"So you felt he would benefit?"

"That was the hope. Do you know anything about the study?"

I shook my head, not wanting to interrupt the flow. He was already more forthcoming than I'd had reason to hope.

"We're looking at the use of three drugs in combination, one of which, Glucotace, we're especially interested in. When Terrence came into the program, we explained we were running a random double-blind study and couldn't guarantee which group he'd be assigned to. One group is given the drug. The control group receives a placebo."

"That's actually one of the questions I had for you," I said. "He seemed to think the medication made him sick."

Dr. Reed said, "So I was told. He was convinced he was on Glucotace. This was week one when we were barely under way. Fifty-fifty chance of it. Subjects aren't told what medication they're taking. Those of us conducting the study also operate in the dark. That's what the term 'double-blind' refers to."

"Really. You didn't know what he was taking?"

"I do now. I'm not sure how familiar you are with research strategies. Since I designed the study and applied for the grant, I have a rooting interest in the outcome, as you might imagine. If we both knew he was on Glucotace, it might influence the questions I asked and the answers he gave. Even if I knew what he was taking and he didn't, the outcome could be affected. We're all suggestible in one way or another. A patient taking a placebo might actually get better because that's the nature of the beast. What we believe affects our physiology. If we're anxious, our heart rate goes up. If we feel safe, our respiration slows."

"I've experienced that myself," I said.

"In a clinical trial, our job is to render an unbiased account of test results. Some of this is based on blood work and other screening procedures, but some of what we track are the subjective reports from the patients themselves."

"If he complained, would you have looked into it?"

"Of course. Absolutely. As you may know, Terrence did complain and we undertook a review. He was seen by three other clinic doctors, and all of us kept a close eye on his lab values and conducted regular physical examinations. If he'd suffered serious side effects, the symptoms would have surfaced."

"So there weren't any?"

"I wish I could reassure you, but he had a problem showing up for his appointments. Completely hit or miss."

"Because of the medication?"

"This was a personality issue. We're meticulous about outpatient monitoring, but we're dependent on compliance. Without that, the numbers mean nothing."

"Was he terminated or did he leave of his own accord?"

"We were forced to sever the relationship. We had no choice. I felt bad about it. He was a good man and we gave him every chance to straighten up. He couldn't seem to manage it."

"He had a friend named Charles Farmer."

"I remember Charles. Same thing with him. He was another of those hard-core cases. Charles showed up for one of his exams so high, he could hardly stand. I have no idea what he was on, but I terminated him that day. Without reliable feedback, we might as well abandon ship. We can't have patients taking meds we know nothing about. Even something as innocent as vitamins or nutritional supplements can skew results."

"Were you alarmed that both men died within months of their enrollment?"

"Of course. That's why I contacted the coroner's office. I was concerned there was an underlying disease process hampering his recovery."

"And was there?"

"Nothing any of us could pinpoint, including Dr. Palchek's postmortem. Subjects aren't always honest about their medical histories. A participant with unsuspected health issues could be at increased risk of an adverse event. We screen as rigorously as we can, but ultimately we can't pick up every warning sign, especially if a patient is hiding something."

"Earlier you talked about suggestibility. Are you saying that if Terrence was convinced he was on daily doses of Glucotace, the symptoms he experienced might have been, what . . . psychosomatic?"

"That's not a term much in use these days. We've come to recognize that the effort to identify disorders as purely physical or purely mental is increasingly obsolete. Many physical illnesses have mental components that determine their onset, presentation, and susceptibility to treatment. Terrence Dace's symptoms were real. The question under consideration has to do with their origin. That's something I can't help you with."

"Understood," I said. I realized I was fresh out of places to take the conversation and I was kicking myself for not bringing in a list.

"What else can I tell you?"

"I guess that's about it." I hadn't pressed him on anything and it was clear I'd never make it as a hard-hitting investigative reporter. We'd covered the subjects superficially, but without anything specific in mind, I was reluctant to take up any more of his time. "Is there anything you want me to tell his daughter?"

"Convey my condolences. I can understand how devastating this must be." He leaned back in his chair. "As long as I have you here, I hope you don't mind if I ask you something."

"Sure."

"When Terrence left the program, he was asked to turn in any medications in his possession."

"So I heard," I said. At that very moment, I had the self-same vial of pills in my bag. My impulse was to avert my eyes, but I held his gaze, filling my head with innocent thoughts instead of the kind that were actually floating around in there.

"He'd just refilled a prescription. That's one way we ensure conformity, insofar as we can do that with patients who aren't under observation twenty-four hours a day. According to the clinic pharmacist, he'd just picked up a week's worth—

fourteen pills. If you have any idea what he might have done with them, we'd love to know."

My little lying self kicked in without missing a beat, an impulse predicated on the notion that it's foolish to give up information that might prove useful at a later date. "No clue," I said. "Do you know what the medication was?"

"I made a point of finding out. From a community-health perspective, it's dangerous—worse than dangerous—it's potentially fatal to have unidentified chemical compounds circulating among the homeless when so many are drug and alcohol addicted."

I said, "I don't know if you're aware of this, but the morning he was found, someone walked off with everything he owned. Some of the items have turned up, but most of his personal belongings are gone. Maybe the pill bottle was in his cart."

"I hope somebody had the presence of mind to toss it in the trash," he said. "Addicts will knock back just about anything if there's a chance of getting high, and most don't worry about the hazards. If his medication turns up, would you let me know?"

"Of course," I said. I glanced down at my shoulder bag and spotted the parking ticket from the lot outside. I pulled it out. "Could I ask you to validate this?"

"Certainly. Hang on a second." He opened his pencil drawer and rooted around for a moment, finally coming up with a small booklet of stamps about the size of those the post office issues. I passed the ticket across the desk. He checked his watch and then tore out three small stamps that he pasted on the back. "These are fifteen minutes each, so you should be amply covered."

"Thanks."

He handed me the ticket. As I slid it back into my bag, I felt a quick jolt. I'd seen one just like it when I was pulling the crap out of Pete's glove compartment. I looked sharply at Reed, but the phone rang just then.

He picked up. "This is Dr. Reed." He listened for a moment and looked up at me. "Can I call you back on this? I have someone in my office."

He listened. "Five minutes," he said. As he hung up, he shot me an apologetic smile as though embarrassed to have to hurry me out the door.

I lifted a finger. "You're the one who called me."

"Come again?"

"June or July. Somebody called me looking for R. T. Dace. I don't know how my number came to light, but I had a brief conversation with a doctor somebody. I didn't catch the name at the time, but I recognized your voice just now."

He shook his head. "Don't think so. Not that I recall. I don't believe we ever had a contact number for him. It might have been someone in the lab."

"Oh. Well, maybe so. It stuck in my mind, but I guess it could have been anyone."

I got up and slung the strap of my bag over my shoulder. "I better let you get back to work. Thanks for your time."

"I'm not sure how much comfort I've provided. If the family have any other questions, I'd encourage them to get in touch. For peace of mind if nothing else." He stood and we shook hands across the desk. This time his grip was ice cold and his palm was damp. "Again, my condolences. I liked him."

"I appreciate your saying so," I replied. I held up the booklet. "Thanks for this."

"My pleasure."

He smiled and resumed his seat, probably already thinking about the call he'd be returning as soon as I was out of earshot.

It wasn't until I reached the door that I hesitated. "One more question if you wouldn't mind. I know this is out of line and if you can't or don't want to answer, please say so."

He watched me and then made a little gesture, indicating his willingness.

"You said you checked on his medications. Was he taking Glucotace or the placebo?"

There was a silence during which he regarded me without expression. I didn't think he'd answer and I could see him weigh the issue in his mind. Finally, he said, "I don't see any harm in telling you. The placebo."

In the corridor, I paused for a short debate. Instead of heading for the exit, I returned to the clinic office. No sign of Greta. I reached over and picked up the appointment book, leafing back through the weeks as though I had every right. August: nothing. Tuesday, July 12: Pete's name was penned into the 1:00 P.M. slot.

Walking back to the parking lot, I gave careful consideration to the exchange. Dace had signed himself out of St. Terry's in June, after which he'd fled to Los Angeles. Dr. Reed had called me in hopes of finding him. Now he dismissed the incident. Plausible deniability is the term, I believe. Covering his ass was my take on it. What he couldn't disguise was the shift from a warm to an icy hand. Slick as he was, he couldn't control the physiology of fear.

I gave Ruthie's front bell a twist and waited. She came to the door in a sweatshirt and jeans with a scarf knotted around her head. She had a dust rag in hand. "Woo. Come in. I could use a break."

She stepped back and I moved into the foyer, saying, "I see you're getting life in order."

She closed the door behind me and I followed her down the hall. "I don't know about that. I have two closets emptied, which I consider a triumph. I don't suppose you have any use for forty-six neckties. I gave him every one of those and he wore the same two all the time."

"No neckties. Sorry 'bout that."

"Too bad. Some are nice. You got my message."

"I was off to an appointment or I'd have picked up right then."

"I hope I didn't sound too cryptic."

"I was properly intrigued."

We'd reached the kitchen by then, which was much as it had been when I'd seen it last. Stacks of boxes, brown paper bags, and plastic bags filled to capacity, the counter littered with odds and ends.

She picked up the sack of birdseed I'd dropped off the day before. She held it in her right hand as though to illustrate a point. "So here's how this went. I decided I'd fill the bird feeder. That was always Pete's job, but I thought what the heck. Poor little things must be starving to death. I had a chickadee bang into the window glass yesterday and it about knocked itself out. Anyway, I get into the bag of birdseed and come up with this."

She pulled her left hand from behind her back and held up

a thick stack of bills folded in half and secured with a silver clip. The outermost denomination was a one. "He keeps small bills on the outside," she said when she saw my look.

"How much?"

"I didn't count. I figured if he robbed a bank, the cops would want to dust for prints."

"You don't really think he robbed a bank."

"I don't know what to think."

"Didn't he say he was setting money aside for a cruise?"

"He said whatever sounded good. He never had this much money in his life."

I stared at her and then stared at the wad of bills.

Sheepishly, she said, "Okay, I did peek just a little bit. The bills on the inside are hundreds. Lots of them."

She handed me the money clip. I sat down at the table and riffled the corners of the bills. "I'd say two or three thousand dollars."

"That's my guess."

She took out saucers and coffee cups and filled both from a thermos. She put a small pitcher of milk on the table and set the sugar bowl close by. Then she sat down. "You know what bugs me? The bill collectors were hounding him. And I mean, *hounding* him. A lot of it was nickel-and-dime stuff. I'm not saying the bills weren't overdue, but some were in the two- to three-hundred-dollar range. There wasn't anything major, except maybe his back rent. It burns my ass to think how many debts he could have paid off with money like that."

"You know how he was. I'm sure in his mind, paying bills wasn't any fun. That's why he avoided it. I'm sure he felt better saving for a trip, which was at least something positive."

"Oh, right, and thanks a bunch, pal. I don't know what I'm supposed to do with that plan."

"If it's any comfort, he probably hadn't booked anything."

"Be thankful for small favors."

I put the clip of money on the table between us. "What are you thinking the source for this is?"

"You go first."

"No, you first. You were married to him."

"I think he was extorting money from someone. Mid-July, he told me business was looking up. He had some kind of job he thought might net him a paycheck. I think 'a handsome chunk of change' is the phrase he used."

"Well, he did pick up a job running surveillance in Reno. That's the work he asked Dietz to cover for him."

Ruthie thought about that while the two of us stared at the wad of money. "Do you really believe that's where it came from?"

"No."

Ruthie actually laughed. "I appreciate your honesty. I thought chances were good that it was hush money of some kind. Who was the victim? Do you have any idea?"

"Pete had only one job in the last six months as far as we could tell. There are two or three people associated with that client, and of those, only one has money—a doctor out at UCST with something to hide. I was in his office less than an hour ago and there's something off. Somehow Pete picked up a whiff of it and cashed in. I can't prove it, of course, but I'd lay odds."

"Honestly, I'm not saying I approve. All I'm saying is if my husband was a crook, I wish he'd been better at money management," she said.

"With Pete, there's always something to forgive," I said.

"So what do you advise? You think I should go to the police?"

"And say what? At this point you really don't know anything for sure. That's part of what I'm trying to work out myself. I do think you have a point about preserving fingerprints. As long as you don't intend to spend the money, I'd leave it alone. Hide it somewhere good."

"Oh, you bet." She propped her chin on her fist. "I wasn't sure you knew about his tendency to play fast and loose. I wouldn't have said anything myself, but you understand where he was coming from."

"I knew him in the good old days and he wasn't exactly a model citizen back then. Sweet guy," I added in haste.

"I can't tell you how much I miss him." Her smile was pained. "I guess one of these days I'll get used to it."

32

When I arrived home, there was a parking spot right in front, which I took as a good sign. As I rounded the corner, moving into the backyard, I saw Henry in the act of closing his garage doors. He turned and picked up his four heavy plastic grocery bags, two in each hand.

"I thought you'd already done your grocery shopping."

"These are for Ed. I'm trying five different brands of wet food to see which he prefers. He turns his nose up at beef. He says cats don't eat cows."

"Opinionated little guy, isn't he? When I came home Tuesday, he popped in for a visit, just to have a look around. I was surprised he was out."

"Ed was out on Tuesday? I don't think so. He was in when I left and he was in when I came home."

"That's because I put him in."

"How'd he manage to get out?"

"Beats me. Cats are mysterious. He might have transmogrified himself and slipped through the cracks like smoke," I said.

"You think he's capable of doing that?"

"How do I know? This is only the second or third cat I've met in my life."

"I'll have to keep an eye on him," he said. "How was your meeting with Dr. Reed? I hope he put your mind at ease."

"I wouldn't go that far. There's still a big chunk of the story missing and he's not the one who's going to fill me in. At any rate, talking to him was a good suggestion. I guess I should thank you for browbeating me into it."

"I'll take full credit."

As soon as I let myself into the studio, I went straight to the phone and called Ruthie. When she answered, I said, "Hey, Ruthie. Kinsey Millhone again."

"Forget the last name. You're the only Kinsey I know."

"Sorry about that. Force of habit. Quick question I should have asked you while I was there. The guy who bought Pete's Fairlane pulled the junk out of the map pockets and the glove compartment. Do you still have that plastic bag?"

"I'm looking at it. I was just about to go through it. I need the proof-of-insurance card so I can call Allstate and cancel the coverage."

"Could you check and see if there's a parking ticket in there? Not a citation—from a pay lot. It'd be an ivory color with pale green stickers on the back."

"Hang on. I'm putting the receiver down, so don't go away."

"I won't."

"I'm turning the bag upside down, shaking everything out on the counter," she called. "Ick. There's a dead bug. What the hell *is* that thing?"

"Take your time," I said.

She came back on the line. "Good news. I found a savings passbook I didn't know we had. Okay, here. I'm looking at a ticket from UCST with stickers on the back."

"Is there a date-and-time stamp?"

"Says July 12. Machine stamped at twelve forty-five P.M. when it was issued, but that's it. No time stamp going out or the machine would have eaten it."

"Hold on to that, okay? I'll pop over there first chance I get and pick it up."

"No problem."

I trotted up the spiral stairs to the loft, where I unzipped my all-purpose dress and stepped out of it. Then I stripped off my pantyhose with a sigh of relief. I pulled on my usual work-aday rags and went downstairs again.

There was a knock at the door and when I opened it, there stood Anna. She wore jeans and a blue knit top that made her blue eyes electric. "I need to talk to you."

"Sure."

I stepped back, inviting her in. "Sit anywhere you like."

She chose a kitchen stool. I moved around the counter to the other side so we were facing each other. I was aware that I was putting a barrier between us, but it felt appropriate. Given her demeanor, I wasn't sure how cozy this chat was going to be. I'd been irritated with her. Now it was payback time.

She said, "I called Ethan to give him Henry's number so he'd know where I was. He has questions."

"And what might those be?"

"Not for you. Ethan thinks I should talk to Daddy's doctor directly. Henry says you have his phone number."

"Dr. Reed wasn't his physician. He's in charge of the research program your father was enrolled in at one point."

"I still want to talk to him if it's all the same to you."

"May I say one thing first?"

"Say anything you like."

"Your father was scared to death of Dr. Reed. He thought the test drug was killing him and that's why he dropped out of the trial. I believe he was right. His friends are convinced of it, too, but of course Dr. Reed won't own up to that. According to him, your father was incapable of adhering to the guidelines and the clinic gave him the boot."

"Why would he say that if it wasn't true?"

"He has an agenda of his own. He came up with a proposal about a drug he thought would be effective in treating addicts. Now it looks like he's being paid big bucks for a theory that isn't panning out."

"Why should I take your word for it? You say Daddy changed his will because he was pissed off at us, like it's our fault and we should just suck it up and let you have everything. I can see how that serves your purposes, but we're getting screwed."

"I don't have a purpose except to see that his wishes are carried out."

"But you never met him. Isn't that what you said?"

"That's correct."

"So you don't know what was going on in his mind."

"That's true."

"How do you know he wasn't suffering from dementia? Ethan thinks he could have been delusional or confused."

"And Ethan's opinion is based on what?"

"The crazy way he behaved. He was mixed up or unbalanced or *something*."

"Oh, I'm getting this. You'd like to think your father was mentally incompetent because that would invalidate the will. You're hoping Dr. Reed will back you up."

"That makes as much sense as your claim. If that medication made him sick, why couldn't it have affected his mental state?"

"Always possible," I said.

"So how do you know Dr. Reed wasn't trying to help? How do you know my father wouldn't be alive today, if he'd done as he was told?"

"I don't know that. Nor do you. You want to talk to Dr. Reed, I can't stop you, but I can tell you right now it's a bad idea."

I crossed to the desk, checked my notes, and jotted down Dr. Reed's number on a slip of paper. I tore the leaf off the scratch pad and presented it to her. "His schedule's clear for the afternoon, so if you run like a bunny, you can talk to him today. Let me know what he says. I'll be interested in his response," I said. "Can I help you with anything else?"

"Get stuffed."

"You, too."

I opened the door for her. This time, she'd barely made it through before I banged it shut behind her.

I closed my eyes, fighting for self-control. I was so irritated, I could barely contain myself.

I sat down. I took a deep breath. In a pinch, do something worthwhile, like clean the entire house.

I let my gaze roam and the first thing I saw was Pete's remaining cardboard box with the big X on the lid, partially covered by the folders I'd decided to keep. Where was I supposed to put the damn thing? I couldn't leave it where it was. My studio, while charming, is a bit short on storage space. In designing it, Henry had provided any number of nooks and crannies, built-in shelves and drawers, the oddly shaped cabinet here and there where a quirk of construction created a bonus cubby. I keep my possessions to a minimum and even so, I'm occasionally forced to beg a few feet of shelf space in Henry's garage. I wasn't going to do that for Pete's junk. I did a 180-degree survey and finally took my foot and shoved the box to the back of the knee space under my desk.

I glanced down and saw the name Eloise Cantrell written on the scratch pad above Drew's phone number. Under her name was a secondary note that said CCU.

I could feel my curiosity stirring along with a flicker of interest. The meeting with Dr. Reed had done little to erase the suspicions Dandy and Pearl had raised. Dr. Reed had met with Pete Wolinsky. Eloise Cantrell was the charge nurse in the Cardiac Care Unit at St. Terry's when Dace had been admitted delirious. Soon afterward, he fled from the hospital and took a bus to Los Angeles. If he'd been frightened of Dr. Reed, she might have known why. Surely, all of these matters were related. I picked up a pen and circled her name. I hadn't put a date on the note because I'd assumed the call was in error, never dreaming the contact might later seem significant.

I opened the bottom drawer and pulled out the telephone directory. I flipped to the Ss in the business listings and ran a finger down the page until I found "Santa Teresa Hospital." There was a general number listed, a number for the emergency room, one for poison control, and then a few department numbers that could be dialed directly, including administration, billing, patient accounting, human resources, development, and public affairs.

I reached for the handset and punched in the general number. When the operator picked up, I asked to be connected to Cardiac Care. I did this without conscious thought, thinking a plan might work to my detriment. Sometimes it doesn't pay to be too well prepared.

The ward clerk answered, saying, "Cardiac Care. This is Pamela."

"Oh, hi, Pam. Is Eloise working today?"

"She's in a staff meeting. Can I take a message?"

"Do you know what time her shift ends? She told me, but I can't remember now what she said."

"She's on seven to three."

"Great. Thanks so much."

I could tell Pam was ready to take a message, perhaps already making a note of the time on one of those "While You Were Out" slips, but I hung up before she had a chance to quiz me. Now all I had to do was figure out what Eloise looked like.

By 2:30, erring on the side of caution, I parked in the lot across the street from St. Terry's and made my way through the entrance and into the lobby. I asked for directions to CCU, and a volunteer walked me to the requisite corridor, where, with pointing and gestures, she explained how to proceed. I wondered if I'd ever be nice enough to volunteer for anything. I was hoping not.

When I reached the floor, I spotted a nurse's aide emerging from a supply room, her arms loaded with clean linens. I flagged her down and asked if Eloise Cantrell was available.

"She's at the nurse's station."

"Is she the little blonde?"

With exaggerated patience, the nurse's aide said, "Noooo. Eloise is six feet tall and she's African American."

After that, it was no trick at all to pick Eloise from among the many white nurses at work. I took a seat in the waiting room within eye shot of the nurse's station and leafed through an issue of a ladies' magazine that was only four years out of date. I was impressed by all the uses there were for instant vanilla pudding. This homemaking business, while beyond my modest aspirations, never failed to amaze.

By the time Eloise left work, I was in the same corridor, lagging slightly behind to allow her to exit ahead of me. I followed her out of the building and tagged along in her wake. There were a number of pedestrians in the area, so she wasn't alerted to my presence. I waited until she turned the corner from Chapel onto Delgado before I closed the gap between us. "Eloise? Is that you?"

She turned, clearly expecting to see a familiar face. Her lips parted as though she meant to speak.

"Kinsey Millhone," I said, pausing in case she wanted to rejoice.

She was dark-skinned, her hair arranged in close lines of head-hugging braids, each of which ended in a sage-green bead that exactly matched her eyes. The hazel irises against the deep chocolate of her complexion was striking. I wouldn't describe her expression as hostile, but it wasn't welcoming.

"You called me a few months ago, looking for information about R. T. Dace."

I waited to see if the name would ring a bell. "I thought you were saying Artie, remember that? But you were talking about Randall Terrence Dace . . . R.T.," I said, framing the initials in air quotes. Still no flash of recognition, so I tried again. "You asked for Mr. Millhone, thinking I was a guy."

I could tell she remembered because she shut her mouth.

"I was curious where you picked up my name and number."

I could see her weighing the pros and cons of a reply.

She said, "You were listed in his hospital chart as next of kin."

"Are you aware he died ten days ago?" I asked.

Her tone was neutral. "I'm not surprised. He was in bad shape when I saw him last."

"I was hoping you might answer a question or two."

"Such as?"

"Did you know he'd enrolled in a drug trial?"

She thought about her answer briefly and then said, "Yes."

"Are you acquainted with the physician in charge?"

"Dr. Reed. Yes."

"Did he come into CCU while Terrence Dace was a patient?"

"Once as a visitor, yes. What makes you ask?"

"Someone told me Dace signed himself out of CCU without the doctor's okay."

Her stare was unyielding.

"Was there any discussion about why?" I asked.

She dropped her gaze, which made her impossible to read.

I plowed on. "His friends tell me he was scared to death of Dr. Reed. I wondered what the problem was. You have any idea?"

She turned and began walking away from me.

I followed six feet behind, my voice embarrassingly plaintive even to my own ears. "I heard Dr. Reed terminated him for noncompliance, but he was sober when he died. No alcohol or drugs in his system, so what was going on?"

She glanced back at me. "I work for the hospital. I'm not affiliated with the university. You want information about Dr. Reed's work, talk to him. In the meantime, if you're hoping I'll sink to the level of rumor and gossip, you're out of luck."

She turned on her heel.

I stopped in my tracks and watched her walk away from me. *What* had she said? If I was hoping she'd "sink to the level of *rumor and gossip*"?

"What rumors?" I called after her.

No answer.

I wasn't giving up on this. Henry had said that if I met with Reed and didn't feel he'd leveled with me, I should talk to someone else. Obviously, in approaching Eloise Cantrell I was searching too far afield. Anything she knew would be hearsay. I needed someone more directly involved with him. The obvious answer was Mary Lee Bryce. She'd know what was going on behind the scenes. The problem was, I had no way to get to her without going through Willard. I could call her directly, but how would I explain who I was or why I was so interested in the work she did? I only knew about her because Willard had hired Pete. The notion of approaching him created a mild thrill of uneasiness. It wasn't my job to keep his dealings with Pete a secret from his wife. I wasn't responsible for protecting either of them. Willard wasn't my client and Pete was dead. There was a certain, subterranean moral code in play, but surely, I could think of a way around that old thing.

When I got home, I sat down at my desk and pulled out the two folders. After a brief search, I found Willard's address scratched on a piece of paper. Cherry Lane in Colgate. I locked the studio, hopped in the Mustang, and headed for the 101.

Next thing I knew, I was knocking on Willard's door. I carried a clipboard, looking (I hoped) like my business was legitimate. In my heart of hearts, I did pray Mary Lee wouldn't answer the door. I wanted to talk to her, but I had other matters to cover first. I knew nothing about Willard. I'd seen photos of Mary Lee, but none of him.

The man who responded to my knock struck me as strange the minute I laid eyes on him. His complexion was ruddy and his skin looked dry. His ginger-colored hair was clipped close to his skull and the tips of his ears were pink. I'd once seen a litter of newborn mice who'd exhibited the same naked characteristics. His eyes were pale blue and his lashes light; white dress shirt with the sleeves rolled up, baggy trousers.

He rested his weight on forearm crutches and one leg was gone. "Yes?"

"Mr. Bryce?"

He didn't own up to it but he didn't deny it, so I moved right along. I held up my clipboard. "I'm a former colleague of Pete Wolinsky's."

Again, no verbal response but his complexion shifted, white patches appearing on a ground of pink. His mouth must have been dry because he licked his lips. I hoped the man wasn't a serious poker player because I could see now he might be a textbook study in physiological tells. "You knew Pete was killed?"

"I read about it in the papers. Too bad."

"Terrible," I said. That out of the way, I went on. "His wife asked me to go through his business files for tax purposes and I came across his report. I wonder if you could answer some questions."

He shook his head. "I can't help. I don't have anything to say."

"But you were a client of his."

"Um, no. Not really. I mean, I knew him and we talked a couple of times, but that was it. More like friends."

Baffling, wasn't it? I looked down at the paper on my clipboard and allowed that little crease to form between my eyes. "According to his records, he collected approximately . . . I can't read his writing here. It looks like two thousand dollars, which you paid him to follow your wife . . ."

He glanced over his shoulder and then eased out the door.

I leaned sideways and peered over his shoulder. "Oh, wow. Is she home?"

"No, she's out. I don't want to talk about this. My wife doesn't know anything and I'd just as soon she not find out."

"Is she at work?"

"She quit her job, if it's any business of yours. She's off at the supermarket. Look, I'll tell you what I can, but you have to be gone by the time she gets back."

"Then we better be quick about it. In Reno, she met twice with a man named Owen Pensky. I gather he's an old high school friend. Do you have any idea what they talked about?"

Lines appeared on Willard's forehead, and his upper lip

lifted toward one side of his nose. "You said this was for tax purposes. I don't understand the relevance."

"Don't ask me. I can't begin to guess why the IRS is looking into it."

"The IRS?"

"This Pensky fellow might be the focus of their investigation. I really have no idea. Pete was obviously concerned enough to make a note of it."

"Well, yes. That was partly my doing. When she got back from Reno, she started shutting herself in the bedroom, making long-distance calls. When I told him about it, he thought there might be a problem."

"Good guess on his part," I remarked. I looked at him without comment, creating a small stretch of silence.

Willard shifted his weight. "So what happened was, he overheard a phone conversation between Mary Lee and Owen Pensky . . ."

"How'd he manage that?"

"What?"

"How could Pete overhear a phone conversation? I'm not following."

He adjusted his crutches and stepped back. "I don't think I should say anything more. Maybe someone else can help."

"Wait," I said. "Hold on. I'm probably out of line here, Mr. Bryce, but in my past association with Pete, there were occasions when he employed a phone bug. Any chance of that here? Because if you gave your consent, you may be facing a serious legal issue."

"I didn't consent. I was against it. I didn't like the idea at all, but he said if there was something going on, we might as well know the truth."

"So you're saying he recorded a private conversation."

"He might have without me knowing it."

"You didn't hear the tape yourself?"

"No way. I paid him and that's the last I saw of him."

"What happened to the tape?"

"He kept it, I guess . . . if there was one."

"I got that already. 'If there was one,' where is it?"

"He didn't say anything more about it."

"He *dropped* the matter?" I said, my tone incredulous.

"Yes."

"He let it go and that was the end of it? You're talking about Pete Wolinsky, is that correct? Because I can promise you Pete never let anything go if there was money to be made."

"Well, there was this other idea he had. He thought she might have something at work. You know . . . like in her desk—letters or something—so he came up with this plan to go into the lab using her employee badge, which I was supposed to give him."

This was unexpected. I studied him with interest. "Really. When was this?"

"August 24, but she turned in her notice that day, so all of a sudden it wasn't any big deal. She quit and that was the end of it. I don't think she's talked to Pensky since."

I said, "Ah."

"I was sick of the whole thing by then anyway. I figured Pete was feeding me a line of bull and I got tired of playing along."

"What was your last contact with him?"

"The next morning. I guess he slept in his car all night because the minute Mary Lee went off to work, he was knocking at my door, all rude and aggressive about why hadn't I handed over her ID. I fired him right then."

"And that night he was shot to death."

Willard lifted a hand in protest. "Oh, no. No, no. It wasn't that night, was it?"

"The twenty-fifth."

"No connection there. None whatsoever."

I stared. "I want to talk to your wife."

"You can't do that."

"She and Owen Pensky had a subject under discussion and she's the only one who knows what it was. Well, no, that's not quite true. Pensky knew, of course. And Pete knew, didn't he?"

"How would I know what Pete knew? Now get away from here. I don't have to talk to you. I only did this to be nice. You have no reason to bother my wife. You want to know what they talked about, call Pensky and ask him."

"Good idea. I may do that, but I should warn you, if I don't get answers from him, I'll be talking to her."

"No. Absolutely not."

"I don't need your permission, Mr. Bryce, so if there's anything you want to 'fess up to, I'd suggest you do it soon."

I took out a business card, slid it into his shirt pocket, and gave it a pat.

I drove home in a state of suspended animation. I was sorry to learn Mary Lee had quit her job, because she'd no longer have access to sensitive information. By the same token, maybe now that she was free as a bird, she'd be happy to blow the whistle on Reed. If Pete had overheard a discussion about the trial or the patients Reed had lost, it would have put him in the perfect position to collect.

At my desk again, I pulled Pete's cardboard box into view and removed the lid. His tape recorder was still wedged in at one end where I remembered last seeing it. I removed it from the box and set it on the desk in front of me. I flipped open the lid and checked the cassette he'd left in place. I could see the bulk of the tape had progressed from the left spindle to the right side of the cassette. I pressed rewind and watched the spindles go round and round until they came to a stop.

I closed my eyes briefly, wondering if there were truly angels up in heaven. Only one way to find out . . .

I pressed play.

The first conversation I picked up was clearly unrelated to my interests. It dawned on me, too late of course, that I should have made a note of where the tape was before I'd so blithely run it back. I played and stopped my way through fifty minutes of other people's business, some of which was downright embarrassing. Finally, I heard a woman's voice and a phrase or two that made my ears perk up. Again, I had to back-and-forth until I caught the beginning of the segment.

The sound quality was decent, but the recorder had picked up only half the conversation. A woman, sounding harried, said, "It's me. I don't have much time, so let's make this quick. What's happening on your end?"

Having never heard Mary Lee Bryce's voice, I had no idea if I was hearing it now.

Her phonemate said something that the recorder didn't pick up. Then she said, "Not yet. I know where they are. I just can't get to them. I'm trying to track the one guy down but it's tough. Can't you use the information I already gave you?"

I heard nothing while the person she was talking to said a few words. I didn't even know if it was a woman or a man. Guess it could have been a dog. Arf, arf.

"Owen, I know that! How do you think I spotted it in the first place? The pattern's there. What I don't have is proof. Meantime, I'm walking on eggshells . . ."

Ah, Owen Pensky and Mary Lee Bryce. How lovely to have you here. Carry on.

She said, "I hope not. You don't understand how ruthless he is. It's fine as long as I'm in the lab, but I can't get anywhere near the clinic."

A question from Owen.

Her reply: "The lab's in Southwick Hall. The clinic's in the Health Sciences Building."

I stopped the tape and scribbled as much as I remembered. I pressed play again. This was like a two-character radio drama. Mary Lee to Owen, Owen to Mary Lee, except that his comments were a blank. She might have been talking to herself.

"Because that's where the subjects are seen for follow-up."

Whatever Owen said in answer was met with derision: "Oh, right," said she. "Talk about a red flag."

"Shit. I'll think about it. Maybe I can come up with some excuse."

And a moment later, "I figured you'd appreciate the finer points."

There was an exchange about a journal published in Germany.

I listened, squinting, but couldn't see the relevance, so I moved past that bit and concentrated on the next.

Mary Lee said, " 'Too bad' is right. What he's doing here is worse. With the grant he got, he can't afford to fail."

Silence.

"Nuhn-uhn. He has no clue I'm onto him. Otherwise, he'd have found a way to get rid of me before now. I mentioned his ripping me off because it's indicative of his . . ."

I stopped the tape again and wrote down what I'd heard. My Aunt Gin had refused to let me take secretarial courses in high school and I was royally pissed off about it now. If I'd been able to take shorthand, I could have made quick work of this. I pressed play again. I missed a garbled sentence or two, but I could have sworn she'd mentioned Glucotace.

"I have his password, but that's it so far."

Owen responded, silently.

"It was written on a piece of paper in his desk drawer. How's that for clever?"

Again, a pause for his response.

"Because I saw the printout before he shredded it."

I pressed stop and play until I heard her say, "Not Stupak's, Linton's. These guys are always circling the wagons. Any hint of trouble, they close ranks. Shit. Gotta go. Bye."

I could see how the deal had gone down. Pete had persuaded Willard to plant a pen mike and this is what it had netted him. If the call had been recorded with a phone bug, both sides of the conversation would have been audible. As for the content, he must have recognized the value of what he'd heard. Given the way his mind worked, how could he not? That's when he must have done his homework, picking up background on Linton Reed and information on Glucotace. I assumed he set up an appointment with Reed afterward so the two could have a cozy heart-to-heart talk.

What I couldn't see was where I might go with this. Linton Reed was wily. He was a cool customer and all he had to do was sit tight. Whatever he'd been up to at work, he was never going to be caught out. If Pete was onto him and had hit him up for money, how would the facts come to light? Pete was dead. The tape would never be admissible in a court of law. Now what?

33

Late Friday afternoon, my curiosity finally got the better of me. I drove to Colgate and parked outside the apartment complex where Willard and Mary Lee lived. I knocked, this time hoping to catch her at home instead of him. She opened the door and regarded me briefly without saying a word.

She was small. Her face was a perfect oval, her features fine. Her red hair was straight, chin-length and cut jaggedly. Her forehead was high. A fine haze of red freckles gave her complexion a ruddy hue. Pale brows, blue eyes with no visible lashes. Very red lips. She was a slip of a thing, so delicately built that it made her feet look too big for her slender frame. "You're the private detective who was here."

"Yes."

Her smile was pained. "You'll be happy to know Willard told me everything. Full confession."

I wasn't sure what to say. I had no guarantee he'd actually told her the whole truth and nothing but the truth so I was reluctant to interject a comment. "Can I have a few minutes of your time?"

"Why not? I'm leaving, so it's lucky you caught me when you did. We can talk while I pack."

I followed her into the apartment. Willard was clearly somewhere else so I didn't bother asking about him. She proceeded to the bedroom, which was small and painted white. The bed was neatly made and a big soft-sided suitcase was sitting open on the spread. This was a room where the couple didn't seem to spend much time. Tidy, but no books. No easy chair, no reading lamp, and no photographs. The closet doors were open, and I could see that the space had been divided democratically: a quarter for him, three quarters for her.

I took a position at the foot of the bed while she resumed her packing. She removed a pair of slacks from a hanger and folded them neatly before she placed them in the right half of the open suitcase. She had a packet of tissue paper on the bed, and she'd stuffed a sheet into the toe of each shoe before she tucked the pair in along the sides. She'd already packed underwear and sweaters.

I said, "Where will you go?"

"A motel for the next few days. After that, I don't know."

"Did Willard explain why I was here?"

"Because you're a friend of the detective he hired."

"Not a friend. He was someone I'd worked with in the past."

"He sure had Willard wrapped around his little finger. I still can't believe he hired a guy to follow me. What was going on in his head?"

"I guess he was feeling insecure."

"He's an idiot. I wish I'd realized it earlier."

"He told me you quit your job."

"That's a move I'll live to regret," she said. "Jobs are scarce. I've been putting out résumés for two months and getting no response. From now on I'll mind my own business, assuming I ever work again."

She returned to the closet, picked two hangers off the rod, and returned to the bed. She removed a dress from each of the hangers and folded them, using tissue paper to minimize wrinkling.

"Pete taped a telephone conversation between you and Owen Pensky."

"That's nice. Did he plant cameras in the apartment so he could watch my every move?"

"He probably would have if he thought he could get away with it."

She moved to the chest of drawers behind me and checked

the first and second drawers. The first was empty. From the second drawer she removed a stack of neatly folded T-shirts that she placed in the left side of her suitcase. "Why are you so interested?"

"I'm distantly related to Terrence Dace."

She fixed a look on me. "I'm sorry. I forget sometimes that life is about more than just me."

"Do you believe Dr. Reed was responsible for what happened to Terrence?"

"Are you asking if I believe it or if I can prove it?"

"Either one."

"I don't think Dr. Reed's responsible in the same way a drunk driver's responsible in a hit-and-run fatality. All he was doing was protecting his own interests. Terrence Dace was collateral damage."

"You know he stole three medical charts. His own, Charles Farmer's, and Sebastian Glenn's," I said.

"I wasn't aware of it, but good for him. Sebastian Glenn was the first death. Linton thought it was a fluke."

"But it wasn't."

"One is a fluke. Three is a pattern."

"Did they have something in common? A condition or a disease that put them at risk?"

"It's possible they had health issues. Prediabetic or undiagnosed diabetes. Heart problems. I really have no idea. Most patients did fine on Glucotace. I had no access to the medical clinic where they were seen. I worked in the same lab with Linton, but not on the clinical trials he ran."

"You told Owen Pensky that Dr. Reed shredded something. I'm not sure what it was. I only heard your half of the conversation."

"Raw data. The printout was sitting on his desk. I caught a glimpse of the graph he'd done, which was a duplicate of one he'd used in an earlier trial. How stupid is that? You'd think if he was going to cheat, he'd be more imaginative."

"So he was, what, misrepresenting his results?"

"It's called trimming. If any values were too far out of line, he made *adjustments*."

"Did you report it to anyone above him in the chain of command?"

"I couldn't see the point. The director of the grants program is the one who hired him in the first place. He thinks Linton is a star, especially since he's bringing money in."

"Actually, I talked to Dr. Reed yesterday."

"And how did he strike you? Is he a buffoon?"

"No."

"Did he sweat? Did his hands shake? Did he hesitate?"

"Once. At the end of our conversation."

"Well, trust me. He was either doing it for effect or trying to figure out an angle before he opened his mouth."

"When we shook hands at the end of the interview, his were like ice."

Her brows went up. "What the hell did you say to him?"

"I was asking questions about Dace. I thought he was being candid. He didn't seem tense or guarded. I know he was bullshitting on one point, but it was minor and I didn't want to press."

She laughed. "That's our boy. Mr. Slick. I'm surprised you picked up on it."

"There has to be a way to shut him down."

"Don't look at me."

"Who better?"

"Not to sound too cynical, but what makes you think anyone would listen to me? I'm the one he jilted. That's according to the rumor he's been spreading around. The first day I showed up for work, word was already out. His claim was we had an affair as undergraduates. That much was true. The way he tells it, I was needy and neurotic. I was jealous of his success, so he broke off the relationship. Now if I say anything at all derogatory, it looks like sour grapes. A woman scorned."

"What's the real story?"

"I broke up with him. He cribbed a paper. He stole my work. That's the kind of guy he is. He diddled with the title, added five coauthors, two of whom I swear to god he made up out of whole cloth. Then he sent it off to a scientific journal. When it appeared months later, I confronted him. Big mistake. You know how many papers I have to my name? Six. He's probably had fifty published in this year alone. That should be another little clue to the higher-ups. With that many, how does he have time to do his work?"

"Why did you apply for the job?"

"I screwed up. Big time. I knew it was his lab, but I'd forgotten how crazy he is."

"But he's a bright guy. Why's he doing this?"

"Why does he do anything? Because he's high ego and he's a narcissist. Dangerous combination. He's not a man who deals well with stress. Something happened in Arkansas a few years ago. I don't have all the details, but a patient died and the error was traced to him. He couldn't face it. He suffered a total nervous breakdown and had to be carted off to the funny farm."

"It didn't affect his career?"

"Not his career; his residency. Check his CV and you'll see the gap. That's when he moved from surgical oncology to research."

"And if it happens again?"

"I hope I'm not around. This turns sour on him, then what? You want my best guess? He'll have a computer crash and lose everything. That way they'll never nail him. Imagine all the sympathy he'll get. An entire year's work down the drain *when he was doing so well.*"

"I thought even with a crash, there were ways to restore the files."

"He could spill a cup of coffee down his CPU or the lab might catch fire. He could go in and change a few numbers. The data could be sitting right there, but he'd be the only one who'd have access because no one else would know the magic key strokes."

"If I told you I had the charts in my possession, would that help?"

"It might. Look, I'm not the only one aware of what's going on. There's a postdoc in the lab who's seen the same things I have. Little signs of Linton's cooking, little things that don't quite add up."

"Would this postdoc agree to talk to me?"

"No. He's married and has kids. You think he'd risk his livelihood? I can promise you he won't. Even if he did agree, you wouldn't have any idea what he was talking about."

"Isn't there anything I can do?"

She smiled briefly. "You can do what I'm doing. Pack a bag and flee."

After I left, I sat in the car as usual, making copious notes. Altogether, I was looking at two full decks of index cards, but this was new. Something had gone wrong in Arkansas. Linton suffered a nervous breakdown and because of it, he switched his career path from surgical oncology to scientific research, which looked like a nice safe place to land. Then Sebastian Glenn had died. Once things started going wrong, he was back in the same place he'd been, only now he was married and had more to lose.

Saturday morning, I drove the Mustang to the car wash to be detailed in preparation for Drew's taking possession. Miguel, who was doing the work, said it'd take an hour and a half. That was fine with me. My schedule was clear and I had time to spare. I told him I'd be in the waiting room, which was replete with two metal folding chairs and a wall-mounted display of car accessories for sale. I took out my paperback and settled in to read. This was a Robert Parker novel in which Spenser and Hawk busted up bad guys so often it cheered me no end.

Ten minutes went by and Miguel appeared. He might have been nineteen, remarkably poised for a guy who was working so hard to grow a mustache with so little to show for it. Miguel's auto-detailing business was called Detailing by Miguel. He wore a black T-shirt with the company name emblazoned on it in red.

He stood with his arms crossed, his hands pressed into opposite armpits. "You want me to leave the gun under the seat or put it somewhere else?"

I ran the sentence through my head, diagramming the parts of speech as I recited it to myself. I keep my H&K in my briefcase, which I knew full well I'd moved from the trunk of the car to the studio before I'd left home. "I don't have a gun in the car."

"Lady, I don't mean to be fresh, but you do now."

"I do?"

I slid the book into my bag and followed him out the back door and across the lot, passing the two lanes where cars were lined up to be vacuumed in preparation for a wash. He ran his one-man enterprise under a temporary awning that shielded him from the sun while he rubbed paste wax onto auto exteriors. With mine, he was still in the process of prepping the interior. The driver's-side door stood open and his Shop-Vac was close by. He pointed and stepped back, saying, "I didn't touch it."

I leaned into the backseat and angled myself so I could see what he was talking about. On the floor under the driver's-side seat there was a .45-caliber semiautomatic handgun nestled up against the rail.

I stared at it for a moment and then backed up a step so I could pull myself upright. I left the car door open. I glanced at Miguel and said, "Hang on."

I hadn't put the gun under the seat. That much I knew. The only .45-caliber semiautomatic I'd heard mentioned of late was one of two guns missing in Pete Wolinsky's shooting death two months before. Cheney had mentioned it Monday night when he showed up at Rosie's. I had no way to calculate how many thousands of semiautomatics were floating around in the world. The number must have been astronomical, so what were the chances of that *particular* gun having been used in the robbery that ended Pete's life?

I hadn't parked the Mustang anywhere near the bird refuge in months. The closest I'd come was the night I'd trundled along at two miles an hour, negotiating the access road along the property line at the back of the zoo. That was the unfortunate occasion when, having suffered a psychotic break, I'd agreed to run interference for Felix and Pearl in their mission to retrieve Dace's stolen backpack from the Boggarts' campsite. Those two locations, the strip of parking spaces near the lagoon and the hobo camp up the hill, were perhaps a quarter of a mile apart. Handguns, as a rule, don't hump from place to place of their own accord. Handgun migration is almost entirely the result of human intervention. But no one had been in the backseat of my Mustang except for Felix that same night.

Miguel said, "You okay?"

"I'm fine. Just give me a minute."

I remembered stumbling onto the scene, having waded through the shrubs to warn them that the big Boggart's arrival was imminent. While Pearl was stomping the makeshift incinerator, Felix had overturned a metal footlocker and the contents were strewn across the ground at his feet. At the moment I caught sight of him, he picked up an item and shoved it into the waistband of his jeans at the small of his back. From that distance and as quickly as he moved, I hadn't identified the object, but later, when he blasted the Boggart with a can of pepper spray, I assumed that's what it was. He'd even admitted stealing the can of pepper spray from them.

Had the Boggarts stumbled across the .45 at the scene of the crime? The bird refuge was part of their turf, so the idea wasn't outside the realm of possibility. Cheney had speculated that the whereabouts of both missing firearms was the function of how far the guy could throw. If he'd tossed one gun in the lagoon and hurled the second one into the dark, it was possible one of the Boggarts had spotted it by day. If that were the case, and if Felix had managed to steal it from them, then the savage beating he'd taken made a sudden twisted sense. That was "if" piled upon "if," but that's sometimes how these things work.

I closed the car door and locked it. I pulled a ten out of my wallet and pressed it into Miguel's hand. "Keep an eye on the car. I'll be right back."

I double-timed it into the building and found a pay phone. I hauled out a handful of change, put a call through to the police department, and asked for Lieutenant Phillips. When I had Cheney on the line, I ran through a highly condensed version of what had happened the Tuesday before last and why I thought the presence of a .45 under my car seat was relevant. I could tell the story made no sense, especially given my attempt to downplay both the raid and my part in it. To his credit, he didn't argue the point. He said he'd be there in twenty minutes and he arrived in fifteen.

I sat in his cubicle at the police department, the two of us eyeing each other warily while I went through my story for the second time. I'd left the Mustang where it was so Miguel could finish his work. Cheney identified the gun as a .45-caliber Ruger. Before he removed it from under the seat, he'd photographed it in place, donned latex gloves, and then eased a pencil through the trigger guard to keep the handling of it to a minimum. Once the Ruger was bagged and tagged, he'd asked me to accompany him to the station. I agreed so I'd appear to be morally upright. He said he'd drop me at the car wash later when we had a better sense of what was what.

The Ruger might not be the missing weapon. It might not be relevant to any ongoing investigation, in which case it could end up in the property room, forgotten on a shelf. But I didn't see how it could be a miss. The stray casing found at the shooting scene was a .45-caliber ACP, which would have been a nice fit for the Ruger.

On our way to his desk, he dropped the weapon off in the lab, where a ballistics expert would test-fire it to see if the slug was a match for the one found at the scene. The Ruger's serial numbers had been noted and someone in Records would run them through the computer in hopes the gun was registered. A superficial examination showed the weapon had been wiped clean of prints and a single round had been fired. When we finally sat down to chat, I said, "How soon will you know who owns the Ruger?"

"Assuming it's registered at all, it may take a while. Records is backed up and I didn't put a rush on the request. I'm fascinated to hear how it ended up in your car."

"I'll give you my best guess," I said. I then laid out an explanation of Terrence Dace's backpack being stolen by the panhandlers, Pearl's spotting it, and her determination to get it back.

Cheney was more patient than I had any reason to hope.

In addition to recounting my participation in the raid and what I remembered of Felix's actions, I used the occasion to talk about the Boggarts' savage attack, which I was now convinced was because Felix had taken property that didn't belong to him.

He said, "You think Felix stole the gun from them?"

"It's the only explanation that makes sense. He was hunched in the backseat as we left the scene and he's the only one who's been back there. I think he was attacked because he came across the weapon at the camp and slipped it into the small of his back. I think the panhandlers bided their time and came after him. If he'd told them where he'd hidden it, they'd have come after me. The owner of that bicycle-rental shop down on lower State saw the whole thing and he's the one who called 911. I talked to him a couple of days ago, hoping he'd be willing to identify the guy. He knows who it was because he's seen the same three bums hanging out at the beach for years. He refuses to help because he's worried about reprisals, and who can blame the man?"

Cheney made a note. "Let me find out who's handling the case and we'll see what we can do. You said three of them?"

"It's the big galoot I'm talking about. Bald guy with a red baseball cap."

"You have a name?"

"I don't, but he's not hard to find. Rush hour, he's usually standing on the side of the Cabana Boulevard off-ramp with a cardboard sign. You can't miss him."

"You think he had a hand in Pete's death?"

"Either that or he stumbled on the weapon after the fact. I can't think how else he'd end up with it."

"Might be completely unrelated," Cheney said. "So far, we haven't confirmed this was the gun used in the shooting. With all the firearms in circulation, plenty aren't registered and can't be traced."

"I'll tell you one thing. Those bums are badasses. They've put together that camp with stolen goods. They've tapped into the zoo's water and electrical supplies and they've co-opted trash pickup. There must be half a dozen ways to bust them."

"We'll do what we can. If the fellow you describe has been in trouble with the law, it will give us some talking points."

"I want to run something by you. I've been thinking about this and I'd be interested in your opinion," I said. "Leaving aside the issue of how I came up with all this . . ."

"All this what?"

"Would you let me tell it my way? This is pertinent."

"Fine." He looked at me steadily. Instead of making eye contact, I found it easier to avert my gaze. I knew what I wanted to say, but I was organizing the story as I went along.

"This may take a while, so bear with me. Originally, Pete Wolinsky was hired by a fellow named Willard Bryce," I said. Then I went through the entire sequence: Pete hiring Dietz, the surveillance, Dietz billing Pete, no pay. I told him about Mary Lee meeting with Owen Pensky, and her quitting her job the same day Pete was shot to death. I told him about the stolen charts. I told him about Eloise Cantrell, who made reference to gossip about Dr. Reed's work. As I worked my way through the narrative, I could see Cheney putting together the bits and pieces. He gave no indication of what he was thinking, but I could feel my confidence erode as I went on.

"Pete had a shitload of debts and he was desperate for cash. I think he got wind of Dr. Reed's problems and saw an opportunity to put the squeeze on him. You know, 'Pay up or I'll tell your boss and I'll contact the NIH.'"

Cheney cut in. "Did Pete actually have evidence of wrongdoing?"

"I don't know. Probably not. He might have suggested that even the *hint* of wrongdoing would tarnish Reed's reputation and impact his career."

"So you think he tried blackmailing Linton Reed over an issue of I-don't-know-what without anything to back it up."

"It doesn't matter if he had anything to back it up. What matters is whether Linton Reed believed Pete would blow the whistle on him. What matters is Reed's anxiety about the kind of trouble Pete could make."

"Are you talking about scientific fraud?"

"That's what it sounds like to me. He's been in trouble before over lesser issues than this."

"You told me Mary Lee Bryce quit her job."

"She did. The same day Pete was killed."

"If she quit her job, where's the threat to Linton Reed?"

"She's more likely to blow the whistle on him now. Besides, I have these medical charts Dace stole. Those should help. In the meantime, I did meet with Dr. Reed."

That caught him short. "Why?"

"I wanted to hear what he had to say about Terrence Dace."

"And?"

"He expressed regret about the deaths. He talked about how the study is set up and why he terminated Dace and his friend. Honestly, he made it all sound reasonable."

"I'm sure he did," he said.

"I'm trying to be fair about this, Cheney. That's what I'm getting at. I'm not demonizing the guy. I'm not even saying he did anything on purpose. He had a theory about Glucotace. When he ran into a roadblock, instead of shutting the study down, he changed the data or deleted it."

"Weak."

"I know it's weak. Most of this is circumstantial, but don't sit there telling me it doesn't count."

"Speculation. No real basis in fact. You think doctors won't stand together in a situation like this?"

"Indulge me, okay?"

He smiled. "I'm already doing that. This is me indulging you."

"Just listen. Ruthie found a wad of cash that Pete stashed away. Suppose Linton's prints are on the bills? Wouldn't that suggest I'm on track here?"

"You're grasping at straws. I don't understand how we get from fraud to homicide."

"Easy. Pete jacked him up for money. Reed paid him once, but he didn't want to pay again, so he killed him."

"Where's the gun? Does Linton even own one?"

"I have no idea."

"You don't even know for sure Pete and Linton Reed knew each other."

"Oh, but I do. Pete met with Reed on July 12 out at UCST. I saw his name in the appointment book, and Ruthie has the properly validated parking ticket, so don't be a shit."

"I am a shit. That's my job. I'm telling you what will fly and what won't. All a defense attorney has to do is come up with a plausible explanation. All he needs is a story that covers the same points but with a different slant. You make it look one way? Fine. He can make it look like something else. Right now, there's no eyewitness and the motive is imaginary. Some guy says he'll expose you, you tell him to take a hike. You don't fork over a couple of thousand bucks and then shoot his ass."

I reached for the bag I had placed at my feet and took out the shrink-wrapped prescription bottle. "This is one of Dace's prescriptions. He believed they put him on Glucotace, along with Antabuse and another drug to reduce his craving for nicotine. I asked Dr. Reed straight out if Dace was taking Glucotace or the placebo. He thought about it briefly and said placebo. Can't you get these analyzed and find out what they are?"

"Why would we do that? There's no case."

"But if the pills turn out to be Glucotace, it would support my argument, wouldn't it?"

"Tenuous at best."

"You have a better theory? You even have a suspect? Because I'm offering both."

"I'm not saying you're wrong. I'm saying I can't sell this. The DA's tough. She won't file if she doesn't think she's got something solid under her feet." I could see him turn the issue over in his mind. "Promise me your access to this information is legitimate."

"Of course." I tucked the pills back into my bag.

"No breaking and entering."

I raised a hand as though swearing an oath.

"You never impersonated an officer."

"I didn't impersonate anybody. When I talked to Willard, I said I was a former colleague of Pete's, which is true. I gave him my business card, so no funny business there."

He shook his head. "An investigation like this would take months."

"I understand. Just let me know if anything new develops. That's all I ask."

"Sure, but don't hold your breath."

34

I didn't hear from Cheney until the following Tuesday morning. "The Ruger's registered to a man named Sanford Wray."

I don't know what I thought he was going to say but it wasn't that. "Who's he?"

"Film producer. He started out as a venture capitalist and he's been involved with Hollywood for the past six years. He lives in Montebello and commutes when he has a project in the works. Jonah's been filling in the blanks. Wray's heavy into charities and he's on half a dozen boards. Big cheese in town."

"Does he have a criminal history?"

"Nope. His record's clean."

"I never heard of the guy. Does the name mean anything to you?" I found myself pacing in front of my desk, telephone in hand.

Cheney said, "Hollywood moguls aren't high on my list. The last movie I saw was *Dirty Harry*, so Clint Eastwood's it."

"How does Sanford Wray know Pete?"

"Remains to be seen. We haven't talked to him."

"When will you do that?"

"Jonah's checking to see if he's in town. Once we track him down, we'll pay him a visit and have a nice long chat."

"I'd love to be there when you do."

Cheney made a sound that said, *Not in our lifetime.* "We

don't know how he's going to react. He could barricade himself in the house, break out a window, and shoot at us. We might end up calling in the SWAT team."

"Or not," I said. I sat down, hoping to calm myself. I couldn't tell if I was nervous, anxious, or excited, but my blood pressure was up.

Cheney said, "The explanation might be innocent. The gun was stolen and he wasn't aware of it, or he knew the gun was gone and he hadn't reported it. If we brought along a civilian, he could file a complaint."

"That was just wishful thinking on my part," I said. "I know I won't be tagging along. Department policy, public safety, or whatever else you care to cite."

"Good girl."

"Will you tell me what he says?"

"Probably. The gist of it at any rate."

"Not the gist. I want you to swear you'll remember everything he says and repeat the conversation back to me. Word for word."

"You got it. Word for word."

I couldn't think what to make of this odd turn of events. I was suddenly facing an information gap. Up pops Sanford Wray and until Cheney filled in the blanks, I had to let go. I returned to the office, happy to be picking up the old routines. No new business yet, but that would take care of itself in due course. I knew William was hard at work on his plans for the two funerals, and I was just about resigned to footing the bill. At least it would be something to occupy my time. I was sitting at my desk in the little bungalow downtown when I heard someone open and close the front door.

Anna appeared. Here it was October and she was in a tank top and a pair of short shorts. "Can I talk to you?"

I hadn't seen her for days, but Henry had told me she'd picked up a job in a beauty salon on lower State Street, which allowed her to walk to work. She was still bunking at his place, but since he had no objections, I didn't see how I could complain.

I said, "Sure. Have a seat. I hear you found work. How's it going?"

She perched on the edge of one of my visitor's chairs. "The job's fine. Still minimum wage, but I like the place."

"Good. What can I do for you?"

"Gee, well, let's just get down to business here."

"Sorry. I didn't know you came to chitchat."

"I think I made a mistake."

This was interesting. I swear if she'd had a hankie in hand, she'd be twisting it. I noticed I wasn't getting the benefit of those big blue eyes of hers. I waited.

"I talked to Dr. Reed. Henry lent me his car and I drove out to the university."

"This was Thursday of last week?"

"Well, yes, but I haven't seen you since then or I'd have told you earlier."

"I wasn't accusing you of anything," I said.

"When I told Dr. Reed I was Terrence Dace's daughter, he was confused about why I was there when he'd already talked to you earlier that day. He got all pissy and said he couldn't understand why you hadn't just passed the information along."

"To which you replied?"

"I was so rattled I don't remember now, but that's not the point. I thought he knew what you did . . ."

"About what?"

"Your work. He didn't know you were a private detective."

"How did that come up?"

"I was just making conversation. I told him I hadn't been in town long. I said I was staying with your landlord, who owns the studio you rent on the same property. I said it worked out well for both of you because you were sometimes on the road. Dr. Reed asked if you were in sales and then I mentioned what you did for a living. He got upset you never identified yourself. He said you acted like you were having any old conversation about a family member."

"That's what it was. I wasn't there in any professional capacity."

"But you asked all those questions about the program."

"He volunteered. I didn't even know enough to ask."

"That's not how he remembers it."

I considered the situation briefly. "I don't see how any harm was done," I said. "I'd have preferred your keeping my personal life to yourself, but it's too late to worry about that now."

"I lied a little bit and said you'd given me some of the information, but what I'd really come to ask him was something else. I told him Ethan's concerns that Daddy's medication might have affected his mind. Dr. Reed blew his stack. The guy's a basket case. He wanted to know why everybody was suddenly so interested. He said my father didn't suffer dementia or any other mental impairment. He was taking a placebo and it wouldn't have had that effect."

"Good news for me and bad for you," I said. "I guess the will's back in effect."

"You don't have to make jokes about it."

"Sorry. I didn't mean to be flip."

"Anyway, I didn't see why he had to get so huffy. I felt like I really put my foot in it. And then to make matters worse, this other business came up."

"Please don't make me guess."

"Well, I knew one of those homeless people gave you a bottle of Daddy's pills . . ."

I cut in, saying, "Who told you that?"

"Henry."

I was close to pressing her further when I picked up the unspoken message. "And you told *Dr. Reed*?"

I was not actually shrieking, but she must have guessed the level of my outrage from the expression on my face.

"I didn't know it was any big secret."

"But why would you do that? Why in the *world* would you do that? Why would the subject even come up?"

"Because he said if I went through Daddy's things I should keep an eye out. He said fourteen pills were missing and I said you had them."

"Is the concept of minding your own business completely foreign to you? I told you not to go out there. I knew no good would come of it."

"I didn't do it on purpose. I mean, I went on purpose, but I didn't mean to make trouble. It just came out. I was trying to help. I was trying to smooth things over."

"So now what happens?"

"Nothing. He'd appreciate it if you'd return them. He says addicts will take any drug they get their hands on in hopes of getting buzzed."

"But those are placebos, so what's the risk?"

"I'm telling you what he said. Daddy signed a form and agreed to abide by the rules."

"But your father *didn't* abide by the rules, Anna, which is why they kicked him out. Dr. Reed was the one who made the decision, so as far as I'm concerned, all bets are off."

"I understand why you're irritated. You already went out there once, but there's no big rush. He said by the end of the week would be fine."

"This isn't a negotiation. I'm not giving him anything. I didn't sign an agreement, so the rules don't apply to me."

"You can't *refuse*. He has a government grant. He has to account for everything. With a clinical trial, you can't just do anything you please. There are strict guidelines."

"Strict guidelines. Wow. I don't know what to say."

"This is stupid. I'm not going to sit here and *argue*."

"That is the best news I've had so far."

"I don't know why you're making such a big deal of it."

"Because I'm having a bad day and you're not helping me, okay? Neither is Linton Reed."

"Well, you don't have to take that attitude. He said if you didn't want to make the drive to the university, he'd stop by and pick them up himself."

"So now he's the pill police?"

"He has a responsibility."

"Well, I don't doubt that. Happily he has no idea where I live."

That's when I got the big blue eyes.

"Do not tell me you gave him my address."

She dropped her gaze. "When he asked, I gave him *my* address. What was I supposed to say?"

I stood up and leaned across the desk. My voice had dropped so low I wasn't sure she'd hear what I was saying unless she knew how to read lips. "Please get out of my office. I don't want to see you. I don't want to talk to you. If you so much as catch sight of me, you better run the other way. Have I made myself clear?"

She got up without another word and left, slamming the door behind her.

After I'd cleaned the office from top to bottom, I realized I'd probably gone too far with her. What difference did it make if he knew where to find me? True, I harbored the suspicion that he might have had a hand in Pete's death, but he didn't know that. As far as I was concerned, he had no power over me and he had no leverage, so what was there to sweat? If he had the gall to come knocking at my door, I'd tell him I'd tossed the pills. That settled, I retrieved said bottle from my shoulder bag, pulled the rug back, opened my floor safe, and locked the pills away.

Cheney called late in the afternoon, saying, "I have a one-hour dinner break. I'm buying if you want to join me."

He knew full well I wouldn't refuse.

I said, "You did talk to Sanford Wray, right?" I held the handset loosely, pen and paper at the ready in case I needed to take notes.

"First thing this morning. Hey, we're old friends by now. He asked me to call him Mr. Wray. That's how tight we are."

"What'd he say about the gun?"

"I'm not doing this on the *phone*. We're starting to cook on this, I can tell you that. We picked up partial prints. Thumb and index finger."

"Oh, come on, Cheney. Don't make me wait. I want to know what went on."

"I'll pick you up in an hour. How do you feel about eating breakfast at dinnertime?"

"I love the idea."

I was home and waiting at the curb when Cheney came around the corner in his red Mercedes-Benz Roadster. I found myself mentally cocking my head. I was thinking about Robert Dietz and his red Porsche, wondering if Jonah Robb had a little red sports car as well. Cheney leaned across the seat and opened the passenger-side door. I slid into the black leather bucket seat and said, "Is this the car you had when I saw you last?"

"That was an '87. This is the '88. A 560SL. You like it?"

"I thought the other one was a 560SL."

"It was. I was so crazy about the car I got a duplicate."

He drove us out onto the wooden pier, the big timbers rumbling beneath his wheels. The restaurant was three blocks from my apartment but it wasn't one I frequented. We ate at a table overlooking the harbor with its modest traffic in power-boats and fishing vessels. Not surprisingly, the restaurant was given over to a nautical theme: black-and-white photographs of sailboats, fish netting draped along the walls, distressed wood, buoys, and other maritime artifacts, including fiberglass fish reproductions—two marlins, three sharks, and a school of sailfish.

As we ate, I wondered idly if you could classify men according to their breakfast preferences. Cheney was a pancake kind of guy: crisp bacon, breakfast sausage, eggs over easy. He piled it all together, poured syrup over the top, and cut it into a big nasty pile that he devoured with enthusiasm. He wasn't a big man but he never seemed to gain weight.

I ordered scrambled eggs, bacon, rye toast, and orange juice. When we finally pushed our plates aside and the wait-ress had refreshed our coffee cups, I said, "Are you going to volunteer the information or do I have to beg?"

"I'm happy to tell you the story, but I'm taking out the filler. You know how it is, you show up at a guy's door asking about a gun, there's all this preliminary bullshit while they decide if they should hire legal counsel before letting you set foot on the premises. Okay, so the nitty-gritty. He answers the door. We introduce ourselves and I ask if he has a .45-caliber Ruger semiautomatic registered to him. This is me and Jonah by the way. He says he does. We ask where the gun is. He says his bed table drawer. We say we'd like to see the weapon if he has no objections. He says, 'None whatever.'

"So far this is going great, but just to be on the safe side, we clarify the request, letting him know he has the right to refuse. By now, he's getting antsy. We reaffirm we have his consent to come in and take a look. He says, 'What the hell is this?' We tell him the Ruger might have been used in the com-mission of a crime, which he says is bullshit."

"I thought you were skipping the filler."

"This is important Fourth Amendment stuff. Something goes wrong, I don't want him claiming we didn't spell it out for him. So there's more back-and-forth before he gets down to it.

"Okay, so after that little verbal skirmish, he decides not to argue the point. We all troop into the bedroom, where he opens the bed table drawer. Sure enough, there's a gun. Obviously not the Ruger because Jonah's holding that in an evidence bag. First thing Wray says is, 'That's not my gun.'

"So we ask if he recognizes the gun and he says of course not, he never saw it in his life. So then we go back and quiz him as to his whereabouts the night of August 25. Turns out he was on location in North Carolina, where his company's shooting a film. We show him the Ruger, which he identifies as his. Now we're making progress. We ask how he acquired it. He says he bought it two years ago after a rash of home invasions in Los Angeles where he was living. Both he and his wife had themselves safety certified before he made the purchase. After that they took shooting lessons. Very conscientious, and we're quick to compliment him for being such a good citizen. We ask him when's the last time he or his wife handled the Ruger, and he names the occasion, which was maybe five months back. They went target shooting and he cleaned the gun afterward."

I leaned forward. "He can prove he was out of town?"

"No question. And please remember, this is coming out of left field, so he's had no time to prepare."

"Okay, so the gun is his, but he was gone. Now what?"

"There's a kicker."

"I hope it's good."

"I don't know how good it is, but it's interesting. I take that back—it's good and it's interesting."

I made that rolling-hand gesture hoping to speed him along.

"Once we tell him the semiautomatic in the drawer might be the one used in a shooting death, he's practically begging us to get the damn thing out of his house. We bag and tag and go back to the station, where we run the serial numbers. And you know what we find?"

"The gun's not registered."

"It is registered. You want to guess who to?"

"Cheney, would you quit this? Either tell me or don't tell me, but don't play games. Whose gun was it?"

"Pete Wolinsky's."

I told Cheney I'd walk home. He had to get back to work and I needed the air. Nothing made sense. How had Pete's Glock

17 ended up in some stranger's bed table drawer? What was *that* about? We'd gone through the story a second time. Once the gun was identified as Pete's, the Wrays were invited downtown for further conversation and they couldn't have been more cooperative. Both agreed to have their prints rolled. Sanford Wray didn't know Pete Wolinsky. He'd never even heard the name. Nor had his wife, Gail. Neither had a criminal history. Both husband and wife were out of state the night Pete was killed. Their home security system had been activated and there were no reports of an alarm. Jonah asked them to make a list of everyone who'd had access to the house in their absence and they'd given it to him on the spot. Not that many, as it turned out. House cleaners, Wray's personal assistant, a couple of family members who were coming in at Jonah's request. In the meantime, Ballistics was now in possession of both the Ruger and the Glock 17, and they'd determine which slugs had been fired from which gun.

It was almost dark by the time I reached home. I'd left lights on for myself, but Henry's place was dark. I figured he was up at Rosie's, so I did a turnabout and walked the half block. I was itchy with anxiety, but I wasn't up to a social visit unless we could talk in private. Rosie's front windows were plastered with the usual beer and liquor ads, but a quick peek revealed Anna sitting at the table with Henry. Except for the boobs, I wasn't jealous of her, but she was getting on my nerves.

Walking back to my place, I passed an unfamiliar turquoise Thunderbird, which I imagined was one of Rosie's patrons taking up valuable parking space. I let myself into my studio and flipped off the porch light. I sat down at my desk, gathered my index cards, secured them with a rubber band, and tossed them into my bottom drawer. With Cheney and Jonah on it, my notes were beside the point. The sole remaining keepsake, if you want to think of it as such, was Pete's cardboard box that I was using as a footrest. I still believed I was right. Given my particular personality disorder, once I get on a thought track, I have trouble getting off.

I felt a nearly irresistible urge to create another, better explanation for Pete's death, but I resisted. Once I'm convinced B follows A and that Y precedes Z, it doesn't matter what I'm looking at, that's what I see. I'd developed a theory about Pete's relationship to Linton Reed and I made sure everything fit . . . which, I realized now, was much the same thing Linton Reed was doing with his data trimming, only without the loss of life.

I wondered (belatedly, I grant you) if I'd been using this entire enterprise as a way of avoiding anxiety about the sudden drop in business. I'd been thinking of these past weeks as unpaid vacation time, immersing myself in the issues of Dace's last will and testament so I could feel busy and productive when in fact I had no money coming in. I was not without ample savings, but I didn't want to go through my rainy-day funds. I'm cheap. I grew up in pinched circumstances. Financial excess is good. Penury is not.

I lifted my head and realized I was hearing a steady stream of cat talk outside. Ed had probably been chatting for some time, but I hadn't been tuned in. I went to the door and peered out the porthole, angling my gaze so I could see the doormat. Sure enough, Ed was sitting there, the two rows of potted marigolds forming a runway on either side of him.

I flipped on the porch light and opened the door, saying, "How do you manage this? I know Henry didn't leave you out."

He said something that I didn't get. He came in, possibly to inspect the premises. He began a leisurely tour, making sure all was in order.

"Hang on," I said.

Maybe Anna had been careless. More likely, the cat had some secret means of ingress and egress.

I grabbed Henry's keys, picked Ed up, and tucked him under one arm, flipping the thumb lock to the unlocked position before I closed the door behind me. My personal escort service might have been his scheme all along since he immediately began to purr. I unlocked Henry's back door and dropped the cat inside. I returned to my place, crossing the patio, which was washed in weak light from my porch lamp. I turned the doorknob and discovered that I'd locked myself out. Well, that was irritating. I must have locked the door when I thought I was unlocking it. My handbag and keys were inside and I was stuck outside. I assessed the situation and realized it was a minor inconvenience easily remedied. I could either let myself into Henry's kitchen and snag his spare keys, which included one for my door, or I could trot up to Rosie's, suffer Anna's company, and have him buy me a glass of wine. I opted for the wine.

It wasn't until I turned to leave that I realized Linton Reed was standing in the shadow of the driveway. He wore a dark overcoat. He looked completely out of place in the midst of such familiar sights. The Adirondack chair and the aluminum lawn chair were still pulled close together, as though William and I hadn't finished talking. There was a trowel on Henry's potting bench that he might have left there two minutes ago instead of the hours it had probably been. Clay pots of marigolds awaited placement around the edges of the patio.

Linton Reed had his hands in his coat pockets and he was completely still. This seemed odd to me. Charming people, like great white sharks, are always in motion. Their charm depends on sleight of hand: a smile, a tone, anything to suggest they have an active inner life that fuels the public image. They depend on motion to give them breath. It's because they're dead inside that they work so hard to maintain the illusion that they have souls.

"Hi, Dr. Reed," I said. "Anna said you might stop by." I moved toward him, showing what a friendly little thing I was.

His reply was late in coming by two beats. "Did she now." His tone wasn't accusatory. It was thoughtful, as though he were contemplating the possibility.

"She said you wanted to pick up that bottle of pills."

Again, the slow response. "When we spoke, you didn't tell me you had them."

"Because I didn't at that point. After you talked about the danger of unidentified medications in circulation, I asked a couple of Dace's friends if they knew what he'd done with his pills. As it happens, he'd given them to a homeless fellow, who turned them over to me. I threw them in the trash. I hope that was all right." He'd triggered the chatty side of my nature, which often comes to the fore when I'm worried I'll wet my pants.

"That's not why I'm here."

"Oh. Well, good. Because the point is, I don't have the pills. If I did, I'd give them to you. I certainly have no use for them myself."

"You led me to believe you had a simple query about a family member when all the time you sat there convinced I'd done something bad. I didn't come here asking about the pills. You jumped to the subject yourself because you're guilty of such deceit."

"I have no reason to feel guilty."

He ignored that comment. "I received a call from Eloise Cantrell, who says you accosted her on the street, asking questions about me."

"I didn't *accost* her. How ridiculous. I ran into her at St. Terry's as she was leaving for the day. I knew she worked on the CCU because she'd called me months ago when Dace was admitted. I asked if she knew you and she said she did. That's all it was. I'd talked to you earlier and it just seemed like a happy coincidence."

I watched his face cloud over.

He shook his head, frowning. "Something's off. Let's go back. You came to my office unannounced hoping to catch me off guard. You presented yourself in a false light, gathering information for reasons known only to yourself."

"I probably should have been more forthcoming," I said. "Here's what happened. I'm sure you know Terrence Dace was suspicious and confused. His behavior was erratic and he harbored paranoid fantasies. I thought I should look into it. It had nothing to do with you personally. I got involved because he'd drawn up a will in which he disinherited his children and left everything to me. I was concerned about a legal challenge, so I was doing my due diligence . . ."

Wincing, he pressed the flat of his hand to the side of his face, like a child with a painful ear infection. "You keep talking and talking. You use talk as a cover for something else, but I don't know what it is."

"Really, I don't. I think you've misunderstood."

"No, I have not. You're devious. I don't know how else to describe your behavior."

"I haven't meant to be devious."

"But it's your nature, isn't it?"

"I don't think so. I wouldn't say that about myself."

"Do you have any idea how perilous your position is?"

"Perilous?"

"I have you to thank for what's happening. It's as simple as that. When we spoke in my office, I didn't grasp your agenda.

I was at fault there for not being quicker off the mark. My apologies."

In a situation like this, it's of little comfort knowing you're right. I was right about Linton Reed. I'd been right all along, but who was I going to tell?

"I don't have an agenda," I said.

"Yes, you do. You talk to people about me. You write things down. You think about things that are none of your concern."

"I haven't done anything to you. I asked a few questions, but only to determine Dace's state of mind when he changed the will."

Dr. Reed was exasperated. "You're lying again. You've undercut whatever credibility you had. I was offering you a chance to explain yourself and you're throwing off all this smoke."

I had a quick little chat with myself, saying: Here's a tip, Self. Do not argue with a lunatic. Arguing with a lunatic simply ensures that you'll climb into his craziness with him when what you want to do is take a big step back.

He held up his right hand. "Do you see this?"

His fingertips were black.

"The police insisted on taking my prints. Can you imagine my humiliation? My wife was there and they took hers as well. The detective was polite, but I hated the way he looked at me. He was taking my measure. He weighed every word I said. I've never been treated like that in my life, but I had to maintain control of myself because I knew he'd be writing things down."

I was getting cold standing out on the patio in the half-light. A thought popped to mind, one of those insights that comes too late to be of any use. This felt like that game show where the contestants are given an answer and asked to frame the relevant question. I said, "Who is Sanford Wray?"

"He's my father-in-law."

I nodded, my mouth suddenly too dry to form a response.

I caught motion on the drive. I looked over and spotted Anna just as she spotted me. She turned on her heel. Linton glanced in that direction. "Who are you looking at?"

I cleared my throat and tried again. "Neighborhood dog. He's always wandering into the yard."

He closed his eyes, testing the truth value of the statement. For once I was lying outright and Linton missed it, so maybe he wasn't as smart as he thought. Maybe I wasn't that smart either because Anna might have helped me if I hadn't read her the riot act.

I said, "You know what? Why don't we forget all this and start from scratch? Somehow I gave you the wrong impression and I apologize."

"Impression? We're not talking about *impressions*. We're talking about the truth of what's going on."

"Which is what? I'm not getting this."

"You're ruining my life. You're tearing down everything I worked so hard to achieve."

I shook my head, saying, "I'm not. I wouldn't do that."

He smiled slightly. "Well. Perhaps you're right. I suppose there's no point in arguing since it won't change anything."

For a moment, I was quiet. Linton Reed was about to declare himself. Then again, so was I. "You know what your problem is?"

He fixed his attention on me. He'd been in that strange little twisted world of his where he was the king. "What's that?"

"You don't know a Ruger from a Glock."

His smile faded and his eyes went dead. He removed a flat silver case from his coat pocket and triggered the lid.

I couldn't bring myself to look. I kept my eyes locked on his. Was there anyone alive in there? My heart had started to bang as though I'd just climbed a flight of stairs.

"Look what I brought for you," he said.

I looked down. The interior was lined with black velvet. In the center was a scalpel. A jolt of ice moved down my spine, chilling every nerve it touched. The effect was odd, like that spritzy jangle you feel when you contact a hot wire.

"This was my specialty. My first love," he said.

He plucked the scalpel from its velvet bed, snapped the case shut, and returned it to his coat pocket. He held the surgical instrument so it caught the light. "I call him 'the Biter.' He's quick and sharp. This blade is my favorite. A number twelve. You see how this portion curves. That's his music. A sweet high note you'll hear when he whistles through your flesh."

His eyes met mine. "No need to be apprehensive. You

won't suffer. He'll see to that. A burning sensation, but so brief. Think of it as lightning, illuminating your soul. A starburst followed by quiet."

I felt tears well. "I bet you introduced him to Terrence Dace when he was admitted to the CCU."

"He was very sick. He was doomed. I offered him a better death. The aide came in so I said good night. I said we'd come back for him."

He lashed out at me so abruptly, I could feel the blade displace the air as it whipped across my face. I jerked back. I put my hand behind me, grabbing the arm of the aluminum lawn chair to keep from stumbling. I glanced down and then swung the chair in a hard arc. I caught Linton by surprise, though he managed to get his arm up to soften the impact. He focused on me with curiosity, perhaps with a touch of respect. I wondered if he thought I'd go down without a fight.

I held the chair in front of me, the four legs keeping him at bay. He paused to consider his options and then lashed out again. He was quick in the way a striking snake is quick. Out and back, hoping to bury his blade in me. I struck him with the chair, driving at him with all four legs. A hard bang as the two front legs jabbed his chest. I backed up and to my left, forcing him to shift right to keep me in range. From the corner of my eye, I saw a touch of white.

The cat was out.

Linton saw him at the same time I did and I watched his eyes flicker toward Ed. I struck again to distract him. Ed paid no attention to either one of us. He sat down and licked his paw, grooming his face with a curling gesture that broke my heart.

Now it was Linton who moved. I knew what he was up to. A demonstration. The Biter cutting to the bone. The simplicity of math. If not me, the cat. My only advantage was that I could devote both hands to the chair I held while his left hand was occupied. A leftie. I'd forgotten. He had his little friend to protect. I lunged, snapping the chair in front of me like a lion tamer. It was too light to do him any harm, but it created a buffer zone between us.

He snatched at the chair and I pushed abruptly, causing him to stumble backward by one step. I leaned left and I grabbed a clay pot of marigolds by the rim. I threw it hard, directly at his face. A gash opened up on his forehead. Scalp wounds really are the most dramatic. No reaction from him. He probably didn't feel a thing. The Biter flew again and I didn't draw back in time. The blade nicked me on the cheek. Linton liked that, drawing blood for blood. I abandoned the chair. I grabbed the big plastic bag of sphagnum moss and held it in front of me like a chest protector. Linton struck and the blade opened up a long slit. Moss bulged through the cut like internal organs being liberated.

I stooped to the mound of lawn mulch and swept upward, an armload of fine dirt flying at his face. He inhaled silt and coughed. He backed up, his body racked as his lungs fought off the insult. The dirt had stuck to his sweaty skin. A minstrel in blackface.

I grabbed a second clay pot and threw it. He deflected it with his arm. Striking him in the head was my only hope. His heavy coat offered him padding. I was in jeans, shirt, and running shoes, my movements unhampered where he had the bulk of his coat to contend with. The only sounds we made were the grunts of two tennis players, putting everything we had into each shot. My body heat had jumped from chill to flame in the space of those few minutes. He was sweating. The Biter must have been slippery in his fingers but his grip was sure.

I saw his eyes flicker again. I'd lost track of the cat whereas Linton had not. Ed had retreated into the shrubs, where he watched us warily. He crouched much closer to Linton than to me. I'd give up before I'd let Linton hurt the cat. My chest was on fire. My heart banged in my ears. I wanted to say, "Don't." I wanted to protest. Linton plunged into the bush and grabbed the cat. This was a mistake. Ed twisted and spat, hissing as he ripped into Linton with his claws. Linton struggled to secure his hold, but Ed propelled himself out of Linton's hands like a whirling dervish. Linton made a sound and the cat was off like a shot. He put a hand to his cheek and then checked his fingertips. He was bleeding. I could see the angry red welt where Ed had made his mark with his rear claws.

I needed a shield. Something between me and the blade. The aluminum lawn chair had folded in on itself to form a flat metal plank. We grabbed for it at the same time, both of us now holding on with two hands. The Biter remained in Linton's grip, but he couldn't maneuver the blade while clinging to the chair. He released his hold, allowing me full possession for all the good it would do. The chair was crudely constructed, not meant to endure much in the way of punishment. It was already growing heavy. My arms burned from the weight.

Linton wanted full access. No impediments. Just me and the small deadly rapier no bigger than his index finger. I heaved the chair at him, but I was too tired to do so with any force. He backed up a step and the chair dropped with scarcely a sound. He lashed and as I jumped, I banged into the potting bench. I snatched the pruning shears from the spot where they were affixed to the garage wall. The second set was bigger, but I had to work with what was closest to hand. I opened the blades and chopped at him. The sound was good, so I chopped at him again.

I swung the shears as though at batting practice. Linton's face was red and his breathing was hoarse. The sound of childhood asthma. I pictured him chubby. A white, fleshy boy. A sissy on the playground. I could have beaten him in second grade, but girls didn't do those things back then. I held the pruning shears low, giving my arms a rest. He struck. I jumped back, angling the shears in front of me. I whacked his left hand full force, hoping his fingers would loosen. He backed up a pace, pausing to catch his breath.

In his hand, the Biter had the look of a claw.

This was the difference between us. He was nuts. I was mad. His thinking was disorganized while I wasn't thinking at all.

I went after him. My only hope was to wear him down. He was heavier than I by a good seventy pounds. I was light on my feet. I was speedier. I would never give up. I would fight to the death if that's what it took. He had his hands on his knees. He panted. I moved toward him, pulling the shears back like a baseball bat. I knew the risk. Linton might not be as tired as he looked. I might not be as strong. I drove at him, aiming for his head. His hand came up to protect his face. I struck the Biter on follow-through and watched the scalpel fly off into the dark. When I looked down, Linton was on his back. His coat was caught under him, leaving his belly exposed. I lifted the shears above my head like a sword.

Someone said, "Kinsey, it's okay. You don't have to do that."

Cheney stood in the drive. He hadn't even drawn his gun. He knew I could do it but trusted that I would not. Anna, white-faced and mute, stood behind him.

EPILOGUE

The district attorney filed first-degree-murder charges against Dr. Linton Reed in the shooting death of Pete Wolinsky. Involuntary manslaughter charges were also brought against Reed for the deaths of R. Terrence Dace, Charles Farmer, and Sebastian Glenn, whose participation in the Glucotace scandal resulted in misdiagnosis and medical mismanagement. The DA theorized that once the first victim died, Reed's continuation of the suspect drug regimen amounted to criminal negligence.

Dr. Linton Reed, through his attorney, declined all requests to be interviewed by the police. He took a leave of absence from the university, where his research was suspended. His wife's family is sufficiently wealthy to underwrite his legal expenses, but after an initial outpouring of protests as to his innocence, his wife has begun to disassociate herself from this once well regarded young researcher whose star fell so swiftly to earth. Better to be married to a bum than a criminal, says she.

Eventually a deal was reached between the DA and Reed's attorney for a plea to voluntary manslaughter with a gun for twenty-one years in prison. Part of the plea deal was dismissal of the involuntary manslaughter charges in the deaths of the three homeless men because all three suffered from multiple debilitating diseases that, individually or together, could have proved fatal. Analysis confirmed Dace's claim that the medication he was taking was indeed Glucotace, which was probably responsible for his failing health and eventual death, as well as that of Charles Farmer and Sebastian Glenn. Nonetheless, the DA's deal with Dr. Reed was supported by Dace's three children, who announced at the same time that they'd reached an out-of-court settlement with Reed, the university, and Paxton-Pfeiffer, the pharmaceutical company that had supported his research. Each of the Dace children received $150,000 in compensation for their pain and suffering.

Dace's will went unchallenged, in part because the legal costs would have been prohibitive, but more importantly, because it would have been inconsistent to claim in a civil suit that their father was of sound mind and body and a victim of premature death at the hands of Reed, thereby justifying a monetary award, and at the same time assert he was so debilitated as a result of drink that he could not competently decide as to the disposition of his assets.

You may wonder (as who has not?) what I did with the half a million dollars that fell into my lap. After less than one minute of consideration, this is the plan I came up with: I made a generous donation to Harbor House and then I put the rest in my retirement account. Do I feel at all apologetic about my good fortune? Of course not. Are you nuts?!

But these are procedural odds and ends, some of them months in the making; dry matters when laid up against the lives of Terrence Dace and Felix Beider. I paid to have their remains cremated with the intention of scattering their ashes at some future date. According to the municipal codes governing this matter, I learned that it is illegal to scatter ashes at a public golf course, a public beach, or a public park. Though it was not specifically spelled out, I was certain that flinging them off a freeway overpass would be frowned upon as well, so I set that decision aside temporarily.

I put William in charge of the memorial service, which was held on the grassy area at the beach where the homeless congregate most days when the weather's good. There was no sign of Ethan, but Anna was in attendance, as were Ellen and her young family, who'd driven down from Bakersfield. The children had never seen the ocean, and they ran barefoot and shrieking to the water's edge under Hank's watchful eye. William was amused by their enthusiasm, smiling to himself as they danced in the surf.

Henry had adapted and copied portions of Dace's botanical folios to create a program commemorating the farewell. Pearl and Dandy were there, along with their new friend, Plato the preacher man. Ken and Belva and other volunteers from Harbor House made an appearance, along with assorted staff members. There was no drinking, of course, and I'm happy to report Pearl only excused herself once for a quick smoke behind a tree.

The day was sunny, the temperature in the midsixties. William wore his best three-piece suit as was fitting for the occasion. His white hair was riffled by the breeze coming off the ocean, and his voice, powdery with age, rang clearly in the open air—in consequence, he later pointed out, of his early mastery of elocution.

William selected and arranged for the music, saying no send-off would be complete without hymns. He'd hired a solo trumpeter (on my dime, of course), who opened the service by playing "Amazing Grace." Strangers passing along the beach path recognized the solemnity of the gathering and paused, looking on respectfully. Cyclists, walkers, joggers, and mothers pushing strollers lingered at the periphery until the crowd numbered close to sixty by my count.

When the trumpeter finished, William welcomed everyone and thanked them for coming. He recited the Lord's Prayer and those who knew it chimed in. He read the Twenty-third Psalm. There was no proselytizing and none of the formalities rested too heavily on the Christian side of the equation. As he said, his purpose was not to convert, but to express the optimism of faith in all its forms. He and Henry then joined in a duet, singing an a cappella rendition of the spiritual "Going Home." Their two strong tenor voices blended in a harmony that was both simple and sublime. I'd never heard Henry sing and certainly not in concert with his brother.

Thereafter, William invited remembrances from those who'd been acquainted with Terrence and Felix. Ellen couldn't bring herself to speak; too shy in a public setting and far too upset to talk about her father. Anna talked about his love of nature, and then Dandy and Pearl both told stories about the two. Their recollections were varied and amusing, with more laughter generated than you'd expect. Or maybe the laughter was exactly appropriate. I've never attended a funeral yet where those present were not bound by both tears and mirth. It was William who captured the sentiment.

William's eulogy was brief.

We are here this afternoon to mourn the passing of two good friends, Terrence Dace and Felix Beider. They were homeless. Their ways were not those we most desire for ourselves, but that didn't make them wrong. We seem determined to save the homeless, to fix them, to change them into something other than what they are. We want them to be like us, but they are not.

The homeless do not want our pity, nor do they deserve our scorn. Our judgments about them, for good or for ill, negate their right to live as they please. Both the urge to rescue and the need to condemn fail to take into account the concept of their personal liberty, which they may exercise as they see fit as long as their actions fall within the law. The homeless are not lesser mortals. For Terrence and Felix, their battles were within and their victories hard-won. I think of these two men as soldiers of the poor, part of an army of the disaffiliated. The homeless have established a nation within a nation, but we are not at war. Why should we not coexist in peace when we may be in greater need of salvation than they?

This is what the homeless long for: respect, freedom from hunger, shelter from the elements, safety, the companionship of the like-minded. They want to live without fear. They want to enjoy the probity of the open air without the risk of bodily harm. They want to be warm. They want the comfort of a clean bed when they are ill, relief from pain, a hand offered in friendship. Ordinary conversation. Simple needs. Why are their choices so hard for us to accept?

What you see before you is their home. This is their dwelling place. This grass, this sunlight, these palms, this mighty ocean, the moon, the stars, the clouds overhead though they sometimes harbor rain. Under this

canopy they have staked out a life for themselves. For
Terrence and for Felix, this is also the wide bridge over
which they passed from life into death. Their graves
will be unmarked but that does not mean they are for-
gotten. The earth remembers them, even as it gathers
them tenderly into its embrace. The sky still claims
them and we who honor them will hold them dear from
this day forward.

In closing, the trumpeter sounded "Taps." When the service ended people hugged and shook hands and wiped their
eyes and blew their noses, connected for that small window in
time. The camaraderie might never rise to the fore again, but
I believe it was heartfelt and genuine while it lasted.

As for the matter of the ashes, William and Henry and
I considered scattering them along the beach, thus committing
an act of civil disobedience, but in the end, Henry came up
with a better idea. We took the ashes home with us, and in a
private ceremony of our own, we folded them into the rich
earth in Henry's flower beds, where they'll nourish the roses
when spring comes again.

Respectfully submitted,
Kinsey Millhone

AUTHOR'S NOTE

A few words about the basic underpinnings of this novel:

Addiction medicine and scientific fraud are both complex issues, and I lay no claim to a comprehensive understanding of the two fields. It's my hope that in folding pharmacological research and crime into the same mix, I do no great disservice to either. For errors, witting and unwitting, I offer my apologies. Insofar as I manage to represent these matters with any accuracy, I am indebted to the following:

Angell, Marcia, M.D. *The Truth About the Drug Companies: How They Deceive Us and What to Do About It*. New York: Random House, 2004.

Bass, Alison. *Side Effects: A Prosecutor, a Whistleblower, and a Bestselling Antidepressant on Trial*. Chapel Hill, NC: Algonquin Books of Chapel Hill, 2008.

Broad, William, and Nicholas Wade. *Betrayers of the Truth: Fraud and Deceit in the Halls of Science*. New York: Simon & Schuster, 1982.

Elliott, Carl. *White Coat, Black Hat: Adventures on the Dark Side of Medicine*. Boston: Beacon Press, 2010.

Graham, Allan W., Terry K. Schultz, Michael F. Mayo-Smith, Richard K. Ries, and Bonnie B. Wilford. *Principles of*

Addiction Medicine, 3rd ed. Chevy Chase, MD: American Society of Addiction Medicine, 2003.

Judson, Horace Freeland. *The Great Betrayal: Fraud in Science*. New York: Harcourt, 2004.

Kohn, Alexander. *False Prophets: Fraud and Error in Science and Medicine*. Oxford, UK, and New York: Basil Blackwell, 1986.